R.L. P

THE CURSED WITCH

NIGHTCASTER CHRONICLES

BOOK ONE

WILLOW HAVEN PRESS

THE CURSED WITCH

THE CURSED WITCH

Copyright © 2021 R.L. Perez

Published by Willow Haven Press 2021

United States of America

Cover Art by Blue Raven Book Covers

ISBN: 978-1-735049-23-6

www.rlperez.com

For Emily, the strongest and most resilient person I know.

1

LEO

THE CITY WAS QUIET. STILL. PEACEFUL. THOUGH MY enhanced hearing picked up every crawling critter and chirping insect in the darkened forest, the noises soothed my ears, inviting a calmness that I shoved away.

Not now. Not tonight.

My eyes were fixed on the Castillo de Coca. The home of Count Antonio de Silva—the man who currently held my brother captive.

I sensed a presence behind me and stiffened. The magic within me prickled to life, preparing to shift me to another form should I have the need to escape.

Then, a whiff of woodsmoke and cinnamon tickled my nose, and I relaxed. I knew that scent.

"Fancy yourself a midnight stroll, Jorge?" I asked without looking away from the castle.

"You've been brooding out here for hours." Jorge silently

approached from behind a large oak tree and followed my gaze. "Still no sign of Ronaldo?"

I shook my head. "He's been gone for two days now. If he hasn't emerged by now, the Count must have him." I took a half step forward, undecided.

Jorge grabbed my shoulder. "If this is true and you interfere, you will surely be captured along with him. You must wait. Trust your brother."

I remained silent. Trust Ronaldo? When he hadn't trusted me to wait? He'd been foolish and reckless to rush in unaided.

His impulsive and stubborn behavior often manifested itself in me as well. But as my elder brother, he should have been the responsible one—the coven's leader. Instead, that responsibility had fallen to me despite being only nineteen.

We needed him back. I couldn't do this without him.

"I could shift to an insect," I said quietly, tying back my long curly black hair. "Creep inside undetected. No one would know I was there."

"Except they can smell you," Jorge argued. "There are warlocks in there. *Light* warlocks trained to smell demons like us."

I flashed a grin at him. "We aren't normal demons, Jorge."

Jorge raised his eyebrows, acknowledging this. "Perhaps not. But with Ronaldo gone, our coven looks to you now. Don't leave us without a leader."

I shook my head, though I didn't know why. I knew he was right.

"How long has it been since you've fed?"

I waved a hand. "I drank from Estrella a few days ago. I can last a bit longer."

"Leo—"

"I still feel her blood inside me," I said sharply. "I know when I'm hungry, Jorge. Don't patronize me."

Jorge fell silent.

I sighed. "Forgive me. Tonight, I am not myself."

"None of us are," Jorge whispered.

I stared hard at the castle as if by my sheer will I could make it move. But it remained still as death. Silent and unyielding like a mountain.

"I need to get closer," I said, surging forward.

"Leo!" Jorge hissed.

I ignored him. Dark magic pulsed within me, roaring to life, and I shifted into my bat form. My body shrank, and my vision darkened, leaving me blind. But I didn't need my sight. Vibrations thrummed and pulsed around me, guiding me toward my destination. Perhaps with my bat's unique senses, I could detect something my vampire form might have missed. My true form was a vampire, but I could shift to various smaller animals thanks to my family's bloodline of shapeshifters.

I flapped my wings fiercely, flying toward the castle. A burst of magic behind me indicated Jorge followed, though I didn't know what creature he shifted to. His magic differed from mine. Not everyone in the coven could shift to a bat like me.

Something crackled in the air, and I wavered, spinning

out of control as if a heavy force barreled into me. The vibrations pulsed so loudly that I screeched in pain. My magic swept over me, shifting me back to my vampire form, and I crashed to the ground.

What the hell was that?

I righted myself, eyes wide as I stared at the castle. A burst of fire poured from one of the castle windows like a waterfall of flames.

"Ronaldo!" I strode forward, but then a mighty shriek filled the air, piercing the night and quieting the sounds of the forest. The cry made my ears throb and sent me staggering back a step.

Lightning flashed in the sky, but it was unusual—this lightning was bloodred, carving jagged, sinister lines in the inky black sky.

A bolt of magic shot through the air toward me, rippling the branches and bushes like a mighty storm. The magic seared through my chest, burning me from the inside out.

I clutched at my heart, moaning as I sank to my knees.

"Leo!" Jorge shouted from behind me, his voice strained.

Another boom shook the ground. Hunks of concrete cracked and fell from the castle, creating a wide crater. Within the hole, something exploded in a burst of flames and dark magic.

I screamed.

2

BRIELLE

I SPENT MY SIXTEENTH BIRTHDAY HUNTING DEMONS.

The day itself had been mundane. A typical Tuesday. Trudging through school, combating my frustrations through an afternoon of kickboxing, forcing a smile as my parents and sister sang "Happy Birthday" and thrust a giant buttercream cake in my face, then pretending to watch TV when my parents left for their coven meetings. The local covens of witches and warlocks in our neighborhood met once a month. Mom and Dad belonged to separate covens since Mom practiced light magic and Dad was a dark warlock—technically a demon.

Even though I possessed light magic like my mom, I was prohibited from attending her coven meetings ever since Joe Velazquez cornered me and beat me to a pulp for being a "worthless witch who was a waste of space."

That was five years ago. And also the day I took up kickboxing.

I drew my hoodie over my face, obscuring my long sand-colored hair. My older sister, Angel, was resting upstairs. She'd had another seizure yesterday and was on a special medication that made her extra drowsy.

It also made it easier for me to slip out unnoticed.

I eased open the door, and the pulse of vibrant Latin music echoed down the street. We lived in the heart of Little Havana. Though my Dad was Cuban, he said the area reminded him of home more than Cuba itself.

I pulled the strings of my hood so that only a small pocket of my face was visible. Though the air was thick with heat and humidity, it didn't bother me. I was always cold.

The weight of my weapons was a comfort to me as I walked. The holsters secured around my waist and chest held my stakes, daggers, and potion vials.

To effectively hunt demons, I needed all three. Especially since I was a "worthless witch."

Joe Velazquez hadn't been completely wrong about me.

I crossed the street to where the music was loudest. A nearby club resonated with energy and enthusiasm. The music pulled me in, lulling me with its upbeat melody and striking rhythm.

No, I told myself. *You're here to work.*

I slid between two clubs and hovered in the alley, keeping myself out of sight. If any demon was hungry for an unsuspecting victim, this was the perfect place. Hidden and secluded. Anyone who stepped outside of the club would be easy prey.

So I waited, shoving my hands into my pockets and

feeling the familiar weight of my favorite blade, a jewel-encrusted athame given to me by my mother when I was twelve.

Back when she still thought I could prove myself a powerful witch.

The blaring music rattled my eardrums. I closed my eyes, allowing the sounds to wash over me like white noise. An array of scents tickled my nostrils—alcohol, sweat, cigarette smoke. My nose filtered through all of these, searching. Hunting.

Then, I found it, and my eyes snapped open. The sharp stench of demon. It reeked of vinegar and onion, practically stinging my eyes.

I drew my athame and hid it in the pockets of my hoodie, surging toward the smell. I followed it down the street, away from the clubs. A gaggle of women stood by the lamppost, laughing and swaying drunkenly to the muffled music. One of them peeled off from the others, stumbling up the road toward the parking lot.

I stiffened, sensing movement nearby. A shadow lingered, watching her.

I shuffled forward, keeping a protective distance—but still close enough to see the woman. Her long dark hair was plastered to her face by sweat. She squinted, looking into the depths of her purse, no doubt trying to find her keys.

A whoosh of air breezed past me, sweeping in a burst of demon stench.

I broke into a run, rushing toward the woman. A black shadow crept toward her, but she paid no attention.

I wanted to shout, to warn her, but if I did the demon would vanish and find someone else to attack.

Just a few more steps.

The shadow was right on top of her. Then, I shouted, "Hey!"

The woman looked up, and the shadow froze, melting backward as it retreated.

The woman blinked, squinting at me. In Spanish, she said, "Do I know you?"

I pressed my palms together as if in prayer and muttered a spell.

"*I summon the magic from spirits on high.*
Reveal the predator lurking nearby."

My hands glowed blue, and a faint vibration tickled my fingers. From behind a black sedan emerged a figure. He straightened, his head whipping around as if trying to locate the source of magic. *My* magic.

My eyes narrowed as I scrutinized the demon. Sallow skin. Bloodred eyes.

Vampire.

I ducked down, using my short stature to my advantage. Creeping forward, I inched around the opposite side of the sedan until I approached the vampire from behind. Then, I flung my athame into his back. It embedded itself just left of his spine. He straightened and cried out with a high-pitched hiss that made the drunken woman yelp.

The vampire staggered backward, looking around until his enraged eyes met mine. Surprise flickered in his expression, and I knew what he was thinking. It was what they all thought when they saw me: *She doesn't have magic.* Otherwise they'd be able to smell me.

They were half-right.

I sprinted, ducking to avoid the swipe of his clawed hand. I yanked my athame from his flesh, and he screeched. I used it to slice his thigh, then his forearm. I spun around to embed it in his stomach when he snatched my wrist, his expression murderous.

"You're no witch," he spat. "Leave me alone and I'll spare you."

I smirked at him. "Not a chance."

I yanked him forward, drawing on the strength from my kickboxing lessons, and flung his body against the pavement. Something within him cracked, and he howled in agony. I lifted my athame, ready to drive it into his gut. Before I could, his foot hooked around mine and pulled.

With a grunt, I tumbled to the ground next to him. I popped up on all fours, trying to wriggle away, but then he snatched my legs, dragging me toward him.

"I warned you," he hissed.

My hands reached out, trying to grab onto something. I snatched the underside of the sedan's bumper and held fast. The vampire grunted from the resistance. His long claws dug into my leg, and I gritted my teeth against the pain seeping into me. I sucked in ragged breaths, trying to calm myself enough to cast another spell.

"*I summon the magic in the air*
To free me from this demon's snare."

A burst of blue light flashed in the corner of my eye.

The vampire shrieked and flew backward, releasing my throbbing leg. I whirled around and brandished my athame. I slid my hand under my hoodie to draw my stake as well.

The vampire scrambled to his feet, his eyes wide and his face slack with disbelief. He pointed a shaking finger at me. "Y-you're—"

"A witch?" I cocked my head and smiled. "Just barely."

I lunged for him, taking advantage of his surprise and hesitation. I slammed into him, knocking him into the concrete and landing on his chest. With one hand, I slit his throat, and with the other I drove the stake into his heart. His chest shuddered and then went still. A moment later, he disintegrated into ash that filled the air, stinging my eyes.

I blinked and wiped my blade and stake on the tires of the black sedan.

Then a piercing scream brought me to my feet. Eyes wide, I looked around and found the drunken woman pointing at me and crying out in such rapid Spanish that I could barely understand her.

Time to go.

I pulled my hood tighter around my face and limped away, ducking into the shadows behind the cars and then darting across the street before anyone could catch me.

It took me a few minutes longer than normal to reach my house, thanks to my injured leg. The pain pulsed through me in waves of agony, and I winced with every step.

If I'd been an ordinary member of the coven, I could've just called our healer to tend to the injury. But I wasn't. Demonhunting without a coven was illegal, and I didn't want to draw attention to myself.

Most witches had an affinity, like an Elemental, a Thinker, a Seer, a Pusher, or a Jumper. I was the oddball; I had no affinity, but I could still perform spells. Somehow.

Which meant I had access to magic, but something within me was broken. Mom and Dad had been hopelessly optimistic, certain my powers would manifest themselves sooner or later.

They hadn't.

I slipped through the front door and immediately hobbled to the kitchen to get some ice. A familiar smell touched my nose as I turned on the light. *Dammit.*

I sighed and met my mother's stern gaze. She crossed her arms, her blue eyes furious and her jaw rigid. Her gaze roved up and down my body, no doubt taking in the bloodstains—a mixture of my blood and the vampire's.

"Where were you?" Mom asked in a clipped tone.

I shrugged one shoulder and sidestepped her to open the freezer. "Out."

"Don't give me that, Brie. *Where were you?*"

"Just around the corner. By the club."

Mom sighed and raised a hand to her forehead. "And the blood on you? Whose is it?"

"Some vampire's."

"*Brielle.*" Mom slammed the freezer door shut before I

could get to the ice tray. "You can't go hunting demons alone! We've been through this!"

"Right," I said, my eyes narrowing. "I can't hunt demons, I can't attend coven meetings, I can't use my magic. What the hell *can* I do?"

"Watch your mouth," Mom growled. "You're barely sixteen. What you *can* do is keep going to school and studying until—"

"Until what?" I snapped. "Until my magic miraculously shows up? Until the Council decides I'm worthless and should be ousted to live as a mortal?"

Mom's lips grew tight, and the fear in her eyes told me all I needed to know. Deep down, she was afraid of this too.

"Why are you home, anyway?" I asked in a monotone, finally easing past her to grab a handful of ice. "You should be at the meeting."

"I left early. I was worried about Angel."

Yeah, I thought bitterly. *What else is new?* My bitterness didn't last, though. Angel was the kindest soul I'd ever met. I could never be angry with her, even if her health problems meant she got more attention from my parents than I did.

I ignored my mom's gaze and poured ice cubes into a plastic bag. Then I hitched my leg up to prop it on the wall and held the ice against my throbbing wound.

"Let me look at that," Mom said quietly.

"I'm fine," I snapped. "I've had worse."

Mom stiffened. "Worse?"

I closed my eyes, cursing myself for letting that slip.

"Brie, how long have you been doing this?"

I pressed the ice more firmly against my wound. My jaw ticked back and forth as I contemplated how to answer. "A few months."

"Merciful Lilith," Mom swore, her eyes darting to the ceiling in exasperation. "You're going to get yourself *killed*."

"I don't care. Dying while Demonhunting is better than dying of boredom. I can't live like a mortal, Mom. I just can't. I'd rather die today than live a hundred years like that."

Mom was silent, but I felt her gaze on me while I stared at the dried blood on my jeans.

She touched my arm. "Brie—"

A loud knocking on the front door interrupted her. I frowned at her, and she looked equally confused.

"Wait here," she muttered before leaving the kitchen.

I hobbled forward, peering around the corner to see who was at the door. Mom opened it and said, "Councilman Solano? What brings you here?"

"I'm sorry to show up unannounced." The old man's wispy voice sounded vaguely familiar. I remembered it from the countless hearings with the Council when they were trying to figure out what to do with me.

"Is everything all right?" Mom asked.

The Councilman hesitated for a long moment, and I straightened as dread rolled through me. "The Council has just ruled on the status of your daughter. She can no longer live among magical beings. I've come to take her away."

3
BRIELLE

"Is this some kind of birthday prank?" I asked, crossing my arms. I was *so* not in the mood.

Councilman Solano's gray eyebrows lowered, his expression grim. "I'm afraid not. It's because of your birthday I'm here in the first place. The Council ruled that if your powers did not manifest themselves by your sixteenth birthday, you would have to be removed from the magical society as a safety precaution."

I blew air through my lips. "I don't need protection."

"As a safety precaution for *others*," Solano emphasized, his eyes widening.

A stunned silence rippled through the room. I stared at Mom, who gaped at the Councilman.

"May I please come inside?" Solano asked. "I can explain everything."

Mom stood back to let him in, her face pale. I watched numbly as Solano strode inside and sat on the sofa, his body erect as if he were having lunch with the President. We sat opposite him on the love seat. I scooted closer to Mom, wanting to lean into her but refusing to give in. Cuddling with her would make me weak. And right now, I needed to be strong.

Solano opened his mouth to speak, but a frail voice whispered from the top of the stairs, "Mom?"

We all looked up to find Angel clutching the banister with both hands, her jet-black hair disheveled. Her dark blue eyes were bloodshot and rimmed with dark circles. Worry was etched in her face as she looked from Solano to me and then to Mom.

"Everything's all right," Mom said with a false smile. "Go back to sleep."

Angel's lips pressed together, obviously unconvinced.

"No, please stay," I blurted before I could stop myself.

"Brie—" Mom said.

"I want her to stay," I said through clenched teeth.

Mom sighed, rubbing her forehead. "Fine." She looked up at my sister. "If you start to feel sick again, go back to bed."

Angel offered a noncommittal grunt and staggered down the stairs. Mom seemed to read the apprehension in my face and moved to the armchair so Angel could sit next to me. My sister was tall and graceful and had the posture and figure of a delicate princess. Her bronze skin, shiny hair, and stunning eyes made her a vision that suited her name. We were both so different. My small form, blond hair, and mud-brown eyes were nothing compared to her beauty.

Even so, I needed her with me now. She slid onto the cushion next to me. Her hand trembled as it touched mine, but I squeezed it and scooted closer until our shoulders touched. Her warmth next to me was a comfort—somehow more comforting than my mother's.

Solano cleared his throat. "I, um, must inform you of protocols within the Council in order to shed light on our unique situation."

Mom held up a hand. "We should really wait until my husband is here. He works for the Council, after all."

Solano winced. "Yes, ah . . . the Council voted him out of these proceedings because we believed he couldn't serve as an impartial voter in this ruling."

Mom stiffened, her eyes flashing. "Well, this is no longer an affair of the Council. This is a family crisis. Any other family, whether employed by the Council or not, would surely have both parents present, wouldn't they?"

Exasperation flickered in Solano's eyes, but he deflated slightly, leaning back against the sofa. "Yes, I suppose you're right."

Mom nodded stiffly. "Give me a moment. I'll call him." She left the room.

I looked at Angel, ignoring Solano completely. "How are you feeling?"

Angel shrugged one shoulder. "Groggy. But my head hurts less." She leaned closer to me. "What's going on?"

"He says he's here to take me away," I whispered. "Because I'm defective."

Angel nudged my shoulder with hers. "Stop that. You aren't defective."

"Aren't I?" Though I smirked, there was truth in my words. And perhaps some bitterness too.

Angel easily detected both and fixed me with a stern look. "Brielle Gerrick, I don't want to hear such self-degrading things coming out of your mouth, you understand? You are a special witch and much more powerful than me, whatever abilities I might have."

"Okay, *Mom*," I teased, but something defensive rose up inside me. Angel wasn't weak, but her condition made it hard to cast spells. She was a Seer, and sometimes her visions were so strong that they caused headaches and seizures. It seemed we were both, in our own way, defective.

The thought made my heart sink to my stomach. Why couldn't we just be a normal, healthy family?

Mom returned, pocketing her cell phone before sitting in the armchair. "My husband is aware of these proceedings, despite your valiant efforts to keep it from him." Her tone was icy as she leveled a glare at Solano. "He says to start the discussion without him."

I sat up straighter. "Perfect. Now the Councilman can tell me where they'll keep me prisoner."

"Brie," Mom hissed.

"What, so you can be snarky but I can't?" I said.

Solano lifted his chin. "We will do no such thing. You will not be a prisoner. You will be sent to the Institute of Impaired Casters for counseling and training."

Impaired Casters. I suppressed a shudder. So what, I was labeled as handicapped? A crippled witch?

"Where is this 'institute'?" I asked slowly.

"Somewhere remote," Solano said. "Only a few of us know of its location, for security purposes. But it's isolated from other communities as a safeguard."

They're talking about me like I'm an atomic bomb, I thought irritably.

"Why does she need to be taken away?" Mom asked. "I don't understand what threat she poses if she doesn't have powers like other casters do."

Solano shifted in his seat, his brow furrowing. "What do you know of Lilith's Curse?"

Mom frowned, and Angel cocked her head, but something familiar prickled in the back of my mind. "Isn't that a myth?" I asked.

"No," Solano said stiffly. "Sadly, it is a part of our history, though many magical families associate it with mythology and lore. Lilith's curse is a—"

"A defect in a witch's blood that marks her as a child of Lilith, cursing her and those around her," I recited. I'd spent years poring over magical texts, hoping that by studying my heart out, my magic would ignite somehow.

I'd been wrong.

"Precisely," Solano said. "We haven't seen a cursed witch in over three hundred years. But the telltale symptom is a witch who is unable to access her magic. It is said that Lilith holds the witch's power until the demon queen sees fit to unleash it."

I blinked at him. "You think . . . *I'm* cursed?"

"That's ridiculous," Mom scoffed.

"You seem well-versed in the story," Solano said, watching me. "Perhaps you can tell us all of the damage a cursed witch is capable of."

I sighed. "The last occurrence unleashed some sort of monster that wiped out an entire country. Councils from all over the world had to unite to subdue the creature and kill the witch to protect everyone from her slaughter." I shook my head. "But that can't possibly be me. How am I supposed to conjure some monster when I can't perform any magic?"

"I don't make the rules," Solano said. "I wish I could grant you the freedom to do what you want, but unfortunately, the risk is too great. We simply can't afford a loss like that. Too many lives are at stake. And if we run this risk, we risk *your* life as well. Should the worst happen, and you unleash Lilith's power, we will have no choice but to hunt you down for the sake of the entire magical world. But if we send you away now to properly train you to access your powers, perhaps you will prove us wrong and tap into your abilities. If this should happen, you are, of course, free to return."

I swallowed, my head spinning. This was starting to feel real. *Too* real. It had felt like a joke before, but now I was genuinely afraid of being ripped away from my family. My home.

The front door opened, and Dad entered, his dark blond hair disheveled and a sheen of sweat coating his forehead. "Sorry," he muttered. "I got here as fast as I could."

He removed his shoes and sat cross-legged at Mom's feet. His scent immediately overwhelmed me. Since he was technically a demon, the smell of him often tickled my nose. But he still smelled like my dad. An outdoorsy scent like freshly mown grass mingled with the sharp vinegar smell of demons.

Dad's green eyes met the Councilman's, and Dad offered a curt nod. "Tony."

"Oliver," Solano said tightly. "We were just discussing—"

"Lilith's curse," Dad said. "Yes, I'm aware. And I think it's insane to send away a child based on this fairy tale."

"I assure you it's no fairy tale," Solano said coldly. "The devastation was very real, as you should know, having served on the Council for several years. The highest officiating Councilmen went to great lengths to cover up the trauma of that event for the sake of protecting the people. As such, the event was tossed aside as nothing more than a cautionary tale."

Dad raised his eyebrows and shrugged. "Perhaps you shouldn't have covered it up then. But I'm not letting you take my daughter."

Pride swelled within my chest, and I tried not to smile at the fire in my Dad's voice. Instead, I stared at my lap. Angel's grip on my hand tightened.

Solano sighed, closing his eyes briefly. "I'm afraid you have no say in the matter. If we must remove Miss Gerrick by force, we will. And your family will be imprisoned for interfering with a motion sanctioned by the Council."

Dad's eyes blazed, and he opened his mouth to argue, but Mom raised a hand.

"Wait, wait," she said. "Can't we go with her? We'll sign some . . . affidavit swearing we'll accept the risks."

"I'm afraid that's out of the question. There are other casters at this institute, and we simply can't allow the presence of loved ones due to a limited capacity in the manor."

"Manor?" I repeated, wrinkling my nose. What was this, some murder mystery?

"Yes, the Institute is a grand, secluded estate," Solano said in a tired voice. "It's meant to serve as a comfortable home instead of a . . ." He trailed off, his face twisting with a grimace.

"Prison?" I raised my eyebrows.

Mom sucked in a breath. "You—you *can't* do this. She's underage!"

"Yes, and the previous cursed witch was only fifteen when she tapped into Lilith's powers," Solano snapped. "We have given your daughter an extra year, but we can't be any more lenient. As I said before, lives are at stake."

"But you said it's been hundreds of years," I said. "How can you possibly think *this* is the year a cursed witch will show up?"

Solano's jaw went rigid. "Because you are the first witch in three hundred years to have no powers."

An icy silence filled the room, chilling me to the bone. *Impossible,* I thought immediately. *Surely there's some other caster who has trouble accessing their power. Surely I'm not the only one.*

But I knew well enough—from the demons who stared at me in shock when I fought them and the witches and warlocks within the coven who'd made my life hell as they taunted my weakness—this was *not* normal. No one else was like this.

Everyone here knew I wasn't a normal witch. And I certainly wasn't mortal either, since I could still utter spells and summon a glow with my hands.

It can't be, I thought, my throat feeling tight. *I can't be cursed. I'd feel it. I'd know! I'd know if Lilith were trying to control me.*

I cleared my throat. "Let's say I *am* cursed by Lilith." I paused, struggling to keep my voice even. "How do I stop this . . . transformation from happening?"

Solano stared at me for a long moment. "If you truly are cursed, then I'm sorry, but there's nothing to be done. Eventually, Lilith will claim you for her own."

My whole body stiffened, and I sat there, frozen for a full minute. I felt everyone's eyes on me, watching me process this information.

I swallowed and leveled a stare at Solano. "Then I'll do it."

Angel gasped, and Mom cried, "No! Brie—"

"It's fine, Mom," I said, grateful I managed to keep my voice steady. "I'm sure it's nothing. Like he said, if I'm *not* cursed, I can just come home. I'll go to this . . . this manor institute thingy, prove them wrong, and come home before you know it." I met Mom's gaze. "I promise."

Mom bit her lip and exchanged a look with Dad. Angel squeezed my hand with trembling fingers.

"Will we—can we keep in touch with her?" Mom asked in a shaky voice.

"Of course," Solano said immediately.

I watched my mom communicate wordlessly with my dad, deliberating this. Though I'd volunteered—though I knew in my heart I had to do this—something within me still shattered, knowing they weren't fighting for me right now.

When Mom's gaze flicked to Angel, I understood why: my sister needed them. She was sick, and if they broke the law to keep me here, no one would be able to take care of her.

I tried to squash the bitterness that swelled in my chest at the thought. As if sensing my conflict, Angel leaned her head on my shoulder, erasing all my anger. I couldn't possibly resent her. It wasn't like she *asked* to be sick.

If she weren't the sweetest person on the planet, I'd probably try to hold onto that anger. But instead, I let it go like a leaf in the wind. I exhaled and closed my eyes, leaning my cheek against her soft hair.

"All right," Mom said in a choked voice. She looked at me. "If you're sure about this—"

"I'm sure."

"I'm going with you," Dad said, his eyes hardening.

Solano sighed like he was talking to a petulant child. "Oliver—"

"I know," Dad snapped. "But let me at least travel with her as far as I can go. Just to ensure she gets there safely."

Solano's nostrils flared and his lips tightened. But, slowly, he nodded.

Relief spread through me. *I won't be alone. At least not yet.*

Mom packed a bag for me, and then I made sure my goodbyes were quick. I didn't want to prolong this, and if I didn't rush out of there soon, I knew I'd break down. Or change my mind.

Or both.

Mom embraced me, and Angel hugged me for a solid minute. I clung to her as if I could take her essence with me.

When we drew away, I pressed my lips into a smile. "I'll be back before you know it." I turned to Solano and Dad, who waited by the front door. "I'm ready."

"I love you, Brielle," Mom sobbed. "We love you so much."

"I love you too," I said quietly. I couldn't look at Mom or Angel again. If I did, I'd never find the will to leave.

I followed Solano out the door. My heart caved inward as the door slammed shut behind us. Dad pressed a hand to my shoulder, and I breathed in deeply. *Not alone yet. Not yet.*

To my surprise, there were two beefy men waiting for us on the porch. Solano's bodyguards, no doubt. As if he'd expected me to put up a fight.

The upbeat music still poured from the club across the street. We walked a block away from my house. My limp kept me from keeping up, but Dad gripped my arm to help me along. He offered to carry me, but I shot him a withering stare.

After a few minutes, Solano stopped, and his guards did as well. I frowned, looking around.

"Hayes will take you from here," Solano said, turning to face me. "Good luck, Miss Gerrick."

"Wait," Dad said, raising a hand. "Where is he taking her?"

Solano looked at Dad. "To the portal."

Dad straightened. "Take me too."

Solano closed his eyes and pinched the bridge of his nose.

Dad's grip on my arm tightened. "I'm not letting her leave without me."

I thought about shaking him off and insisting I was a big girl and could handle myself. But instead, my heart swelled. *He's fighting for me.*

In this moment, I needed to know that.

Before I could process anything, the guard closest to me grabbed my arm. I clutched Dad's hand tightly. With a small *pop*, my surroundings faded, and my body jerked forward on its own. Magic spun around me, making me dizzy.

We landed in an enormous, empty warehouse larger than three football fields put together. The guard guided us forward, and our footsteps echoed. A single fluorescent light illuminated the eerily still surroundings.

"What is this place?" I asked, my voice bouncing off the walls.

The man called Hayes said nothing. He urged me forward to the very end of the warehouse. Only then did I notice the strange purple glow emanating from the wall. A large hole gaped at me from the wall in the back corner of the warehouse, and it glistened with power. Magic sparked in the air, but it was unlike any magic I'd ever smelled before. It wasn't like the foul stench of demon or the citrus scent of light magic. This smelled like ash, onions, and seaweed. It stung my nose, swirling within me and filling me with dread and apprehension.

"What the hell is that thing?" Dad demanded.

"A portal," Hayes said. "It will take Miss Gerrick to her destination."

I shot Hayes a bewildered look. "You're a Jumper! Can't you just take me there?"

He shook his head. "There are wards preventing Jumpers from reaching it. It's heavily protected. This is the only way." We stopped, finally facing the portal. A faint vibration thrummed around it as if it let off some kind of frequency.

I swallowed as uncertainty numbed my bones. Something didn't feel right.

"Mr. Gerrick," Hayes said softly.

Dad stiffened and looked at Hayes, who stood a few feet behind us. "What?"

"You must remain here."

My body felt numb. "I have to jump through that weird thing . . . alone?"

Hayes nodded like this was the simplest thing in the world. "You are the only one authorized to. Only those admitted to the Institute are permitted to enter."

Unease spread through me. I turned back to the portal. My body froze. Something within me screamed that this wasn't right, that I shouldn't go through.

No way am I stepping through that thing by myself. I knew nothing about this portal. For all I knew, it could take me to a pack of ravenous werewolves.

I looked at Dad, whose panic matched my own. *This isn't right.*

"Go on," Hayes urged.

I hesitated, searching inwardly for the resolve that had pushed me to agree to this in the first place. But it was gone. "No," I said.

Hayes stiffened. "You must."

I shot him a sharp look. "Like hell. I'm not going there unescorted. Do you even know where that portal goes? What if I'm attacked?"

Hayes reached for me, but Dad swatted his arm away. "She said *no.*"

Hayes fixed a fearsome scowl at him. "It's the Council's orders. She doesn't have a choice."

I backed away from the portal, my limbs itching to break into a run. "You go first so I know it's safe," I said to Hayes.

"Miss Gerrick . . ." Hayes reached for me, and I bolted.

Dad took my cue and sprinted next to me, carrying half my weight as we ran in a weird sort of gallop.

With a *pop*, Hayes appeared in front of us, arms outstretched to grab me. Dad shoved the man aside, and I ducked underneath him to keep running. Over my shoulder I cast a spell.

"Magic above and powers that be,
Freeze this man who's chasing me."

My hands glowed blue, and Hayes cried out with a roar of anger and frustration. I kept running, ignoring the pain searing up my leg and the stitch that formed in my side.

"Run, Brie!" Dad shouted, his voice muffled. I knew Hayes was fighting with him, and for a moment, I hesitated. "Get out of here!" Dad cried. "Hide!"

My survival instincts kicked in, and I kept running, my injured leg pulsing with pain. I didn't know what I would do or where I would go, but I knew that portal meant nothing good for me.

Another *pop* made me stop in my tracks. A new man appeared, his thick eyebrows lowered and his jaw rigid. He closed a hand around my wrist, his grip firm and unyielding. I thrashed and yanked my hand, but it was no use.

He Jumped, and we were back in front of the portal again. I struggled, kicking and flailing like a toddler, but the man dragged me forward. Then another *pop*, and Hayes was by his side with my enchantment broken. They each grabbed one of my arms and hauled me toward the portal.

"Dad!" I screamed.

"Brie!" His voice was faint. Too far. He wouldn't reach me in time.

The two Jumpers hauled me forward, and I struggled uselessly against their steely grips.

"What are you going to do, throw me like I'm a piece of garbage?" I shouted loudly. My voice echoed in the empty warehouse, mingling with Dad's shouts. He was only a few yards away now. Maybe he would reach me in time.

The purple portal warbled at my approach, and a fresh wave of panic overcame me.

"Stop! Please!" I dug my heels into the floor, but still they pushed me forward. "*Dad!*"

"I'm sorry, Miss Gerrick," Hayes said with a grunt.

And they shoved me forward through the portal and away from the life I knew.

4

BRIELLE

My stomach churned. Lights spun in my vision, and I squeezed my eyes shut. Nausea built up inside me until I was certain I'd puke.

Then everything stopped. Something hard collided with my face, and pain split through my head like an ax. I groaned and shifted, my head throbbing. Slowly, I opened my eyes and found a wide expanse of elaborate marble. My face was planted right in the middle of some decorative octagon with an array of bright colors and tiles.

I sat up, my head spinning. The ground was cool to the touch, and I suppressed a shiver. The injury in my leg pulsed as I tried to stand. I looked up, craning my neck to view the magnificent ceiling high above me, surrounded by ornate sculptures. A balcony wrapped around the room I was in, indicating there was at least a second floor—maybe more, judging by the height of the ceiling.

Where am I, some sort of castle?

"Bloody hell," said a voice.

I jumped and found a boy about my age standing opposite me near a narrow hallway. Short, copper hair framed his face, and his blue eyes were wide as he stared at me, his face white as paper.

I swallowed and frowned at him. He wore a gold overcoat that fell past his butt, decorated with gleaming buttons. On his neck was a white ascot of some sort—maybe a cravat?

He seriously looked like some royal courtier from a play. If I hadn't known any better, I would've expected him to start belting Shakespeare or burst into song.

"Who are you?" I asked.

The boy blinked and looked behind him like he thought I spoke to someone else. Then he turned back to me, gaping. "Uh, my name is Riker. Riker Wilkinson." He spoke with a thick, British accent. Which explained the "bloody hell."

"Where are we?" I looked around the vast room again, taking in the small details like the grand paintings hanging on the wall and the beautiful rugs lining the floors of the hallway. Something sharp stung my nose. Something familiar.

There were demons here.

I stiffened, my fingers itching to grab weapons I didn't have. Unfortunately, Solano had forbidden me from bringing any.

"Where are we?" I asked again, louder this time. I

stepped toward Riker, prepared to slap the shock off his face if I had to.

"The Castillo de Coca," Riker said. Fear stirred in his eyes at my approach.

I blinked. "What?"

"It's a castle located in the province of Segovia. Central Spain."

I staggered back a step. *Spain?* This top-secret Institute was located in *Spain*? "Mother of Lilith," I whispered, feeling faint again.

"You're unwell." Riker strode toward me and offered his arm. "Allow me to escort you to the guest room."

I shot him a bewildered look. "Escort me? I'm perfectly capable of walking myself."

"Most of us weren't well enough to arrive without vomiting," Riker said in a conspiratorial whisper. "So, it's not a question of your capabilities, Miss . . .?"

I sighed. "Gerrick. Brielle Gerrick."

Riker raised his eyebrows. "Brielle? Are you French?"

I snorted. "No. My mom just has an odd sense of humor. I'm Cuban, actually."

Riker frowned and cocked his head, eyeing me up and down. "You seem rather fair for a Cuban."

I nodded, rolling my eyes. "Tell me about it." I stilled and narrowed my eyes at him. "What do you mean, you didn't arrive without vomiting? There are others who . . ." I trailed off, unsure of how to word my question.

Riker nodded. His gaze darted down to his elbow, which

was still extending toward me. "I'll explain on the way. It's quite a long walk."

As much as I wanted to shove him away and find the guest room myself, I knew I wouldn't last very long with my injured leg. Begrudgingly, I rested my hand on the inside of his arm, surprised by the strength I found there.

"We all arrived at different times," he said, guiding me down the hallway he'd just come from. "Armin was the last to arrive. He came from Mumbai and he's been here about three years."

I tried to focus on his words and not the number of statues we passed that put the statue of David to shame. "Arrive how?" I didn't want to outright say "through a magical portal," on the off chance he was just a mortal.

Riker smirked. "I think you know. An abandoned warehouse with a glowing purple light? We were all taken there."

"So, this . . . castle is really the Institute then?"

"Ah, yes. The Count doesn't like the term 'Institute.' He thinks it diminishes the grandeur of such a place. Honestly, he treats it more like a shrine."

"The Count?"

"Count Antonio de Silva. He runs the place. So, ah *Miss Gerrick,* what time are you from?"

I stared at him. *What time?*

Riker glanced at me and then stopped walking. "We're in the year 1735. The portal you stepped through sent you through time."

I raised an eyebrow, waiting for the punchline. When he

didn't say anything, I said, "Do you really expect me to believe that?"

Riker laughed. "We all questioned it at first, but it's true. You'll see soon enough." He patted my hand and continued walking.

I gazed at the tapestries and paintings through narrowed eyes. Whoever decorated this place certainly went all out. There was nothing modern about it.

Which could only mean that someone desperately wanted me to believe I was in a different time period.

But I was no fool.

"So, tell me more about the rest of you," I said, hoping to get him talking so he could feed me useful information. "You're all . . . handicapped somehow? Something's wrong with your powers too?"

Riker nodded. "I'm a Seer who can't control his visions. They're often violent. Sometimes others get hurt. Sometimes I hurt myself." He shrugged, but his eyes darkened. "Others have it much worse. One bloke sets himself on fire spontaneously and has no control over it." He looked at me. "What about you?"

I pressed my lips together. "I don't have any powers. Well, not an affinity. I can cast spells, but that's it. No specialty. No gifts."

Riker frowned. "How peculiar." He faced forward again as we climbed a giant stone staircase.

I watched him as we walked, but he said nothing else. Nothing in his expression indicated discomfort or fear or even disgust.

Relief swelled in my chest. He didn't think I was a freak. A defect.

Of course he wouldn't. Everyone here is defective.

I tried not to let that thought squash my spirits.

"Why did you seem so surprised to see me?" I asked.

"Well, like I said, we haven't had a newcomer in three years. It was startling."

"No one told you ahead of time?"

Riker chuckled. "We don't have reliable communication in the eighteenth century. And certainly no way to communicate with other time periods."

I tried not to roll my eyes again. *Right. This time travel nonsense.* "I see."

Riker's smile widened, and he winked at me. "I know you've still got your doubts. You probably think I'm insane. Don't fret, I don't think any less of you for it. We all had to come around in our own time."

We reached the top of the staircase and passed by several doors with gold handles and elaborate, swirling patterns carved into them. I gazed down the long hallway lined by a crimson carpet. It seemed to stretch on for miles.

"How many others are here?" I asked.

"A dozen."

"And where are they?"

"Training. They sent me to fetch more blankets to keep Izzy warm."

I frowned, and he laughed again.

"Izzy's hands keep turning to ice. Yesterday it was fire.

I'm sure tomorrow it will be something else. Perhaps her wind will be uncontrollable. Who knows?"

Unease spread through me. He was suspiciously cheerful about a girl who might die of frostbite at any second. "Shouldn't you go help her? What if she freezes to death?"

"She won't. The Count has the situation well in hand should the worst happen."

"Who is this Count? And why is he in charge?"

"He's a . . . distant relation of some duke or other. He owns the castle."

"And what time is he from?" I tried to hide the scorn in my voice, but Riker winked at me again.

"This time. He's one of the founders of Spain's magical Council."

My eyes widened. I knew from my lengthy studies of the American history of magic that our Council wasn't founded until the early 1800s. A dozen questions and doubts circled my mind, and I shook my head to clear them.

"I know it's a lot." Riker stopped and jerked his head toward the closed door in front of us. "Go rest. I'll make sure someone sends a meal up for you." He patted my hand.

I swallowed and nodded numbly. Though I still didn't believe him about the time travel, I somehow knew something was off about this place.

"1970s?" Riker asked.

I stared at him. "What?"

"Are you from the '70s?"

I shook my head. "2020."

Riker sucked in a breath. "Blimey."

I frowned. "Why? What time are you from?"

"1981."

My gaze moved up and down, taking in his outfit that seemed fit for royalty. "Right."

Riker snorted and gestured to his clothes. "Don't mind this. It's all they have here, and the Count likes to keep to his rules. I showed up here in jeans just like you did." He exhaled, shaking his head, his eyes full of humor and amazement. "2020. Bloody incredible." He pointed to the closed door in front of us. "This is your guest room. I'll inform the Count and the others that you're here."

He didn't move. Then his arm shifted, and I realized I still had an iron grip on him. I relaxed my fingers, but my hand shook.

"You'll be fine, Miss Gerrick." He bowed his head to me. "We'll help you transition. Don't fret." He offered a charming smile and turned on his heel before disappearing down the hallway.

5

BRIELLE

I ENTERED THE ROOM AND CLOSED THE DOOR BEHIND me. A large four-poster canopy bed rested in the middle of the room. A chaise sofa was on the opposite end, flanked by mahogany end tables with vases that surely cost a fortune. The walls were decorated with swirling crimson and gold paint that stretched around the entire room.

I sucked in a breath at the sheer elegance of it all and slid my bag off my shoulder. I pulled out my cell phone from my pocket and tried calling Mom. No signal. No bars. I couldn't connect to the internet or even send a text message.

Then again, this place was supposed to be super remote. Maybe that was why I had no service.

Groaning, I flopped down on the bed and rubbed my eyes. Despite the sun streaming through the window, I was exhausted from the effort of Demonhunting and saying goodbye to my family. My stomach twisted at the thought.

How was I supposed to contact them if there wasn't any

signal out here? Perhaps there was a landline somewhere, but if they were keeping up this whole "eighteenth century" ruse, then I highly doubted there would be a phone anywhere.

Maybe I could convince someone to escort me to the nearest town and find a phone or computer to use. After all, I wasn't a threat if I had no powers, right?

I wanted to collapse and sleep right then and there, but my outfit was still covered in blood, and I needed to check out my injured leg. With a sigh, I undressed, wincing as I slid my stained pants off my legs. Three long gashes marred my shin, courtesy of the vampire's claws. The bastard.

I dug through the bag Mom had packed for me and found a first aid kit. *Thank you, Mom.* Gritting my teeth, I dabbed my wound with an alcohol wipe and then wrapped it in a bandage. Then, I hobbled over to the magnificent wardrobe on the left wall and eased open the doors. Dozens of silky satin gowns hung before me in a rainbow of every color imaginable. I swallowed down bile at the thought of dressing in those frilly, dainty dresses. *Over my dead body.*

Thank goodness Mom had packed me extra outfits. If I found a way to wash them myself, I'd never have to wear a dress.

I reached into my bag until I found an extra pair of jeans and a tank top. After changing, I collapsed on the giant bed, which smelled of honey and roses, and instantly fell asleep.

∾

A light knock sounded at the door.

"Mmm?" I grunted sleepily, turning over on the pillow.

"*Su criada, mi señora,*" said a soft voice.

I opened my eyes and frowned. "*Criada?*" Handmaid?

"*Sí, mi señora. ¿Podría entrar?*"

I cleared my throat and sat up, patting down my hair. "Um, yes. *Sí.*"

The door opened, and a dark-skinned woman entered. A white bonnet covered her black hair, and she wore a plain gray dress. She carried a tray with fruits, bread, and cheese and carefully set it on the table next to the bed.

I watched her, racking my brain. Was she magical? Ordinarily the innate translation charm among casters allowed foreigners to understand one another. In my case, I was fluent in both English and Spanish, so I wasn't sure how that worked for me.

It was also possible she was mortal.

In Spanish, I asked her, "What's your name?"

"Maria." The woman offered a curtsy and clasped her hands in front of her. Her brow furrowed when she looked at my outfit. "May I help you dress?"

"No thanks. I'm fine wearing this."

Maria's lips tightened. "The Count will not like it, my lady."

The Count can shove it up his ass. I cleared my throat. "How long have you worked here, Maria?"

"I have been in the Count's service for seven years, though it is hard to keep track with the blight, my lady."

"Blight?"

"Yes. The curse." Her eyes darkened, her brows pinching, and I knew she would speak no more of it.

She must believe in this crazy time jump too. I refrained from rolling my eyes.

Maria bent and gathered my bloodied outfit into her arms. "Shall I wash these for you?"

"Um, yes. Thanks."

Maria bobbed another curtsy and headed for the door. "Dinner is in one hour, my lady. The Count expects all guests to attend." She cast another disapproving look at me, her eyes raking over my bare shoulders and arms, before she left, closing the door softly behind her.

I shook my head. A *handmaid*? Seriously?

With a sigh, I slid over to the tray of food and popped a few grapes in my mouth. The cheese tasted fresh and the bread was buttered to perfection. Within minutes, I'd eaten everything.

I ran a hand through my brittle blond hair and sighed, rising from the bed to take a look in the mirror. My hair still looked a bit wild, so I used the brush on the vanity to pull the tangles free and make it look a bit more presentable. Goosebumps tickled my arms, and I dug through my bag until I found a light jacket. After putting it on, I rubbed my arms and looked around, my hands itching to do something.

I approached the bed and straightened the comforter and the sheets, then rearranged the pillows neatly. Then I put the first aid kit back into the messenger bag and slid it out of sight under the bed. My eyes roved around the room. It looked as untouched as when I'd first entered.

For some reason, this brought me satisfaction. And with it, a sense of peace that eased my anxiety.

I can do this.

The holsters around my chest and waist felt empty, but I tried not to dwell on it. I kept them there on the off chance I could find a dagger or two during my stay here. With no powers, weapons were all I had to protect myself. Or a well-written spell.

After taking a deep breath, I heaved open the heavy door and hobbled into the hallway. Voices echoed below me, and I peered over the balcony to see a few figures disappear around the corner. I recognized the bright red hair of Riker.

I crept down the staircase and followed the hall to where I'd seen the others. It opened up to a magnificent dining hall filled with medieval-style tables that could seat twenty people each.

I lingered in the hallway, peering around the corner to take in my surroundings first. A single figure stood at the head of the table, his fingers clasped in front of him as he watched the gaggle of people enter. He had long brown hair swept up in an elegant ponytail and a beard that fell to his collarbone. He was adorned in a regal white overcoat and a crimson cravat. A sword was belted at his waist.

Twelve people approached the man—who was most likely the Count—with Riker among them. Many of them looked to be teenagers. When I thought about it, it made sense; the Council had told me I had until my sixteenth birthday for my powers to awaken. Perhaps the others had had a similar deadline.

One of them seemed to be an older woman. She had stark-white hair pulled up in tresses that beautifully framed her face. But then she turned her head to laugh at something, and her face was youthful and wrinkle-free. I realized she was also young—she just had white hair for some reason.

The guests all looked so different. Some had dark brown skin, others lighter brown or merely tan, and some were pasty and pale like Riker and me. It seemed like this ragtag band of misfits had come from all over the world.

They were all dressed like courtiers. Even the white-haired girl wore a smooth satin dress and sparkling jewelry.

It really did feel like I'd stepped into another time period.

A burst of light made me gasp. Flames erupted in the center of the room, engulfing a boy with shaggy, blond hair. Then, just as suddenly, the flames died and he shook his head, his body and clothes untouched from the fire.

"Watch yourself, Mr. Porter," the man at the head of the table chided. He spoke in a deep, booming voice and a thick, Spanish accent. "We'd rather not have you burn our food."

"I apologize, Your Excellency." The boy inclined his head. His accent was American, like mine.

The guests gathered around the Count, seating themselves in front of the empty plates and bowls.

I took a deep breath and emerged from around the corner, keeping my head held high.

The Count, who had just sat down, rose again, his eyes lifting to meet mine. His lips tightened, and he looked over my unorthodox appearance. He sniffed.

"Ah. You must be our newest arrival." He stretched his hand to the empty seat next to the white-haired girl. "Please, join us."

I hobbled forward and slid into the seat without preamble. The Count wrinkled his nose, no doubt offended that I didn't curtsy or address him.

The white-haired girl glanced at me with raised eyebrows, her charcoal-colored eyes amused. I looked around at the others. One boy had dark skin and dread-locks. Another had light brown skin and short black hair. Next to him sat Riker, who winked at me. On his other side was a short, chubby boy with jet-black hair and a round nose. Then, the shaggy-haired blond named Porter, a tall and skinny brown-haired boy, a boy with shoulder-length black hair, another blond with light facial hair, a boy with skin as dark as the one with dreadlocks, a pale-faced boy with sandy-brown hair, and a short and stocky blond who looked like he could belong on the wrestling team at my high school.

I knew I'd never keep all of them straight. My head spun just looking at them all, so I directed my gaze to the shining silver plate in front of me.

"We are pleased to have another guest here," the Count said. "I am Count Antonio de Silva, son of the twelfth Duke of Alba. My brother is Fernando de Paula de Silva Mendoza y Toledo, who is the tenth Duke of Huescar."

Lilith, what a mouthful. My eyes widened for a moment before I realized the Count expected an answer. I inclined my head politely. "Pleased to meet you."

"You may address me as 'Your Excellency.'"

I cleared my throat. "Um, okay. Your Excellency."

I hadn't meant to sound sarcastic. Honest.

But he still heard the bite in my voice, and his lips tightened again. He lifted a hand to the boy with dreadlocks next to him. "This is Abraham Abernathy. Next to him is Wesley Cunningham. Then Riker Wilkinson, who I believe you've met. Elias Wood, Harrison Porter, Jacques St. Clair, Juan Arévalo, Alexei Petrov, Armin Patel, Samson Schubert, Christopher Knox, and Isabel Stark." He finally gestured to the white-haired girl, who smirked at me.

Ah, I realized. *This must be Izzy.*

I nodded, offering a smile I knew looked fake. But I couldn't help it. "It's nice to meet all of you. I'm Brielle." I considered asking them to call me "Brie," but my throat felt tight as I thought of my family. They were the only ones to call me that— even people at school called me Brielle—so the words died on my lips.

The Count cleared his throat and shifted in his seat. "I understand there are certain . . . customs where you come from. But here we abide by the principles of this time and do not use Christian names."

I raised an eyebrow. *Yeah, right.* I met Riker's gaze across the table, and half his mouth quirked up in a knowing smile. He'd used the name Izzy with me earlier. There was no way they all followed this rule.

I realized the Count was waiting for me to respond, so I said, "Uh, okay. Miss Gerrick is fine then."

The Count nodded and directed his gaze to the door, where several servants poured in carrying trays laden with food: a roast pig, potatoes, seasoned vegetables, sliced bread and cheese, and fresh fruit. The aromas wafting from the food swirled in my nose, making my mouth water even though I'd just eaten.

When a servant placed a heaping plate in front of me, I immediately started eating. The flavors burst on my tongue, and I had to suppress a moan of satisfaction.

The Count cleared his throat loudly at the head of the table. I looked up and realized no one had started eating yet. Riker was smirking at me again.

I set my fork down and raised my eyebrows expectantly.

"We say Grace before each meal," the Count said stiffly.

I had to refrain from rolling my eyes. *Of course. Keeping up the time travel facade.*

The Count bowed his head and said a prayer in what sounded like Latin. When he finished, several others around the table whispered, "Amen." Many didn't, however, including Isabel next to me. The Count crossed himself and then began eating. I stared at him, frowning. Once again, the translation charm hadn't converted his words to English. I made a mental note to do some research with whatever texts I could find here about the translation charm and how it worked.

"It's nice to finally have another girl around here," Isabel said, nudging me with her elbow. Her skin felt ice-cold.

I looked at her, trying to place her accent. "Australian?" I asked.

Isabel grinned. "Pure Aussie right here. You're American, right?"

"Yep."

"You can call me Izzy, if you like," Isabel said. "It's Brielle, isn't it?"

I nodded, taking another bite of food.

"Just so you know," Izzy said, pointing with her fork, "St. Clair, Arévalo, and Petrov don't speak English." She gestured to the skinny brown-haired boy, the one with shoulder-length black hair, and the blond with facial hair. "Patel speaks some broken English, but he's still hard to understand." She pointed to the dark-skinned boy next to Petrov.

Armin Patel, I remembered. The newest one here besides me.

"What do you mean, they don't speak English?" I asked. "The translation charm should allow us to understand each other, right?"

Izzy shook her head. "It hasn't been invented yet."

I gaped at her. "Invented? But . . . it's built into our *bodies.*"

"Right. But it developed from some serum in the late eighteenth century that the Council mandated we inject ourselves with. From there, all magical offspring were born with it in their bloodstream."

A chill swept through me. *It hasn't been invented yet.*

Lilith, it couldn't be true. It just couldn't.

"You're looking kind of pale there, Brielle," Izzy leaned closer to me. "You all right?"

I swallowed. "Uh, what . . . year are you from?"

"1968."

I closed my eyes, suddenly feeling sick.

"You?" she asked.

"2020."

"Crikey." Izzy whistled. "What's it like? Do we have vehicles that fly? Or communication devices small enough to fit in our ears? Or a cure for the deadliest disease?"

Merciful Lilith. I can't breathe. I ducked my head, sucking in sharp gulps of air, trying to ignore the way her questions circled through my brain. She was right about all but the flying cars.

"It's true then?" I asked in a raspy voice. "This really is—"

"The year 1735. It's a bloody inconvenience. There isn't a single dunny around here."

I blinked, feeling dizzy. "Dunny?"

"Right, uh, latrine. Toilet. John. Loo. Whatever you Americans call it."

"I'm gonna be sick," I muttered.

Izzy just laughed. "We've all been there, Brielle. Trust me. You'll get over it."

I gritted my teeth. "I don't want to get over it. I want to get the hell out of here."

I jumped up from my seat so fast that the dishes clattered on the table. The chatter surrounding me died, and the Count looked at me, his dark eyes sharpening.

"I'm sorry," I said loudly. "I just . . . I can't do this."

Without preamble, I fled from the room as fast as my injured leg would allow.

6

LEO

"ARE WE CLOSE?" I ASKED.

"Yes," Jorge said, poring over a thick text of Spanish spells. "Just a few more ingredients, and the spell will be complete."

I nodded, looking around the vast, homey cavern of our library until my gaze rested on my cousin, Guadalupe. "Do you have it?"

Guadalupe lifted a large, ceramic bowl. "A drop of blood from everyone here."

I knew this, of course. I could smell the unique tang to every creature's blood—both from my vampire coven as well as our human Donors.

But I needed reassurance all the same.

"Are you certain the right spell is in Spanish?" Jorge asked, glancing up at me. "What if he used Latin?"

I shook my head. "Latin spells are risky. There are too

many variables. Too many interpretations that might go awry if cast incorrectly. If the Count wanted to be certain the spell would work, he would use his native tongue. I'm certain of it."

Jorge pressed his lips together doubtfully but made no argument.

Estrella strode into the cavern, her cheeks still flushed from our last feeding. "The other Donors are secure." Her warm brown eyes met mine, and my blood boiled, coming to life from her proximity.

The bond between vampire and Donor was a volatile thing. And too dangerous for me to toy with during an event as important as this.

I waved a hand at Estrella. "Thank you. Please go to your quarters and stay hidden until we are through."

Estrella bowed her head, reading the need in my voice, and left the cave quickly. She understood the bond too. It thrived within us like a living creature. Awakening when we drew near. Growling when we parted.

I shoved the discomfort down and willed my blood to take control again. My body was always chaotic after a feeding, but I had to be sure I was at full strength.

Today was the day we would break through the Count's barrier surrounding the city. I was sure of it. We'd been trapped in his magical dome for months now, unable to travel outside the province of Segovia.

But no more. Today we would break the enchantment and free ourselves.

I clapped my hands together, grinning at Jorge and Guadalupe. "The time is near, my friends. Gather round and bring the ingredients."

Guadalupe hefted the large bowl and strode toward me. Jorge brought the book and the cauldron of ingredients, which reeked of mucus and rotten leaves. Jorge placed the large text on the table in the center of the room. Guadalupe set the bowl on the floor and used a dagger to etch runes into the cavern floor.

I stood over the cauldron, running my hands along the rim. Black wisps of magic poured from my fingertips and settled on the mixture within. Power thrummed from the cauldron.

This is it, it seemed to say.

Guadalupe rejoined us once the runes were complete. She slid her dagger along her palm and passed it to Jorge, who did the same. I followed suit, ignoring the stinging cut against my skin that quickly healed itself. The three of us clasped hands. Though a full coven would be more powerful, I couldn't risk it if something went wrong. Besides, we were part shapeshifter and part vampire. Two lines of magic flowed through our veins.

Our power would be enough.

I peered at the text and the notes I'd jotted down on the edge of the page. Then, I uttered the spell in Spanish.

"Magic above, I call upon thee
Respond to this spell
Seal this blood and free us

Unlock the curse and enchant us
Eliminate this force that traps us
And break us free of this magic."

More magic poured from my fingers like smoke, engulfing the cauldron and the bowl of blood. The ground trembled. Magic crackled in the air around us. Guadalupe's hand tightened in my grip. Energy thrummed in my chest, swelling and growing until—

Like a snuffed-out candle, the magic vanished. The cave grew still, and the energy seeped out of my body, leaving me cold and empty.

"No," I whispered.

"It didn't work," Guadalupe said in a hollow voice, releasing my hand.

A flash of heat bolted through my chest, and I sucked in a breath. I looked at Jorge with wide eyes. His stunned expression indicated he'd felt it too.

"That feeling," he murmured, his eyes unfocused. "I have felt it before."

"I have too," I said, struggling to remember. Images flashed through my head. Bits and pieces of memories I couldn't grasp.

Then, finally, an image I recognized: the Castillo de Coca. That same bolt of heat seared through me the last time I'd entered the castle, which was several miles away from our caves.

I stiffened and stared at Jorge, finally putting the pieces together. I hadn't considered the Count had enchanted the castle as well as the city.

A wide grin stretched across my face.

"The *castle* was enchanted?" Jorge asked slowly.

"Yes," I said, laughing at this unexpected victory. We might still be trapped within the city, but at least we had another advantage. "And we've just broken that enchantment."

7
BRIELLE

I DARTED DOWN HALLWAYS AND UP AND DOWN staircases, trying to find the marble floor I'd appeared on earlier. I had to find a way back through the portal. My injured leg throbbed with each step. Panic raced through me, urging me to go faster.

Footsteps echoed behind me, but I kept going.

I have to get out of here. They're all insane. Every one of them. It really is *an insane asylum.*

I thought of the food I'd ingested. Had it been drugged? Was I about to take part in the same collective hallucination?

"Brielle!" a voice shouted. Izzy.

Ignore her, I told myself. *Keep going.*

I rounded the corner, and there it was: the colorful octagon of tiles on the floor, shining in the moonlight pouring from a window up high.

Rushing forward, I got down on all fours and lay on the

ground, just as I had when I'd arrived. I knew I was being ridiculous, but I didn't care. I had to get home. Now.

I took a deep breath, waiting for the familiar thrum of magic. When nothing happened, I wiggled my fingers and murmured,

"Magic above and powers that roam
Surround me here, and bring me home."

Magic crackled from my fingers, and a blue glow emanated from my hands. But then it flickered and faded like a burnt-out light bulb.

"No," I whispered. I closed my eyes and tried again.

"I call on magic within my soul,
Carry me home and make me whole."

Still nothing.

I swore and spat another spell.

"Magia rota, sana y devuélveme
Llévame a casa a dos mil veinte."

Again, nothing happened.

A frustrated scream tore against my throat. I lifted my hands to my forehead and tugged at my hair, trying to ignore the mounting panic within me.

Have to get out. Now.

I sucked in a breath and bolted, racing down hallways and passing stunned servants until I finally found a giant set of oak doors.

Yes! The way out.

I reached for the doors, but a servant stepped toward me.

"May I help you, my lady?" he asked in Spanish.

"I have to get out of here," I muttered, trying to sidestep him. But he continued to block my exit.

"I'm afraid His Excellency has strict orders for the guests to—"

"I don't give a *damn*!" I roared, clenching my fingers into fists. "Either step aside, or I will *fight* you."

The servant stared me down, his dark eyes shifting from apathy to genuine fear. He swallowed and quietly shuffled out of my way.

I threw open the doors, and a cool evening breeze rippled over me. Just a gulp of fresh air was enough to soothe the hysteria in my mind.

I can do this. I can find a way out of here and get back home.

Voices echoed behind me. I surged forward, slamming the doors shut. Then, I sprinted down a massive set of concrete steps. The faint light of the moon in the sky illuminated the path before me. Neatly trimmed hedges lined the stairs, and a plethora of floral scents flooded my nose, though it was too dark to make out any flowers.

I flew down the steps. My breaths came in sharp wheezes, and a sheen of sweat formed on my brow despite the chill in the air.

When I reached the bottom, I stopped short. A lush forest surrounded a narrow dirt road, but something tickled the air. Something *magical.*

Slowly, I moved forward, following the scent. It crackled and shifted in the air like it was alive.

I took another step, and something invisible slammed

into me. I bounced backward and almost fell over. Stumbling back a few steps, I righted myself and rubbed my throbbing head.

What the hell was that?

A familiar smell tickled the air, and it took me a moment to place it. Ash, onions, and seaweed. It smelled the same as the portal I'd fallen through.

Frowning, I inched forward again, this time extending my hand. My fingers met something soft and cool that fluttered against my skin like a curtain. When I touched it, a faint green light flashed, zapping my fingers as if I'd been electrocuted.

I jumped and jerked away, shaking my hand to rid myself of the numbness.

I rubbed my forehead as the panic started to overwhelm me again. "Why can't I get out of here?"

"Because of my wards," rumbled a voice from behind me.

I looked over my shoulder to find the Count standing there watching me. His eyes glinted with interest. Behind him, I noticed Riker and a few of the others.

"Let me *out*," I growled, glaring at him. "You can't keep me here like a prisoner."

"I'm afraid I can't release you until we've conducted a thorough assessment of your abilities," the Count said quietly. "You see, the guests in my home often pose a threat to others. So, it isn't safe to simply allow you to run amok in the city."

My fists shook, and I stared hard at him.

"Miss Gerrick," the Count said, stepping toward me. "I believe it's time we spoke in private so I can explain the situation to you."

I briefly considered trying to fight him, but between the other teenagers behind him and the host of servants in the castle, I knew I was outnumbered.

Begrudgingly, I followed the Count back inside the castle and into a vast library with shelves climbing higher than my house in Miami. We sat across from each other in grand armchairs next to a crackling fire. I wrung my hands together on my lap, itching to tidy something. With these bookshelves surrounding me, all I wanted to do was spend a day reorganizing them. Oh, the satisfaction that would give me.

"So, Miss Gerrick," the Count said, rubbing his bearded chin. "You were trying to return home?"

"I can speak Spanish, if that's easier for you."

The Count smiled, though it didn't reach his eyes. "I am quite comfortable speaking English. Don't trouble yourself."

I sighed and slumped back in the chair. "Yes, I was trying to leave."

"I fear I must inform you that that's impossible."

I stilled. "Why?"

The Count stared pensively into the fire for a moment before responding. "What do you know of Lilith's curse?"

My blood ran cold. "I know she is said to possess a witch and harness her powers to summon a demonic monster."

The Count chuckled, sounding impressed. "Well then, you know much more than my other pupils did when they arrived. You see, in 1735, a monster was unleashed upon the province of Segovia, slaughtering thousands. My magical comrades and I did everything we could to prevent the destruction, but we were too late. One of us, a powerful dark warlock, cast a wild and uncontrollable spell that turned into a curse. He wanted to bring back those who were lost, but he didn't word the curse carefully enough. Instead, his magic trapped the entire province in a sort of . . . 'time loop,' as Mr. Wilkinson would put it. The same year repeats over and over again. None of us can leave the province. At the end of every year, the beast attacks and we can do nothing to stop it. Then, the year resets again, and everything is restored to what it was before. We are trapped here, forever preserved in time as we relive the same year again. And again."

I narrowed my eyes. "A time loop. Really." *And all because of Lilith's curse? This can't be a coincidence. Someone is playing a joke on me.*

The Count shook his head, smirking. "I realize how truly inconceivable this all sounds."

"What about the rest of the world—outside of Segovia? Are they frozen too?"

"No."

My brow furrowed. "How do you know?"

"We have been to the barrier separating the province from the outside world. We can see through it, though no one can see us."

"And you can't get through it? You don't have a Teleporter who can Jump you through it?"

The Count wrinkled his nose, no doubt offended by the offensive term 'Jump.' "No. There are no Teleporters here, otherwise I would've had one Teleport us to the other side of the barrier long ago."

"And your wards—"

"They are there to protect the city from any, ah, accidents my guests might cause."

"But if the year resets, won't the civilians just forget whatever happened?"

"Yes, but each year I'm hopeful we can find a way to break this curse. When we do, everyone in the city will keep their memories. It is a risk I'm unwilling to take."

I crossed my arms, raising an eyebrow. "So, the Council just sent me into a portal through *time* to a place that was frozen in the year 1735?"

"The Councils across time are not aware of the situation. We have no way to communicate our problem to them, and even if we could, we aren't sure the message would get through the barriers of the curse."

"Why is there even a portal to begin with? Can't someone close it to stop people from coming here?"

"We've tried. When I first established this as a refuge for injured casters, I proclaimed it as a rehabilitation center, welcoming any who needed assistance with their magic. I'm not sure how that proclamation traveled through years and even centuries, but it seems that even in your time, the Council still sees this as a refuge for those with magical maladies."

"What about the Council here? Riker said you founded them. Did you tell them of this place?"

"Of course I did."

I scoffed, letting my arms fall on my lap. "That was a stupid move. They've obviously passed on the information for generations. *That's* how the word was spreading."

The Count's eyes tightened. "I assure you that had I known we would be cursed, I never would have shared the information."

"So, who designed this portal in the first place?"

The Count straightened in his chair. "I did. But no matter what spell I attempt, I have no way of accessing the portal on this end while we are cursed."

I remembered the familiar smells of the portal and the wards. It made sense—if the Count created both, they would smell like his magic.

"Can't someone reverse the curse and free you?" I asked.

"Unfortunately, the dark warlock who cast it wasn't in his right mind. He wrote the spell himself. It would be impossible for us to reverse it without knowing the exact words he used, and he is dead."

"Mother of Lilith." I ran a hand through my hair and laughed without humor. "This is a real sick prank you're pulling on me, *Your Excellency.*"

"I assure you, it is *not* a prank." He fixed a stony stare on me.

A small part of me wanted to wither under his scrutiny, but I firmly held his gaze. "And you all just carry on here like normal then? Training these inept and broken witches and warlocks?"

The Count lifted his hands. "What else am I to do?"

My hands curled into fists on the arms of my chair. "So, there is *no way* for me to get home? No way out of here whatsoever?"

"I'm afraid not."

The panic rushed inside me like a dam had burst. *I can't get home. I can't leave.* Mom might already be freaking out because I hadn't contacted her yet.

My palms started to sweat. I had to move. I had to do something.

I jumped up from my seat and approached the nearest bookshelf, pulling out several books at a time. I took a moment to inspect each one—some were in Greek or Latin, so I focused on the color instead. *Green books over here. Blue over there. This one's bluish green. Yes, right there.*

"What in Lilith's name are you doing?" the Count asked.

I just shushed him and continued reorganizing. When I'd created an aesthetically pleasing shelf of rainbow books, I stood back to admire my work. My heart rate settled into a steady rhythm, and my body felt less restless.

I took a deep breath and slowly sat back down again, meeting the Count's bewildered stare.

"It's how I cope with stress," I snapped. "It's either that or kickboxing, but I don't imagine you'd like me doing that in your precious castle."

The Count wrinkled his nose. "No, I would not."

I blew out a breath through my lips, puffing out my

cheeks. "So, what am I supposed to do? You expect me to just sit around and hope this curse will end on its own?"

"Of course not," the Count said coldly. "I have a coven working tirelessly, trying to find a way to end this dark creature that emerges every year. We believe that, through the monster's demise, the curse will be broken, since the dark warlock's magic is tethered to the creature."

I stilled, staring hard at the flames in the fireplace. "And what of . . . this cursed witch? The one who summoned the creature in the first place?"

The Count scoffed, waving a hand. "She is an abomination. A crime against nature. She doesn't deserve to live. When the creature dies, so shall she. Lilith's power will be cut off and she will be sent back to the underworld."

A lump formed in my throat. *An abomination. A crime against nature.*

The Count eyed me, his expression calculating. "I heard you utter those spells earlier. You're quite talented at wordsmithing. I could use your help in our endeavor to break the curse."

I swallowed. "Help? What am I supposed to do about it?"

The Count leaned forward. "First and foremost, I must know why you're here. Why did your Council send you?"

I froze, my brain working furiously. I couldn't tell him I was suspected of being Lilith's cursed witch. He would murder me on the spot.

Instead, I took a breath and said, "My powers aren't working. I'm an Elemental, and they were working fine

74

until about five years ago. Then they just flickered and . . . died. I haven't been able to access them since."

"Hmm." The Count stroked his chin again. "Fascinating. I've never heard of such a problem. And you are quite certain your gifts were of an elemental nature?"

I nodded, dropping my gaze. "Yes, of course."

"I see." He dropped his hand. "Well, a few examinations and trainings should sort you out. Several of my pupils have already greatly improved, so much so they are able to help me in my efforts to protect this city and restore the timeline. You, of course, must remain here in the castle and abide by our rules." He wrinkled his nose, his eyes roving up and down my body. "Please note that we adhere to the customs of this time period and you must blend in if you are to remain here."

I grimaced. Just imagining having to wear one of those frilly dresses made me feel nauseous. I shifted in my chair. "Fine."

The Count's eyes sharpened. "So, you'll assist me?"

I waved a hand vaguely. "Sure, I guess. I don't have much of a choice, do I?"

The Count smirked, sitting back in his chair. "I'm glad we understand one another."

8

BRIELLE

Despite my begrudging acceptance of my circumstances, I couldn't help but check my cell phone when I got back to my room that night.

Still no service.

Agony laced through my chest, bitter and all-consuming. Emotions choked my throat as I pulled up my photos and scrolled through pictures of Angel, my parents, and a few friends from school.

I would never see any of them again.

I shut my eyes against the onslaught of panic threatening to drown me.

I can do this. I can get out of here if I figure out how to break this curse.

As the Count said, I was excellent at wordsmithing. I'd spent my whole life writing spells because it was all I *could* do.

If I could handle fighting demons on my own, then I

could handle this too.

A light knock rapped at the door.

I cleared my throat and pocketed my phone. "Come in."

Maria entered, holding a stack of blankets and a long metal object with a pan attached to the end. A bedpan maybe?

My knowledge of the eighteenth century was woefully lacking.

"Ready to undress, my lady?" Maria asked, setting the pile of blankets down on the night table.

I crossed my arms and eyed the bedpan-looking thing. "Am I . . . do I need to pee in that?"

Maria's eyes widened, and a blush bloomed across her face. "Oh no, my lady. This is a warming pan. To ward off the chill in the winter."

"Winter?" I frowned. My birthday was September 7, which was the day I'd left. "What—what month is it?"

"January, my lady."

I stared vacantly at the wall just behind Maria, trying to focus on breathing.

"Pupils always arrive when the year resets," Maria went on, placing the warming pan into the fireplace.

"But—but it was September when I left."

Maria nodded. "No one is quite sure how it works, my lady. A caster steps through the portal, and time speeds up to arrive precisely at this time."

I shook my head. *This is insane. Absolutely insane.* I sat on the edge of the bed, bouncing my leg up and down. "So, uh, where exactly do I . . . do my business?"

Maria looked at me, the corners of her mouth pulling into a smile. "The chamber pot, my lady." She gestured to what looked like an ornate pot for plants in the corner of the room. "If you like, I can come back in a few minutes and empty it for you. So you don't have to smell it as you sleep."

My face burned, and I nodded. "That'd be great. Thanks."

Maria offered a kind smile and set the handle of the warming pan down on the floor. She curtsied and left the room.

I sighed and undressed before squatting and doing my business. Instead of putting my jeans back on, I slipped on a pair of sweats from my bag and climbed into bed before Maria returned.

She stopped short when she saw me in the bed. "Are you undressed, my lady?"

I nodded.

Maria opened and closed her mouth. "Won't you need my assistance?"

I smiled. "Not tonight. I'm still adjusting. I know the Count has his rules, but can you let it slide just this once? I'm a little overwhelmed."

Maria's eyes filled with sympathy, and she smiled again. "Of course, my lady."

Using the tongs by the fireplace, Maria placed several coals into the warming pan. Then, she slid the pan under the sheets just past my feet. Heat tickled the tips of my toes, and I sighed with contentment.

Maria bustled about for a few more minutes, snuffing candles and tending to the dying fire. Then, she turned to face me and curtsied again. "I'll be back in the morning. Sleep well, my lady."

I thanked her before she left. The door closed, and silence pressed in on me, along with the wintry chill. Spain had always struck me as a hot place like Miami, but this was colder than any of our winters. I rolled a little to one side, then the other, pulling the blankets more snugly around my body and pressing my toes into the warm sheets.

The next morning, I woke with aches in my body from sleeping in an unfamiliar bed. My head throbbed from sleep deprivation. I'd tossed and turned, my head swarming with thoughts and worries well into the night.

Maria helped me dress in one of the ridiculous frilly gowns. When she asked my color preference, I told her to pick. She'd chosen a deep coffee brown, claiming it would bring out my eyes.

Yes, I thought grumpily. *My duller-than-dirt brown eyes.*

Maria wrapped a stiff brace around my midsection and pulled. I sucked in a gasp and choked as my back arched and tremendous pressure slammed into my chest. "What the hell is this?"

Maria released a small yelp at the swear word and laughed nervously. "Be at ease, my lady. This is a corset. You'll adjust to it."

I don't want to adjust to it.

When she finished, I was standing up much straighter than normal. Already the muscles in my back ached from holding myself up so high.

Lilith help me.

Then Maria fitted me with petticoats before fastening the dress on top of that. The skirts poofed out, making me look like a brown marshmallow—or a giant turd. To be honest, I felt like the latter. My sleeves were a mass of lace and itchy fabric. And the neckline was much lower than I would have liked, accentuating the flatness of my chest.

"A vision," Maria said, beaming at me. "How would you like your hair, my lady?"

"No!" I blurted. "Please, don't. Leave it as it is."

Maria's smile faded, her face looking as forlorn as a kid who found out Christmas was canceled.

I sighed, dropping my arms. "Fine. But make it as plain as possible. No fuss."

Maria inclined her head. "Yes, my lady."

Despite my insistence for simplicity, it still took almost an hour to get my hair done. Maria stuck a few tools in the fire to warm them, then pinned my hair up into an elaborate knot. She pulled a few chunks of hair loose from the top and dampened them using water from the pitcher. Then she removed the tools from the fire and used them to curl the loose pieces of my hair. She pinned those as well, so they rested against my cheeks, delicately framing my pale face.

I peeked in the mirror and had to refrain from gagging. I looked like freaking Marie Antoinette. Feminine. Weak.

Ridiculous.

"You are stunning, my lady," Maria breathed, her eyes sparkling.

I cleared my throat. "Um. Thanks."

I was seriously starting to reconsider agreeing to abide by the Count's rules. At this point, even facing Lilith's beast seemed more appealing.

I strode downstairs, but between my injured leg and the mountain of fabric surrounding me, it was slow work. Gritting my teeth, I hefted up my vast skirts to give my legs some more room. It didn't make breathing any easier, though.

Curse this time period.

I was halfway down the staircase when I had to pause and catch my breath, gripping the banister tightly.

"Need a hand?" a voice behind me asked.

Panting, I looked up to find Riker behind me, offering his arm and looking gallant as ever in his waistcoat and cravat.

I rolled my eyes. "I'm perfectly . . . capable . . ."

Riker snorted and looped his arm through mine. "You're not fooling anyone, Brielle. May I call you that?"

"It *is* my name. Just don't let the Count hear you."

Riker chuckled. "You're catching on quick."

Together we strode down the stairs. I had to admit, it was a lot easier relying on someone else to carry my weight.

Riker glanced down at my leg, then back up at me with

a frown. "You're limping. Are you hurt?"

I sighed. "It's nothing."

"Blimey, Brielle. You should have said something. The Count has healers who can tend to your injury."

"I'm *fine.*"

Riker laughed, his blue eyes shining. "You are too much, Brielle. You know, I won't think less of you if you ask for help now and then."

My nostrils flared, but I said nothing.

"You're ravishing, by the way." Riker cast me a warm look.

I groaned. "I look like a freak."

Riker released a loud snort, then raised his free hand to his mouth, his eyes wide with embarrassment. He cleared his throat. "You'll get used to it. But no matter how long we've been here, we all look forward to the days when we can wear trousers."

I raised my eyebrows. "The Count allows that?"

Riker nodded. "Only on the days when the demons attack."

I froze, and for a moment Riker pulled me forward a bit before he noticed I'd stopped walking. I asked, "The demons attack? When? Where do they come from?" Despite my suffocating clothes, I felt naked without my weapons on me. *I knew I'd smelled demons when I first arrived.*

"A few days every month, the local demon coven attacks the castle," Riker said. "We aren't sure why. Maybe they think we've grown too powerful with how many we have living here. Or maybe they're enemies of the Count. But either way, because of the time loop, all events are fixed, so we know when they'll strike. We're able to prepare ourselves against their attack."

I stared at him, eyes wide. "They . . . they don't remember any previous attacks?"

"From the year before? No. Once the year resets, they do too."

"Then, how come you haven't killed them off yet?"

"We've killed a few out of necessity, but they've just come back when the year restarts again."

"So, if one of them kills one of us, then we come back too?"

"Ah." Riker rubbed the back of his neck. "That gets tricky. You see, the Count cast a powerful spell on the castle to keep us immune from the time loop—so that we remember and don't reset at the beginning of every year. But because of that, it means we're vulnerable, unlike those outside of this bubble. It was the only way for us to see any progress with our ailments, you see."

"But the demons you kill—"

"Are not considered part of the castle's enchantment. Only those who pass through the time portal are immune. The enchantment is linked to the portal."

I nodded, though I felt only more confused. My head spinning, I took a step, and Riker followed my lead, guiding me toward the dining hall.

"The Count mentioned training and examinations," I said. "What are those like?"

"Oh, it's not that bad. A few spells, a bit of blood work.

The training can get a little taxing, but . . ." He trailed off, glancing at my injured leg. He smirked. "I'm sure you've suffered worse."

I nudged him with my elbow, but my lips quirked upward in a reluctant smile.

We reached the dining hall and found half the guests were already there, including Izzy. She waved me over eagerly, and Riker obliged her, steering me toward the other side of the table to join my new friend.

"You look like a princess," Izzy said, bursting into a fit of giggles. It sounded more like an insult than a compliment.

"Thanks," I grumbled, trying to maneuver my skirts around the chair to sit down. I looked her over. She wore a bodice trimmed with lace and deep purple skirts cascaded over her legs. "You don't look much better."

Izzy snorted and drank deeply from her goblet.

"How's the ice today, Iz?" Riker asked, sliding into a seat next to me.

"Melted," Izzy said. "But I think it's because the fire's come back. We'll see."

A few of the other boys entered—the one with dreadlocks and the chubby one with dark hair. I squinted, trying to remember their names, but Riker leaned closer and whispered, "Abe and Elias."

I nodded. "How come there aren't as many girls?"

Riker shrugged one shoulder. "What does history tell you about witches? They were persecuted and hunted for so long. It was only in the last decade or so that they were more widely accepted in society. If there *were* witches with ailments like ours, I doubted the Council would offer to do anything about it before my time."

I raised an eyebrow at him.

Riker grinned. "I'm a bit of a history enthusiast."

"And do you share that opinion about women?"

Riker's smile vanished. "Lilith, no. My mum was the first female member of the Council in my country." He straightened, his eyes glinting with pride.

I couldn't help but smile in return. "That's pretty impressive. My dad serves on the Council as well."

"That's Alexei and Jacques," Riker said, gesturing to the skinny brown-haired boy and the blond with light facial hair. "Those blokes are mates because they're the only ones who speak French."

"You don't?" I raised an eyebrow.

"*Un peu, ma chérie,*" Riker said, winking at me.

I blushed and looked away. I knew little to no French, but I knew enough to understand he was flirting with me.

"That's Wes, Harrison, Sam, and Chris," Riker said, pointing to the tan boy with black hair, the shaggy-haired blond, the pale-faced sandy-haired fellow, and the one who looked like a wrestler. "I call them the Four Musketeers."

I raised an eyebrow. "But weren't there *three* musketeers?"

"Ah, that's the thing." Riker grinned at me. "The book is called *The Three Musketeers*, but when you add D'Artagnan it's actually four. Anyway, those four are inseparable. They're all from America."

My eyes widened. "Really?" I glanced at the others and

pointed to Abe and Elias. "What about them?"

Riker cleared his throat and rubbed the back of his neck. "Also American. But . . ." He trailed off, looking uncomfortable.

I frowned at him, then looked back at Abe and Elias.

Izzy leaned forward and chimed in, "The Musketeers aren't the friendliest of blokes. And they're a bit judgmental."

Realization settled in my stomach like a heavy weight. *Oh.* Abe was black and Elias was overweight. They were the outcasts.

"That's ridiculous!" I said, balling my hands into fists.

"Shh," Riker said hastily as the boys seated themselves around the table. "Keep your voice down. You're right. But the Four Musketeers don't see it that way. They're from the early 1900s. They see things differently than you and I do."

Idiots. My eyes narrowed as I watched the four boys grin at each other and sit at the table. One of them—the wrestler, Chris—swept his gaze over me and flashed a leering grin in my direction.

Douchebag. I gave him the finger.

Riker choked on his drink, spitting onto the table. He grabbed my hand and shoved it out of sight. The table groaned as Chris rose to his feet, his brows lowering over angry eyes.

"I beg your pardon, miss?" he growled.

Riker chuckled nervously, waving his hand. "Pay her no mind, mate. She's still adjusting from the transition."

Chris shot a nasty look at Riker before sitting back

down, his jaw tense.

The last guests to enter were Armin and the boy with shoulder-length black hair.

"Armin and Juan," Riker said to me. He leaned closer. "Try not to insult them, okay?"

"No promises."

Riker sighed with exasperation, but his eyes danced with amusement.

As soon as Juan sat down, servants appeared with fruit and bread to serve us. Riker immediately started scarfing down food, but I looked around, remembering my grave error from last night.

"Where's the Count?" I asked.

Riker waved a hand. "He stays in his room through most of breakfast. Be as 'unladylike' as you wish."

I laughed and leaned forward to take a bite, but my damn corset stopped me from slouching over like I usually did while eating. I lifted my arms and scooted forward, then swore so loudly that half the table stopped eating to look at me in shock. I ignored them and managed to lift the plate to my face to take several large bites.

Frantic footsteps echoed down the hallway, and I looked up from my plate. Riker's face was equally curious, so I knew this wasn't the norm.

The Count himself appeared in the dining hall, his cravat untied and his shirt untucked. Fury darkened his expression. "Forgive my imprudence, but we must leave at once. My mages have just informed me the demon coven has broken one of the time loop's enchantments."

Shock rippled across the table. Several boys gaped at the Count, and Riker's face paled. My heart thrummed anxiously in my chest. "What does that mean?"

The Count leveled a hard look at me. "It means they *remember* the events from last year, Miss Gerrick. And they could attack us unawares at any moment."

Riker jumped to his feet. "What do you want us to do, Your Excellency?"

"Mr. Wilkinson, Mr. Cunningham, Mr. Abernathy, and Mr. Knox, I want you all to launch an offensive attack to catch them off guard. Strike them first before they strike us."

Riker straightened, his jaw stiff with determination. Wes, Abe, and Chris also rose to their feet.

Chris inclined his head. "Yes, Your Excellency." His lips curled upward in a satisfied smirk.

"What about the rest of us?" I asked loudly. A few heads turned to look at me with derision.

"You will remain here, Miss Gerrick," the Count said stiffly. "My mages will see to your training and protection." He bowed his head as if this ended the discussion. Chris, Wes, and Abe followed him out of the dining hall. I caught Riker's arm before he moved to join them.

"You're going *to* the demon coven?" I hissed. "Isn't it dangerous to leave the castle?"

Riker offered a half smile. "Your concern for me is touching, Brielle. But don't worry. We've done this before." He patted my shoulder before sprinting forward to join the other men.

9
BRIELLE

I SAT BACK IN MY CHAIR AND RUBBED MY FOREHEAD. My tightly wound hair was giving me a headache, and my shoulders ached from sitting upright for so long.

Next to me, Izzy ruffled her white hair and sighed. "You'll get used to it. The Count always favors the men."

At least he isn't completely racist, though, I thought bitterly, remembering how Abe was one of the warlocks the Count had taken with him.

"Riker says they've done this before?" I asked her.

Izzy nodded. "A few times. The Count sometimes needs certain spell ingredients from the demon lair."

"Is it safe for him to take those warlocks with him if they—" I stopped, unsure of how to word my question.

"Chris, Abe, and Wes have made the most progress with their training. If it weren't for the time loop, the Count says they would've been free to return home thanks to their rehabilitation. And Riker—well, his problem only arises when he has a vision."

I raised my eyebrows. "What if he gets a vision while fighting demons?"

Izzy shot me a bewildered look. "How many Seers have you met? They rarely have visions in battle, especially if they're trained like Riker. Something about the adrenaline."

I pressed my lips together, chagrin heating my face. The only Seer I knew was Angel, and she'd never battled demons before because of her condition. But now that I thought about it, what Izzy said made sense. Angel never had visions when we were playing or hanging out at the mall. They only plagued her at home and in her sleep.

Angel. A swarm of suffocating emotions filled my chest, threatening to drown me. Grief choked my throat, gripping me tightly like a demon's claws. I closed my eyes, gritting my teeth against the agony within me at the thought of never seeing my sister again.

"You all right?" Izzy asked, touching my arm. Her touch snapped me out of my haze.

I opened my eyes and sucked in a breath. "Yeah," I said tightly. "Just fine, thanks."

Izzy leaned forward, her eyes glinting. "So . . . how'd you do that last night? Come up with spells like that?"

I frowned. "What spells?"

Izzy gestured to me. "You know, when you were trying to get back home yesterday. And what language was that?"

"Spanish."

Izzy whistled. "Crikey. You can do that?"

I sighed. "Do what? Cast a spell? Sure, can't you?"

Izzy propped her chin on her hands. "Well, yeah. But I didn't recognize those spells from the Grimoire. Unless they're spells from your time?"

"No, I wrote them myself. It's . . . a gift I have. Because of my magical issues, I needed to find *something* I was good at, so I worked at writing spells." I shrugged.

Izzy's face split into a huge grin. "That's really sick, mate. Good on ya. Wish I could do that."

Her smile was so infectious that I couldn't help but return it.

After breakfast, those of us who remained were ushered by servants into a ballroom with windows stretching from floor to ceiling, bathing the bare wooden floors in sunlight. Our footsteps echoed in the empty room.

The servants who escorted us left without a word, slamming the doors shut with their departure. Elias stood off to the side while Sam and Harrison muttered to each other. Jacques and Alexei started speaking rapidly in French, and Armin stood alone, his eyes fixed on Izzy. She didn't seem to notice.

I looked at Juan, who was watching me with a peculiar look in his eye.

"Something wrong?" I asked him in Spanish.

He blinked, his face splitting into a huge grin. "I thought I heard you speaking my native tongue earlier." He bowed his head, his hands sweeping backward in a grand gesture. "A pleasure to meet your acquaintance, Miss Gerrick."

I raised my eyebrows. "And when are you from?"

"1772. Spain."

"Ah, so you're not too far off from the Count's time then?"

"Not at all. In fact, he's acquainted with some of my relatives near the area."

I offered a fake smile. "How nice."

He cocked his head at me. "If you don't mind me asking, how is it you come to speak this language?"

"My father taught me. He's from Cuba."

Juan's eyes widened. "Cuba. I have heard stories of the little island in the Caribbean, though I have never been myself. What's it like?"

"Hot," I said flatly.

Juan stared at me, obviously waiting for more. When I said nothing, he burst into laughter. "Very amusing, Miss Gerrick."

I refrained from rolling my eyes.

Izzy nudged me with her elbow. "Making friends?"

"Hardly. What are we standing around here for?"

"Waiting for the Count's mages to come work with us. No one else is allowed in here in case we injure someone."

"Who are these 'mages'?" I asked. In my time, the term wasn't used, but I'd often read stories of mages. The Great Mage War had taken place barely a decade prior to this time.

"Fancy word for 'scholarly casters.' They train and abstain from marriage like monks, pledging their life to serving royalty in honor of guiding those with magic."

"Do you have mages where you're from?" I asked curiously. I knew quite a bit about American and Spanish magical history due to my heritage, but I didn't know much about other countries.

Izzy shook her head. "No, my country eliminated them about the time of the Great Mage War. Similar to yours, I'd wager."

The large oak doors burst open, and four bald men in sweeping purple robes entered, their postures stiff and regal and their heads held high. One of them approached me and bowed so low I thought he'd fall over. When he straightened, he clasped his hands in front of him.

"Miss Gerrick," he said softly in accented English. "It is a pleasure to meet the newest guest of the Castillo de Coca. Please follow me to complete your preliminary examinations."

My stomach did a backflip, but I nodded and limped toward him. He frowned and eyed my injured leg. "Are you well, my lady?"

My lady. Was I technically his superior? I shifted my weight uncomfortably. "I'm fine."

"May I heal that for you?"

I sighed and nodded. "Yeah. Sure." As much as I wanted to prove I was capable of letting it heal on my own, it *would* be nice to be able to walk freely in this monstrosity of a castle without feeling like I might fall over at any minute.

"Please remain still," the man said, kneeling in front of me. "This will only take a moment."

He moved his hands in the air directly in front of my injured leg, performing grand sweeping motions that tickled my nose with magic. His voice was low as he murmured words I couldn't understand—it sounded a bit like Latin to me. His hands glowed blue, and my leg stiffened as pain shot up my body. I gritted my teeth and closed my eyes.

Then the pain was gone, and with it my injury. I exhaled and stretched my leg. I felt nothing at all.

A relieved smile spread across my face. The man stood and bowed to me.

"Thank you, Mr. . . . ?"

"Ignacio Cortes."

"Mr. Cortes." I nodded to him.

He stretched his hand toward me. "Come this way, please."

I followed him out of the ballroom, casting a glance over my shoulder at the others. Izzy, Wes, and Elias crowded around one mage while the rest of the guests spoke with the other two mages. I vaguely wondered how they were grouped before the ballroom disappeared from view.

"How long have you worked for the Count?" I asked Ignacio.

"Many years," Ignacio said in a hushed voice as if we were in some sort of sacred chapel. "I am one of the few mages left in his employ after the Great War."

We strode down an empty hallway and turned into the library where I'd spoken with the Count the night before. Ignacio scooted a small table forward and placed it between the two armchairs. Then, he gestured that I sit. I hefted up my skirts and awkwardly backed into the seat until I flopped backward onto the cushion with an "oof."

A tiny smile pinched the corners of Ignacio's mouth, but he said nothing as he sat across from me. "Tell me of your magical ailment, Miss Gerrick."

I cleared my throat, trying to remember the details I'd told the Count the night before. "I'm an Elemental. My powers were working fine until I turned eleven. Then they faded and stopped working altogether. I can still cast spells and summon my blue magic, but nothing else. I've tried taking potions and writing my own spells to summon my magic back, but nothing's worked."

Ignacio nodded, his gaze directed to the floor as he contemplated this. "And when your powers were intact, you were able to conjure each of the elements without difficulty?"

I shifted in my chair. "Yes."

"Did you have an affinity for one over the others?"

"Fire," I blurted without thinking. It had been the first thing that popped into my head. Dad had told me he'd had the same affinity, and his father had as well.

Ignacio's eyebrows lifted. "I see. Did you ever find this fire uncontrollable? Did it ever take over your body?"

I shook my head. "No, I always had control over it. But my father can set his entire body on fire without feeling anything. Maybe it's genetic." I shrugged, avoiding Ignacio's gaze.

Ignacio nodded thoughtfully. "Interesting. Miss Gerrick,

would you mind if I cast a few spells upon you? They are not harmful and will not alter you in any way."

Discomfort wriggled in my stomach. "Um, sure."

"May I have your dominant hand?"

I stretched out my right hand, and he gripped it in his. His palms were calloused, but his long, thin fingers were soft. He flipped my hand over and ran a finger down several lines in my palm. I suppressed a shiver at the feeling of having this stranger touch me so gently.

Ignacio clasped my hand in both of his and muttered another spell in Latin. A blue glow encompassed our clasped hands, and a sudden tightness gripped my chest. I tried sucking in a breath, but no air came. Spots danced in my vision. My lungs struggled for air.

Finally, the pressure in my chest eased and I sucked in several gulps of air. "What was that?" I choked.

Ignacio released my hands, his brows knitting together. "I tried accessing your affinity, but I was blocked by another source."

I stilled. "Another . . . *magical* source?"

"I cannot tell. It is most likely the cause, although I have encountered a few individuals whose physical ailments blocked me from accessing their affinity."

Again, I thought of Angel and her illness. Would her condition prevent a spell like that from getting through?

"Has this happened to anyone else?" I asked.

Ignacio nodded. "It is quite common for impaired casters to be blocked somehow. That was just the first test.

For the next one, would you mind reciting the cloaking enchantment for me? If you don't know it—"

"I know it." I leaned forward and closed my eyes.

"Magic above, I summon thee,

To obscure me from this enemy."

As my hands started to glow blue, Ignacio waved his fingers in the air in front of me, conjuring purple sparks that stung my nose. The sparks flew closer to me, and I held my breath, afraid I might accidentally inhale them.

Then, the sparks flew back toward Ignacio's hand, surrounding his fingers until they disappeared.

I watched with wide eyes, waiting for some kind of explanation. When it didn't come, I asked, "What was that?"

"I was trying to discern whether you *have* an affinity or not. In rare cases, a person's aura blocks me from looking closer because there is nothing to see. Sometimes traumatic events cause a person's affinity to vanish completely."

A lump formed in my throat. "And . . . did you find something there?" *This is it. This is where he tells me I'm broken beyond repair. I'm defective.*

"Yes."

My head reared back, my heart thundering in my chest. "*What*? Really?"

"Yes, there is certainly something there. I presume it is your elemental abilities, but I cannot yet determine what is blocking them."

I took several deep breaths. My eyes felt hot, and I rubbed my nose. I wanted to laugh and cry at the same time. Relief blossomed through me. *Thank Lilith.* I wasn't *completely* broken after all.

Ignacio rose to his feet. "Come."

Blinking, I stood. "Is that it?"

"For now. I have determined you are not a danger to the rest of us. But you do have powers that are inaccessible, which means we should be able to help you."

Together we strode out of the library and back down the hall. "Have you ever encountered someone who you couldn't help?"

Ignacio slowed his steps and glanced at me. "Once."

"What happened to them?"

"They died."

My heart lurched in my throat. I waited for more information, but Ignacio's tight-lipped grimace told me he wouldn't share anything else.

Instead, I tried to focus on my relief. *That won't be me. He says there's something there, waiting to be accessed. I'm not doomed.*

Ignacio suddenly gripped my elbow, stopping me in my tracks. A second later, a foul odor stung my nose.

I stiffened and met Ignacio's wide eyes.

"Demons," he whispered. "They're here."

My heart racing, I gritted my teeth. "I need weapons."

Ignacio's mouth opened and closed, his face pale.

I gripped his arm tightly. "*Ignacio!* Where are your weapons?"

"I . . . uh . . . the armory. Downstairs. Past the kitchen."

I gathered my skirts and ran, grateful Ignacio had healed

my leg earlier. I took several wrong turns and swore loudly. The stench of demons grew stronger. Shouts and crashes echoed around the castle. I thought of the other casters here and the ailments that kept them from battling properly.

They needed my help.

I pushed faster, my chest aching from the damned corset restricting my air flow.

At long last, I descended the staircase and found an armory stocked with shields, armor, swords, daggers, pistols, rifles, and stakes. There were some more menacing weapons with spikes and chains that I skirted away from. Instead, I snatched a small dagger and a stake and slid them inside my bodice, allowing them to take up the room my flat chest provided.

I hurried back out and came face-to-face with a demon.

10

LEO

I STOOD FROZEN IN THE DOORWAY OF THE ARMORY, stunned, as I watched the girl with straw-colored hair sift through weapons.

How had I not smelled her? Was she mortal?

I'd been quite certain the area was empty. Otherwise I wouldn't have risked going to the armory.

Jorge, Miguel, Eduardo, and I had split up to cause more chaos. Jorge and Miguel had been closest to the staircase, so I left to grab weapons while my men searched for my brother.

If he was here.

It was probably better that I gather supplies. The Count's men would be looking for me—the coven leader. I could provide a distraction from the important task at hand.

But I hadn't expected to find a young woman in a mahogany gown reaching stiffly for weapons she looked far too small to handle.

The girl rose and whirled to face me, then took a startled step backward. Her face drained of color, and I sensed her heartbeat quicken. The way the blood pulsed in her veins called to me, but I squashed it down. I watched her scrutinize me as I had her just moments ago. Her eyes raked up and down, taking in my leather attire and boots, my curly hair tied at the nape of my neck, and my silver-rimmed eyes. The eyes were always a shock upon first glance. Though I'd been born with dark eyes, my vampiric and shapeshifter forms added a ring of silver around my eyes that glowed like moonlight.

I bowed deeply to the woman, smirking when I straightened. "Forgive me, my lady. I did not expect to see someone as elegant as you down here."

To my surprise, the girl fixed a fearsome scowl at me and brandished her dagger. I almost laughed. She was so petite that wielding such a weapon looked utterly ridiculous.

I raised my hands in mock surrender. "Please, my lady. Have mercy."

The girl's nostrils flared, and she lunged for me. Surprised, I jumped backward with a yelp, but she was quicker than I'd thought. Her blade sliced into my arm, and fire burned from the cut.

Little viper.

I laughed to mask my shock, pressing a hand to my wound. Blood glistened on my fingers. "Impressive." I looked at her, assessing the fire and determination blazing in her eyes. Like she had something to prove.

I'd taunted her, and she hadn't liked it. Perhaps that could work in my favor.

"You're a fiery little thing, aren't you?" I asked.

The girl attacked again, but this time I was ready for her. She aimed a kick at my chest, but I caught her foot in my hands and twisted until she collapsed to the floor in a heap of satin skirts.

Chuckling again, I stepped over her toward the weapons. Then a sharp pain exploded in my shoulder. Hissing, I stiffened and glanced back at her. She'd flung her dagger into my shoulder.

"My, my," I said through clenched teeth, groping blindly in search of the dagger. "You *are* persistent."

The girl jumped to her feet and tackled me. Together, we collapsed on the floor. She landed a punch squarely in my face with a *crack*. Blood poured from my nose. I dodged her next blow and smashed my forehead against hers.

Dazed, she reared back, her eyes wild and incoherent. Her brows knitted together, and her expression crumpled in pain. I almost felt bad for her.

I gathered the weapons that had fallen to the floor, taking advantage of her injury. I strode toward the doorway, but then the girl uttered a spell.

"*Magic within me, gather near,*
Trap this man and keep him here."

Her hands glowed blue, and my eyes widened. *She's a witch.* How had I not smelled her magic?

I hurried to leave, but some invisible force blocked me.

Though I strained and struggled, I couldn't move past the doorway. A faint blue glow hovered in front of me.

I sighed. How had I managed to fail at this one, simple task?

Slowly, I turned to face the girl, whose eyes were burning with hatred. I cocked my head at her. Her spell had been in English. Adopting her language, I asked, "Just how many languages do you know, my lady?"

The girl blinked at me, shock etched into her face. "I could ask you the same thing. *My lord.*"

I laughed. "I'm no lord. I am Leonardo Serrano, the leader of this coven." And I'd make sure she never forgot it.

"That's nice," she said in a monotone. "Now give those back." She pointed to the weapons in my arms.

I grimaced, feigning sympathy. "Unfortunately, *mi amor,* I must leave with these. You see, the fate of my coven depends on it." *It's not entirely untrue. We do have great need of these weapons.*

The girl dragged another dagger from off the wall and brandished it at me.

I exhaled in exasperation. "Must we do this again? I've already bested you."

"Hardly," the girl growled.

She burst forward, kicking my legs out from under me. I collapsed in a clash of metal as the weapons fell from my arms.

This has gone on long enough, I thought. My dark magic swirled around me, taking over and shifting me to my bat form. I flapped blindly around the room, using my other senses to guide me. With another swell of magic, I reappeared in vampire form and barreled into the girl.

She fell to the floor again with an "oof," crashing into a suit of armor.

I vanished again in a puff of black smoke, changing back to my bat form. I sensed her bewilderment as she tried to find me, but I flew away from her and toward the doorway.

"You're a shapeshifter," she spat, rising to her feet. I detected her magic crackling through the air. *She's casting another spell!*

The girl's voice vibrated against my body as she spoke.

"Vile demon of unholy crimes,

I banish you—"

I shifted back to my vampire form and slammed into her. She stumbled backward into the wall with a groan.

How dare she? I thought, seething. *She tries to banish me? She thinks she can just defeat me in the blink of an eye?* Fury roared within me, and I felt her pulse quicken from my nearness. I pressed an arm into her collarbone, pinning her into place.

"See, that's where you're wrong, my lady," I whispered in her ear. "I've committed no unholy crime. If you're searching for a lawbreaker, why don't you ask your precious Count what crimes he has committed against my coven?"

The girl thrashed against my grip. I knew she would only keep fighting me. Despite how she infuriated me, I didn't want to kill her. Though I was certainly a monster, there were some lines I didn't want to cross.

I had to escape. Even though it broke the rules of my coven, I had no choice if I wanted to let her live. So, I leaned in and sank my teeth into her throat.

Blood flooded in my mouth, sweet and delicious. I hadn't expected to feed today, and my body thrummed with excitement from the prospect. The tangy fluid gushed down my throat as I swallowed it like nectar. The girl's body fell slack in my arms as she responded to the numbness of my venom.

While I drank, something odd settled in my mouth. A sharp, bitter taste that puzzled me. I'd never tasted anything like it before.

This girl was no ordinary witch. I'd tasted witch blood before, and this was much more unusual.

I drew away before the bloodlust overcame me, and the girl stiffened from the jolt of my withdrawal. Blood dripped down my chin and onto her dress. A trickle of crimson liquid oozed down her neck.

"That's . . . interesting," I whispered, licking my lips.

The girl merely blinked at me, her eyes foggy.

"What are you?" I murmured, drawing closer to her. Her tawny eyes stared drunkenly at me with the same wonder I felt.

"What . . . are *you*?" she asked weakly. Her eyes flicked over my face unabashed. Then, she shook her head as if trying to regain clarity, but I knew it would be no use for her. She would need days to recover from the blood loss. It was a shame to see her so dizzy and incoherent. She'd been a fierce opponent.

But she'd occupied my time long enough. I sensed a crackle of dark magic in the air—a signal from Miguel.

We needed to leave. The Count would be returning soon.

As if spurring me on, heavy footsteps sounded nearby, and I turned toward the noise. *Out of time.*

I grinned at the girl. "Until next time, *mi amor.*"

With another puff of black magic, I vanished and reappeared as the bat. The blue shield the girl had summoned earlier flickered and vanished, no doubt a result of her diminished powers thanks to my feeding. I flew in a circle before darting out the doorway.

Just before I left, I heard the girl mutter angrily, "Bastard."

11

BRIELLE

"BRIELLE. *BRIELLE*!"

My eyelids fluttered open, and an explosion of pain followed. I winced, raising a hand to my head.

"Ow," I muttered, shifting and trying to rise. "What—where am I?"

"The armory. Looks like a vamp got you." I recognized the Australian accent.

"Izzy?" I said. Slowly my vision cleared, and Izzy came into view, her white hair in tangles around her face. Soot covered her cheeks, and a bloody gash ran from her forearm to her wrist.

"The very same," she said with a grin.

"Where—the demons!" I shot to my feet, then swayed as my vision blurred again.

"Easy now." Izzy caught me by the shoulders. "Don't push it. Let your body recover from the blood loss."

"Where'd they go?" I asked. "What did they take?" My

eyes fell to the pile of weapons. The strange vampire, Leonardo, had just left them there.

"Dunno. But the Count's back. We think the demons vanished when our reinforcements showed up. Looks like they tried attacking when our numbers were few."

"Is anyone hurt?" I asked as Izzy looped my arm around her shoulders to help me hobble out of the armory.

"A few cuts and bruises, but we're all right. We might not be experts at fighting demons, but we can certainly cause some chaos." She eyed the puncture marks on my neck. "So, who got you, eh?"

"Leonardo Serrano."

Izzy stopped walking and sucked in a breath. "You fought *Leo*?" She whistled. "What was that like?"

Anger and shame washed over me as I thought of how useless I'd been. How cocky and arrogant he was. How I'd just fallen limp in his arms while he drank my blood from me. I shoved the thoughts away and looked at Izzy. "You know him?"

"Yeah, he's the coven leader. Shapeshifting vampire."

"Yeah, so I gathered." *Eventually.* I remembered how close his face had been to mine, the way his dark eyes gleamed with silver. His light goatee had tickled my neck when he'd drunk from me. I suppressed a shiver. "I've never met one like that before. I thought the only shapeshifting hybrids were gargoyles."

"Most are, yes. But some, like Leo, come from a powerful demon heritage. His bloodline's as pure as they come."

"Pure?"

"Pure *demon*. No light magic in him at all."

Something icy slithered in my chest. "So, how do you know about him?"

"The Count had us study up on the coven's history to help us prepare. Leo attacks on a regular basis, always searching for some powerful weapon the Count doesn't have. This is the first time they've caught us off guard because—"

"Because they found a way out of the time loop."

"Right."

We slowly climbed up the stairs and found the wide room I'd first arrived in. Vases and paintings were smashed, leaving the floor covered in debris. I could barely make out the decorative octagon on the tiled floor.

We dodged the wreckage until we returned to the ballroom where the others were huddled together, speaking in low voices.

Riker looked up when he saw me. A small cut above his eyebrow bled freely, but he otherwise looked unharmed.

"Brielle!" He rushed to my side and took my other arm. "What happened?"

"Leo," Izzy said darkly.

Riker's eyes blazed and his jaw tensed. Apparently, he didn't need any more information. He leaned forward and traced a finger along my neck. The puncture wounds throbbed slightly from his touch. I shuddered. There wasn't enough vampire venom in me to do much damage, but still

—just knowing that bastard's poison was inside me made me want to puke.

Riker drew his hand back, his face contorted with anger. "I'll kill him."

"Not if I kill him first," I growled.

Surprise mingled with satisfaction in Riker's eyes, and the corners of his mouth twitched.

The Count was speaking with one of the mages in rapid Spanish. Both of them looked up at my approach. The Count's eyes widened, but he quickly recovered. He snapped his fingers and said, "Ignacio, tend to her wounds."

Ignacio appeared before me and looked me over. "Where is the most pressing injury, Miss Gerrick?"

I shook my head. "I'm fine. Just blood loss from a vampire."

Ignacio's lips tightened, and I knew we were thinking the same thing: blood loss was one of the few things that couldn't be healed by magic. Only time could help me now.

"I'll send for your handmaid to escort you to your chamber." Ignacio strode out of the ballroom, his purple robe sweeping behind him.

I wanted to object, but the persistent throbbing in my head urged me to comply. As soon as I recovered, I could figure out who those demons were, what they wanted, and how to stop them.

I still saw Leo's taunting smile in my head, his patronizing laughter as he mocked me.

I'd make him regret underestimating me. Even if it killed me.

I woke up with my cell phone clutched in my palm, though I didn't remember going to bed with it. When I tapped the screen, I found a picture of Angel and my mom. My throat tightened with emotion. I gritted my teeth and turned off the phone. My battery would die soon. Even though my phone didn't work in this time, the idea that the screen would go dark forever made me feel lost inside. It was my only connection to my time, besides the bag I kept stashed under the bed.

I groaned and sat up, rubbing my forehead. A dull ache throbbed there, but other than that I felt stronger. More coherent. I didn't even remember climbing the stairs and getting into bed. The sheer nightgown I wore meant Maria must've helped me undress. I suppressed an eye roll at that. If I'd been in my right mind, I would've insisted on getting ready by myself.

Leo's black and silver eyes flashed in my vision, and I flinched.

I balled my hand into a fist. He *had* bested me. I didn't want to admit it, but he'd won. It had been years since a demon had beaten me in a fight. Since I'd taken up kickboxing, I'd triumphed almost every time.

I gritted my teeth and jumped out of bed, eager to throw myself into a new task to get my mind off my failure. After sliding my messenger bag out from under my bed, I reached inside to grab my jeans. I didn't care about the Count's stupid rules today. Perhaps if I'd been in more comfortable clothes, I would've beaten Leo yesterday.

I'd just pulled out a T-shirt when a light knock sounded at the door. Maria edged inside, holding a tray of food. Her eyes widened when she saw me crouched on the floor by the bed.

"My lady!" she breathed, hurrying inside to place the tray on the table. "You shouldn't be out of bed. You need rest!"

"What I *need* is to get dressed and figure out how to be useful," I growled, digging through my bag for a pair of underwear. When I looked up, Maria's brows were knitted, and she opened her mouth to object. I raised a hand. "Don't try to dress me in one of those death traps again. Please, for the love of Lilith, I beg of you—"

Maria shook her head quickly. "No, my lady. The Count has allowed the guests to wear, uh"—she lowered her voice to a whisper—"trousers." She swallowed as if she'd just spoken an offensive word. "At least for the time being. In case we are attacked again."

I heaved a sigh of relief. "Thank Lilith for that." I resumed rummaging through my bag.

Maria cleared her throat and shifted her feet. When I looked up at her, she muttered, "He insists you wear the trousers of *this* time, my lady."

I groaned and threw my bag down on the floor. "Of course he does."

She helped fit me into a pair of trousers that fit surprisingly well. When I inspected myself in the mirror, I realized they were riding pants—or whatever they were called in this time period. I also wore a light, airy tunic tightened at the waist like a corset but more breathable. Maria helped me find a pair of boots that fit as well. When the ensemble was complete, I looked at myself and half expected Maria to insist I wear a riding helmet and crop as well.

I snorted and shook my head at my reflection. When Maria gave me a pained look, I sighed and waved my hand. "Do whatever you want with my hair." I plopped down on the vanity chair.

Maria beamed at me and got to work while I tried not to wince as she tugged at my thin hair. My mind returned to the fight with Leo and what he'd said about the Count— that he'd committed unholy crimes as well.

Though I didn't trust a word Leo said, I didn't necessarily believe the Count was a complete saint either. He gave me the creeps.

Whatever was going on, I was determined to find out.

When Maria was finished, I offered a small smile, hoping to appease her. Her frequent grimaces made me realize I was probably being too harsh with her. She didn't deserve it. If anything, *she* should've been exasperated with *me*. I was making her job so much harder.

When she curtsied and made to leave, I said quickly, "Maria, wait."

She paused at the door, her eyebrows lifting. "Yes, my lady?"

Slowly, I rose from the seat, briefly registering how much easier it was to move in these clothes than what I'd worn yesterday. I smoothed my pants and wrung my hands together. "I, uh, never thanked you for taking care of me yesterday. I don't really remember what happened, but . . ." I trailed off, unsure of where I was going with that sentence. I cleared my throat. "Um, thanks. For everything."

A warm smile lit her face. She curtsied again, her brown eyes glowing. "A pleasure, my lady."

After she left, a tightness wound inside my chest, and I rubbed my nose. My hands itched to do something, so I reorganized the accessories on the vanity and then repacked my messenger bag and hid it from view. Maria had already made the bed and taken away the breakfast tray, so my room was tidy. *Too* tidy.

I knew it was insane, to prefer to have a mess just so I could clean it. But that's how I felt.

I huffed in exasperation and left the room, clenching and unclenching my fingers into fists as I made my way downstairs to the dining hall.

When I arrived, several guests were already seated and chatting amiably. Some had bruises and cuts on their faces, but it seemed everyone was all right.

A quick glance around the room told me Izzy and Riker weren't there. Discomfort swelled within my chest, but I squashed it down. I was a big girl. If I could handle fighting demons, I could handle this too.

I spotted Juan, who grinned eagerly in my direction and waved me over. I suppressed a groan but moved toward him. The Four Musketeers—or rather, the Four Douchebags

—didn't seem happy to see me, so sitting with Juan was my best option.

As I took my seat, Juan looked me over, his gaze lingering on my chest and waist. I almost slapped him right then and there.

"You are unharmed, Miss Gerrick?" he asked.

Right, I thought sarcastically, placing a handkerchief on my lap. *I'm sure he was only staring at my chest because he was looking for injuries.* "Yes. And you?" I looked him over and found his face as spotless as before the attack.

Juan's smile widened. "I thank you, yes. Those demons could not hold their own against me." He sat up a bit straighter.

Did he think that impressed me? I forced a smile. "Great. Glad to hear it."

Juan leaned closer conspiratorially. "I heard you faced off with Leo Serrano."

"I did."

"Was it terrifying?"

"No. He's unusual, but he's just another demon."

Juan's eyes widened. "Just another demon? He's a shapeshifting vampire! Is that not alarming?"

I shrugged one shoulder. "No."

Juan's smile faded. "It does not frighten you, Miss Gerrick, to face demons?"

I leveled a stare at him. "No. I face one every day. My father's a demon."

Juan's eyes grew wide, his face slackening. "Your . . . *father?*"

My eyes narrowed. "Yes. He follows the law, though. He doesn't pose a threat to anyone. It's the criminal demons that are the real threat."

Juan swallowed and looked away. Discomfort mingled with horror in his eyes.

Lilith, he acted like having a demon for a father was the worst fate in the world. I wasn't an idiot—I knew more demons caused trouble than light casters. But there were plenty of law-abiding demons who kept to themselves and didn't harm anyone. That was why my dad served on the Council: to keep the peace between both sides.

Juan subtly scooted away from me like I was contagious. After a few minutes, he muttered something about speaking with someone and moved to sit by the Douchebags. *Fine by me,* I thought.

Izzy entered the dining hall, and I smiled and waved her over. She flashed a grin and slid into the seat next to me, also dressed in riding pants and a loose tunic.

"Love the new fashion here," she said with a snicker, tossing her white hair over her shoulder. "Makes me think of home, wearing dacks again."

I leaned closer to her. "So outside of training and examinations and whatever it is you all do here, are we free to . . . roam the castle? And the grounds?" *Specifically, can I go outside and check out the Count's wards?*

Izzy frowned. "Sort of. The Count doesn't like us being outside. He says it runs the risk of exposing who we are to the civilians. He doesn't like us exploring the lower levels either, but we can visit the main rooms and the guest quarters. Why?"

I deflated. If the Count was so strict about people going outside, I probably wouldn't be able to slip out unnoticed. *All right then. Plan B.* "I . . . I was just thinking of doing some research in the library later."

Izzy wrinkled her nose. "Ugh, why?"

I laughed. "I just want to catch myself up with the history here."

"Want some help?"

I stilled, then quickly shook my head. "No thanks. I'll be fine." I didn't like the idea of having an audience while I searched for information about Leo's coven and how to take them down. Besides, I wanted to research Lilith's curse as well, and it'd be hard to do that with someone watching me. I didn't want to arouse Izzy's suspicions.

"I've been here longer than you," Izzy said, raising an eyebrow. "I can show you around the library and help you navigate through all those books."

I pressed my lips together. "I'm really okay."

Izzy rolled her eyes and leaned forward. "Come on, Brielle! What else am I supposed to do, hang out with those idiots over there?" She waved a hand toward the Douchebags at the end of the table, and I knew her voice was loud enough to be heard. A few of them glared in our direction.

I couldn't stop myself from smiling. With a sigh, I muttered, "I guess I could use some help."

Izzy beamed. "Excellent." She cocked her head at me,

her eyes glinting. "You know, the person who knows the most about everything is probably Riker. He's a bit of a history geek and knows the castle and the area better than anyone."

I made a face. Though I was fond of Riker, he made my stomach spin in ways I didn't like. I waved a hand, feigning nonchalance. "I don't want to bug him about this."

Izzy raised her eyebrows but didn't press me about it. I knew I was a terrible liar. But I couldn't even explain it to myself why I didn't want to involve Riker. I just didn't like feeling uncomfortable or thrown off, especially not now when I was so focused on finding out more about Leo and his coven and how to stop them.

As if summoned by my thoughts, Riker himself entered the dining hall, wearing a gold waistcoat that made his hair look exceptionally red. His blue eyes roved around the room until they settled on me.

When the butterflies swarmed in my stomach, I cursed under my breath.

Oh, Brie, you've got to be kidding me, I chided myself. I wasn't ordinarily the type to swoon over a guy, but I had my fair share of crushes. I was a sophomore in high school, for crying out loud. How could I not?

I subconsciously straightened in my chair, then clenched my fist on my lap to scold myself. *Stop it. You barely know him. You just like him because he was nice to you. Stop. It.*

"Good morning Izzy," Riker said, sliding into the seat opposite us. He nodded at me. "Brielle."

I pressed my lips together in the barest attempt at a smile.

"How are your injuries faring, ladies?" Riker asked, straightening his waistcoat.

Izzy responded by shooting a jet of wind over Riker's shoulder. She swore. "Sorry, mate." After flapping her hand rapidly, the wind died down, but not before shattering a plate on the table behind Riker. A few chuckles and murmurs rippled through the Four Douchebags.

Izzy's cheeks reddened, and she slid lower in her chair, tucking her hands in between her legs. "Bloody powers. They strike at the worst time."

Riker laughed. "Don't fret, Izzy. No harm done. I'm lucky you didn't blast me against the wall."

Izzy snorted. "I'm surprised I didn't."

Servants entered and served us breakfast. Riker took several large bites of fruit and pointed his fork at me. "You haven't told us what your magical problem is yet, Brielle." He eyed me up and down. "I haven't witnessed any accidents yet."

I swallowed my food and cleared my throat. "Oh yeah. Well, it's kind of boring. I don't have any powers."

Izzy and Riker stared at me, their eyes wide.

"Anymore," I added quickly. "I don't have them anymore. Used to be an Elemental, but years ago, my powers just vanished." I dropped my gaze and took another bite. *Stupid, stupid, stupid.* With Lilith's beast roaming free at the end of every year, *of course* everyone would be on high alert for anything remotely related to Lilith's curse.

Izzy exhaled and laughed. "That would be a nice problem for me to have. It would mean I'd stop hurting people."

"Yeah, well, it's not that great," I grumbled. "I'm not mortal, so I don't fit in there. But I'm not allowed to be part of my mom's coven, so . . ." I lifted my shoulder in a shrug.

"Your mum's coven?" Riker asked. "What about your dad?"

"He's a demon, so he belongs to a different coven."

Riker's fork fell on his plate with a loud clatter. Several voices fell silent as some of the other boys turned to look at us. Riker chuckled and said loudly, "Bit my tongue. Don't fret over me, you lot."

A few of the Douchebags rolled their eyes before returning to their food. Riker leaned closer to me over the table and hissed, "Your dad's a *demon*?"

I nodded. My throat felt dry. I met Juan's gaze from farther down the table, and he quickly looked away. Remembering his reaction when I'd mentioned my father, I whispered, "You guys hate *all* demons then? Even the ones who follow the law?"

Riker shook his head, closing his eyes. "It's not just that, Brielle. The Count believes all demons are inherently evil. That they're all going to Hell no matter what. Remember what time period you're in. Religion is a lifestyle for these people. They think demons are crimes against nature and can't be cured. It doesn't matter if your father is the most charitable saint in the world. He's a *demon*. And you need to be careful."

"If the Count finds out," Izzy said quietly, her face grave, "there's no telling what he'd do."

My blood ran cold as I looked at Juan again. He was speaking with Armin and avoiding my gaze. But I couldn't help remembering that he was from the eighteenth century. He knew the Count. It was only a matter of time before he shared the information with him.

If he hadn't already.

I've got to find a way out of here. Fast.

12

BRIELLE

AFTER BREAKFAST, THE COUNT ANNOUNCED WE HAD the day to ourselves while he and the mages repaired things from yesterday's attack—and no doubt scoured the castle to see if anything important had been stolen.

I found it odd that the Count volunteered to do this himself instead of leaving it to the help, but I wasn't going to complain. Not when it provided me a full day of research.

Knowing I might be in some kind of trouble because of my demon lineage, I was even more determined to find out more about this stupid time period and how to escape.

Izzy showed me to the library so I could get to work. The room itself was as big as a cathedral and had shelves climbing all the way to the ceiling. It made me feel grateful for the help, though I'd turned my nose up at it earlier. Tackling it on my own seemed way too intimidating.

"The books are arranged by topic and then date," Izzy said, stretching out her hand to gesture to the monstrosity of books. "But very few of them are in English." She smirked at me.

"I have a way around that," I said quietly, approaching the nearest bookshelf and squinting at the titles. Under my breath, I uttered a spell.

"*Magic above and powers that be,*

Translate these words here before me."

My hands glowed blue, and the titles shifted before my eyes. I read through labels of medieval magical battles and warfare, then strode past them to the next set of shelves.

Izzy let out a low whistle. "That's amazing." She approached the shelf and frowned, cocking her head. "It still looks the same to me."

"It only works for the caster," I said absently, running my finger along the old leatherbound texts as I searched.

Izzy chuckled. "That's a shame. I was thinking you could invent the translation charm early."

I didn't answer. My brow furrowed as I moved past the books about wars, medicines, indigenous cultures, and education before I found a book about the history of demon covens. I hefted the large book off the shelf and wiped dust from the surface, coughing as the particles filled the air.

I slammed the book on the table between the two armchairs.

"Can I cast the spell too?" Izzy asked, squinting at the foreign text. "Then I can help you."

I hesitated for a moment, but the eagerness in her eyes told me she wouldn't back down. I sighed. "Yeah, you can cast the spell yourself."

"Fantastic. What am I looking for?"

"Any information about this time period—Leo and his coven and where they came from, the dark warlock who cursed the city with the time loop . . . anything that might help." I returned to the shelves and scoured them until I found what I was looking for: demon mythology and origins. I glanced over at Izzy and found her poring over the book, leaning closer as her eyes narrowed with concentration.

My heart racing, I selected a book and pried it open, holding it against my chest as I flipped through pages. Then I found it.

Lilith's curse.

My eyes flew back and forth as I quickly read through the section, skimming for anything helpful. *Lilith only possesses female witches . . . A beast is conjured, wreaking havoc and destruction . . . The witch never regains her powers when Lilith takes control . . . The only way to stop the beast is by killing the witch.*

My blood chilled as I read. But the more I studied the passages, the more my heart sank in my chest. It didn't mention anywhere how to defeat Lilith or resist her influence, nor did it say how to stop the beast without killing the cursed witch.

A lump formed in my throat. If I truly was Lilith's cursed witch, then I was doomed.

And if I wasn't, I had no way to prove it. Once the Count found out I had demon blood in me, he was sure to jump to the conclusion that I was responsible for unleashing the horrible monster that kept destroying the city.

I flipped through pages, trying to find any information about what kind of creature was unleashed. I spotted words like *dragon, phoenix, wraith,* and *hellion,* though it was all speculation. No one knew for sure.

Right, I thought, determined. *Time to switch gears and find a way out of here.*

"What are you two doing in here?" a voice asked.

I slammed the book shut and fumbled to keep it in my grasp. My wide eyes looked up at the intruder.

Riker stood there, leaning against a bookshelf, his eyebrows raised.

Izzy shot me a glance before she responded. "Research. Want to help?"

I suppressed a groan and shelved the book I was reading.

"With what?" Riker asked, striding toward the table where Izzy was sitting. He peered over her shoulder and wrinkled his nose. "Blimey, Izzy. This is in *Greek.* I didn't know you could read that!"

Izzy snickered and shared an amused glance with me. "Courtesy of Brielle's ingenious enchantment."

Riker looked up at me with wide eyes. Half his mouth lifted in a smile. "You translated this?"

I shrugged, looking away. "Just a little charm. It'll wear off soon."

"That's brilliant."

I tried to suppress my smile, but I was hopeless. My

cheeks warmed, and I inwardly cursed myself. *You aren't doing yourself any favors by liking him,* I told myself. *Especially if you're just doomed to die anyway.*

"How can I help?" Riker asked, taking the seat opposite Izzy.

"She wants information about Leo Serrano and his coven," Izzy said.

Before I could correct her and mention I wanted information about *more* than just Leo, Riker perked up. He straightened in his chair. "Why are you picking through these dusty old things? I can tell you everything about the coven."

I sighed and pulled up a chair to join Riker and Izzy. There was no use avoiding it now. *I might as well take advantage of what he knows.*

"Who is Leo Serrano?" I asked, clasping my hands together on my lap. "Where did he come from? And what does he want from the Count?"

Riker grinned. "Ah, well, it's quite a long story."

I raised my eyebrows expectantly while Izzy rolled her eyes and returned to her reading.

Riker sat forward with an eager glint in his eyes. "Just after the Great Mage War, covens from both sides were severely depleted. Leo's brother, Ronaldo, rose to power. He was a shapeshifter, just like Leo, but he was young. Barely eighteen years old.

"The light coven, led by the Count and his mages, tirelessly hunted the Serrano coven until the demons were forced underground to wait out the search. Ronaldo was . . . inexperienced. He believed he could ambush the Count and launch an attack, but many of his demon followers doubted they would survive. Several defected to another coven, leaving the Serrano brothers with only half the numbers they originally had.

"According to the history I studied, Leo and Ronaldo had a falling out. Leo wanted to abandon the idea of an assault and rejoin the demons who had left, but Ronaldo was determined to prove himself. Leading just a few men, Ronaldo crept into the Castillo de Coca and slaughtered many of the soldiers. He stumbled upon something large and powerful that caused a great explosion, reducing many of the rooms to rubble and ash. When the area was cleared, Ronaldo and his men were gone. Never found.

"It is said that ever since then, Leo has regrouped his coven and launched attack after attack, trying to find the weapon his brother had stumbled upon to get it out of the Count's hands. The historians of my time were never certain if Leo sought revenge or somehow still believed his brother was alive."

I frowned, staring hard at the smooth mahogany of the table. "And . . . *is* there a weapon hidden here?"

"Lilith, no," Riker said with a laugh. "I've seen the Count's mages perform some powerful, explosive magic. I'm certain that Ronaldo was attacked and cursed into oblivion and that's what caused the explosion. Leo is as stubborn and persistent as his brother, but he's clever and patient as well. He hid away for years, training and recruiting more demons to his coven to rebuild his numbers. Every attack of his was planned and calculated, and even though we always saw them coming, they were quite a challenge for us."

"And what about the time loop?" I asked. "When did that happen?"

Riker stroked his chin thoughtfully. "After Ronaldo's death, I believe. Lilith's beast emerged right around the same time Ronaldo was killed, so Leo's counterattack was put on hold as the city was under siege by the beast. Then, the dark warlock trapped the city in the time loop, and . . ." Riker sat back and spread his hands wide. "Now you're all caught up."

My brows knitted together as I tried to sort through all the information. Leo's brother snuck into the castle, there was some huge explosion, then Lilith's beast emerged, and the dark warlock cast the spell, locking everyone into the time loop.

Which meant Leo's brother wouldn't come back. Because he died before the time loop started.

Sheesh, what a mess.

"Did Leo and his coven remember anything when the time loop started?" I asked.

"I assume not. Otherwise why would they keep attacking? My guess is the loss of his brother is still fresh, which is why he continues his offensive. But it certainly changes things now that he's found a way out of the time loop."

I leaned forward. "What *is* Lilith's beast? Have you seen it?"

Riker shook his head. "None of us have. It only emerges

at night. It has a great roar that shakes the trees and the ground, and it rains fire down from the sky. Many believe it to be a dragon. Others think it's a mutant Elemental—like a shapeshifter hybrid, similar to Leo."

"You don't try to hunt it down or stop it?"

"No. Since we're exempt from the time loop, if we die, then"—he shrugged—"we don't come back. The Count thinks it's too risky. He's more intent on finding the cursed witch and stopping the monster that way."

I kept my gaze fixed on the table as I asked quietly, "And who is the cursed witch? Have you found her yet?"

"No. We assume she's a demon, though. The Count has led several attacks on the demon's coven but hasn't found any clues yet. But now that the demons have broken free from the time loop, he fears that Lilith's cursed witch will find a way out of the city. If she survives . . ." He closed his eyes. "She could destroy the world."

A foul taste filled my mouth, and I swallowed. *She could destroy the world. I could destroy the world.*

No, I argued with myself. *It's not true. It isn't me. I would know.* Someone *would know.*

I cleared my throat. "What about . . . this dark warlock? What do you know about him?"

Riker blew air through his lips. "Nothing. According to history as I know it, this time loop never happened. So, whoever cast it never went down in history. Now, I *do* know about the demons of this time period—the Serrano brothers, of course, and their predecessor named Fernando Castillo. He was a bloody awful bloke. He used to torture light casters—for *fun*." Riker shuddered. "Then, the one before him, Santiago Suares, he—"

"I found something," Izzy interrupted, lifting a finger in the air. "This here says the Serrano brothers had a sister."

Riker sat up straighter, and I sucked in a breath. "A sister?" I repeated.

Izzy nodded. "Lucia Serrano."

"What happened to her?" I asked.

Izzy shook her head. "It doesn't say. It's just listed here in their family tree."

Riker frowned, his eyes contemplative. "I haven't heard her mentioned in the stories. Perhaps she died young."

"How does Leo's story end?" I whispered, almost afraid to ask. "Who prevails in this battle between his coven and the Count?"

Riker looked up to meet my gaze. "You have to keep in mind, Brielle, that history has been affected because of the time loop and because of everyone's arrival here. If the dark warlock had never cursed this place and if the Councils around the world had never sent impaired casters here, things would be very different."

"That doesn't answer my question."

Riker paused, pressing his lips together. "Eventually, the Spanish monarch sends an army to assist the Count. They slaughter all the demon covens in the city."

The news should have brought me relief, but it didn't. A hollow feeling settled in my chest, and I looked away from him.

Leo would lose his life and his coven. He would never avenge his brother or find out what killed him.

Riker leaned closer to me and brushed his thumb against my neck. I suppressed a shiver.

"He bit you?" he asked quietly.

I nodded.

"Be careful. Your blood can be tracked."

I hesitated. "I'm not sure that it can."

Riker stared at me. "Why not?"

"He said he tasted something . . . different about my blood. Something unexpected. He didn't tell me what it was, though."

"It probably has to do with your ailment," Izzy said.

"Probably." I felt Riker's gaze on me, but I stood and returned to the bookshelf to find something else to peruse.

13

BRIELLE

I stayed in the library past lunch. Izzy left to eat and when she came back, her wind became so uncontrollable that she kept billowing through the pages and ruffling our notes. She excused herself to find a mage to help calm her powers.

To my surprise, Riker stayed with me in the library. Both our stomachs growled, but we continued our research. After a few hours, Riker ran a hand through his red hair, ruffling it slightly.

"This is so frustrating," he muttered. "Not a thing about Lucia Serrano. She didn't just *vanish*. If she'd died, there would've been an obituary, death certificate, or some kind of record from the local parish."

"Maybe the family kept quiet about it."

"That doesn't sound like something the Count would just let slide, though. He was watching the Serrano family for ages. He would've wanted to know for sure."

"Maybe he keeps documents like that under lock and key." I looked at Riker, widening my eyes. "There *are* places we aren't supposed to explore in this castle, right?"

Riker squinted at me in suspicion. "Why Brielle Gerrick, I'm surprised at you. Are you suggesting we snoop around?"

I shrugged, biting back a smile. "Aren't you curious?"

Riker offered a low chuckle. "Maybe. But not curious enough to incur the Count's wrath. We all keep our memories when the year resets, so it's not like he'll forget about it if you cross him. He'll carry that grudge *forever*."

"I'm new here, though. I can just pretend like I didn't know the rules yet."

Riker crossed his arms and smirked at me. "And what about me? What's my excuse?"

"I dragged you against your will, threatening to cut you open if you refused." I flashed a grin.

Riker snorted. "It'd be more believable if we claimed you'd seduced me."

My face flushed, and I looked away, though I felt his eyes on me.

"What?" he said quietly. "You don't believe that's possible?"

I raised my eyebrows and said nothing. My face still felt unbearably hot.

"You're right," Riker said, his tone suddenly serious. "It would be better to convince them it was *my* idea and *I'd* seduced *you*."

A loud snort burst from me before I could stop myself. I

clapped a hand over my lips, giggling madly. Riker joined in, pointing at me with glee all over his face.

"Very ladylike," he choked, wiping a tear from his eye. "Just add it to your long list of charms and wiles you use to ensnare men."

More laughs poured from me. "Love at first snort."

Riker barked out a laugh that echoed through the library. In a smooth, narrator-like voice, he said, "And he knew right then and there—when he met her gaze and she squealed like a pig—that he was truly enamored with her."

I slumped forward onto the table, slapping my palm against the surface as I giggled uncontrollably. "Lilith, it's a wonder I haven't lured the Count under my control by now! With my charms, I'm *unstoppable*. He would escort me to his secret lair immediately."

Riker's face was now as red as his hair. He hunched over, his shoulders shaking as his chuckles turned into high-pitched wheezes. Tears streamed down his face as he croaked, "Now I'm picturing . . . the Count . . . with a lovesick look in his eyes . . . while you're snorting and grunting like a warthog!"

Envisioning the stern Count with his rules and propriety watching *anyone* with lovesick eyes was too much for me, let alone imagining him smitten by someone as awkward and unladylike as me. My eyes filled with tears, too, and my stomach ached from laughter. For several minutes, we succumbed to the endless chuckles and grins, our breaths becoming weaker and our voices hoarser. My face hurt from smiling, and when the laughter finally faded, I felt suddenly tired.

The library was quiet when we settled into silence. The sky darkened outside, casting shadows on the bookshelves. I glanced upward out of habit only to realize there weren't any lights—someone would have to light candles.

My stomach growled, no doubt spurred on by our laughter. I sighed and rubbed my eyes. "We should probably call it quits."

Riker nodded, rising to his feet and stretching. My eyes were drawn to the pull of his biceps before I realized I was staring and dropped my gaze.

Riker approached me and offered his hand. "My lady," he said with a smirk.

I rolled my eyes but returned his smile, taking his hand and allowing him to help me to my feet. He looped my arm through his, and for once, I didn't mind at all.

Together, we strode from the library just as several servants entered. I glanced over my shoulder and found them lighting candles around the room.

I guess we could've stayed a bit longer, I thought wistfully, wondering what else Riker and I might have talked about. But the groaning of my stomach said otherwise.

"You never told me what happened," I said. "When you all raided the demon coven."

Riker shrugged. "Not much. It was a trap. They intentionally fed us information about their spell to break out of the time loop so we'd come to them. We arrived in their caves and found the place empty. We only got back just in time."

I suppressed a shudder at the thought of Leo having even *more* time to drink my blood.

Riker noticed the unease in my expression, and his eyes darkened. "I won't let him hurt you again."

I scoffed. "It's not your job to protect me. I can protect myself."

Riker raised his eyebrows. "I'd argue with you, but if you held your own against Leo Serrano, then you're probably right."

We walked through the halls in silence for a few minutes, passing by the occasional servant or two.

"I'll do it," Riker said suddenly.

I looked up at him, frowning. "Do what?"

He met my gaze, his blue eyes solemn. "I'll help you get into the Count's forbidden chambers."

My mouth fell open. "You . . . you will? What changed your mind?"

Riker's jaw tightened. "If Leo Serrano's coven found a way out of the time loop, it means they can be stopped. They can be *killed*. It means we can put an end to these attacks once and for all." His eyes blazed, and my stomach churned in response. "If we can find information the Count has kept locked away, then I want to be a part of it."

My mouth felt dry. I swallowed. "Okay. Then let's do this."

~

Riker and I joined the others in the dining hall. The Count stood at our arrival, his lips tightening with displeasure. I realized we were the last ones to arrive and quickened my pace to sit at the table next to Riker. Izzy nudged me with her elbow, her lips twitching.

"Now that all our guests have arrived," the Count said, his nostrils flaring, "we may say Grace." He closed his eyes and spoke the same prayer he'd said before. Then, he crossed himself and began eating.

Riker and I hungrily tore into the turkey and sliced bread, barely saying a word.

Izzy burst out laughing when she looked at us. "So, did you two find anything interesting?"

Riker met my gaze and then looked away.

I shrugged, keeping my eyes fixed on my plate. "Not really."

I felt Izzy's stare but pretended to be intently focused on my meal. Riker looked at me again, a question in his eyes. I shook my head slightly.

"How are *you*?" I asked Izzy, changing the subject. "Did the mages fix your wind problem?"

Izzy sighed and nodded. "Yeah. A temporary enchantment to keep things under wraps. It'll probably wear off tomorrow." She glowered at no one in particular, so I didn't press the subject.

We ate in relative silence, but I felt Riker's gaze still on me. I gritted my teeth and kicked him under the table. He choked on his drink and spit all over the table.

I snorted and covered my mouth. Izzy chuckled, and a few others joined in.

"Sorry," Riker muttered, shooting a glare at me. I nudged his foot again, gently this time, and he laughed.

Izzy raised her eyebrows at us, her eyes glinting. When Riker wasn't looking, she winked at me. I rolled my eyes.

It didn't take me long to fill my stomach. I took one last bite and sat back in my chair, grateful I wasn't wearing the dreaded corset anymore. My eyes fell on the Count, who was muttering something in Spanish with Juan at his left.

I grew still and watched them. Their expressions were both solemn, but neither of them looked my way. Perhaps they were talking about the demon situation. I wasn't close enough to distinguish what they were saying.

It was probably nothing.

I cleared my throat, suddenly feeling exhausted. Slowly, I rose from the table. The other boys surrounding me stood politely, though the Four Douchebags looked a bit peeved at having to rise.

"I'm finished too," Riker said, jumping to his feet as well. "I'll walk you up."

My face was hot as I felt Izzy's eyes drilling holes into me. Forcing a smile, I nodded, trying to ignore my sweaty palms. Riker offered me his arm, and I took it as we left the dining hall together. I felt several pairs of eyes on us as we exited.

"You know, they're probably talking about us," I muttered to him when we reached the hallway. "Entering and leaving together is practically a scandal in this time."

Riker laughed. "Let them talk."

I couldn't help how my stomach contracted at those words.

Riker steered me off to the side in an alcove filled with paintings of waterfalls and mountains. My heart raced as he ducked his head to meet my gaze.

"Should we include Izzy in this?" he whispered.

Momentary confusion flickered in my mind. Then, I understood. My heart plummeted, and I swallowed down my disappointment. *Of course he wants to get me alone to talk about our plan.* "I'd prefer not to."

Riker frowned. "Why?"

"Her powers are uncontrollable. What if she hurts someone? Or hurts herself? Besides, I wouldn't want to implicate her in this. The fewer people involved, the fewer people might get caught."

Riker nodded. "Yes, you're right. Besides, that would put a damper on our story of how I seduced you to perform my bidding."

I chuckled and slapped his arm. "Oh, stop."

Riker's eyes glittered with mischief. He leaned closer. "Well, if you change your mind, I'd be happy to revert to my original suggestion: claiming I was powerless against your charms."

My breath caught in my throat. His face was much too close to mine.

"It wouldn't be hard, you know," he went on, capturing a lock of my hair and tucking it behind my ear. "You do have the most captivating smile. And the most alluring brown eyes."

Lilith, I can't breathe. I really can't breathe. My face was an explosion of heat, and I couldn't move my tongue to speak at all. I realized my mouth was open, and I clamped it shut. Even if I *could* talk, I had no idea what to say.

Riker smiled as if he could sense my awkward speechlessness. He took my hand in his, bent his head, and pressed his lips to my fingers. A shiver of pleasure raced up my spine, and I sucked in a breath.

"Until tomorrow, Miss Gerrick." Riker winked at me, and then he was gone.

I lingered in the alcove for an extra moment or two to clear my head of the all-consuming fog of Riker's presence. I was such an idiot. A hopeless idiot.

I clenched and unclenched my fingers into fists and took several deep breaths. My eyes closed as I conjured images of fighting demons, spilling blood, and diving into the adrenaline-filled battle I craved. Slowly, my body returned to normal and my head cleared. My heart still raced, but it was from something different—something familiar that I felt when fighting. An excited energy, but one I could control.

Satisfied, I ducked out of the alcove and ran straight into one of the Four Douchebags. He staggered backward with an "oof" and then straightened to glare at me.

I stared at him and backed up a step. "Uh, sorry. Didn't mean to bump you."

It was the pale-faced boy with sandy brown hair. I

couldn't remember his name, though. He straightened his waistcoat, his gaze raking up and down my figure with unnecessary slowness.

"That's quite all right," he said, his lips spreading into a smile that looked more like a leer. "Miss . . . Gerrick, is it?"

"Yeah. Sorry, what's your name again?"

"Samson Schubert at your service." He bowed low and popped back up to smirk at me.

"Right. Well, I should be—" I tried to move past him, but he blocked my path. He towered over me by at least a foot, and the size of his biceps told me I couldn't exactly shove past him.

"Why are you running off? We've barely gotten to know each other."

I glared at him. "You and your friends haven't shown any interest in getting to know me."

"Well, it wouldn't be much fun like that, would it? Then, I'd have to share you with them." Samson grinned widely at me, leaning closer.

I sucked in a breath, suddenly realizing what was happening. His arm pressed into the wall behind me to corner me into the alcove.

I dropped to the ground, ducking under his arm, and raced toward the staircase. Samson snatched my arm, his fingers gripping me like a vise as he tugged me back toward him.

"You're a slippery little thing, aren't you?" He smiled as if my escape attempt were endearing to him. "Do you know how long I've had to go without decent female company?"

He yanked me closer and pressed his face against my hair, inhaling deeply.

Nausea and anger swirled in my chest. I jerked my head up, smashing into his face with a sickening crack. Samson yelped and stumbled backward, releasing my arm. I ducked low, using my small size to my advantage, and slammed my fist into his kneecap. He howled and swung his arms toward me, but I dodged and aimed a kick straight into his gut. He collapsed onto the floor in a heap, moaning and clutching at his stomach.

I stepped closer to him and nudged him with my foot until he rolled onto his back, glaring at me.

"I don't care what kind of company you keep, asshole," I hissed. "Stay the hell away from me."

Fury burned in his eyes. "You're dead, bitch."

I spat in his face and turned on my heel, leaving him lying there like a baby. A slither of satisfaction crept through my chest. I hadn't realized how much I'd missed beating someone in a fight.

14
BRIELLE

Darkness plagued my dreams that night. Smoke and ash engulfed me. Flames burned against my skin, charring my flesh. I couldn't breathe. I couldn't see through the haze of smoke. Screams surrounded me, begging for mercy. Blood and death pressed in on me, suffocating me. My ears throbbed from the cries of the wounded. My eyes burned from the ash in the air. A familiar scent stung my nose along with a sharp, vinegar smell.

Everywhere around me was pain. Destruction. Tragedy.

When I awoke, I was covered in sweat, my heart racing a mile a minute.

Panting, I peeled my sweaty hair off my face and rolled over, squinting at the purple rays of dawn peeking through my window.

I'd had nightmares before, but never like this. Something crackled within me like a living thing had awoken inside me, clawing to the surface of my mind.

I sat up, crossing my arms to keep my hands from trembling. My shoulders shook. I bent over, sucking in deep breaths to calm my nerves.

In the dream, I had smelled demons as sharply as if they were breathing down my neck. I still smelled them now even though I was awake.

My eyes burned and my throat tightened. All I wanted was to see Angel. Whenever we had nightmares, we often crawled into each other's bed for comfort. I didn't do it as much anymore, but when she had a particularly nasty vision in her dreams, she would still come to my room.

I needed her now.

I closed my eyes and rested my forehead against my knees. *Just a dream,* I told myself again and again. *It wasn't real.*

I lifted my head, my hands itching to do something. But my room was already frustratingly tidy.

Sliding on a robe, I eased open my door and crept downstairs. The hallway was eerily quiet. Small candles cast a faint glow to illuminate my path down the staircase. The decorative vases along the hallway left ghostly shadows against the wall. I shivered, wishing I had a jacket with me.

My bare feet whispered against the floor as I made my way to the library. I peered inside hesitantly. Several candlesticks were lit, and a fire burned in the hearth, but the room was empty.

Exhaling, I sat in front of the fireplace for a moment to warm myself, my eyes captured by the movement of the flames. Then, I rose to my feet and approached the nearest shelf, whipping out book after book and creating stacks of different colors and sizes. After a while, the numbness of my mind took over, and I lost focus. My body moved in a familiar rhythm as I reorganized the shelf. Dust tickled my fingertips and hovered in the air in front of me. Some texts were worn and frayed, and others were fresh as if they'd never been opened.

At long last, I finished a satisfying rainbow shelf of books and stood back to admire my work. In my heart, I felt at peace. None of the horrors from my nightmare could touch me now.

I nodded once, then turned and let out a yelp.

A dark figure stood opposite me, facing a bookshelf. He turned at my shout, his face hooded.

Fear climbed up my throat. I patted my waist but I had no weapons.

"Who are you?" I demanded.

The figure chuckled and crept forward, lowering his hood.

I gasped. It was Leo Serrano. His hair was down, falling just past his chin in thick curls. His silver-rimmed eyes speared right through me.

"Forgive me," he said, bowing low. "I was expecting His Excellency. Not you." He smirked, his eyes roving over my body. Though I wore my shift and a robe, I suddenly felt naked under his scrutiny.

"What do you want with the Count?" I asked, edging back toward the fireplace. I arranged a frightened look on my face. Better to make him think I was afraid of him instead of trying to grab a weapon in the form of a fire poker.

Leo took a step toward me. "That's none of your concern."

"It is if you're about to attack me for being in the wrong place at the wrong time."

Leo lifted his hands, his eyebrows raising. "Who said anything about attacking you?"

I scowled. "So what, you'll just let me go? I find that hard to believe."

Leo grinned widely. "Well, if you assured me you would let my intrusion here go unnoticed, then I'm certain we could come to an arrangement."

I glared at him, and he laughed.

"I figured as much." He drew closer. I bumped into the bookshelf next to the fireplace, my hand groping blindly for the tongs. "You don't want to fight me," I growled.

"I bested you before."

"You did *not*," I snapped before I could help myself.

Leo chuckled again, his eyes alight with amusement. "It bothers you, doesn't it? That I triumphed against you." He cocked his head at me, his eyes moving up and down my body—much more slowly this time.

I resisted the urge to cross my arms. My nostrils flared. *I wish people would stop doing that.*

"For a small thing like you, that's surprising," he murmured thoughtfully. "Do you fight many demons, *mi amor*?"

"Don't call me that," I said.

"Then, what should I call you?"

My fingers clasped something cool and metal, and I offered Leo a half smile. "Your worst nightmare." With a shout, I lunged, swiping the poker at him. It sliced into his cheek, and he stumbled back, his eyes wide with shock. A trickle of blood trailed from the cut on his cheek. He pressed a hand to it in disbelief and then laughed.

He actually *laughed.*

Anger roiled within me, and I advanced, swiping again and again. But he was ready for the fight now. Black magic pooled from his hands like shadows, engulfing him until he shifted. When the magic faded, he was gone.

I blinked and stepped backward. He hadn't just *vanished*; he was a shifter.

So, what had he shifted *to*?

Thinking quickly, I recited a spell I'd written,

"Surrounding magic, guide my eyes,

Reveal this enemy's deceptive disguise."

My hands glowed blue. A jet of magic speared from my fingertips, hovering momentarily in the air until it shot forward, colliding with something invisible.

No, wait. Not invisible. *Miniscule.* He must have shifted to an insect.

Leo shifted back to his human form and grunted as the force of my spell slammed him against the bookshelf. He was out of breath but still grinning.

"Reveal this enemy's deceptive disguise?" Panting, he straightened his sleeves. "That's clever. I've never heard of that one before."

I lifted my chin. "That's because I wrote it." I stepped forward, brandishing the poker. "Care to try again?"

Leo arched an eyebrow, his eyes glinting. "Tell me, Miss, uh, *Worst Nightmare*, what is your affinity? I fear I hold an unfair advantage over you by shifting." He spread his arms wide. "But I feel you have not responded in kind. Surely, you must be holding back."

My jaw went rigid. Glaring, I muttered another spell,

"Magic above, surround this space,

Freeze my enemy and hold him in place."

Blue jets of magic spilled from my hands and surrounded Leo in a bright glow. He froze in place, still wearing that infuriating smirk on his face.

I bounded forward and rammed the poker into his shoulder. It went right through his flesh. Something unreadable flared in his eyes, but he didn't so much as flinch.

I yanked the poker free and lunged again, but this time my spell wore off. He collapsed to the floor, moaning as he tried to rise. Blood poured from the wound in his shoulder.

A weary chuckle escaped his lips. Groaning, he climbed to his feet and clutched at his injured arm. "Impressive," he said hoarsely. Amusement still danced in his eyes, but his face was wary. Nervous even.

It brought me a tiny bit of satisfaction to see his expression shift, even if the change was subtle.

I raised my eyebrows, challenging him.

Leo's chest heaved with ragged breaths. His face looked

paler than usual, and when he stepped toward me, he winced, his expression crumpling.

I smiled, cocking my head at him. "Again?"

He breathed an airy laugh, shaking his head. "You are a worthy adversary, Little Nightmare. I'm sorry I underestimated you."

"Not sorry enough," I growled, stepping forward.

A door slammed, echoing in the hall behind me. For once, Leo's smile slid off his face. I stilled, watching him. Waiting. My hand felt slick with sweat as I gripped the poker tightly.

"Until next time," Leo whispered. Before I could react, he vanished in a puff of black smoke.

I gasped. My head whipped back and forth as I looked for him. I heard a faint buzzing sound near my head. I whispered hastily,

"Surrounding magic, guide my eyes,
Reveal this enemy's deceptive disguise."

Blue magic poured from my hands again, circling the room, but nothing happened. Eventually, the light faded, and my magic vanished. Swearing, I whirled around to look for Leo, but I already knew I wouldn't find him.

He was gone.

My face was covered in sweat. Panting, I looked around. Footsteps echoed in the hall. I was gripped by the sudden urge to hide or conceal my weapon, but I didn't know why.

Then, I focused on the tip of the fire poker. I hastily drew it closer and wiped the tip with the sleeve of my shirt. Now it looked like *I'd* been injured.

I had no idea why I'd done that. But something told me I needed to keep Leo's blood. And I didn't trust the Count with it. If I could use it for a locator spell—or some spell of my own invention—maybe I could hunt Leo and his coven down myself.

Several figures appeared in the doorway of the library. The Count stood in front, dressed in a satin robe. His hair surrounded his face, and his eyes were wide and bloodshot.

"Miss Gerrick." He looked around the room. Aside from a few books that had fallen from their shelves, the library was otherwise undisturbed. "What happened here?"

I wiped my forehead. "Leo Serrano was here. We fought. He left."

"You . . . you *fought*?" The Count sputtered, glancing over his shoulder. Just behind him I recognized Ignacio and a few others who were obscured by shadows.

"Yes," I said through clenched teeth. "I wounded him, and he left."

The Count rubbed his chin, his eyes wide and calculating. Then, he turned from me to whisper something to Ignacio. Ignacio nodded and left, followed by another mage.

"Mr. Wilkinson, would you be so kind as to search the premises for any other demons?" the Count muttered.

My heart lurched. *Riker's here?* A figure stepped out of view, vanishing into the shadows before I could get a better look. I swallowed down the lump in my throat.

The Count turned to face me again, his eyes narrowing. It was just the two of us now. I felt I should put the poker back, but it gave me a strange sense of comfort. I ran my thumb along the cool metal handle.

The Count's eyes followed my movement, fixing on the weapon I wielded. "You fought him off with only that?"

"And my spells," I muttered.

The Count's eyebrows lifted. "Most impressive, Miss Gerrick. Perhaps we should bring you along with us when we next attack."

My heart lifted, and I straightened a bit.

"Come and sit." The Count gestured to the chairs surrounding the fireplace.

We sat in the armchairs, similar to when we'd first met. I carefully placed the poker back against the wall next to the fireplace and clasped my hands on my lap.

"You are hurt," the Count gestured to the blood on my shirt.

I cleared my throat. "It's barely a scratch. I can't even feel it."

"Even so, you should have Ignacio take a look."

I nodded, eager to move on from this subject. "I will."

The Count scrutinized me. I forced myself to meet his gaze, trying to arrange my face into something carefully neutral.

"So, you spoke with Serrano?" the Count asked, his voice barely more than a whisper.

I nodded.

"What did he say to you?"

"Just that he wasn't expecting me. He was expecting *you*."

The Count frowned. "And . . . what *were* you doing in the library at this hour?"

I shifted in my chair. "I couldn't sleep. As I've told you before, arranging books helps my mind relax. I was hoping it could help me get back to sleep."

The Count watched me for so long that my eyes started to water, but still I didn't look away. I was telling the truth. I had nothing to fear.

At long last, he nodded. "Did he say what he wanted?"

I shook my head. "He was cloaked. I didn't recognize him at first. I think . . . I think he came alone. This wasn't like before when they all attacked at once. I feel like he crept in here on his own."

"Why?" the Count whispered, stroking his chin.

Though I had the feeling he asked himself the question, I still answered it. "Maybe he was looking for something."

The Count stilled, his eyes shifting to me and sharpening. Distrust and uncertainty flickered in his expression.

I watched him, and something roared within me. *I was right. He's hiding something. Something Leo Serrano wants.*

"Perhaps," the Count said slowly. "I will have to consult with my mages and examine the extensive evidence and research we've collected on the coven over the years. This incident was isolated, but perhaps it will help me to see the bigger picture."

He looked away from me, and I understood his implication: my opinions weren't wanted. And he knew more than me about this.

I pressed my lips together and nodded. If I wanted to avoid his suspicion, I needed to act compliant.

Especially if Riker and I would be snooping through the Count's things later.

"That is all, Miss Gerrick." The Count waved his hand. "You may return to your chambers."

I stood and left the library, anxious to be alone and decompress from the whole ordeal. When I entered my room, Maria was already inside. She yelped when she saw me, raising her hands in the air.

"Oh my lady, I was so frightened! The other servants said they heard fighting and then I came here and couldn't find you—" She broke off, shaking her head. Tears filled her eyes and she sucked in several breaths.

I smiled and took her hands in mine. "I'm all right, Maria. Thank you for your concern. But I've been up for a long time and would like to rest now, if that's okay." I glanced toward the window and found sunlight bleeding into the room.

Maria followed my gaze and squeezed my hands. "It's all right. His Excellency is always more lenient after demons attack. I'm certain he won't mind if you rest a bit longer." She exhaled and wiped her hands on her apron.

"Relax, Maria," I said. "Everything's fine. It was just one demon, and he's gone now."

Maria offered a wobbly smile. "I only need my nerves to settle, my lady."

"You go and rest too. I don't need your help undressing or anything. I'll be fine, I promise."

Maria looked at me, her eyes wide and fearful.

"Really." I fixed a stern look at her. "I insist."

Maria chuckled shakily and curtsied. "Thank you, my lady."

Then, she left.

I heaved a sigh and strode to the window. Rolling hills and small concrete buildings stood in the distance, surrounded by a thick forest. Just barely visible near the horizon were the peaks of small mountains. The air smelled of dust, dirt, and decaying leaves. I gripped the edge of the window, staring for a moment at the scene below me. How had I never wondered what this city looked like? The one time I'd been outside, I'd been in a panic and intent on finding a way back home. I hadn't really appreciated my surroundings.

Resolving to explore later, I drew the curtains closed and settled into bed, my mind and body so exhausted that I didn't think once of my nightmare before drifting off to sleep.

15
BRIELLE

I slept well past noon. Maria came to fetch me when lunch was being served. She helped me dress in a shirt and pants similar to what I'd worn yesterday. She also insisted on pinning my hair up into something elegant.

I entered the dining hall and realized I was the last to arrive. Everyone had already begun eating, including the Count. The men all stood at my entrance and then sat down when I seated myself between Riker and Izzy.

"You will forgive us for dining without you, Miss Gerrick," the Count said, nodding toward me. "I thought it best to let you sleep after your ordeal last night."

I inclined my head politely. "Thank you, Your Excellency."

I ate in silence, though I felt Izzy's gaze on me during the meal.

Just before I stood from the table to excuse myself, a

blinding light exploded from the other end of the table. A boy was completely on fire.

I sucked in a gasp, looking around in horror for something to douse the flames. After barely a minute, the flames died, revealing the shaggy-haired Douchebag.

I swallowed down the panic in my throat, pressing a hand to my chest. Several boys jumped up to pat down the flames on the table and chairs with their waistcoats.

Vaguely, I remembered this same boy setting himself on fire my first day here. His name was Porter. I stared at him, wide-eyed. Chagrin filled his face as he hurried to help clean the ash and soot lingering on the table from his accident.

The Count waved a lazy hand toward the door, and a mage appeared. "Take him." He pointed to Porter.

Red splotches appeared on Porter's face, but he nodded in dejection and followed the mage from the room.

"Where are they going?" I whispered to Izzy, slowly lowering myself back in my seat.

"Probably more training. That's what they do for me. If they can't subdue his flames, they'll give him a sedative. It's happened to me once or twice." She rubbed her nose, dropping her gaze.

"It's nothing to be ashamed of," I said sternly. "We all have problems here. It's not your fault."

Izzy offered a bitter smile. "It doesn't feel that way when someone you love gets hurt."

I stared at her as she took another bite of food. Horror climbed up my throat. I didn't know what to say. Sure, I'd had my own problems, but I'd never hurt someone else. If anything, *I'd* been the one hurt so many times because of my incompetence.

The tightness in Izzy's jaw and the darkness in her eyes told me she didn't want to talk about it. So, I didn't pry. But my heart twisted in agony for whatever tragedy she'd suffered.

On my other side, Riker nudged me with his elbow. "You all right?"

I nodded, offering him a weak smile. "I'm fine."

"Last night," he said, then paused and swallowed. "I . . . I'm sorry I wasn't there."

I frowned. "Why?"

"To help you fight him, of course."

I snorted. "I don't need help. In case you couldn't tell, I *beat* him. He bolted."

Riker's brows knitted together. "Or he fled because he heard the other guests waking up."

I shot him a glare. "You think I can't handle myself in a fight?"

Riker raised both hands in surrender, the corners of his mouth curving upward. "I said no such thing, my lady."

His mocking tone and disarming smile easily soothed my anger. "Good," I muttered, but I couldn't help but smile back.

Riker chuckled. "You are a feisty one, Brielle Gerrick."

My face warmed at his use of my full name, but I said nothing.

After the meal, the mages met with us again. This time I was grouped with Armin, Abe, Elias, and, to my disgust, Samson. His eyes were full of fire when he looked at me, which told me he hadn't forgotten about our altercation the night before.

We sat in a circle as Ignacio coached us through some tedious breathing exercises. He chanted some words in Latin while lifting his hands as if in prayer. I wouldn't be surprised if he and the Count actually believed we could be cured through some divine intervention.

He urged us to take deep, cleansing breaths and point our hands toward him, who was to be a conduit to our powers.

As I expected, nothing happened. And when we were dismissed, I grumbled to myself about what a waste of time that had been. I could've spent that hour researching or exploring the Count's wards.

The days turned into weeks. After the incident with Leo's coven, the Count had been relentless with our training, claiming that if the demons could attack at any moment, then we had to work nonstop to master our powers.

I could hardly call it "training," though. It was really more like yoga and meditation, and it made me gag every time. For the next week, when I wasn't busy listening to Ignacio spout on about "deep breathing" garbage, I was creeping around the castle at mealtimes as I tried to find a way out. But the Count's guards were stationed at every door.

I often spent time in the armory practicing with weapons. I couldn't exactly use a punching bag in this time period, so I had to release my frustrations through other means. My favorite was the small dagger. With my stature, I couldn't wield a heavy sword easily. Sometimes Izzy would join me, and I'd teach her some basic sparring moves. I was never satisfied until I'd broken a sweat.

Juan often avoided me or shot me frightened looks, which was fine with me. I had no desire to become close friends with him. But after a while, unease wriggled through me, especially when I saw him chatting with the Count like they were best buds.

After a few weeks, I knew I had to clear the air. Even if he'd already told the Count about my father—I *had* to know.

After dinner one night, he darted out of the dining hall, and I hurried to catch up to him.

"Juan!" I called out, then clamped my mouth shut. "I mean, ah, Mr. Arévalo. Can I speak with you?"

Juan went still, his eyes guarded as he looked at me. "Of course. What can I do for you, Miss Gerrick?"

I glanced around before drawing closer to him, trying to ignore how he leaned away from me like I was contagious. "I want to apologize for speaking so . . . freely about my father and his dark magic." I dropped my voice even further. "Can you forgive me for being so blunt and forward? I realize now it was a mistake to discuss something so sensitive with you."

Something like relief flickered in his eyes, but he remained wary. "Not at all, Miss Gerrick. Think nothing of it."

He turned to leave, but I hissed, "Wait! Please. There's something else."

Juan stopped, his brows knitting together. "Yes?"

"I must ask that you keep the information to yourself." I tried to look innocent and weak, but I was sure it came off as more of a pained grimace. "I realize now the error of my careless comments, and I would hate for it to offend someone else."

Juan straightened, and something unreadable stirred in his eyes. "I'm afraid I cannot make such a promise, Miss Gerrick. I do not feel comfortable keeping secrets from my peers and my superiors."

Panic swirled within me. "Juan, please," I whispered, dropping the prim and proper act. "I'm in danger here. I swear to you, I practice *light* magic. I don't follow in my father's footsteps. Please."

"Miss Gerrick, as you're well aware, the Count despises demons. Even if I *didn't* share his beliefs, I would feel like I was betraying his trust if I kept this information from him. He is already on edge due to his efforts to find a way to free us from this blight, and since he doesn't know much about the dark warlock who cast the spell, the task has proven difficult. I cannot add another burden with my deceit."

Juan's lips tightened, and he stepped away from me. "I'm sorry."

And then he left. I stared after him numbly until his words struck me like a blow.

Demons. The Count despises demons.

If he hated demons, then of course he wouldn't know anything about the dark warlock who cast the spell.

But surely *someone* did. Someone who also practiced dark magic.

Someone like Leo Serrano.

16

LEO

Estrella's light snores filled the cave. Satisfied that she was deeply asleep, I rolled out of bed and slid my trousers and tunic on. I glanced at her sleeping form, momentarily overcome with envy and nostalgia.

Lilith, I don't even remember what it's like to sleep.

I shook the thought from my head, instead focusing on the satisfying pleasure I'd shared with her just moments ago. It had been a welcome escape to step away from my conflict with the Count and allow my body to experience the passions of mortals. To forget myself and everything around me.

And to revel in Estrella's pleasure too. Since she was my Donor, we shared a bond through which I could sense her heightened emotions. It made the experience so much more enjoyable for me.

I'd hit another dead end. Thanks to the Little Night-mare, I'd been unable to find any information in the Count's study about spells or enchantments he might've used to seal the barrier to the city. We'd had a minor victory breaking through the defenses of the castle and catching the occupants off guard, but now we were at a loss how to proceed.

I needed to know the particulars of the Count's spell. Otherwise I was simply guessing.

I ran a hand through my untidy hair and carefully tied it behind my neck. Estrella shifted in her sleep, her face still pink from exertion. I felt her blood thrumming through our connection, calling to me. Beckoning me back into her bed.

Not now. I only submitted to the call of her blood when I needed something to take my mind off my duties to the coven. Estrella knew that. It was something we agreed on when she acquiesced to become my Donor. I never forced myself on her, though. I always ensured she agreed before sharing her bed.

She hadn't refused me yet.

I wasn't sure if it was because of our connection or my insanely expert skills in bed. Perhaps both.

I slipped soundlessly out of her chambers. Well, rather, her cave. Centuries ago, my ancestors had carved out cavities within these caverns, forming the perfect hideout. And with the Count's magic surrounding the city, we couldn't form a home anywhere else, so we made the caves fit for living quarters. The walls had been smoothed and lined with lanterns, and each small cavern had been fully furnished.

Despite being cut off from the forest outside, it felt like home to me.

I weaved my way through the dark tunnels, my vampire vision allowing me to see the path perfectly. Then, I entered my library where Jorge sat in an armchair studying a book.

"Enjoy your dalliance?" he asked in a bored voice without looking up. Jorge didn't approve of my arrangement with Estrella. He had several committed Donors, but they kept a very distant and professional relationship. Sometimes Jorge was so much like Ronaldo that it made me ache. Both so pious and formal. Both frustratingly rigid with rules—unless breaking a rule provided an opportunity to be a hero.

"Very much," I said with a grin, sliding into the armchair across from him. "Have you found anything?"

Jorge slammed the book shut and ran a hand through his short, brown hair. "No."

Of course not. Another dead end.

We couldn't keep looking for answers that weren't there. We had to make a move. *Now.*

The time for waiting was over. The solution to the Count's spells wouldn't present itself to us, then we'd seek it out through other means.

Jorge read the determination in my eyes. "Leo, what are you thinking?"

I rubbed at the facial hair along my jaw. "Prepare the coven at full force."

Jorge straightened. "For what?" But the hardness in his face indicated he already knew.

"For battle. We strike the Castillo at dawn."

17
BRIELLE

OVER THE NEXT FEW DAYS, I STEWED OVER MY realization that Leo Serrano had information I needed. I didn't like it. If I found a way to talk to him, what would stop him from killing me? Or me from killing him?

But I should've thought of it earlier. The danger of being as narrow-minded as the Count was that you only saw things from one side: the side of light magic.

So, if a problem arose involving dark magic, you were screwed.

My hours of research in the Count's library were worthless because it only contained historical texts about *light* magic.

At least—those were the only ones available to the public. If the Count *did* have any helpful information, it would be hidden.

Instead of even considering the idea of tracking down

Leo Serrano, I focused on my plan with Riker to dig up any skeletons the Count had hidden in his closets.

A week after my conversation with Juan, I had just finished training with Ignacio when Riker waved me over to the other end of the ballroom, his expression eager. I hurried forward, trying to ignore the way my stomach flipped when his blue eyes fixed on me.

"What's up?" I asked.

Riker took my elbow and guided me to a corner of the ballroom where we wouldn't be overheard. Around us, the training groups scattered, some leaving and others lingering to chat like us.

"My valet told me this morning that the Count is taking a journey tomorrow," Riker said breathlessly. "He'll be visiting a village on the other side of the city to converse with his other mages."

My eyes grew wide. "He has *other* mages?"

Riker nodded. "Apparently he stationed them around the city to monitor things and ensure nothing is different about the time loop. My valet said he plans to take his servants with him, since this journey will take longer. I think the demons breaking free of the time loop have made him anxious."

I couldn't blame him. My brows furrowed. "So . . ." My heart lurched as I realized what he was implying. "We can snoop around while he's gone."

Riker nodded, his eyes glinting. "Indeed we can, my fair lady."

I grinned at him. "When should we do it?"

"Let's give the Count a day, just in case he comes back claiming he forgot something."

I nodded eagerly. "And what about the mages?"

"Just stick to our story. You didn't know the rules and will apologize profusely. I'll claim I was smitten by your charm."

I rolled my eyes. "Riker—"

"No, really. That's appropriate in this time. Let me say I was worried for your protection and wanted to keep you safe. I tried to stop you." He raised an eyebrow as if asking my permission.

I sighed, my cheeks warming. "All right. That's fine."

Riker leaned closer to me and whispered, "What do you think we'll find?"

My skin felt hot with his nearness. I swallowed, but my throat felt dry. "I, uh, I'm not sure. Maybe some sacred shrine?"

Riker snorted. "A shrine to *himself.*"

A loud laugh burst from my lips, and I covered my mouth. A few of the lingering guests looked in our direction.

Riker winked at me, and I slapped his arm. He stuck out his elbow, and I laced my arm through his as we marched regally to lunch. All the while, my heart fluttered in anticipation. Perhaps I'd finally be able to discover what exactly the Count was hiding.

∼

The next day, my entire body seemed to thrum with anticipation. I was up before dawn and dressed myself, making my way to the library to rearrange books and keep my restless hands busy.

At breakfast, Riker and I sat next to each other, casting excited glances back and forth. Izzy, ever alert, eyed us with suspicion. She caught my arm after breakfast, holding me back while everyone else exited the hall.

"What's going on with you two?" she asked, jerking her chin toward Riker's retreating form.

I blushed. "Nothing."

Izzy raised her eyebrows. Her eyes were stern as they drilled into me. "You can't lie to me, Brielle. You two are flirting *constantly*."

My mouth opened in indignation. "We are not!"

"Are too."

I sputtered incoherently. "I—we—I don't even know *how* to flirt."

Izzy crossed her arms. "You certainly do. Whatever you do around Riker, that's called flirting."

I swallowed. "I—do you think *he* knows it's flirting?"

Izzy leaned forward conspiratorially. "I'm pretty sure he knows. And he likes it too."

My tongue turned to sandpaper, but I couldn't stop the goofy smile from spreading across my face.

Izzy laughed. "Crikey, you are so *green*, Brielle. Have you never had a chap before?"

My blush deepened. "No," I muttered. "I've never even kissed a guy."

Izzy's eyes grew wide, and I wanted to smack her. "Fair dinkum?" she said loudly, gaping at me.

I shushed her, waving my hands to keep her quiet. "I don't know what that means."

"It means, 'Are you telling the truth?'"

I shoved her shoulder, and she laughed again.

"No worries, Brielle. I'll teach you everything you need to know about your first pash." She patted my shoulder and offered a condescending smile.

I gave her my most withering stare. "You talk funny."

Izzy laughed, and I couldn't help but join in as she steered me out of the dining hall.

We participated in our training as normal. I kept stealing glances across the room at Riker. Oftentimes I found him with his jaw rigid and a determined fire in his eyes that made my stomach churn. Other times, he caught my eye and winked or grinned at me, which also sent my insides spinning.

I hated myself for being so twitterpated. For losing focus during my training and not even feeling remotely sorry when nothing happened during Ignacio's exercises.

Get a grip, Brie! I told myself. *This is why you're here.*

But I was also here because I was suspected of being cursed by Lilith. And if the Count had any information hidden about it, I had to find it.

Then why was my heart racing and a ridiculous smile spreading across my face?

You're such an idiot, I thought.

Training ended, and the mages excused us. Riker immediately bounded toward me, his face alight and his eyes dancing. "How did training go?"

I rolled my eyes. "I couldn't focus."

"Me neither," he said breathlessly.

We grinned at each other, our eyes locking for a moment longer than necessary.

Then, he cleared his throat and rubbed the back of his neck. "I, uh, figured the best time would be during lunch when the others are preoccupied."

I nodded. "Good. Yes. I agree." *Stop talking, Brie. Just shut up.*

Riker chuckled nervously. "I'll meet you on the staircase at noon, okay?"

"Okay."

We both smiled again. Neither of us moved. He inched closer, his smile fading. "Are you sure about this, Brielle?"

I swallowed. "Yes. I need answers."

He stared at me for a moment. "About what?"

I hesitated. "About the Count and what he wants hidden. And if it might possibly have anything to do with me and my ailment."

Riker frowned. "Brielle, why would he hide that?"

I opened my mouth to speak but then thought better of it. I still wasn't ready to open up to him about my fears or my secrets. Instead, I chose something else. "You already know my father's a demon. I thought maybe . . . something about me having demon blood might be affecting my magical issue. I can't exactly go to the Count or mages about it because—"

"Because they hate demons." He grimaced and nodded. "Right."

"And the Count seems like the type of person to keep anything demon-related hidden away to keep up appearances." I shrugged. "I figured it was worth a shot."

Riker's expression warmed. "I don't think any less of you, you know. For having a father who's a demon."

I blinked. "I didn't think you would."

We stood there staring at each other for another long moment. Slowly, the warmth within me faded. I cleared my throat and muttered something about changing my clothes before I dashed off.

Though I did change into a lighter tunic, I really wanted to slip into the armory and load up on weapons just in case. I didn't expect any trouble, but one could never be too careful, and I felt more comfortable fully armed. I swiped a few athames and stakes and then hunted for holsters. When I found a few that fit, I pocketed the sheathed weapons and made sure they were secure in my trousers.

For the next hour, I busied myself in the library, rearranging books to keep my mind at ease. At long last, the clock chimed, jolting me from my therapeutic organization. My heart racing, I darted back up the stairs and tried to stand as casually as possible while waiting for Riker.

It didn't take him long. He spotted me from the opposite side of the guest rooms and strode toward me. Something in my chest squirmed, seeing his gaze fixed on me as he walked toward me with such purpose and vigor.

"Shall we?" he whispered, glancing around. His cheeks were pink, and his eyes glinted.

I nodded, my throat too dry to say anything.

I took his arm out of habit, and we descended the stairs. When a babble of voices erupted nearby, he tugged me off to the side in a dark corner where we hovered, waiting for the group of guests to pass. My breath caught in my throat. Riker's chest pressed against mine. He smelled of mint and soap, and it made my head spin.

"We're clear," he whispered, his breath brushing against my forehead.

I grunted something incoherent, my throat closing off in the process. Luckily, Riker didn't seem to notice.

He steered me toward a lower staircase I hadn't noticed before. It was tucked between two large pillars flanked by ostentatious paintings. The stairs were cast in shadow from the pillars, obscuring it from view—unless you were looking for it.

We descended the stairs, and a chill swept over me. At the bottom was a door. Riker jiggled the handle and swore. "Locked."

"Here." I dropped his arm and lifted my hands, closing my eyes before I uttered the spell.

"*Magic above and spirits herein,*
Release this lock and let us in."

My hands glowed blue, and the energy crackled through me. With a soft *click,* the door swung open.

Riker looked at me, his face full of awe. "That was bloody incredible."

I bit back a smile. "Thanks. Come on." I took his arm again, and we strode through the open door.

A long, narrow tunnel stood in front of us. Darkness wrapped around me, pressing in toward my bones. I suppressed a shiver as the cool air swarmed around me, numbing my body. We crept forward slowly and carefully, afraid of making a single sound. The hallway was lit by torches, which cast eerie orange glows on the wall like flames threatening to engulf us.

Echoes whispered past us. Muffled shouts and moans. Sobs.

"Do you hear that?" I breathed. I couldn't be sure if it was in my head or not. Perhaps it was just the wind.

"Yes." Riker's arm shook in my grip. "It's spooky. You think this place is haunted?"

I knew he was trying to lighten the mood for my benefit. I shoved his arm, but a sense of foreboding gripped me like a vise.

The tunnel stretched on and on, and we inched forward a few steps at a time. My limbs ached from quivering so much, and goosebumps erupted on my arms.

Focus, Brie, I told myself. *You've fought demons before. You can do this.*

Finally, the hallway opened up to another staircase that plunged into a black abyss below. Riker and I stopped and shared an uncertain glance. Part of me feared that if I stepped forward, I would fall to my death.

I sucked in a breath. "We've made it this far."

"My thoughts exactly." But Riker's voice cracked,

betraying his uncertainty. He adjusted his arm so his fingers laced through mine, squeezing some warmth back into my body.

I closed my eyes and took another breath. We moved forward. Our feet met a solid step. Then, another. Soon darkness completely swallowed us up. I couldn't even see Riker next to me.

This is madness.

I froze. "Hold on," I muttered. "I'm an idiot." I closed my eyes—though it made no difference—and uttered another spell.

"Surrounding magic and powers that be,
Provide us light with which to see."

My hands glowed blue again, and this time the glow intensified and held like a lantern. It illuminated a vast cavern at least a hundred feet below us. The stone steps wound downward in a spiral. I squinted, trying to make out what was at the bottom. All I could see was giant metal bars, like a cage.

A howl of agony split through the air, and my heart lurched in my chest. The sound echoed, blaring against my ears—much closer than before.

They weren't ghosts. Someone—*something*—was down there.

Riker's breath hitched. "Are you sure about this? Brielle, if there's a creature down there, I don't know if—"

"We'll be fine," I whispered. "I'm armed."

He shot me an unreadable look but said nothing.

What could the Count possibly be hiding down there? I

was expecting a locked library or study, perhaps a few scandalous letters, but not *this*.

Too late to turn back. Curiosity melted my fear, and I surged forward, dragging Riker with me. Using my hands to light the way, we crept downstairs, stepping carefully to avoid slipping. The chill only worsened the deeper we got, and the moans and noises intensified. But something within me resonated with the creepiness of it all. My brain suddenly switched modes, and now this was a mystery to be solved instead of a horror to be feared.

Riker's hand trembled in my grasp, and this time I squeezed his fingers for comfort.

"Almost there," I muttered.

When we descended the last few steps, my eyes widened at the scene before me.

It wasn't a cage—it was a *prison*. An array of criss-crossing metal bars stood in front of us, each cell holding a small cot and a table with jars and tools. The air reeked of demons, stinging my nose and filling me with dread.

Dropping Riker's hand, I hurried toward the first prison cell and peered inside. A low voice sobbed from the other side.

"Hello?" I called. "Who's there?"

The sobbing stopped for a moment, but whoever it was said nothing. I squinted, holding up my hands to see better, but all I could make out was a massive shape crouched on the ground, facing away from me.

"Brielle, over here."

I followed the sound of Riker's voice to another prison

cell. When I lifted my hands to provide light, Riker and I both gasped.

Inside the cell was a vampire. His eyes were all-black, and his fangs dripped with blood. A huge gash ran from his eye socket to his jawline, oozing blood down his shirt.

"Bloody hell," Riker choked.

Horror numbed my bones, chilling me worse than the cold air. I hurried to the next cell and found a werewolf tied up with silver thread. The next one held a woman whose eyes were closed, but her shoulders rose and fell with labored breaths. Then, another vampire, some troll-like creature, and a shapeshifter, his skin riddled with so many pus-filled boils that he could no longer shift forms.

I covered my mouth, holding back bile, and rushed back to Riker's side. His face was ashen, and his mouth turned downward in a nauseous grimace.

"Brielle, look at the tables next to their beds," he hissed, pointing. I held up my hands and noticed the jars held liquids of various colors. The tools looked like thin skewers and blades, and some of them glinted with fresh blood.

"This isn't just a prison cell," I whispered, horrified. "This is a torture chamber."

18

BRIELLE

"WE NEED TO LEAVE, BRIELLE. *NOW*." RIKER TUGGED on my arm.

"We have to help them!" I gestured to the prison cells. My eyes fell on the sharp instruments coated with demon blood. How long had these prisoners been here? How long had the Count been torturing them?

A door slammed shut high above us, echoing throughout the cavern. Riker and I froze and exchanged a horrified look.

"We have to leave," he hissed again, grabbing my hand. "If we're caught down here . . ."

I stared at the vampire with the bloody gash. Bile and regret rose up inside me, threatening to strangle me. I couldn't just leave them.

Footsteps echoed. Someone was coming down the stairs.

"Brielle," Riker whispered, pulling on my hand. "We can

find a way to free them later. But we can't help them if we're caught."

A lump formed in my throat. I nodded and ran with Riker toward the staircase. The footsteps drew nearer and nearer. I muttered a quick spell to extinguish the lights on my hands.

When the footsteps were practically on top of us, I grabbed Riker's arms and held him still. Together, we skirted the edge of the staircase and waited, holding our breaths. In a low whisper, I muttered,

"Magic above, conceal us here,
Hide us from those who draw near."

Magic crackled within me, sweeping over me and Riker. I felt power emanating from our bodies, proof that my cloaking spell worked.

We held perfectly still until a dark figure loomed just in front of us. Riker's hand shook in my grasp. We backed up, allowing the figure to pass. My heart lurched when I recognized him—Ignacio.

Ignacio stopped for a moment, his head turning as he looked around. Terror gripped my body. I closed my eyes and clenched my teeth.

At long last, Ignacio continued down the steps until he faded from view. His footsteps became a mere echo in the cavern.

"Come on," Riker whispered, and we hurried up the steps. I resisted the urge to glance over my shoulder to see if Ignacio noticed us.

"What's he doing down here?" I asked.

"No idea," Riker said.

Nausea swirled in my stomach at the thought of the mages working *with* the Count to torture demons. If Ignacio was down here, it meant he knew exactly what was going on.

I shoved my thoughts away, trying to keep my emotions at bay until we reached the top. Riker held my hand as we continued our climb. The door was still ajar, and we pushed it open, climbing up the final staircase and emerging in the hallway adorned with paintings. Light filtered through the windows, momentarily blinding me in contrast to the darkness below.

I pressed my back against the wall, gasping for breath while my heart raced a mile a minute.

"What . . . the bloody hell . . . was that?" Riker panted. His eyes were wide, and his face had completely drained of color.

I shook my head numbly. The fear within me subsided, and anger slowly took its place. "How could the Count *do* this?"

"You knew how he felt about demons, Brielle."

"That doesn't excuse this!" I cried, waving a hand toward the staircase. "He's *torturing* demons! And why? Because he thinks they're an abomination? Maybe I should torture *him* for the same reason!"

"You don't know anything about those prisoners," Riker said softly. "They could be criminals. Murderers."

"Even so, they don't deserve that! They don't deserve to

be cut up and experimented on! They deserve a fair trial and a humane sentence."

Riker threw his hands in the air. "These are unprecedented times, Brielle. I'm sure that, were it not for the time loop, they would be getting justice right now. But—"

"Who decided the Count should be in charge? Light casters break the law too, but I didn't see any down there!"

Riker rubbed a hand along his face. "Brielle, I understand your father is a demon and you're protective of casters like him. But you can't ignore the statistics. Demonhunters hunt *demons*. Because demons are more likely to commit crimes. Creatures like vampires and werewolves thirst for blood. The urge to bite and feast is almost uncontrollable. Light casters don't have that same problem."

"I don't need a lecture on demons," I snapped. "This is still wrong. You can't deny that, Riker."

"No, I can't." He sighed. "But we need more information before we do anything about this."

My nostrils flared. I crossed my arms and didn't answer.

"Please, Brielle. Promise me you'll wait. I swear I'll work with you to solve this and free those prisoners, but we need *time*."

My jaw ticked back and forth, and I exhaled. "Fine. I'll wait."

Riker's eyes swam with relief. Suddenly, his whole body stiffened, becoming so tense that his tendons and veins stood out. His back arched, and his mouth opened in silent agony. His jaw went rigid, and his eyes rolled back until they were all white.

"Riker?" I said, stepping toward him.

His arms swung forward, knocking me backward. I fell to the ground, my chest throbbing from his blow. *What the hell?* When I rose to my feet, I found him twitching and convulsing.

He was having a fit.

My blood chilled as I remembered his ailment: he had violent visions.

I reached for him, but I knew if I got closer, he might hit me again.

"Riker!" I shouted, trying to get through to him. But his white eyes didn't even blink. His body continued thrashing until he slammed against the wall. The paintings rattled from the impact.

I took a deep breath and muttered,

"Magic above, surround this space,

Freeze my friend and hold him in place."

My blue magic surrounded Riker until he went completely still, his mouth still hanging open and his face taut with agony. His limbs were outstretched at odd angles.

He looked completely alien. Like some creature instead of the Riker I knew.

My stomach swirled with terror. Was the vision hurting him? Was he in pain right now?

I had to do something before the spell wore off. I glanced up and down his body, knowing he was too heavy to carry by myself. My heart pounding, I looked down the hallway and peered around the corner. My eyes fell on the open doors of the library. Perhaps I could drag him there.

For a moment, I glanced in the other direction toward the dining hall. Soft voices echoed as the others finished their lunch.

But I couldn't ask for help. I didn't trust the Four Douchebags, and I certainly didn't trust the mages anymore.

I had to do this myself.

I took a deep breath and carefully lowered Riker so he lay on the floor. Then, I lifted his arms and dragged him. His backside slid easily on the polished wood floor. My arms quivered from the strain of pulling so much weight, but I gritted my teeth and pressed forward. Sweat coated my face and neck. Pain flared in my arms.

You can do this. You can do this.

Finally, I reached the library. I gingerly lowered Riker's arms so he lay in front of the fireplace. Then, I collapsed next to him, gasping for breath. Energy seeped out of me. The spell was wearing off.

I shifted and sat up, hovering over Riker's inert form. My hands fluttered uselessly over his chest and face. I wasn't a healer. I had no idea how to help him.

My mind raced with possibilities—all the spells I'd written. I closed my eyes, muttering under my breath until I remembered one I'd tried years ago. Clearing my throat, I placed my hands over Riker's body and whispered,

"*Magic above, I call upon thee,*

To heal this man in front of me."

I waited, then opened my eyes. Nothing happened.

I swore under my breath. Part of me had known that a

person couldn't just be *healed*. You had to have the right abilities and, often, the right ingredients as well. Perhaps with no affinity it was an impossible task for me.

I inhaled and tried again,

"Magic above, hear my call,

Relax this man and make him calm."

Still nothing. Though Riker was frozen, his body was still stiff and in obvious pain.

Panic swelled within me. *You can do this.* I watched him for a long moment. Slowly, the blue glow surrounding him faded. I was out of time.

What had Riker told me? He often had violent *visions*. Which meant a vision had taken over his mind.

Angel had the same problem. Her visions caused her pain and anguish. Mom had once said that when that happened, it meant the vision had overpowered her mind— that her brain wasn't capable of processing it on its own.

Maybe Riker had the same problem.

Closing my eyes again, I placed my hands over his chest and whispered,

"Magic above, empower his brain.

Release the vision that causes him pain."

Power thrummed through me, vibrating like an engine. I gasped and opened my eyes. The blue glow surrounded Riker again, and my magic rippled like water.

Then a sharp, rattling gasp poured from Riker's mouth. His body quivered, but he no longer thrashed. Instead he shook violently as if he were freezing. Gradually, his face relaxed, but his eyes were still white.

He sat up slowly, facing me with those terrifying empty eyes. My breath caught in my throat.

In a hoarse, ethereal voice that wasn't his own, he said, "Three months hence, a choice will be made. A threat will emerge, powerful and afraid. Darkness will rise and cover us all. And then her magic will make us fall."

A chill raced through my body. I stared at Riker, numb with shock. He exhaled, his body drooping. When he crumpled, I lunged forward to catch him before he face-planted. I held up his shoulders and propped him up against the wall next to the fireplace.

He sucked in several ragged breaths. His eyes closed, his mouth open as if he were asleep.

Worry clenched my stomach. I scooted closer to him and took his hand in mine. It was cold and clammy.

"Riker?" I whispered.

He inhaled deeply, his eyelids fluttering open. Then, his blue eyes fixed on me, filled with confusion. "Brielle?"

"Oh, thank Lilith." I leapt forward, wrapping my arms around him and clutching him tightly. "I was so scared."

"I . . . I . . . oh, bloody hell, tell me I didn't . . ."

I nodded before pulling away from him. "You had a vision."

Riker's eyes closed. He ran a shaking hand through his hair. "Damn it. What happened? Did I hurt you?" He opened his eyes, looking me over.

"No." I paused. "You . . . you don't remember?"

Riker shook his head.

"I cast a spell on you to freeze you in place. Then, I dragged you here. By the way, sorry if your butt hurts."

Riker looked at me in bewilderment, but amusement flickered in his eyes. "That's incredible, Brielle. No one has been able to subdue my visions before."

I bit my lip. "That isn't all. I cast . . . another spell." I took a deep breath and recited the spell I'd used to wake him up.

Riker stared vacantly at the bookshelf behind me. "Interesting," he muttered, his gaze far away.

"Nothing else was working," I went on, unable to stop myself from babbling. "I realized I had to address the cause behind your fit, which was the vision. My sister, Angel, suffers from the same thing. She's a Seer and her brain can't handle her visions, so her body reacts by seizing. She has to take a special medication, and sometimes she wakes up with migraines. Most visions she doesn't remember at all, and . . ." I trailed off, realizing I was rambling. My mouth clamped shut. "Sorry."

Riker smiled at me. "It's all right, Brielle." He leaned forward, tucking a lock of hair behind my ear. "Thank Lilith you knew what to do in this situation. It could've been a lot worse."

I clutched his hand against my cheek, relishing the warmth of his palm on my skin. "You really had me worried, Riker."

Riker chuckled. "You? Worried? Well, then I've achieved the impossible."

I shook my head, grinning. "Your humor's back. That means you must be feeling better."

His smile faded, and he looked at me with warm eyes. "I am."

For a moment, I was lost in his gaze. Then, I cleared my throat and looked away. "Riker, your vision . . ." I paused and took a breath before telling him what he'd said in that strange, mystical voice.

Riker's brows knitted together. "How peculiar."

"Do you know what it means?"

He shook his head, frowning. "My mum told me I sometimes recited something similar when I had visions, but she could never decipher them."

"Did they ever come true?"

Riker shrugged one shoulder. "It's hard to tell. If you can't decipher the words, then how do you know if it came true? According to Mum, I once foretold of a great battle between gods and monsters, but obviously that never came to pass. Now, if you interpret 'gods' as Lilith's beast and 'monsters' as demons, well then . . ." He trailed off and shared a grimace with me. We both knew what he was referring to.

I thought of the line he'd spoken: *A threat will emerge, powerful and afraid.* The word "afraid" had struck me. How often did you imagine a terrifying and powerful adversary that was *afraid*?

I sighed and shook my head. "Whatever your vision meant, I'm glad you're all right."

"What an exciting afternoon this has turned out to be."

Riker grinned at me, and we both laughed. He took my hand. "I'm glad you're here, Brielle."

My smile faded as we stared at each other. Heat churned between us. My heart pounded a frantic rhythm in my chest.

He leaned forward. I spotted a sprinkling of freckles across his pale cheeks. His blue eyes bore into mine.

We were so close that I could taste his sweet breath. His minty smell enveloped me like a caress.

Somehow, my body knew what to do, though my limbs felt frozen. I closed my eyes and leaned into him. His lips covered mine, timidly at first. Just barely brushing against my mouth.

Then, we drew closer, our chests touching and our arms wrapping around each other. My lips moved over his, exploring and searching. His breath was hot and sweet as it mingled with mine. My hand wrapped around his neck, and I slid my fingers through his soft hair.

He moaned against my lips, and I pushed against him, climbing on his lap. I couldn't stop. Heat scorched over every inch of me. I pressed my palm against his cheek, which was prickly with stubble. His hands snared my waist, pulling me closer. Our heavy breaths pulsed around us until it was all I could hear.

A door slammed, echoing in the hall, and our mouths broke apart. My heart jumped in my throat, and my lips felt numb. I was suddenly aware of my body wrapped around Riker's like some whore. His hands were on my waist—no wait, they were *much* lower than my waist.

Alarm raced through me, and I scrambled off him, my eyes wide. I couldn't meet his gaze.

"Brielle," he said, his voice low and husky.

"I'm . . . I'm sorry. I haven't—" I stopped before I blurted out that I'd never kissed anyone before.

"Hey." Riker scooted forward and touched my hand. "It's all right. Brielle, that was—that was amazing. I've never kissed anyone like that."

I tried to ignore the way my stomach clenched as I realized he'd kissed other girls before me. *Of course* he had.

I swallowed. My mouth was dry. Why couldn't I speak?

"Do you"—Riker cleared his throat—"do you regret it? I mean, uh, was it enjoyable for you?" He winced and looked at me with anguished eyes. "I'm sorry if I made you uncomfortable."

Slowly, the panic inside me subsided. I took a deep breath. "No, you didn't. I wanted to. I enjoyed it a lot, actually." My face burned as I dropped my gaze.

Riker laughed nervously, reaching forward to stroke my cheek with his thumb. "Good. So did I."

We shared a smile, our gazes locking again. That same heat returned, swirling between us like something tangible.

Footsteps echoed in the hall. I gasped and jumped to my feet, prepared to bolt if I had to. Then, I stopped, realizing how ridiculous I was being. I wiped my sweaty palms on my pants and extended a hand to Riker.

Riker grinned and took my hand. I helped him stand, and he extended his elbow toward me. "Shall we get some lunch, Miss Gerrick?"

I nudged him but took his arm, biting back another smile. "Yes, Mr. Wilkinson."

The next morning, I found Riker waiting for me outside my bedroom. He was dressed in a gold waistcoat, and his arms were crossed, causing the fabric to bunch around his biceps.

I stopped short when I saw him. Heat immediately flooded my cheeks. I rubbed my nose. "Hey."

Riker offered a low bow. "Miss Gerrick."

I elbowed him. "Stop that. The Count's nowhere near us."

"Good." He leaned in and brushed his lips against mine.

Fire exploded within me, but I clung to the small shred of sanity left inside me and drew away from him.

His eyes opened, and they flashed with hurt. "What's wrong?"

"You shouldn't—*we* shouldn't—" I stopped and shook my head, unable to find the words.

"No one has to know. We can keep it a secret."

The idea sent flames of desire rippling through me, but I shook my head again. "It's not a good idea. If the Count finds out about my Dad *and* finds out about us, he'll target you too."

"Brielle—"

"I mean it, Riker." I looked at him with wide eyes. "It's too dangerous."

Riker pulled away from me, his lips pressing into a thin line. "If you don't want me, just say so."

I sucked in a breath. After glancing up and down the hall to ensure we were alone, I leaned in and brought my mouth to his. I pressed myself closer, sinking into his arms as they wound around me. His lips moved more urgently, and a low, sexy sound rumbled from his throat.

It took all my strength to pull away. I broke the kiss with a gasp, my head spinning.

"Tell me you felt that," Riker said breathlessly.

The skittering in my heart was undeniable. "I did," I whispered, closing my eyes.

"So, you *do* want me then." Triumph glittered in his eyes.

A lump formed in my throat, and I nodded. "But Riker, it's not safe. I already have a target on my back, and—" I broke off. I couldn't tell him I suspected I was Lilith's cursed witch. But if I was being honest with myself, that was the real reason I was pushing him away.

I was either doomed to die or doomed to kill an entire city. I couldn't get close to him.

I pressed my palm against his cheek and smiled sadly. "Please just trust me. At least for now, it's safer if we don't."

He stared at me for a long moment, his expression unreadable. His eyes bore into mine as if he could see right through me. At long last, he nodded and offered a tight smile before extending his arm to escort me downstairs.

19
BRIELLE

FOR THE NEXT FEW WEEKS, I SLID INTO THE USUAL routine I'd grown accustomed to. Training with Ignacio remained the same, though I noticed the wording of his Latin spell sometimes changed. At the end of every day, I returned to my room and tried to write down the words I remembered. I was too afraid to ask him outright—especially since I knew he had a hand in the Count's imprisonment of demons.

Riker and I didn't speak much of the demons we'd found underground. Whenever I brought it up, he changed the subject or begged me to wait until we got more information. But as time passed, I grew more and more impatient. What information did he hope to gain by doing *nothing*?

My mind kept returning to those wounded demons trapped below the castle as they awaited further torture from the Count and his mages. I *had* to do something—but I didn't know what. I couldn't get back home, and I was the only one in the castle who gave a damn about demons and their well-being. If the Count or his mages found out about my demon bloodline, I would surely end up locked in the dungeon too.

Recently I'd been plagued by nightmares similar to the one I'd had of the blood and destruction. I tried to ignore them, but one night it got so bad I had to do something about it.

In my dream, my hands were covered in blood. Fire burned in my veins, waiting to be unleashed. When I couldn't contain it any longer, jets of flame poured from me like lava, reducing the city to ash. Children screamed. Women sobbed. Men gathered weapons and tried to fight me, but they were insignificant compared to my power. Magic and energy surged through me, so foreign and yet so *exciting*.

I woke up in a cold sweat and found myself facedown on the floor of the library. Next to me, a fire crackled in the hearth. A stack of books lay scattered on the floor next to me.

Panting, I peeled my sweaty face off the floor and sat up, my head spinning. "How the hell did I end up here?" I muttered aloud. My eyes fell to the stack of books on the floor. They were all a different shade of green.

I'd been organizing books. It sounded like something I would do, but I had no memory of coming down here.

Panic flooded through me. I grabbed the books, placed them back on the shelf, and wiped my sticky hair off my face.

Don't panic, I told myself. *You'll be just fine.* My mind raced as I tried to formulate a plan, but everything I could think of would only make things worse.

Tell the mages? Nope. Not only did they imprison demons, but the Count was on high alert for anyone exhibiting signs of Lilith's curse. This would definitely raise some red flags.

Tell Riker? No way. He was my only ally here, and if he even suspected I was cursed, I wasn't sure what he would do. I trusted him in almost every sense, but his apathy toward the imprisoned demons made me hesitate about being honest about this side of me.

Find a cure? *How?* I'd already scoured the library and sneaked into the Count's private quarters, but the only thing he was hiding were prisoners—not books or information.

I sank into an armchair and wiped my sweaty palms on my shift. My head throbbed, and I covered my face with my hands. I was so alone here.

"Hey."

I jumped to my feet, my heart lurching in my chest. Izzy stood at the doorway in a nightgown, her white hair disheveled and her eyes sleepy.

"What're you doing up?" I asked.

"I could ask you the same thing."

I shrugged, slumping backward in the chair. "It's hard for me to sleep here. Sometimes I come here to organize books. It relaxes me."

Izzy strode forward and sat in the armchair across from me, her gaze fixed on the flames in the fireplace. The light danced in her eyes, making them appear the color of coffee instead of their usual inky black.

She glanced at me carefully, then looked back at the fire. "I heard you."

My gaze snapped to her. "What?"

"You were shouting something in the hallway. It woke me up, so I followed you here."

My heart froze. Swallowing, I said quietly, "What was I saying?"

"I don't know. It sounded like a different language. Spanish maybe? Or Latin?"

My heart raced uncontrollably. I tried to control my breaths, but they came hard and fast until I felt like I might pass out. Again.

Izzy leaned forward, propping her arms on her knees. "Brielle, what's going on with you?"

I closed my eyes. How could I hide this from her? I couldn't come up with a believable excuse for my behavior. I didn't quite understand it myself. Part of me was in denial, certain I couldn't possibly be Lilith's cursed witch. The other part of me was convinced that if I *was* cursed, I could find a cure before I hurt anyone.

"I don't know," I admitted in a whisper. "I just . . . blacked out. I don't remember coming down here." My gaze darted to her worried expression. "Please don't tell anyone."

"But Brielle, the mages—"

"No," I said sharply. "Not the mages. *Please.*"

Izzy pressed her lips together in a thin line.

I sighed, rubbing my forehead. "I don't want to attract any extra attention. You know my dad's a demon. If they find out—" I broke off, shaking my head. "I can't risk it."

"But Brielle, you aren't well. What if this gets worse? What if you hurt yourself . . . or someone else? That's why we're here—to be healed."

"I know." I closed my eyes. Sorrow built in my chest so severely it sliced like a knife. "I wish I could go home and see my family. They would know what to do." Even as I said it, I knew it wasn't true. My parents had always been at a loss for how to help me.

But I felt safe with them. I never felt like I had to hide my problems.

Izzy took a long breath, her eyes fixed on me. Concern and affection glistened in her eyes, and for a moment, I was reminded of Angel. The kindness in Izzy's face was so similar to what I saw in Angel's.

"I know you feel alone here," Izzy said softly. "But I want you to know I'm here for you. I don't have any allegiance to the Count or his mages or anyone here. I'm here for myself. To be healed so I can stop hurting people. If you need a friend—someone to talk to, someone to turn to when you're scared—you can always come to me."

A lump rose in my throat. I couldn't speak. My eyes felt hot, so I dropped my gaze.

"You're always so closed off," Izzy went on. "You think I don't notice, but I do. You keep things from me—from everyone. I know better than to ask. But I hope one day you'll trust me with the truth. You can't do this alone, Brielle."

I closed my eyes, knowing that if I looked at her, I would start to cry. I wanted to say, *Yes, I can.* I was so used to taking on everything by myself. But a foreign and frightening uncertainty filled my chest like icy water. For the first time in a long time, I felt helpless. Cold. Afraid.

Weak.

I despised the feeling. I needed to feel capable and powerful again.

I needed to fight a demon and beat him. Which was ironic, since all I could think about were the poor demons the Count had imprisoned and tortured.

I'm not like him, I told myself, though I wasn't sure I believed it.

Unbidden, my mind turned to Leo Serrano. I hadn't seen him or his coven in over a month. He was suspiciously quiet, and it made me wonder if he'd found what he was looking for.

Or if the Count had found a way to neutralize the threat. If I crept downstairs again, would I find Leo and his coven trapped with the other prisoners? I suppressed a shiver at the thought.

When I opened my eyes, Izzy was gone. It was just me and the roaring fire.

I wrapped my arms around myself and stared at the fire until I fell asleep.

∾

I mulled over Izzy's words over the next few days, knowing she was right—and knowing I had to do something before these blackouts got worse. As much as I wanted to believe it was an isolated incident, a chilling feeling inside me told me it wasn't. It would happen again.

I couldn't do this alone.

The cold winter days melted into early signs of spring, thawing the icy walls of the castle. I tried not to think of the prisoners down below and how they must be suffering in their freezing prison cells.

One night, another nightmare overcame me. This one was much stronger than the others. So vivid. An explosion of fire consumed me. Screams echoed. Blood poured from my body, but I felt nothing. Someone was sobbing. Begging for mercy.

But I refused to give it. Something within me roared with satisfaction hearing these pitiful mortals beg.

Because it meant I was powerful. Unstoppable.

I jolted awake with a gasp. The thrill of my vision made my heart race and my blood boil, and it took a moment to settle my body back down. Gradually, horror crept into me, making me feel sick.

Swallowing down bile, I bolted out of bed and ran a hand through my hair. I didn't want to go back to sleep. I feared I'd return to the nightmare. The thought made me shudder.

Wrapping my robe around me, I slid out of my room and crept downstairs toward the library.

A small, insane part of me hoped Leo Serrano would

show up again. Not because I particularly wanted to see him, but because he was a demon. He might have answers for me.

An ache built in my chest as I thought of how alone I felt here in this giant castle. I was the only person in this stupid place who gave a damn about demons and what happened to them.

I missed my dad.

Like a little girl, I missed him. I missed his comforting smell—the way I could still tell he was a demon, but it was mingled with something outdoorsy that was just so *him*. I missed his levelheadedness and the way he proved that demons could live a moral life.

Being in this place made me long to see him, to know he was okay. To know there was somewhere out there where demons didn't have to live in fear.

"I figured you wouldn't be sleeping."

I nearly dropped the stack of books in my hands. Whirling around, I found Izzy standing at the open door of the library.

I exhaled, my heart racing. I hadn't realized how much my body had tensed and seized at the thought of an unwanted guest joining my midnight shelving. Slowly, I relaxed and offered a weak smile.

"Do you organize them all by color?" Izzy asked, approaching me with her arms crossed.

I nodded. "I don't have the energy for the translation spell. Plus, if I don't pay attention to the titles, it helps me . . . zone out. Forget about everything."

Izzy nodded. "Can I help?"

"Sure. You do the blues."

Izzy grinned and slid a stack of navy and pale blue books over toward her. We worked in silence for a moment as we organized our rainbow books.

"I might be cursed," I whispered.

I didn't know why I said it. I hadn't even registered I'd spoken at all until Izzy froze, her hands hovering over a book with a sky-blue cover.

I clamped my mouth shut. What the hell was wrong with me? But something like relief wormed its way into my chest, and I couldn't hold back now that I'd started.

"Lilith's cursed witch," I said, meeting Izzy's wide eyes. "It might be me."

Izzy's face drained of color. "What are you talking about?"

"I've been lying to everyone. I never had any powers. I've never been able to access them. But I couldn't say anything because—"

"Because they're looking for the cursed witch. To stop the monster." Izzy's voice was hushed, and she swallowed. "But . . . that can't be you, right? I mean, you just got here. The monster's been attacking the city for years now."

"But it's a time loop," I whispered. "How do we know how it works if it just resets every year?"

Izzy shook her head. "Brielle, it *can't* be you."

I pressed my lips together and dropped my gaze. "I can't do this anymore. The lies, the fear, the demons—"

"Demons? What demons?"

I took a breath and told her what Riker and I had found in the dungeon.

Izzy's face turned ashen. "Crikey. That's bloody insane, keeping them locked up here."

I looked at her carefully. "Because they might escape?"

"Well, that too. But because they belonged to someone's *coven*. A demon coven. The Count must be nuts to risk retribution like that."

I stilled at her words. *A demon coven.*

I remembered what Izzy had said after the first attack: *Leo attacks on a regular basis, always searching for some powerful weapon the Count doesn't have.*

What if he wasn't searching for weapons—but *demons*? What if he was searching for his own people?

Like his brother.

I dropped the book I was holding. My hands shook. I couldn't ignore this any longer. It was my only option.

"Brielle?" Izzy stepped closer to me and touched my shoulder. "You look pale. Come sit by the fire."

I shook my head and looked at her with wide eyes. "I need to talk to Leo Serrano."

20

LEO

"How many sentries?" I asked Miguel. We stood in the shade of several oak trees nestled deep in the forest less than a mile away from the Castillo de Coca.

"A dozen, but I slipped by unnoticed. Easily." Miguel scratched his chin. "Are you certain about this? Usually the Count has more than that. This feels like a trap."

I grinned. "All the more reason to proceed. We wouldn't want to disappoint the Count and all his careful planning, now, would we?"

Miguel shared a doubtful look with Jorge, their expressions equally rigid.

My smile faded. *Sometimes I'm the only one here with a sense of humor.* I sighed. "The Count can't possibly know we're coming. We've swept the forest twice and found nothing. The castle grounds are quiet. We've taken a slow journey through the woods to ensure we weren't followed or spied upon. Our time to act is *now*."

Guadalupe swooped down on us in eagle form and shifted when she touched the ground. "The Count's carriage and several horses are missing."

I stiffened, my skin prickling with suspicion. *Perhaps this is a trap.* It rang with familiarity, reminding me of when we'd lured the Count to our home only to attack the castle in his absence.

How could he possibly know?

I shook my head. "He must be visiting the other mages in the city. Though I don't know why." I rubbed my jaw. We'd tracked the Count's movements often over the past several months. Ordinarily he only visited the mages once every two months. But this was an unusual visit. What was so important it couldn't wait another month?

Jorge, who was sharpening his knife, glanced at me briefly. "Do you want me to track him and see where he's gone?"

Something in me yearned to say yes, to succumb to the curiosity. But I shoved the thought away, thinking of Ronaldo. *That's exactly the kind of thinking that got him captured. Impulsive. Reckless. I need to be smarter than that. For his sake.*

"No," I said quietly. "We proceed as planned. If this is to be our final strike, we'll need our full force."

Jorge nodded, sliding his knife into his holster.

Once again, my skin prickled, and I stiffened. I inhaled deeply, searching the air for scents—for anything that seemed amiss. But the familiar forest smells surrounded me. Nothing out of the ordinary.

My ears tingled, listening. Waiting.

A faint whisper hissed among the wind. A voice.

"Do you hear that?" I asked.

My comrades shook their heads, frowning at one another. I closed my eyes, focusing on the sound. It was a small voice—perhaps that of a child. My brows knitted together in concentration. Then, I realized the voice was uttering a spell.

"Magic above and powers that be,

I call on you and summon thee,

To locate this being and bring him near,

So I may communicate with him here."

My eyes snapped open. "No—"

Before I could finish my protest, a blue light engulfed me, blinding me. I flinched against the brightness. The light drew me out of the forest and into the blazing sun I'd tried to avoid during our journey.

I fell forward, and my palms met concrete. The sun beat down on me, scorching my skin. I gritted my teeth, groaning in agony. My hair fell forward in front of my face. Slowly, I raised my gaze to find myself in the courtyard of the Castillo de Coca. I glanced around to see who had summoned me.

Of course. I should've known.

A familiar figure approached me, crouching down to my level. She cocked her head. "Hello."

The smugness in her voice made my blood boil. I tried to meet her gaze, but the intensity of the sun made me drop my head again. I managed a weak chuckle. "What have you done to me, Little Nightmare?"

The girl shifted, and I sensed her blood pulsing in irritation. She hated the nickname.

Good, I thought with pleasure. *I'll keep using it then.*

"I've summoned you here," she said. "I have some questions for you."

I wanted to look around, but the brightness of the area burned against my eyes. Instead, I focused on my sense of smell. An oddly familiar metallic scent reached my nose.

My blood. This girl had my blood. It must've been how she'd summoned me.

Then, something else, something more lethal burned my nostrils. A sharp, foul stench. I recoiled, sucking in a rattling gasp. *Garlic.* A circle of garlic surrounded me. "Lilith, are you trying to kill me?"

"It's only a precaution," the girl said. "To make sure you cooperate."

I lifted my face just enough to glare at her. "Have I not been cooperative until now?"

The girl snorted. "Hardly."

I laughed again and dropped my head. My whole body throbbed with pain, and it took all my strength to keep my voice level. "Ask your questions, Little Nightmare. I will answer."

"What do you know about Lilith's cursed witch?"

I grew very still. The silence between us was only punctuated by my rasping breaths. Though I didn't need to breathe, it was an innate habit of mine—especially when I was weak. "Lilith's cursed witch?" I repeated slowly. *She knows,* I thought in a panic. *She knows about Lucia. Why else would she ask about this?*

"Yes." She sounded impatient. "You come from a long line of demons. I know you've heard the story. What do you know about it?"

I sucked in a breath. "We call them Nightcasters. Or *brujas de la noche.*"

"Why?"

"Because when Lilith takes hold of her witch, she starts slowly when the witch is most vulnerable—at night when she sleeps."

The girl froze, and I sensed the thrumming of her blood responding to my answer. For some reason, this struck her. And frightened her.

I peered at her through my long hair. "Why do you ask, Little Nightmare?"

The girl said nothing. She remained frozen.

An unfamiliar voice interjected. "Is there a cure? Can a cursed witch resist Lilith's influence?"

My eyes shifted to the second voice. Another girl. I recognized her. She had a strange accent and stark white hair.

"According to legend, no," I said. Though this wasn't entirely true. In working with my sister, I had found several possible cures. But I wasn't about to share this with the two who held me captive.

The first girl—the Little Nightmare—sagged lower to

the ground, and I felt the agony pulsing in her blood. The devastation.

I frowned. No, this wasn't about Lucia. This was personal for the girl. She was desperate.

I wasn't sure what possessed me to speak—pity perhaps —but I added, "There are rumors that a Nightcaster can survive Lilith's curse . . . through the monster."

The girl straightened. "The monster who attacks this city every year?"

My blood chilled. "Every year?" I whispered. *What in Lilith's name is she talking about?* There had been whispers of a fiery monster emerging, but no one had been attacked. Yet.

The girl avoided my question. "Do you mean the monster that's threatening the city? How is that supposed to help a cursed witch?"

I shook my head, and my locks swayed back and forth. "I don't know. The rumors are . . . unclear. They only say the monster and the witch are one. But usually the witch is powerless, and Lilith takes over completely. Controlling the monster for herself." I lifted myself up on my hands and knees. My arms trembled, and sweat dripped down my face. The fire burning along my skin was too intense. "Please," I rasped. "The sun. It—" I choked on the words, swallowing down the burning ache in my throat.

The Little Nightmare didn't move at first. Her blood reeked of suspicion. Did she honestly think I was trying to trick her?

"Brielle," the second girl hissed.

Brielle. The name sounded French and yet the girl spoke Spanish? How peculiar.

The girl called Brielle sighed and uttered a spell.

"*Magic above, shield this light.*

Cloak us with the dark of night."

Brielle's hands glowed blue, and a shadow fell on us, blocking the sun like a parasol.

I glanced up, my eyes wide. A large, black oval hovered in the air, perfectly shielding the three of us from the sun. Slowly, I shifted my gaze to Brielle. "Incredible," I murmured. Something within me pulsed with excitement, but I was too weak to pinpoint why.

"It won't last long," Brielle said. "But I have one more question."

I sat up and brushed the hair from my eyes. Then, something stung my nose. A familiar scent of cinnamon.

Jorge.

The coven was close. I had to keep Brielle and her friend distracted. I leveled a gaze at the Little Nightmare and said, "Ask it."

"What is it you're looking for in the Institute?"

I cocked my head at her. "Institute?"

She sighed. "The Castillo de Coca."

I watched her, my skin prickling with suspicion again. *This girl knows too much. I just can't tell* what *she knows.* "Why do you ask?"

Brielle scowled and brandished a dagger toward me. "I'm asking the questions here. Answer me."

Though I knew she was a capable fighter, seeing her try

to appear intimidating made me laugh. "You don't frighten me, Little Nightmare."

Her blood boiled from my condescension. She lunged forward, swiping her dagger so it nicked my cheek. I hissed and raised a finger to the blood dripping down my face. But still I smirked at her, knowing it fueled her anger.

"You are fierce," I admitted. "And strong. But not frightening."

She blinked, clearly taken aback by my compliments. *Good.* Her confusion would muddle her senses and keep her preoccupied. Jorge's scent grew even closer, mingling with the lavender smell of Guadalupe and Miguel's familiar rainy leaves scent.

So close.

Suddenly Brielle whirled, sensing the disturbance. Miguel barreled into her, knocking her backward and shoving a dagger into her shoulder. The rest of the coven advanced, all wielding weapons. Pride soared within me at the sight of their fierce expressions and eyes blazing with determination. *My family.*

Jorge reached me first. He looked over me, no doubt assessing any injuries I had. Then, his gaze fell to the circle of garlic, and his jaw went rigid.

"I'm unharmed," I said.

The fire never left his eyes. He brought his hands together, summoning a wave of black magic that dispersed the garlic, creating an opening for me to pass through.

I hobbled forward, my skin still hot from the sun's touch.

"Liar," Jorge growled, grabbing my arm and hefting it over his shoulder.

I shook my head. I was a Second Tier vampire—meaning I had performed a specific blood ritual to access a higher power of dark magic. It strengthened me against small, offensive magic like garlic and sunlight. But those things still weakened me.

If I'd been a First Tier vampire, I would've burned up immediately.

Brielle and her friend were busy trying to extract the blade from Brielle's shoulder. Jorge moved as if to whisk me away into the forest, but I stopped him. Waving my hand at the others, I gestured toward the two girls, indicating they surround them. My men obeyed, forming a tight circle so the girls had no way out.

With every ounce of effort, I straightened to my full height, ignoring the trembling in my limbs. I had to appear strong in this moment.

The white-haired girl summoned fire to close Brielle's wound. Brielle screamed, but it wasn't the shrill, pitiful sound I expected. It was raw and angry. Somehow, it made her sound stronger.

Brielle's friend helped her to her feet, and they both faced me. Fear struck the white-haired girl's face, but Brielle clenched her teeth, glaring at me.

This girl has such spirit, I thought gleefully. I would almost regret parting with her. "As always, Little Nightmare, it's been a pleasure."

"You never answered my question," she snapped.

A few of my men shifted and grunted. Jorge summoned a ball of black magic in his hand, and I knew he would hurl it at her.

"Jorge," I said sharply, shooting him a warning glance.

Jorge dropped his hand, and his magic faded. But he stared at Brielle with hatred in his dark eyes.

"I've answered plenty of your questions, my lady," I said softly. "Despite the, uh, inhospitable circumstances of our conversation. Should you have any further questions for me, you are more than welcome to call upon me in my home. My coven will be eager to host a feast in your honor." I grinned widely, revealing my fangs. Several of my comrades chuckled.

Brielle's blood raced with fear, but she didn't even flinch. Her nostrils flared, and she whispered, "Go to hell."

I threw my head back and laughed. "*Adios, mi amor.*"

In a burst of black magic, I shifted into a raven, unable to shift into bat form in the blinding light. I flitted in the air, circling above the girls before taking off toward the mountains. I sensed a few of my men shift as well, including Guadalupe and Jorge. The rest of them sprinted forward on foot toward the cover of the forest, just beyond the courtyard of the castle.

21

BRIELLE

AFTER LEO AND HIS FELLOW DEMONS LEFT, I FINALLY relaxed my arms. The magical shade hovering above Izzy and me vanished, and the blinding sun took its place. My arms trembled, and I slumped sideways into Izzy.

Izzy shifted her weight to hold my arms steady and cleared her throat. "That was fun."

But I wasn't listening. My eyes narrowed as I watched the demon coven flee from the castle grounds. Izzy fidgeted next to me, but I didn't move. I just watched. And waited.

There it was. A bright green glow that burst in the air for only a moment. Like a tiny firework. They'd made it through the Count's wards.

In a flash, I took off after them, ignoring Izzy's shout behind me. The demons ran farther and farther away until they were nothing more than specks like ants on the ground. But still I hurried after them, ignoring the ache in my shoulder and the throbbing in my head from the exertion.

This is it. This is my chance. Izzy and I had been lucky enough to slip outside due to the Count's absence. Wherever he'd gone, he'd taken most of his guards with him.

Which meant as soon as he returned, my opportunity was gone.

I ran through the gardens, weaving through hedges like a maze until I slammed against the same invisible force I'd hit my first night here.

I stumbled backward, eyes wide, and glanced up and down as if I could see the top of the ward. Then, I dropped my gaze to my shirt, which was covered in scorch marks and blood. I found some blots of blood that were still wet, and I dipped my fingertips in them like I was finger-painting. Then, slowly, I lifted my bleeding fingers to the invisible ward.

A green glow burst against my eyes, but this time it encompassed my hand just like my normal blue magic did. I felt it thrumming through me like electricity. I held my breath, waiting for the power to shock me as it had before.

But it didn't. It pulsed through me like an invitation.

Waiting for the spell to break the enchantment.

Swallowing, I said the first thing that came to mind.

"Magic above and powers that be,
Remove this ward in front of me."

A bolt of electricity shot through me, knocking me off my feet. I tumbled backward, rolling in the grass. My limbs felt numb. I stared vacantly at the clear, blue sky and just lay there on my back for a moment.

Idiot, I thought. *Of course the Count would use a spell in Spanish to break his ward.* I stood up, brushing the dirt and grass off my clothes, before stepping forward to try again.

"Brielle!" a frantic voice shouted behind me.

I turned and found Izzy, her eyes wide with panic. Panting, she pointed behind her and said, "The Count. He's back."

Izzy and I sprinted back toward the castle. Outside, a grand carriage pulled up, flanked by half a dozen horses and footmen.

"Come on." Izzy tugged my arm away from the entrance and toward the ballroom where the mages were. When I looked at her in confusion, she muttered, "We have some time. It takes forever for him to climb out of that stupid carriage."

We approached Ignacio and asked him to heal me, claiming Izzy and I had had an accident with her fire. He looked a bit shocked at my appearance but readily agreed.

Soon after Ignacio healed me, His Excellency strode through the front door, flanked by an entourage of servants and valets. The Count's deep crimson robes swept behind him with all the elegance of a king.

I had to refrain from rolling my eyes.

On the staircase I noticed Riker, his hand on the banister and his mouth set into a grim line. His eyes flicked to me. I tried offering him a smile, but he looked away before I could.

"Abernathy, Wilkinson, St. Clair, Petrov, and Arévalo, come with me please," the Count said curtly, waving his hand. He strode past me and Izzy without a glance.

"Your Excellency—" one of the Douchebags came forward. It was Chris, the wrestler-looking guy.

"Not this time, Mr. Knox," the Count said, brushing past him.

Chris's face reddened. Another Douchebag—Wes Cunningham—stepped forward.

"You stay as well, Mr. Cunningham," the Count muttered before he vanished down the hall.

Riker, Jacque, Alexei, and Juan quickly followed. I stared at Riker, who flashed me a brief smile before he left.

Then, it was just Izzy, Armin, Elias, the Four Douchebags, and me.

Eager to get away from the others, I dragged Izzy by the arm into the library.

"Why—" I started.

"Did he leave Wes and Chris behind? Sometimes he alternates. From what I've seen, Alexei and Jacques have been making great progress with their magic. Maybe this is a test for them."

"And Juan?"

Izzy shrugged. "He and the Count have been really chummy lately. Dunno why."

My stomach dropped as I remembered Juan's refusal to keep my secret. If he and the Count were getting so close, Juan certainly would've revealed my demon parentage by now.

"Miss Gerrick?" a soft voice asked.

I jumped and turned to find Ignacio and the other mages standing in the open doorway. A chill of foreboding rippled through me.

"Yeah?" I said.

"Can you come with us please?" Ignacio bowed his head as if this made his request less threatening.

It didn't.

I swallowed and shared an uneasy glance with Izzy. "Why?" I asked.

"There is another routine examination we need to administer."

I glanced at Izzy again, and she shook her head, her brows furrowing slightly. If she was confused as well, that meant she had no knowledge of this 'routine examination.'

My body refused to move. Though the mages' hands were clasped and their heads inclined in submission, I knew they could easily overpower me if needed.

"Miss Gerrick is still recovering from the incident she suffered," Izzy chimed in. "Can I come with her for support?"

"I am afraid this examination must be conducted in private," Ignacio said.

An awkward silence passed between us. I took a deep breath and nodded, forcing my lip to tremble just a bit. "I, uh, let me just say goodbye." I turned to Izzy and embraced her.

Izzy made a startled noise, but I clutched her close and

whispered, "If I'm not back in half an hour, come get me. Please."

I released her. She met my gaze, her eyes wide, and nodded slightly.

I swallowed and turned to the mages, following them out of the library with a sense of numbing dread.

The mages' cloaks whispered on the floor as we walked down the hallway. We passed the ballroom where we conducted our usual training. I clenched my fingers into fists, trying to control my breathing. In my mind, I recited a few spells I kept handy in case of emergencies.

"So, the Count left here pretty quickly," I said nonchalantly.

"He has uncovered some developments from the demon coven," Ignacio said. "It was prudent to act immediately."

I frowned. What developments?

Then, my insides froze. I'd abducted the coven leader, and his friends had come to rescue him.

Had that left their home defenseless? Had the Count found out they'd all left and decided to seize their territory?

An uncomfortable feeling wormed its way through me. Though I despised Leo and his condescending smirk, I'd never meant to turn him over to the Count. Leo was an asshole, but at least he was open about it. The Count, however, kept secrets—too many secrets. And to me, that was far more dangerous.

"When will they be back?" I asked.

"I'm not sure, Miss Gerrick," Ignacio said.

"Shouldn't we wait until His Excellency returns before

conducting this examination?" I asked. "Won't he want to know the results?"

"He has authorized me to conduct this in his stead." Ignacio stopped in front of an open door and spread his arm, gesturing I enter first.

I swallowed and stepped into the small room. It looked like a tiny study, which was unusual for a castle this size. A desk sat in the corner along with a high-backed armchair and a set of small shelves stacked with papers.

I entered and backed up against the shelf to allow room for the other mages. To my surprise, only Ignacio entered. He closed the door behind him—and *locked* it.

That's why I've never seen this room before, I thought. *It must always be locked.*

Being in a room alone with Ignacio made me feel more at ease. I knew I could take him down in a fight.

Then, my eyes flew to the door, and I realized why the other mages had followed us. They were standing guard right outside.

"Do you do this examination with the other guests too?" I asked, rubbing my arms.

"No." Ignacio strode toward me with his hands outstretched. "Your hands please, Miss Gerrick."

I placed my hands in his, and he gripped them tightly. His eyes closed as he muttered words in Latin I'd heard before but couldn't translate. "*Invenire sint. Invenire sint.*"

What does that mean? I cursed myself for not searching the library for books in Latin that might help me.

A sharp pain sliced into my palms like my hands were

splitting open. I winced, trying to withdraw my hands, but Ignacio held them tightly. Blood welled on my hands and dripped onto the floor, but still Ignacio didn't move.

"*Invenire sint,*" Ignacio whispered again.

Something within me lurched and roared like a writhing, living thing. It stirred and growled until I threw my head back and screamed. Energy seeped from me, spiraling toward the ceiling in a burst of blue magic.

I clamped my mouth shut, stunned as I stared at my magic. It hovered above us like an orb. Then, spirals of black magic exploded within it like fireworks.

Horror settled in my stomach. *Dark magic.*

But I was a light witch. How was that possible?

Gradually, the magic dispersed, though the air around us still crackled with energy. Ignacio dropped my hands. I looked at my palms, but the blood was gone. It had even vanished from the floor.

"I—what—what was that?" I panted, gasping as if I'd just run a mile. The thing within me still stirred restlessly. It felt like Ignacio had unleashed something inside me, and now that it was awake, it wanted to be freed.

The thought chilled me to my bones.

"Interesting," Ignacio whispered. His dark eyes bore into mine, and I resisted the urge to shrink under his scrutiny. I had to remind myself he couldn't read my thoughts. "That is all, Miss Gerrick. Thank you for your cooperation."

My mouth fell open. "That's it?"

"Yes. You may go."

I frowned, but he didn't need to tell me twice. After he unlocked the door, I swung it open and hurtled past the other mages as fast as I could.

I found Izzy pacing in front of the hearth in the library. Her eyes widened when she saw me, and she strode toward me. "Brielle! What happened? You okay?"

I nodded, still out of breath. In a rush, I explained to her what had happened.

Her face drained of color. "You don't think—"

"It's Lilith's beast," I said in a hushed voice. "I'm sure of it. Izzy, what else could it be?"

Izzy shook her head. "Brielle, you're a *light* witch. Why would Lilith possess you?"

"My magic turned *black*," I told her. "I saw it." Panic surged in my chest. "I have to leave. I have to get out of here or the Count will imprison me like those other demons."

"No, Brielle, you can't leave yet. Just—just wait until the Count gets back. Wait for Riker."

My head reared back in surprise. "Riker? Why?"

"He's in the Count's good graces. He can vouch for you. He's been reliable and obedient ever since he got here. The Count will listen to him."

"But—"

"The mages won't do anything without the Count," Izzy said. "I'm sure of it. They aren't in charge here. If they *did* find out something from this test, they'll have to report the findings to him first."

"Izzy—"

"Where will you go?" Izzy demanded. "To the Serrano coven? To the village that'll be burned by the beast at the end of the year?"

I fell silent, knowing she was right. I had nowhere to go. I'd rather drop dead right here than seek out Leo and his coven for help.

"Let me do some digging," Izzy said in a whisper. "Let me ask around and see what I can find out. I've been here a while. I know how to talk to people."

I swallowed and nodded slowly. "All right."

"Just keep your head down for the next few days, okay? It'll be fine. I promise."

I wanted to believe her. I really did.

Three days passed with extreme sluggishness. My brain ached from constantly looking over my shoulder, waiting for the mages to grab me and throw me in the dungeon. My limbs throbbed from the tension of being on edge for so long.

And the nightmares returned. During the first night after Ignacio's examination, I woke up on the floor of the dining hall in a cold sweat. Luckily, the room was empty, but I couldn't risk that again. After waking up and rushing back upstairs, I'd knocked on Izzy's door and asked to spend the night in her room. She agreed without objection.

"You've been talking in your sleep," Izzy muttered to me at breakfast on the third day. "Something in Latin."

I stilled and looked at her. "By any chance is it *invenire sint*?"

Izzy stiffened, her eyes wide. "Yeah. That's it. Do you know what it means?"

I shook my head, but I knew it couldn't be anything good. Especially if Ignacio had been chanting it to me.

He'd awakened the beast inside me. And there was nothing I could do to get rid of it.

After breakfast, Izzy pulled me aside in the hallway before our usual training with the mages. Her eyes were wide as she glanced around nervously.

"What is it?" I asked, my heart racing.

"I heard Chris and Sam talking," she whispered. "They know the mages performed some weird test on you." She paused. "They said it's the first time that's happened. Most of the blood tests have been small, like the pricking of a finger. And it's always done in public. Nothing like what you went through."

I swallowed as fear numbed my bones. *That's not good news.*

"Does anyone know what it means?" I hissed.

Izzy shook her head, her eyes filled with concern.

My blood ran cold. If I was the only one the mages had administered this test to, then that meant they'd found something unique. Perhaps something they'd been looking for for years.

Lilith's cursed witch.

Panic solidified inside me, hardening to resolve and

determination. *If I don't find out anything by the time the Count returns, I'll beg for Riker's help.*

And then I'll flee this place forever.

22

BRIELLE

Two days later, the Count and his Demonhunting party returned to the castle. Izzy and I hurried to the entrance to greet them. My stomach churned with anxiety as my eyes flitted from each person, searching for Riker.

There. His face was covered in soot, but he seemed otherwise unharmed. Exhaustion tugged at his expression, but his eyes brightened when he saw me.

"I need to talk to you," I muttered, stepping close to him and trying to ignore the sharp vinegar stench emanating from him.

Riker's eyebrows lifted. "Oh, nice to see you too, Brielle. So glad you're safe and all that."

I rolled my eyes. "Why else would I be standing here if I weren't worried about you?"

Riker leaned closer and dropped his voice to a conspiratorial whisper. "It wouldn't hurt to say nice things to me every now and then." He winked, and a blush bloomed across my face.

I heaved a sigh. "Riker Wilkinson, I was so worried about you and I'm so relieved you've returned safely so you can joke and tease me some more. Is that better?"

Riker chuckled. "Much."

I glanced over his shoulder as Abe and the Count strode through the doors. I tugged on Riker's arm and pulled him closer to the staircase.

"I need your help."

Riker stared at me, his brows knitting together. "Of course. What's wrong?"

"The mages conducted some weird blood test on me, and I'm—I'm really scared." Just saying the words made my chest shudder with revulsion. I couldn't look at his expression, not after I'd just admitted how weak I was. "Can you . . . can you talk to the Count? Izzy says you're on his good side."

Riker was silent for a long moment. I finally peered up at him and found his eyes guarded and his lips pressed together.

Dread pooled into my stomach. "Riker—"

"I can't, Brielle."

My chest caved inward, practically suffocating me. "Why not?"

"Because the Count told me he knows about your father. He's already suspicious of you. Even I can't convince him not to be."

"*What?*"

"I'm sorry, Brielle."

Panic raced through me. "No, Riker, this can't be happening! Do you—"

"Miss Gerrick," said a cool voice.

I froze and slowly turned to face the interruption. The Count stood in the hallway next to the alcove wearing a gold waistcoat and matching gloves that looked untouched from the mission, despite the bedraggled appearances of the other guests who'd arrived.

"Your Excellency." I curtsied.

"Might I have a word with you?"

My blood chilled. *Not a chance in hell.* I cleared my throat. "I'm afraid I'm not feeling well today. I think something I ate—"

"It will only take a moment," the Count insisted, offering his arm to me. His cold gaze told me there would be no negotiating.

I glanced around and found the mages just behind him as well as several servants and guards.

Merciful Lilith. I'd never make it out of here.

I exchanged a worried glance with Riker before I said quietly, "Certainly."

I took the Count's arm and followed him into the hallway. Glancing over my shoulder, I widened my eyes at Riker and mouthed, "Help me!"

He simply stared back at me, stunned.

"My mages have reported some interesting findings," the Count said, drawing my attention back to him.

"Oh?" I rubbed my nose with my free hand.

The Count guided me toward the same small office where Ignacio had conducted his weird test. "Yes. They tell me something has awoken inside of you, Miss Gerrick." His keen, dark eyes appraised me. "Can you enlighten me?"

I tried to arrange my face into something innocent, but I knew I was failing. "I . . . I don't know what you're talking about."

"Ignacio tested your blood." The Count smirked, and all warmth fled from my body. "Do you know what we discovered?"

My mouth felt so dry I couldn't answer. I simply shook my head.

The Count's eyes glinted. "Dark magic."

"But . . . but my magic is *blue*."

"Indeed." He looked like he was thoroughly enjoying this. "But upon further inspection, we not only discovered the presence of dark magic—but also the presence of another *soul* residing with yours."

My heart lurched in my throat, and I was so surprised I came to a full stop. "*What*?" I said too loudly.

Irritation flickered in the Count's expression. He glanced around the hallway. "Do keep your voice down, Miss Gerrick."

"How can another *soul* be living inside me?" I hissed through clenched teeth.

"I was hoping *you* could provide the answer to that question." The Count leveled a hard stare at me, his eyes so calculating I felt stripped naked standing in front of him. I felt like he could see *everything*.

I shook my head numbly. "I don't—"

"Before you try to lie to me about this, Miss Gerrick, let me make something clear. It is in your best interest to be forthcoming about your abilities and your magical ailment because as of this moment, your future at the Castillo de Coca is looking quite grim indeed."

I swallowed. Fear crept up my throat, and I couldn't breathe. I rubbed my chest and whispered faintly, "Your Excellency, I have done nothing wrong. I have broken no rules, and I—"

The Count raised a narrow hand to stop me, his cold eyes drilling into me. "Listen to me carefully. This beast continues to destroy the city without fail every year. Innocent lives are taken. Families are destroyed. The victims of this city are *innocent*. I long since abandoned any hope I had for rescuing whatever poor, dark soul is responsible for bringing such terror to my city. I have come to accept that the life of one innocent is worth the price of thousands."

"Please—" I rasped.

The Count's grip on my arm tightened, and his fingernails dug into my skin. "Hell is waiting for you, Miss Gerrick. You may not deserve it, but it is the unfortunate truth. The Dark Lady you've succumbed yourself to will be destroyed, and you along with her."

Something sparked within me at his words, thawing the shock that had frozen my body. Flames roared within me. I gritted my teeth. "Don't you dare threaten me."

The Count's eyebrows lifted in surprise.

I tried wrenching my arm free, but he held fast. Rage

boiled my blood, bringing my senses back to life. Adrenaline pulsed through me, and I felt the familiar thrill of Demonhunting coursing in my veins.

I swung my head back and smashed my forehead into the Count's face with a satisfying crack.

The Count stumbled backward, clutching his nose and moaning.

I didn't pause to see how he would react. I turned and bolted down the hallway, grateful he hadn't taken his guards or mages on the little stroll along with us.

A small *pop* tickled my ears, and the Count appeared in front of me. Blood flowed from his nose, and his eyes were blazing.

My mouth fell open. "You're a *Jumper*?" I backed away from him, but with another *pop*, he appeared behind me. He wrapped one arm around my neck, cutting off my air supply. The other arm he wrapped around my waist, pinning me in place.

"I think you've caused us enough trouble, Miss Gerrick," he hissed, his voice thick with blood.

I struggled against his grip, but then my stomach dropped as something tugged within my chest, yanking me forward. The walls spun around me, and nausea swirled in my gut. I closed my eyes, and with another *pop*, I found myself in the dungeon. The barred cells housing the other demons surrounded me, and darkness engulfed me completely.

A chill of horror swept through me. I whirled around, but the Count was gone.

"No," I whispered, rushing forward. As my eyes adjusted, I barely made out the staircase Riker and I had crept down.

It was on the other side of the cage I was in.

I gripped the iron bars surrounding me and shook them. They wouldn't budge.

"*No!*" I screamed. I sucked in a deep breath and stepped back, trying to clear my head. Then I lifted my hands and uttered a spell.

"*Magic above and powers that be,*
Unlock this prison and set me free!"

My hands glowed blue, but the light flickered and then died like an overused light bulb. I stared blankly at my hands and shook them as if I could wake my magic back up.

This can't be happening. Energy drained from me, and the smell of magic tickled the air, but it wasn't *my* magic. It was something else.

Sniffing, I followed the scent until my nose touched the metal bars.

Magic emanated from my prison cell. The bars were enchanted. Somehow, they'd sucked my magic from me.

I was trapped.

"Hello?" I shouted. My voice echoed in the damp dungeon. "Is anyone there? Can you hear me?"

The only response was a low moan from a few cells over. I edged to the other side of my cell, peering through the darkness. "Who's there? Are you hurt?"

No response. Somewhere in the dungeon, a demon coughed—a foul, wheezing sound.

"How long have you been here?" I tried again.

Still no answer. Either the demons were ignoring me, or they were too unwell to respond. I dropped my hands in resignation.

I tried not to dwell on what the Count had in store for me. If he wanted me dead right away, he would've just snapped my neck or had his mages do the deed.

He wanted something from me. To torture me perhaps. The thought made my skin crawl, and I pushed it from my mind.

For hours I paced the length of my grimy cell, which was about as big as a bathroom. Every few minutes, I approached the bars and tried uttering another spell, but nothing worked. Each attempt left me a bit more drained than before, and after a while I gave up, knowing that if I kept trying, I'd pass out from exertion.

Fear crept into my skin, crawling up my spine like a giant spider. It clawed at my chest and stomach until the itch to move and *do* something was so strong it was almost painful. I envisioned the library upstairs and closed my eyes, mentally traveling there and organizing books by color. I remembered the exact shades of navy, robin's-egg blue, sky blue, and baby blue. In my mind, I set these books aside, arranging them from light to dark. Then, I thought of the purple and green books I'd found the other day. Forest green, hunter green, kelly green. Then lavender, indigo, plum, and violet.

It helped, but not by much. The panic still swirled within me.

Footsteps jarred me from my imagination. I jumped, racing toward the bars and squinting to see who had arrived. I clutched the rusted bars with trembling hands.

Soft, hurried steps echoed in the dungeon. Gradually, a tall figure came into view as it scurried down the steps. The motions were frantic—like they didn't want to be spotted.

I swallowed, trying to quell the fear in my bones.

When the figure drew nearer, I gasped in recognition. *Riker.*

"Thank Lilith," I whispered, exhaling.

"Brielle!" Riker hurried to me, clutching the bars that separated us. His wide, blue eyes were terrified as he looked me over. "Are you hurt?"

"No, I'm fine." I wanted to sob with relief. "Thank you for coming for me. The bars are enchanted, but it might be just from the inside. Can you cast a spell to set me loose?"

Riker didn't answer. He watched me with an unreadable expression.

"Riker, come on. We have to hurry before someone finds you."

Still, Riker hesitated.

"What's wrong?" I asked. Uncertainty swept over me. There was a tightness in his eyes that terrified me. *Why is he here?*

"The Count says he found Lilith's cursed witch," Riker whispered. "Is it true? Is it *you*?"

My blood ran cold, and I went very still. I didn't know how to answer him. I couldn't lie, but if he knew the truth—

I didn't have a choice. He deserved to know. "I'm sorry," I said. "I should've told you before. I don't know for sure, but . . . I think it *is* me. But—but I'm looking for a way to cure it. To resist her influence and—"

"Brielle, what the *hell*?" Riker hissed. His jaw was rigid, and he released the bars from his grasp. "How could you keep that from me? You *know* there's a monster that destroys the city every year! It's the whole reason why we're stuck in this time loop! And for months, you've been prancing around like nothing's out of the ordinary. Like you aren't the one who's going to slaughter thousands of innocent mortals."

"We don't know it's me," I snapped. "It could be someone else." But unease crept into my voice. I knew he heard it too.

"*That's* your defense?"

I closed my eyes and sighed. "I'm sorry. But . . . I'm trying to find a way out. A way to get out of here so the people in the city don't get hurt."

"That's even *worse*, Brielle. At least in the time loop, the people you'll kill will come back next year. If you leave and unleash the monster someplace else, then you'll just kill other innocent people who *won't* come back."

A knot formed in my chest. I knew he was right. "But Riker, there's a way to overcome it. Leo Serrano said—"

"*Serrano*?" Riker swore and rubbed his forehead. "Lilith, you've been talking to Serrano? Brielle, do you have any idea how bad that looks?"

"There's a cure! There's a way to stop it, and I swear I'll find it."

But Riker was shaking his head. It was hopeless. "I can't believe you kept this from me." His voice was laced with hurt and regret.

He was saying goodbye.

"Riker." I stepped closer, trying to reach him through the bars. "Please. *Please.* You can't leave me down here."

Agony flared in his eyes. "I don't want to, Brielle," he said in a choked voice. "You know I care about you. But . . . you're just one person. Responsible for killing thousands. I—I have to do the right thing here. I'm sorry." His eyes glistened with tears, and he swallowed. "Goodbye, Brielle."

He turned away from me and hastened up the steps.

"Riker!" I shouted after him, my voice breaking. "*Riker!*"

But after a few minutes, his footsteps faded, and then I heard nothing but silence.

He was gone.

23
LEO

I COLLAPSED INTO THE HIGH-BACKED ARMCHAIR IN my quarters, my body still humming with excitement from the recent feeding with Estrella. As much as her body had called to me, I had to refuse. I'd been spending far too much time indulging with her. If I didn't withdraw, I risked giving her too much of my venom, which would Turn her after her death.

And that was more than she or any Donor had bargained for.

As luxurious as it was to be immortal and shapeshift, I wouldn't wish it on anyone.

A familiar cinnamon scent tickled my nose. I half turned. "Finished feeding already? Poor Marco."

Jorge sighed and strode into my cavern. "Marco is fine. We didn't feed today. I only require his blood once a week now, and he does just fine on the blood I give him in return. Which is how it *should* be." He leveled a stern gaze at me.

I stared hard at him. Then, I offered a false smile. "Forgive me. I thought *I* was the coven leader. For a moment, it sounded as if you made the rules."

Jorge rubbed his face. "That isn't what I meant. You need to be careful with Estrella."

I waved a hand. "I know. I sent her away for a while. I'll find another Donor."

Jorge crossed his arms, still watching me even after I'd dropped my gaze to the smooth, gray floor. "Do you want to talk about it?"

"About what?"

"The girl."

I stilled. "What girl?" But I knew who he meant.

Jorge slid into the armchair across from me. "She abducted you. She *summoned* you and tortured you for information! She's a threat, Leo."

I laughed. "She's not a threat. I've bested her twice now."

"Hardly. From what I heard, she's proved a worthy adversary in a fight."

I slouched back in my chair. "She's not a threat," I repeated. I couldn't explain it. No matter how many times we fought, I never felt like my life was in danger around the girl. Perhaps it was because she was a light caster. Based on my dealings with the Count, I knew better than to blindly trust someone who practiced light magic.

"What did she want with you?" Jorge asked. "What kind of questions did she ask?"

He'd asked me this before, and I'd merely told him she

wanted answers about the Count. Even now, I still couldn't bring myself to tell him she was asking of Lilith's cursed witch.

No one in the coven—not even Jorge—knew about my sister. And I didn't trust myself to speak so freely of Lilith's curse without arousing Jorge's suspicions.

So instead, I said, "She wanted to know why we kept attacking the castle. What we were looking for." It wasn't entirely untrue.

"And what did you tell her?"

"I told her nothing."

Jorge nodded and then frowned. "How did she abduct you? I've never heard of a witch who could do that."

"She had my blood," I said. "I smelled it in the air. She must've cast a . . . reverse locator spell."

Jorge arched an eyebrow at me. "Such a spell does not exist, Leo."

I leaned forward, propping my arms on my knees. "I know," I admitted. "But it wasn't the first time she's used . . . unusual spells around me."

"Unusual how?"

"Spells I've never heard of. Spells that sound and feel *different*. I can't explain it."

Jorge's dark eyes sharpened. "Similar to the Count's spells?"

I stiffened, my eyes shifting to his. "What do you mean?"

"We've hit another dead end, Leo. We are nowhere closer to breaking the Count's enchantment, and our surprise attack on the castle was ruined by this girl's interference. What if she can help us?"

"No," I said tightly.

"Leo, you said it yourself, she casts unusual spells. What if—"

"We are *not* discussing this." I rose from my chair and paced the length of my room, avoiding Jorge's gaze. "You were just explaining what a threat she is, and now you want to make her our ally?"

"I want to eliminate the threat and use her skills at the same time." Jorge rose to his feet too.

"She despises our coven. She would never agree to help us."

"If we have the right leverage, I'm sure we can coerce her."

I shot him an accusing stare.

"She did the same thing to you," Jorge snapped.

"It's a slippery slope, Jorge. Soon you will be suggesting we adopt the Count's methods as well. We have our own rules to abide by."

"Then, let's use our rules to coerce her," Jorge urged, stepping toward me. "We'll free her from the castle and from the Count. In exchange for her freedom, we'll ask for her help."

I shook my head. "Jorge, I'm not bringing in a stranger —an *enemy*—into this coven. Facing her in a fight is one thing. When I'm alone, I know I can handle myself against her. But bringing her *here,* where our people are supposed to be safe? No. For all we know, she's working with the

Count, and my abduction was merely a way to deter our attack. I won't endanger our family by bringing her here. We'll find another way."

Jorge's jaw went rigid. His eyes blazed as he stared at me. Then, after a long moment, he inclined his head, submitting to my decision.

Fire burned in my blood. I clenched my fingers into fists and strode out of the cavern, desperate to escape from Jorge and the reminder of our predicament.

24
BRIELLE

I WASN'T SURE HOW MUCH TIME PASSED. I DRIFTED IN and out of a fitful sleep, slouched on the dirty floor with my head propped up on the bars. I didn't doze for long, and when I did, I was plagued by visions of the beast, covered in blood and roaring in triumph. I smelled death and black magic, and the scent lingered even after I'd woken.

When I wasn't sleeping, I either paced my cell or tried new spells to escape. I didn't care how drained I was—if I died trying to get out, it would be preferable to the torture the Count had planned for me.

My stomach growled with an endless groan like my body was caving in on itself. I tried to squash the ache of hunger, but it grew worse with every passing hour.

After what felt like days, I finally succumbed to the weakness in my body and curled up in the corner of my cell. I drew my knees against my chest and shivered. My very bones seemed to quiver from weakness and hunger. It felt like an animal clawed at my gut, desperate for nourishment. With no food around, it decided to feast on my innards instead.

I tried not to think of the *actual* beast inside me. The one that would slaughter thousands of innocent civilians in a few months.

Riker was right. I deserved to be in here. Though I longed to escape, what could I do? How could I stop myself from killing all those people?

Leo said there was a way. There has to be a way.

But even Leo had said it was a myth. How could he help me? How could anyone help me?

I miss my family. I miss Mom, Dad, and Angel so much.

I closed my eyes, pressing my forehead against my knees. But I wouldn't cry. I refused to cry.

Loud footsteps jolted me from my misery, and I jumped to my feet, heart pounding. Unlike Riker's, these steps were slow and careful. Measured. Calculated.

Whoever was down here *belonged* down here. So, it couldn't be anyone who would help me.

I swallowed and drew closer to the bars, squinting in the darkness as a tall figure came into view. Even before I could make out his features, I knew it was the Count. His graceful, elegant strides and upright posture reeked of royalty and pretentiousness.

I struggled to keep my breaths calm and remain upright, even though my body ached to crumple back into a fetal position.

The Count approached my cell with a calm expression, his eyes appraising me with mild interest. As if we were sitting by the fire in the library instead of this horrifying prison cell.

"Miss Gerrick," he said softly. "I wish I could say it was a pleasure. It's a shame things couldn't happen differently."

"I highly doubt that," I snapped, but my voice came out as more of a croak. "You never liked me."

The Count frowned and raised his eyebrows as if in agreement. "Perhaps this is true. But I knew from the beginning you were keeping secrets."

"Can you blame me? Look what happened when you found out who I was."

"Yes, but keeping it a secret only made you look guiltier," the Count hissed, leaning closer to me.

"You're saying if I'd been honest from the beginning, things would've turned out differently?" I spat.

The Count's silence answered my question.

"I thought so," I said. "Just get on with it." I turned away from him and crossed my arms, trying to squash down the fear trembling in my bones.

"Before we begin, I have some questions for you," the Count said softly. He waited, but I said nothing. He sighed and continued, "How long have you known that you were Lilith's cursed witch?"

I chewed on my tongue, refusing to answer.

"It's in your best interest to comply, Miss Gerrick. I don't think I need to tell you what will happen if you don't cooperate."

I thought of the vampire with the bloody gashes on his body. The dark witch who was too weak to even move. I took a shuddering breath. "I don't know. I haven't known for sure. But I started having visions—nightmares—a month or so ago."

"Visions of what, precisely?"

"A beast. A monster." I swallowed. "Something with fire that slaughtered people."

The Count was silent for a moment. "Have you exhibited any other symptoms?"

"Besides my lack of magic? No."

"Ignacio says he found traces of another soul in your blood. Have you felt another presence inside you? Something other than this beast?"

"You mean like Lilith? *No.* I think I would know if there was someone else in my head."

The Count scoffed like he didn't believe this. "When you have these visions of the monster, do you have any control? Any sense of yourself and who you are?"

I was silent for a moment. I knew I had to answer. In a whisper, I said, "No."

"I see."

I turned to face him and found a pitying expression on his face. But within his eyes lurked a darkness that reminded me of the demons I'd hunted in Miami. A dark hunger that yearned for blood. For pain and suffering.

I resisted the urge to back farther away from him.

"You have no idea what a relief it is," the Count said in a

soft, dangerous voice, "to have finally found you after all these years."

I shuddered with revulsion. "Glad I could offer some comfort," I said, trying to sound bored. I rubbed my arms. "What're you going to do with me? Kill me?"

The Count cocked his head at me. "Not yet. I've searched for you for so long. It would be a waste to dispose of something so . . . fascinating."

I didn't like the glint in his eyes. Like I was some machine he wanted to take apart and study.

"I—do you"—I swallowed—"do you think you can heal me? That you can . . . get Lilith out of me? Make me normal again?"

The Count chuckled, but the sound was more like a growl than a laugh. "No, my dear. I fear your fate is already sealed. As a crime against nature, you are doomed to a painful death. But . . . perhaps you can offer something to me before you leave this world and atone for your sins. Perhaps you can provide answers. A key to unlocking Lilith's curse and keep her from returning and inhabiting another soul. You will not die in vain, Miss Gerrick. Of that I assure you."

He smiled at me like a predator eyeing its prey and then turned to leave.

"Wait!" I blurted, rushing to the bars and clinging to them in desperation. "Food. I need food. I'm starving."

The Count glanced at me over his shoulder, his face apathetic. "No, I think you'll do just fine without sustenance. The less nourishment you have, the more desperate the beast—and Lilith—will become. I'll return shortly."

He turned away again and climbed up the steps.

"Please!" I screamed, gripping the bars so tightly my knuckles turned white. "Please don't leave me here!"

Several more days passed, though everything became a blur. Eventually, I grew too weak to pace my cell or even stand, so I sat crouched in the corner with my head against the cool metal bars, trying to ward off the chill and the weak starvation clawing through me. My vision darkened, and I often saw strange things—creatures creeping down the steps toward me. My mom and dad smiling warmly at me. Angel laughing at me.

None of it was real.

At one point a shrill scream pierced the air, echoing in the dungeon. I ignored it, dismissing it as another hallucination. But it persisted, rattling against my eardrums with such violence that for a moment I wondered if it *was* real.

I crept toward the sound and shouted, "Hello? Who's there? What's wrong?"

The scream gradually subsided, and broken sobs took its place. "Cold," a deep voice cried. "So cold!"

"What's so cold?"

"The darkness. Can't escape. Can't get out. It's everywhere."

I edged forward until my face was pressed against the bars. "Who are you? How long have you been down here?"

"Too long. Forever."

I was silent for a moment. The demon's sobs filled the dungeon again.

"My name is Brielle Gerrick," I said. "They say I'm Lilith's cursed witch."

The sobbing stopped abruptly. Then, the demon uttered a sharp gasp. "They found you?"

"Yes."

There was a soft scuffling noise as the demon shifted. "How did you get here? How did they find you? We tried so hard to protect you."

I stilled, my bones chilling at his words. "Protect me? Why?"

"These light casters know nothing. They only know light and dark. But we demons know better. Lilith is more than just a demon witch. She's a *prophetess*. Her chosen vessels are marked for greatness."

My skin crawled at his words. "Marked for greatness? You mean the greatness of becoming a beast and killing innocent people?" I couldn't keep the edge out of my voice.

"No, no," the demon said in an awed whisper. "Lilith cannot inhabit those who are weak. The reason it takes her hundreds of years to resurface is because the vessels she chooses sometimes reject her spirit. The rejection kills the host, and she has to try again.

"But you, Miss Gerrick—you're strong. If you're strong

enough to let Lilith in, then you're strong enough to push her out too. We demons revere Lilith's vessels because they are the epitome of strength and power."

"That doesn't make sense," I said. Anger stirred within me, but I was too weak to speak in anything more than a mumble. "How can I be strong if she takes over my body? How can I be strong if I can't resist her influence? Or resist the monster she unleashes?"

"I don't know," the demon admitted. "But we tell the tale for a reason, Miss Gerrick."

"Call me Brielle."

I could sense the distaste in his voice when he said, "Ah, I'd rather not."

"We're both in prison and about to die. Formalities are kind of useless down here, don't you think?"

He sighed. "Very well, *Brielle.* The story is passed on for generations of Lilith's chosen vessel. The marked witch who embodies two souls."

I shook my head even though he couldn't see me. "You speak of my curse like it's a *gift.* Like I should be thankful. But I don't feel strong. I feel weak. Like I'm letting someone else take over my body."

"If you're strong enough to let her in," the demon said again, his voice surprisingly firm, "then you're strong enough to push her out."

I swallowed. "What's your name?"

"Ronaldo Serrano."

Something within me splintered and shattered. "*What?*"

I hissed. For the first time in days, my body felt alive with energy. "You're—you're Leo's brother?"

"You know Leo?" Ronaldo shifted again as if he could scoot closer to me. "How is he? Does he live?"

I opened and closed my mouth, choking on my words. Finally, I sputtered, "I—yes, he's alive. But . . . you *died*. How are you not dead?"

"I didn't die," Ronaldo said bitterly. "But I should have. My sister, Lucia, died in my place. I was trying to rescue her. The Count thought she was Lilith's vessel, and he abducted her. When I came to rescue her, she—she—"

"She died," I whispered.

"No, not . . . not like that," he said in a tortured voice. "Lilith claimed her, but she wasn't strong enough. Her body gave out, rejecting Lilith as a host. Lilith must have moved on to you instead."

Horror numbed my body. I couldn't speak. Couldn't breathe.

Then, I remembered what Ignacio had told me months ago when I'd asked if there had ever been a caster he couldn't help. *Once,* he'd said. *They died.*

"Tell me of my brother," Ronaldo said, his voice cracking with desperation. "Please."

A sour taste filled my mouth. How was I supposed to tell him I hated his brother's guts? That the only encounters we'd had were when we'd attacked each other? "He's . . . strong. Powerful. And he has an odd sense of humor."

Ronaldo barked out a laugh, which quickly turned into a fit of coughing. He wheezed so loudly that I jumped.

"Are you all right?" I asked.

He ignored my question. "My brother's humor always irritated me. But now I long for his ability to make light of dark situations."

Something cold settled in my chest. "What did the Count do to you?"

Ronaldo was silent for a long moment. Then, he whispered, "Something too terrible to speak in a lady's presence."

"I'm not a lady," I snapped. "I'm a prisoner just like you. Tell me. I'd rather be prepared."

Ronaldo hesitated before he said, "He cut me apart. To test my blood and my skin. He—he didn't tell me why, but I imagine it had to do with my sister and why Lilith marked her as a possible vessel." He paused. "Then . . ." He drew a shuddering breath. "He forced me to drink the blood of . . . all kinds of creatures. He wouldn't tell me where the blood came from, but perhaps that's for the best. I fear . . . I fear he's given me the blood of my sister." He broke off with a sob.

Agony swelled in my gut, and I closed my eyes as Ronaldo's broken cries echoed in the dungeon.

"He wanted to see how my body would react to drinking different forms of blood," Ronaldo went on, sniffing. "When he found blood that left me weaker than normal, he focused on this and now it's the only sustenance he offers me. My body decays more and more every day."

"Do you know what kind of blood it is?" I asked in a hushed voice.

"Whoever this blood belonged to is no longer living. If it's from a vampire like me or someone who is deceased, I do not know. But a vampire cannot survive without the blood of living creatures."

Ice hardened in my chest. *Ronaldo is dying. Leo's brother is dying.*

"What does the Count want from you? Information about the coven? About Leo?"

"At first, yes. But he quickly learned I wouldn't relinquish any such information. Now, I think he sees me as a test subject. One on whom he can experiment to find particular brands of torture for other demons. Demons like my brother."

The ice in my chest sharpened like daggers cutting through me. "He wants to use it on Leo."

"Yes."

I sucked in a shaky breath. Whatever ill feelings I had toward Leo, he was a saint compared to the Count.

Which was ironic, given how religious the Count claimed to be.

I opened my mouth to ask Ronaldo another question, but footsteps echoed on the staircase. I stiffened, my eyes wide as I tried to make out who it was. The footsteps multiplied into a muffled scuffling sound. It wasn't just one person.

Ronaldo went completely silent on the other side of the dungeon, and I didn't blame him.

At long last, the figures approached my cell. The Count stood in front, looking strangely informal without his waist-coat. His sleeves were rolled up to his forearms, and his hair was tied behind him. Three mages stood next to him, though I couldn't make out their faces in the darkness.

"Miss Gerrick," the Count said softly, his mouth widening into a disturbing smile. "Shall we begin?"

25
BRIELLE

I TRIED TO SUMMON MY BRAVERY, BUT I WAS TOO weak to do more than just look at him blankly. The recesses of my mind screamed at me to do something, to lash out or jump at him. To shout insults or spit in his face.

But I just sat there, my head lolling like a rag doll.

The Count nodded toward one of the mages, who stepped forward and unlocked my cell door. When he drew closer, I recognized him as Ignacio.

Though I'd kn he'd been a part of this, I naïvely hoped he'd grown fond of me during our trainings together. Fond enough to want to free me. Or to be repulsed by what the Count might do to me.

But his face was a smooth, blank mask as he swung opened the door and entered my cell. He clasped my arm and hoisted me off my feet. My head spun and I teetered, but Ignacio righted me and guided me out of my cell. His touch was so gentle that it was easy to pretend like he was helping me. Freeing me.

Until he led me away from the staircase and toward another cell. We passed several other prisoners. Most of them were motionless heaps. Some of them groaned or sobbed. Then, my eyes fell on Ronaldo, who watched us pass with a grim expression. His long hair was dank and matted with grime, blood, and sweat. A jagged, bloody gash ran down his face, and I realized I'd seen him before. When Riker and I had first been down here.

I struggled against Ignacio's grip, but I was so weak from hunger and thirst that he barely had to tighten his hold to keep me in place. Some small part of me registered that I was no longer within the enchanted cell—which meant I could use magic.

I wiggled my fingers, but I felt nothing inside me. No prickle of magic. No buzzing.

I was too weak. *That's why the Count starved me. So I couldn't use my magic.*

Damn him.

I closed my eyes and let Ignacio drag me, not caring where we ended up or what they would do to me.

If this is how I die, I won't give any of them the satisfaction of seeing me beg. Of seeing me become a coward.

Ignacio finally led me to an empty cell with a long, narrow table inside. My eyes fell on a bench at the end of the cell with a tray of sharp-looking instruments.

I swallowed, trying to quell the growing fear inside me.

Without warning, Ignacio grabbed me by the waist and

lifted me so I was sitting on the table. I fidgeted under his grasp, but the other mages were there in a flash, holding me, then pushing me to lie down on the table. The mages hunched over me, binding my torso tightly with something leathery, like a belt.

Panicked breaths pulsed through me. My insides felt cold and numb with terror.

The Count stepped toward me, watching me with mild interest. "Let's see what lives inside you, Miss Gerrick."

He closed his eyes and placed his palms against my chest. I struggled, trying to move away from his touch, but the restraint kept me in place.

The Count spoke a spell in Latin. I squinted, trying to pay attention to the words.

"Magicas spiritus invoco

Et daemonium pythonissam

Fidenti eam animo

Invitare per eam."

A blinding white light burst from the Count's fingertips, searing my chest like a hot iron. I cried out, my voice a strangled scream as the heat scorched me from within. The light faded, but long tendrils of inky black smoke took its place, slicing through the light like claws.

Dark magic.

Something within me lurched at the sight, bounding forward. I no longer had control. An ethereal voice poured from me and shouted, "Yes!"

My vision darkened, and I slumped backward against the table. My body couldn't move. I couldn't feel anything.

But my eyes remained open, fixed on the cell bars to my right.

And then I was gone. Flying in the air. Whipping through the moist clouds and the fog coating the sky. Darkness surrounded me, punctuated by the faint glow of the moon.

It was a cloudy night—perfect to avoid detection.

My wings spread widely at my sides, slicing through the misty clouds. Fire rumbled in my belly, but I quieted it. *Not yet,* I told myself.

I flapped my wings and burst forward with a surge of speed, gliding lower. Just low enough to make out the rooftops of the village below me.

The smell of fresh humans filled my nostrils. They called to me. Beckoned to me.

How could I resist?

With a mighty roar, I lowered myself below the cloud cover and rained fire down on the unsuspecting mortals. Their screams filled me, satisfying that endless hunger within me. My claws and fire tore through the buildings like they were nothing. The pitiful humans fled from before me, but it was useless.

They were all mine now.

I jerked awake. My entire body was covered in sweat, and my clothes clung to me, drenched in my own filth.

I couldn't tell if it was *only* sweat, or if I'd soiled myself. I didn't want to know.

The Count and his mages were gone. But I was still strapped down to the table. I flexed my fingers and wriggled my wrists, but the leather strap held fast.

Panic welled in my throat, and I glanced around in desperation. My heart stopped. On the wall opposite me was a giant, black shape. I squinted, trying to make out what it was. Then, my blood ran cold.

It was a scorch mark. A round imprint. Something had charred the wall and left a mark the size of a person. If I could stand, I imagined this mark would be bigger than I was.

What the hell caused that?

As I thought the question, something burned within me. The echo of the fire in my vision.

Bile rose in my throat.

I had made that mark.

I closed my eyes and turned my head, pressing my cheek against the cool surface of the table underneath me. All I wanted was to disappear—to vanish until my body caved inward on itself.

I was the beast. I was the monster who destroyed the city. Thousands of innocent lives would be lost.

Because of me.

Any fight I had left in me was gone. Even if I'd been strong enough to find a way out, in that moment, I didn't want to. If staying here and giving myself up to the Count and his horrifying methods meant keeping the city safe, then I'd do it.

Tears rolled down my cheeks, and a strangled sob poured from my mouth.

"Brielle?" a soft voice asked. Ronaldo. "You're—you're alive?"

"Yes." I swallowed. My lips trembled as more tears poured down my face.

"Are you hurt?" he asked. His voice sounded farther away than before.

I cleared my throat. "No."

Silence. Then he asked, "What happened?"

"W-what do you mean?"

"What's the last thing you remember?"

I shook my head, trying to drive the memory from my mind, but it resurfaced on its own. The screams. The roaring hunger within me. The destruction and devastation.

It couldn't have been real. *Please don't let it be real.*

A knot formed in my stomach. I sucked in a breath. "I don't know. Ronaldo, I don't remember anything that happened after the Count cast that spell. What—what did you see?"

Ronaldo hesitated before responding. "A burst of flame. A roar that shook the dungeon. Then, the fire lunged forward. The Count and his mages had to dive out of the way to avoid being burned. You—your body was on fire, Brielle. Even after they all left, your body still glowed like a flame. For days."

My heart stopped. I couldn't breathe. *Days.* How long

had I been out? I lifted my head, trying to examine my body for burns. But I felt nothing but the tight pull of the restraint on my body.

"I—how?" I asked weakly.

"I don't know. But something similar happened to my sister. When the fire consumed her, she . . . she would glow. For days, sometimes weeks at a time. We could never rouse her during her fits. At times we thought she was dead. But she always woke confused and disoriented, as you did."

What in Lilith's name is happening to me? I said nothing, struggling to contain my panic. The silence pressed in on me, threatening to swallow me whole. My mouth stretched wide as silent sobs poured from me, shaking my shoulders and tearing through my chest. All the sorrow and pain I'd kept hidden for so long was unleashed in that moment. Each tear I shed was an emotion I'd tucked away to hide my weakness from the world. My defective magic. The bullies I'd faced over the years. The lack of attention from my parents. The portal that tore me away from my family forever. The fear of being found out. The realization that I was exactly what everyone feared: Lilith's cursed witch.

And above all, the fact that no one was coming for me. Riker believed I belonged down here. And now, so did I.

A high-pitched squeal made me jump. I lurched, trying to sit up and look around, but I couldn't move. Instead, I held my breath and waited.

A small flash of light burned from the top of the staircase. Then, someone hissed, and the light went out.

My heart thrummed painfully against my chest. Hasty

footsteps shuffled down the stairs. When the figure drew closer, my pulse was louder than thunder in my ears.

Another burst of light. *Fire.* The flames illuminated the figure in the dungeon, and my heart twisted.

Izzy.

"Brielle!" she hissed, looking around. "Are you here? Are you alive?"

"Izzy," I croaked.

Izzy gasped and hurried forward, using her fire as a flashlight. When she reached me, her eyes widened, and her face drained of color. "Crikey, Brielle! What did that bloody count do to you?"

I shook my head as more tears leaked from my eyes. I couldn't stop them once I'd started crying. "You shouldn't have come down here. It's *me*. I'm the one who—"

"I know," Izzy interrupted, stepping toward the bars of my cell. "You're Lilith's cursed witch. Whatever. I'm still getting you out of here."

"Izzy, *no*—"

"Shut up, Brielle." Izzy lifted her hands and summoned fire again. Then, she placed her hands against the cell bars.

With a sharp yelp, she jumped backward, shaking her hands as if she'd been shocked. "What the hell?"

"It's enchanted. I can't use my magic in here."

Izzy only hesitated for a moment before she said, "What about a spell? Can you come up with one I can use?"

My brain felt like mud. I shook my head slowly. Even if I wanted to, I didn't have the energy to come up with any spells. "I—I can't."

Izzy exhaled loudly. "Okay. I'll go back up there and find the Count's keys. I'll come back for you, Brielle."

"Izzy, don't!" I shouted, finally finding my voice. Izzy stiffened in surprise. "Please. If you get caught, the Count will kill you—or torture you. I can't have another innocent life on my conscience, Izzy. I'm begging you. Just leave me here. It's safer for everyone."

Izzy clutched the bars and leaned closer to me. "I don't believe that for a second. I don't believe you're doomed to destroy this whole city with no say whatsoever. That's bullocks. Don't be a drongo, Brielle. Let me help you."

"Izzy—"

Izzy lifted her hands and stammered,

"Magic above that—and powers that be,

Let her go . . . and set her free!"

Her hands glowed blue, but the light faded and then went out like a dead bulb. She swore and shook her hands as if she could wake up her magic.

"It won't work," I said. My mouth felt so dry.

"Magic above—"

"Izzy!" Something tickled my throat, and I coughed loudly. It sounded like an old man's wheeze. "You—you can't," I croaked. "Even if you got me out, I'm too weak. I won't be able to stand on my own, let alone run away."

Izzy went still, watching me with agony in her eyes. "Oh, Brielle." She clutched at the bars and pressed her face against them, her eyes filling with tears. "I can't just leave you here."

"Yes, you can."

Izzy shook her head and pressed her lips together. She opened her mouth to speak, but then loud footsteps echoed in the dungeon.

My heart stopped. "Izzy, go!" I whispered. "Hide!"

"Brielle—"

"Now!"

Izzy backed away from me and vanished in the shadows. The newcomer descended the steps and quietly drew closer to my cell. I swallowed, looking around for Izzy. I knew if I could see her, then so could the visitor.

"Hey," I said loudly. My voice was still scratchy, so I cleared my throat and tried again. "Hey!"

The footsteps stopped. Then, the figure came closer to me.

It was Ignacio.

I swallowed. "I need water. Or food. Please, I'm begging you."

"I'm sorry, Miss Gerrick, but I—"

"Listen to me!" I shouted. In the corner of my eye, I noticed a shadow edging toward the staircase. I had to keep talking to mask the sound of her footsteps. "I've been down here for who knows how long. You've starved me and imprisoned me. I can't sleep or eat or drink. I'm scared. I just want to go home. I haven't done *anything* wrong. Have I killed anyone yet? No! There's still hope for me, Ignacio. Please. If there's any mercy in your heart at all, please help me. Just a small cup of water or a piece of bread. *Anything.*"

Ignacio's lips tightened. I heard a faint scuffle and then

silence, which meant Izzy had gotten out. I exhaled and closed my eyes, no longer caring what Ignacio said.

"I must obey my master's orders, Miss Gerrick," he said softly. "I am truly sorry. But if it's a matter of saving you and saving the city, I choose my city."

He quietly stepped away from me and drifted down the row of prisoners. A jangle of keys and a loud creak told me he'd entered another cell. I turned my head, trying to make out who he visited. Was it Ronaldo?

A low moan pierced the air. Ignacio whispered something. Then, the moan intensified until it was a howl of agony.

It wasn't Ronaldo, though. That much I could tell.

My head slumped backward against the table as I struggled to drown out the screams of my fellow prisoner.

26

BRIELLE

IZZY SNUCK BACK DOWN OFTEN TO BRING ME FOOD. The table I was strapped to was just close enough for me to stretch my fingers and catch the rolls and cheese she passed me. But the ornate goblets from the dining hall were too big to slide through the metal bars. Instead, I asked Izzy to pour some water into my cupped hand, and then I brought it to my mouth. I only managed to gulp down a few drops before someone started descending the steps. Then, I reprised my role as disgruntled prisoner, shouting at whoever had come down here that I was being mistreated—all so Izzy could get out.

Each time she came to see me, I begged her not to come back. But she never listened. And despite how much I wanted her to leave me down here, a tiny, selfish part of me clung to the knowledge that someone was fighting for me. Someone cared for me. Even if it meant nothing—even if I would still die down here—I grasped that knowledge and held it close within me.

I wasn't alone.

Izzy never mentioned Riker, and I never asked about him. Our silence confirmed what I already knew—he believed I deserved to be down here. That I shouldn't be set free.

I agreed with him.

But it still stung, knowing he'd given up on me so easily.

I wasn't sure how much time passed. Each day Izzy came to see me, she told me how long it had been since her last visit. Three days after her first visit. Then, two days after that.

When she didn't come back for a long while, I worried she'd gotten caught. My heart twisted with anxiety, and the fire inside me roared hungrily as it tried to come to life again. The presence within me had been awakened by the Count, and it wouldn't stay hidden any longer.

My chest burned so intensely that I was covered in sweat despite the chill of the dungeon.

Ronaldo spoke to me, but our conversations were stilted and brief. Neither of us had much to say. I told him what I could of his brother's coven, and he told me everything he knew about the Count and Lilith's cursed witch—but it wasn't much, and most of it I already knew.

Eventually, we both realized we were just trying to keep each other talking to avoid the inevitable—that we would both die soon.

After what felt like a week, Izzy came to see me again.

Her steps were slow and clumsy, like she carried something heavy. When she reached my cell, she had several items in her hands: a knife, a potion vial, and a few sandwiches.

"Sorry it took me so long," she panted. "I was working on a potion for you, and I kept messing it up. Here." She slid me the sandwiches and I hungrily shoved them in my mouth. "This is a vanishing potion." She held up a vial of orange liquid that I recognized. I'd used a few while Demonhunting to escape some particularly tricky situations. "And I also swiped a knife from the dining hall. It's a butter knife, so it might not work so well, but—" She shrugged and slid the knife to me handle first.

I swallowed the last bite of sandwich and took the knife and vial. "Izzy, you shouldn't have done this."

"Shut up, Brielle. You're my friend, and I'm not going to leave you to rot down here." She paused and glanced back toward the stairs. "I may not visit for a while, though. The Count's been asking me questions about you and about what I know, so I need to keep my head down. But that's why I brought you the knife and the potion. If you get a chance to escape, *do it*. You hear me?"

"Izzy—"

"I'm serious, Brielle. I'm not giving up on you, so if you decide to stay down here, I'm just going to keep coming until I get caught."

I swallowed and closed my eyes. Agony and fire clouded my mind. I couldn't think. "I . . . Izzy, I . . ."

"Look, Brielle, I've got to go. But know that I love you and I'll find a way to get you out. Just hang on for a bit longer, okay?" She pressed a kiss to her hand and stretched through the bars to grasp my fingers. My lips trembled as I squeezed back, though there was little strength left in me.

Then, she was gone.

For hours, I lay there strapped to the table, my stomach growling so loudly it felt like the whole dungeon quaked. The food Izzy brought had staved off my hunger, but now my stomach demanded more as if I'd been taunting it. I clutched the handle of the knife in one hand and the potion vial in the other. My grip was so tight my palms started sweating, but by now I was used to the heat. The fire rumbled within me so consistently it felt like a rhythmic heartburn that never left. And stirring just beneath the surface was the monster. Just longing to be unleashed again.

I tried to take my mind off it, but the scorch marks on the wall kept drawing my gaze. *I did that.*

If I would destroy an entire city, then I deserved to be down here.

But if I didn't try to escape, then Izzy would keep coming for me until she got caught. And I shuddered to think what the Count would do to her.

I closed my eyes as tears rolled down my cheeks. This was the most I'd cried in years, but once I started, I couldn't stop. The tears kept coming until they formed a waterfall cascading down my face, mixing with the grime and sweat already plastered to my skin.

I miss you, Angel. I missed her warm, comforting presence. The way she shone a light on any situation no matter how grim. How she was always optimistic and cheerful even though her body often failed her and she had plenty of reasons to complain.

Though I longed for her in that moment, I felt a slither of gratitude knowing she had no idea where I was or what I was enduring. It would break her to know this. At least if I died down here, she would never know. She could imagine me living somewhere else and working on my magic. Living happily.

Loud footsteps jolted me awake, though I didn't remember falling asleep. The knife slipped from my grasp, but I tightened my grip before it fell. My heart lurched in my throat as I rubbed the smooth vial still clasped in my other hand. Then, I let out a breath. If I'd let those fall because I'd been dumb enough to fall asleep, then I deserved to die down here.

I shifted and wriggled until my hands were behind my back, still clutching my secret weapons.

I'll get out, I vowed. *I'll get out for Izzy. And then I'll find a way out of this city, so no one gets hurt.*

I held my breath, waiting for the Count and his mages to return to my cell. But when the door creaked open, it wasn't mine they entered.

"No," moaned a voice. "No, please . . ."

My heart stopped. It was Ronaldo.

Something metal clinked. Then, a burst of blue light, and—

Ronaldo released a piercing scream that shook me to my core. My blood chilled as his anguished cries resonated in the dungeon. My eyes clamped shut, and I clenched my teeth so hard my head throbbed. For several minutes, Ronaldo shrieked in pure agony.

At long last, I cried out, "Stop! For the love of Lilith, just *stop*!"

Miraculously, Ronaldo's screaming stopped, and a terrifying stillness swept over the dungeon. Then, footsteps shuffled, and Ronaldo's cell door creaked open and shut again. The footsteps drew nearer, and my limbs tensed in preparation for some kind of retaliation.

My cell door opened, and the Count whispered, "Do you pity them, Miss Gerrick? The demons?"

I swallowed. "I pity anyone who's tortured like that."

"Even those who are already damned? Those the devil himself has claimed?"

I turned my head and spat in his direction. "I'd rather go to Hell with all the demons in the world than spend a minute more with the likes of you."

The Count merely chuckled, igniting the anger within me. "You will get your wish soon, Miss Gerrick. But not yet. We must draw Lilith out. She responded so eagerly last time."

A blue light blazed to my left, and I turned my head, my neck aching from the stiffness of being latched to the table for so long. Two mages were huddled over a small bowl that emitted a strange blue smoke.

"What—what is that?" I couldn't hide the terror from my voice.

"Essence of Mr. Serrano," the Count said, his voice

reeking with pride. "His bloodline lured Lilith once before. I want to see if combining it with *your* blood will provide an even stronger incentive for her to emerge."

Oh please, no. I thrashed against my restraints, but it was no use. My hands were slick with sweat, but I still gripped the knife. I just needed the opportunity.

The Count faced me, watching me with sharp eyes. If I pulled the knife out now, he would see. And my attempt would be over in a second.

"What're you going to do with that?" I jerked my head toward the bowl while the mages muttered a spell in Latin.

The Count's mouth stretched into a wide, sinister smile. "Feed it to you."

Bile swirled in my stomach, and I shook my head. "No. No, please!" I wriggled again, trying to slide my hands out. I no longer cared if the Count saw me—I *couldn't* let him feed me the mixture in the bowl. My stomach crawled just thinking about it.

But before I could slide the knife out, a mage approached me and pressed a hand against my chest, locking me in place. I screamed, but then another mage drew nearer with the bowl, ready to pour the mixture into my mouth. I clamped my lips shut and turned my head away, trying to avoid the contents of the bowl. The bowl gave off a sharp vinegar smell—clearly demon—along with a metallic, copper scent that I knew too well.

Blood.

One of the mages gripped my jaw and turned my face toward the bowl. I fought and lurched, but there were too many of them. The Count took the bowl from a mage and thrust it toward me. I tried turning away, but it was no use. Someone pinched my nose, but still I resisted. My body pleaded for air, my lungs screaming in protest, until finally my lips parted, and the awful gooey substance slid down my throat. I gagged and choked, but I swallowed the mixture. Then, a hand closed my mouth and held it shut like a muzzle. Bile climbed up my throat, threatening to spew out, but the grip on my mouth kept it down. I swallowed, and my eyes burned. The gritty, sour taste filled my mouth, and spots danced in my vision. My head throbbed and ached, pulsing with its own rhythm of agony.

The presence within me burst forward with a mighty roar. My body seized and bucked so violently that one of the mages stumbled backward in alarm.

"Hold her!" the Count yelled.

My body shook more intensely. My head rattled, and my vision swam.

Then, all I saw was fire. Fire and death. Screams surrounded me. The flames licked my skin, charring my soul.

But it was beautiful. It was *freeing*.

I found myself grinning. Laughing so hard that tears sprang to my eyes. Glee I'd never known before swept over me, a soothing caress compared to the agony I'd endured.

"I am fire," I hissed. But it wasn't me. It was a foreign voice that poured from my lips. "I am death. And I am free."

27
BRIELLE

THE FIRE CONSUMED ME, EATING AWAY AT MY FLESH, and I was too powerless to stop it.

But I didn't *want* to stop it.

The blissful release from the agony of starvation and fatigue was a comfort I clung to. I hadn't realized how much of a strain it had been to keep this presence at bay, but relinquishing my hold, my control over myself was so easy. Effortless.

Why had I fought this for so long?

The beast within me roared its assent and spread its wings wide. Flames surrounded me like an ethereal glow, but they no longer harmed me. The flames were a *part* of me.

I am fire. And fire is me.

"Brielle," a voice whispered.

Suddenly the flames stopped as if someone had frozen time. I went very still, and the voice within me fell silent.

"Brielle," the voice said, louder this time.

Mom.

"Come back, Brielle!" Mom shouted. "You must come back!"

I shifted, trying to bring the feeling back to my body, but the flames roared in protest. The beast within me clawed at my mind, trying to take hold again.

"Brielle! You must resist!" Mom's voice was changing. It was deeper and . . . *closer.*

"Silence him," a different voice muttered nearby.

In a flash, I was back in the dungeon. Though my body was on fire on the inside, the flames had vanished from my vision. The darkness of the dungeon took over, slamming into me with such force that my head throbbed.

"What?" I whispered dizzily.

Then, Ronaldo screamed again, and I froze.

He'd been calling for me. He'd been the one trying to bring me back.

"Stop," I mumbled, trying to shout, but my mouth was too dry. Numbness took over my body.

Ronaldo's screams intensified.

I shook my head and gritted my teeth. "Stop!"

The Count leaned close to me, his foul breath hissing against my face. "I will not let that vile demon stand in the way of *everything* I've been working toward these many years."

I stared at him, trying to ignore the way my vision swayed. Then, I frowned. "Many years? What the hell are you talking about? You told me you've been trying to find a way out of the time loop all this time."

Ronaldo's screams subsided into sobs. A creaking sound told me whoever had hurt him was leaving his cell now.

The Count leaned away from me, and a slow smile spread across his face. "Foolish girl." He laughed. "*I'm* the one who cast the time spell."

Ronaldo's sobs suddenly went quiet.

My heart turned to ice, and I stared numbly at the Count, not comprehending. "You—*you*?"

The Count shrugged, but his face oozed smugness. Like he was proud of what he'd done. "I had to do something to protect my city. This was the only way to keep everyone *here*. So I could weed out Lilith's cursed witch myself. Of course, it did complicate things, having so many male pupils in my castle when I was looking for a *witch*." He shook his head. "But my years of waiting paid off. I finally found you."

"Found me," I repeated, my eyes widening. "You sent for us? For *all* of us? You *meant* for us to come here?"

The Count nodded. "I needed to draw her in without arousing suspicion." His eyes gleamed. "And it worked."

Her. Meaning Lilith.

The presence inside me.

"You're a Jumper," I remembered suddenly. *Of course.* I'd once asked him why a Jumper hadn't just used teleportation to get everyone out, and he'd made up some excuse about not having a caster with that kind of ability.

But *he'd* had the power this whole time.

Horror numbed my body, freezing over every part of me. Crumbling my resolve and determination to escape. Quenching even my disgust toward the beast inside me.

All these people—all of us who'd been trapped in this castle. It was the Count's fault. He'd done it—*on purpose.*

"You asshole," I spat at him. "You *son of a bitch!*"

"Silence her," the Count said, looking over me at one of the mages.

"You're a monster!" I screamed as a pair of hands clutched my shoulders. "I hope you burn in Hell!"

Something warm pressed against my chest. Blue magic tickled the air, flashing against my eyes.

Then, a cloudy emptiness filled my mind, and my head slumped over as I blacked out.

"Brielle," hissed a voice.

I mumbled incoherently, turning my head. Maybe whoever it was would go away if I said nothing. Sleep overcame me, beckoning me forward.

"Brielle!" the voice said more urgently.

My eyes snapped open, and the familiar darkness of the dungeon filled my vision. Drool and sweat stuck to my face. Something in my arm throbbed, and when I glanced down, I found a trail of blood running from my shoulder to my elbow.

I shuddered. What the hell had the Count done to me while I was unconscious?

Mercifully, my hands were still tucked behind me, though I'd lost my grip on the knife. Scrambling, I fumbled until I found it wedged on the right side of the table. Then, I exhaled.

"Brielle, you must wake up." It was Ronaldo.

"I'm awake." I turned my head toward his voice. "Are you all right? What did they do to you?"

"Worry not for me, Brielle. You *must* get out."

I released a hollow chuckle. "Yeah. I'm aware."

"No, you don't understand." Metal clanged as if he'd gripped the bars of his cell. "The Count has cursed this city. He is responsible. You *must* get to my brother and tell him this."

I frowned. "Why?"

"Leo has been working on a counterspell. To lift the curse. If he knows who cast it, it might help him succeed."

I shook my head. "Ronaldo, I can't—"

"Brielle, this is the most important thing," Ronaldo said, his voice laced with desperation. "I beg of you. When the Count returns, please go. Find my brother and warn him. He can save you. He can save everyone in this city."

I went still. "When the Count returns?" I whispered. "Ronaldo, what're you going to do?"

"It's of no consequence to you."

"The hell it is!"

"I'm already dying!" he roared. "The only reason I haven't given up yet is because I cling to some hope that if the Count is busy with me, he will not search for my brother. But now—God has given me this opportunity. To

303

serve you. To help you escape. If I can play a part in saving this city from his wretched curse, then I'll do it."

"God has nothing to do with this," I growled.

"You may believe that. But I do not."

I clenched my teeth and made no response. Though a part of me believed in an afterlife or a great beyond or something else out there waiting for us, I wasn't sure I believed in God. How could I believe in a god that approved of what the Count did here? He was as devout as they came, but I could never follow a religion that condoned such vile acts.

"Nothing you say will change my mind," Ronaldo said softly. "Whatever you decide, I will be dead soon. But I hope and pray you will take advantage. I pray I will not die in vain."

"Ronaldo—"

"I heard your friend. I know she gave you a means to escape. I beg of you to take it. Please, Brielle."

I said nothing. My eyes burned, and I closed them against the agony throbbing in my head. My heart twisted.

"I know you're afraid. I know you think you deserve to stay here. But you don't. There is a way to push out Lilith's influence. I am sure of it. If anyone can help you, it's my brother."

"What the hell can he do about this?" I snapped.

"Demons believe differently than light casters," Ronaldo said. "Light casters believe Lilith's cursed witch is doomed no matter what. But demons . . ." He paused. "We don't see it the same way. Leo is a scholar. He knows more about the legend than I do. He can help you, Brielle."

I remembered what Leo had told me—that Lilith possessed the witch at night, but the witch could fight off her influence by uniting herself with the beast.

He'd claimed he hadn't known much about the rumors. And I hadn't pressed him on it. But what if he *had* known more and hadn't been willing to tell me? I hadn't exactly been friendly toward him.

And for good reason. He was practically begging me to show up on his doorstep so his coven could feast on my blood.

"He'll kill me," I said at last.

"He won't," said Ronaldo. "Not if you tell him I sent you."

I didn't answer. As much as my mind screamed to refuse, I had no alternative. And Ronaldo was right—I had to do something about this. The whole reason we were stuck in this damn time loop was because no one knew who cast the spell.

But not anymore.

With this knowledge, I could help reverse the curse. I might even be able to return home.

Home. The word rang in my head, and a pang of longing stabbed right through me.

"My coven lives at the base of the mountains," Ronaldo said in a weak voice. "Head for the three mountain peaks. The caves of my coven are in the center of them." He paused. "When you see my brother, tell him what happened to Lucia. Tell him I tried to save her."

I nodded without realizing it. "I will."

Ronaldo sucked in a breath. "So, you'll do it?"

"Yes. But I'm taking you with me."

A loud clang echoed in the dungeon, and I wondered if Ronaldo had slammed his head against the bars. "For Lilith's sake, Brielle. You'll get yourself killed trying to get me out."

"I can't just leave you here to die!"

Ronaldo exhaled long and slow. "They removed my legs, Brielle."

I stiffened. My blood chilled as I mulled over his words. "They—"

"They cut off my legs. The wounds are bound to stop the flow of blood, but I'm not long for this world. I can't run or walk. You can't free me, Brielle."

"But . . . but can't you heal?" One thing I knew about vampires was that they couldn't be killed without a stake or a banishing spell. They could heal from their injuries.

"Not if my legs aren't here to be reattached. I cannot grow the limbs back. They took my legs with them to ensure I couldn't heal."

Bile crept up my throat. *They freaking chopped off his legs* . . .

I crammed my eyes shut to ward off the sting of more tears. "Ronaldo." My voice broke.

"Don't weep for me, Brielle. With your escape, you'll

give me a purpose. I can carry that with me into the next world."

I clenched my teeth. It wasn't enough. I didn't even know if I fully believed in an afterlife. This might've been *it* for him. This horrible, wretched dungeon would be the last thing he ever saw.

I opened my mouth to speak, but footsteps on the stairs stopped me. The steps were loud, and they multiplied. It sounded like the Count had returned with his mages.

My heart raced, thrumming incessantly against my chest. For once, the presence within me was silent, though the heat from the flames still burned my insides.

"Prepare yourself," Ronaldo hissed.

I slid the knife out from behind me. My arm was numb from being wedged under my back for so long. Gritting my teeth, I slid the blade against the leather strap. Agony flared in my head, but I gripped the knife more firmly and pressed harder, though I felt weaker than a dry twig.

The footsteps were getting closer.

Faster, Brie. I quickened my pace, sawing frantically through the leather. Then, with a light snap, the restraint fell off. I relaxed against the table as if I were still restrained.

I thought of Ronaldo sitting in his cell and waiting to be killed. Clinging to the hope that I'd carry out his final wish.

What if I failed him?

I choked on more sobs and bit my tongue to keep myself from crying.

You can do this.

I held my breath as the footsteps drew nearer,

wondering what I would do if the visitors went into a different cell. There were other demons here, after all, though it seemed they were either too injured or too incoherent to make conversation like me and Ronaldo.

The footsteps grew louder and louder, matching the rhythm of my heartbeat.

Then, my cell door swung open.

"Excellent," the Count said quietly. "You're awake. We can resume our work."

Before I could say anything or even look in his direction, a blood-curdling scream wailed throughout the dungeon. My heart lurched in my throat as I looked around.

But it wasn't Ronaldo.

Another shout pierced the air, mingling with the first.

Then, came Ronaldo's voice. "Help me! *Help*! Get it off me! Something is attacking me!"

Moans and howls filled the dungeon as if the whole place were haunted. Under different circumstances, it might've been funny.

But in this instance, it made my skin crawl.

The Count hollered something at the mages, who all darted off in different directions.

Now! I lunged for the Count and slammed the knife into his chest. He screeched and stumbled backward, but I didn't wait and see if he recovered. I yanked the knife out of his chest, hurried out of my cell, and smashed the vial of orange liquid on the floor. A plume of amber smoke engulfed me.

My stomach dropped, and then I was weightless,

floating in the air. The orange mist surrounded me, shielding me from view. The Count's roar of fury mingled with the noises of the other demons in the dungeon.

I closed my eyes, succumbing to the vanishing potion. *Take me away,* I urged it.

I soared upward like a balloon. The stench of the dungeon left me, and the cacophony of sounds grew fainter. For a brief moment, I thought I heard Ronaldo's voice shouting something at me, but I couldn't make it out.

Then, something heavy pressed against my chest, squeezing the air out of me. I couldn't breathe. Couldn't think.

A blinding light struck my face, and I squinted, raising a hand to shield my eyes.

My breath caught in my throat. I was in the hallway by the staircase. I was aboveground.

For one stupid moment, I stood there frozen. *Izzy.* I had to get her out of here!

Then, shouts echoed from below me, and I knew I was out of time. I swore under my breath.

Forgive me, Izzy.

I bolted down the hallway, praying I wouldn't run into anyone. I had no idea what time it was, but perhaps everyone was dining right now. Maybe luck would be on my side.

"Oof!"

I slammed into someone and stumbled backward. My mouth fell open, and my eyes widened in terror.

"Brielle." It was Riker. He looked me over, his face draining of color. "What—"

I tried to sidestep him, but he stood in my path. I stared up at him, trying to look fierce despite my numbing fatigue. "Get out of my way."

He watched me, and something like pity stirred in his eyes. It only made me angrier.

"Don't make me fight you, Riker."

Riker shook his head. Muffled shouts echoed behind me, and my heart stuttered in panic.

My anger fled from me. "Please," I whispered.

Riker glanced over my shoulder and looked at me again. Then, he stepped aside. "Be safe, Brielle."

I surged forward and then stopped to look back at him. *I have to tell someone.* "The Count cast the spell. He created the time loop."

Riker's face slackened in utter shock, but I turned away from him before he could respond. With a sudden burst of energy, I sprinted down the hall toward the giant front doors. Sucking in a breath, I hauled them open, slid outside, and slammed them shut behind me.

28

BRIELLE

MY LEGS THROBBED, AND EVERY INCH OF MY BODY pulsed with agony. But still I ran. The sun beat down on me, blazing against my vision that had grown so accustomed to the darkness of the dungeon.

Keep running. Keep running.

I pushed on until my lungs burned. My vision darkened and my head spun, but still I ran. I raced down the steps and flew past the gardens, past the spot where I'd trapped and questioned Leo Serrano.

Sweat poured down my face, mingling with grime and blood as it formed a sickening paste.

A stitch formed in my side, but I couldn't stop or even slow down. If I did, I knew I wouldn't be able to run again. I'd be too weak.

Shouts echoed behind me, and panic sliced through my chest.

Keep going.

At long last, I reached the wards surrounding the castle. I finally allowed myself to come to a stop, remembering how the wards had rebounded me last time I'd tried to get through.

Gasping for breath, I doubled over. My heart thumped so painfully it felt like it would burst from my chest. Agony crashed over me in waves, threatening to drown me.

Come on, Brie! I told myself.

I straightened and brushed my fingers against the bloody gash on my arm. My fingers trembled, and the wound throbbed from my touch. Then, I lifted my fingers to the invisible ward, reaching forward until the tickle of its magic whispered against my skin.

I closed my eyes and muttered a spell in Spanish.

"*Magia arriba, te convoco*

Rompe este encanto."

A burst of blue light flashed, and magic prickled against my hand. Then, with a loud crack, a ripple of electricity bolted in the air in front of me like lightning. The smell of ash tickled my nose.

Hesitantly, I stepped forward.

Nothing stopped me. The wards were down.

More shouts echoed behind me.

I surged forward and then turned back to face the castle. Raising my bloodied hand, I muttered another spell.

"*Alta Magia, te convoco*

Restaura este encanto."

I had no idea if it would work—perhaps I needed the Count's blood to secure the wards. But to my surprise, something rippled in the air, forming a hazy film in front of me like a layer of clear plastic.

My heart surged with relief, but I wasn't safe yet. I'd only restored the Count's wards. If that were the case, he could easily remove them.

But it might've bought me some time.

I broke into another run, weaving through grass and shrubs that thickened until I reached a large wood. But I didn't stop there. Still I ran, avoiding tree roots and low branches. My skin itched and burned. The smell of dirt and dead leaves filled my nose.

I couldn't last much longer. The small mountains in the distance were miles away. The pain rippling over my body would claim me, and I'd pass out soon.

But I had to find a good place to hide in case the Count's men found me.

I finally found a huge oak tree with low branches, and I started climbing. Though my limbs burned from exertion and the darkness crept into the corners of my eyes again, still I climbed.

When I was high enough to be concealed by the leaves of the branch beneath me, I stopped, settling onto a thick branch with my back resting against the massive trunk of the tree.

I leaned my head on the tree bark behind me and closed my eyes, my breaths coming in sharp wheezes. My chest burned with each breath I took, and my heart wouldn't stop racing. My legs ached, the muscles stiff and tense as if I were still running.

I lifted my shaking hands and whispered another spell.

"Magic above and powers that be,

Conceal me from my enemy."

My hands glowed blue, but the light flickered slightly like a fading light bulb. A warm pressure enveloped me like a blanket. The cloaking spell had worked. But I wasn't sure how many more spells I could cast while I was so weak.

I wanted to rest my head and close my eyes again, but I couldn't risk sleeping and falling from this height. Instead, I wriggled out of my loose tunic and tore at the laces and strings, pulling them free. Then, I draped the tunic back over me, though now it was nothing more than a large piece of fabric. Locking my legs together over the tree branch, I tied the strings around my thighs, binding them together over the tree branch. I formed several strong knots and shifted my legs to test them. The strings held, but I could easily break them if I used enough force.

I just had to trust I would wake up in time to catch myself from falling.

Swallowing down my unease and terror, I leaned back against the tree trunk and let the darkness overtake me.

Flames burned against my face. A mighty roar consumed me. A triumphant laugh poured from my lips.

I jolted awake, and something snapped. My arms flailed, wrapping around the tree branch just before I slid off. My heart raced a mile a minute as I glanced down and noticed my knotted string falling to the ground.

I gripped the tree branch tightly, trying to calm my panicked breathing.

Dusk had fallen. The wood was cloaked in darkness. Owls hooted nearby. Insects chirped. The sounds were eerie, but I tried to take comfort in them—it meant the forest was undisturbed. If I was being pursued, the insects and other creatures would fall silent.

I took a moment to clear my head. I climbed back into a sitting position and rested my forehead against my knees. The frantic pounding of my heart was a warning rhythm. The shock of almost falling out of the tree wasn't the only thing that rattled me.

I'd dreamed of the beast again. I'd felt *her* inside me again.

The fire within me had been suspiciously quiet since the Count's last experiment. I didn't like the silence. The stillness inside me. It screamed at me that something was wrong. That something big was coming.

I'll deal with that later. Right now, I had to focus on finding food. And, eventually, refuge.

My stomach churned at the thought of seeking refuge with Leo Serrano. I had no doubt they would see my presence as a threat. After all, the Count had led many attacks against their coven.

My only hope was that they would pause long enough to hear my plea before imprisoning me. Or killing me.

Sucking in a deep breath, I wriggled off the branch until

my feet found the branch below me. With slow, careful movements, I climbed down until I was low enough to the ground to hop down.

I froze at the base of the tree and waited. Being on the ground again made me a target. If the Count or his mages were lurking nearby, now was their chance to grab me.

But nothing happened. The sounds of the forest consumed me like white noise. I exhaled.

It was slow work navigating through the forest in the middle of the night. In the moments when I feared I was lost, I cast my light spell to use my hand as a flashlight. Each time I did this, insects swarmed around me, and I worried about drawing too much attention. But I had to make sure I was headed in the right direction.

Occasionally, I paused to climb up another tree and check that I could still see the mountains. Each time I did, I was discouraged by how *far* I still was from my destination.

After hours of walking, I couldn't ignore my hunger any longer. I found a large bush and crawled inside, using the foliage to conceal me from view. Then, I waited.

I tried to squash my discomfort and unease at the thought of hunting. I'd never hunted animals before.

But the fear swirling within me only made me angry. *You're a Demonhunter, for Lilith's sake. Get a grip. If you can stake a vampire twice your size, then you can catch a few animals.*

So, I waited. After a few hours, fatigue crept in my mind, and my eyelids drooped. I shook my head, trying to wake myself up. *You can do this.*

A rustling nearby made me stiffen. I stared through the brush, eyes wide, as a large rabbit hopped into view. I swallowed, trying not to make a sound. Slowly, I lifted my hands and uttered in a hushed whisper,

"Magic above and powers that be,
Strike this animal in front of me."

A bolt of blue light flashed from my fingertips and struck the rabbit. It jolted and seized before collapsing on the ground, motionless.

I approached the creature and poked it to make sure it was dead. Then, my mouth twisted with a grimace. I had no idea how to skin a rabbit. Or cook one. What parts of it were safe for me to eat?

I pulled the knife from my pocket and crouched next to the animal. Holding my breath, I forced the knife into its fur and cut.

Hours later, I trudged through the woods as the sky lightened with approaching daybreak. The guts and blood of the rabbit still coated my hands up to my forearms, but I'd eaten. The rabbit's fur had been surprisingly easy to cut through, even with my dull kitchen knife. Aside from a few hairs and some bones I had to spit out, the meat had been satisfying. I'd prepared kindling and used my magic to summon sparks before cooking the carcass. Then, I'd put out the flames, eaten what I could, and continued my journey.

I tried not to smile as I thought of how shocked Angel would be if she could see me now—braving the back-country and hunting for food. But as soon as I thought of her, my smile vanished, and an ache of longing filled my chest.

I would never see her again. Even if I *could* end the time loop, I couldn't very well return home when I knew Lilith was inside me, just waiting to be unleashed. I couldn't doom my family and my city to that kind of destruction.

No, I vowed to find somewhere secluded to live out whatever time I had left. If Leo could help me, then great. But I was skeptical. Part of me knew I was living on borrowed time.

I'll help break the curse and then find a safe place to unleash Lilith. Somewhere no one will get hurt.

The idea of surrendering myself to her—of giving up my soul and dying—hadn't yet settled in my mind. It still seemed like a faraway idea. Almost like a fairy tale. Or a bad dream.

But it was there, lurking in the shadows of my mind. Waiting to crash down on me.

A few days passed. I trudged through the woods, stopping often to rest, eat, and relieve myself. Anytime I felt tired, I succumbed and took a break; if my energy was too depleted, I wouldn't be able to cast spells. And I was almost certain the Count's men would follow me.

How could they not? The Count claimed he'd been looking for Lilith's cursed witch for years. If this was what he'd been waiting for all this time, he couldn't just let me go.

At night, I sought out large bushes for cover and slept on the forest floor. The fitful sleep was far from refreshing—between the bug bites, mud, and chilly air—but it was enough for me to keep going.

At last, the mountains grew so close I could see them through the trees without even climbing. Relief soared in my heart, and I surged forward, eager to reach my destination before nightfall.

Something prickled my ears. I stiffened and scurried behind the nearest tree, waiting. Listening.

I shut my eyes and trusted my hearing and sense of smell. Then, I caught it. A faint whiff of ash and magic.

I swallowed and patted myself out of habit. But, of course, my only weapon was the dumb kitchen knife. Still, I clutched it in my sweaty palm and sucked in several deep breaths.

Soft footsteps crunched on leaves and twigs. My brow furrowed as I concentrated on the sounds.

There were multiple sets of footsteps, but I couldn't tell how many. Two or three perhaps.

You can do this, Brie. It's just another hunt.

When the footsteps grew close enough for my skin to prickle, I lunged from my hiding spot and swung my knife. One of the men ducked, avoiding my blow. I drew back, ready to strike again, and my eyes fell on my opponents.

All five mages faced me. Ignacio stood in the front with his arms raised. "Please, Miss Gerrick."

I hesitated, but only for a moment. I wielded my knife again, my arms lifted in a fighting stance.

"Please *what*?" I snapped. "Please return with you so the Count can torture me some more? So he can unleash the monster inside me?"

"The lives of everyone in this city depend on it," Ignacio pleaded. There was such sorrow in his eyes, such torment and devastation, that something within me faltered.

I'll be responsible for thousands of deaths, all because I wouldn't give in. Because I was determined to find a way out.

But what if there isn't a way out? What if by escaping, I've doomed this entire city?

Ignacio edged closer to me, and my arms lifted again, sensing an attack.

"Don't come any closer." My voice sounded feebler.

"You are no killer, Miss Gerrick," Ignacio whispered, stepping closer toward me. And this time I didn't draw away from him. "I know you'll do the right thing. Would you really put your life above the lives of everyone here? Above the lives of your friends in the castle?"

Izzy. A hard lump formed in my throat. "They won't die," I said. "The castle is protected."

"Yes, but they are all trapped there indefinitely until this threat is contained. Which means they will live out their lives away from their homes and families. Unless you submit yourself and eliminate the monster."

My eyes shifted to the mountain base still visible through the trees. I was *so* close.

"What if there's a cure?" I asked. "What if there's a way to defeat Lilith? To push her out?"

Ignacio smiled sadly, his eyes full of pity.

Anger roared within me, and I gritted my teeth. The mages behind Ignacio tensed, obviously sensing my intent to attack.

Something unreadable flashed in Ignacio's eyes. Blue magic burst from his fingertips, spearing through the air and straight into my chest, knocking me backward. I fell to the forest floor with an "oof," but in an instant, I was back on my feet.

The mages surged toward me, their cloaks billowing. I ducked and kicked the legs out from under Ignacio. Then, I swiped my knife, cutting the sleeve of another mage. I aimed a high kick into the chest of a third mage and finally broke free, sprinting toward the mountain as fast as my legs could carry me.

Magic tickled the air, and I ducked instinctively as another flash of blue magic seared toward me. Heat stung the top of my head, and I knew I'd narrowly avoided a spell.

Sucking in sharp breaths, I pushed onward, weaving through trees and using the foliage for cover. Gasping, I cast a spell.

"Magic above and powers that be,
Conceal me from this enemy!"

A faint blue glow surrounded me, but the usual warmth of my magic felt feeble and thin. Like the simplest spell could break through it.

I wouldn't last much longer.

The forest grew thinner. I was almost free. Almost there.

Something sharp lodged itself into my shoulder, and I fell over with a yelp. The knife flew from my grasp. Warm blood soaked my shirt. I wriggled on the ground and glanced over my shoulder to find a dagger buried in my flesh. Already, blood blossomed on my shirt.

I crawled forward, but pain sliced into my shoulder with each movement. Sobs poured from me as I slithered along the ground. Footsteps approached. I glanced behind me and found the mages surrounding me, blocking my escape.

It was over.

29
LEO

From the shadows of the trees, I hovered, watching the events unfold. The Count's mages had caught up to the Little Nightmare. They'd used excessive force— she was bleeding freely from a wound in her shoulder.

The terror and anger in her face struck something within me.

"What should we do?" Guadalupe asked from behind me.

"Nothing. Let them take her."

"But Leo—"

I fixed a steely gaze on her. "She isn't our responsibility." My shadows swirled around me, prepared to shift, when I caught a whiff of something that made me freeze.

Fresh wood chips and honey mingled with the sharp, metallic smell of blood.

Ronaldo.

It was the faintest hint of him like it was swept away with the wind. As if he had only shared air with someone.

Someone like this girl. Like Brielle.

"Attack," I hissed to Guadalupe before I could change my mind.

Her eyes widened in shock, but she recovered quickly. In a flash, she vanished in the brush, communicating with my other brethren hiding nearby.

I burst forward in an explosion of shadows. I felt the mages' blood racing when they saw me, and their fear shot a thrill through me. I shifted to bat form and flitted around until I hovered behind them. Then, I shifted back to vampire form and lunged for the first mage. With a shout, I pounced, knocking him over before sinking my teeth into his neck. I only allowed a moment of satisfaction before I stopped drinking his blood and moved on to the next one. I wasn't here to feed, and there was something foul about their blood. It was tainted in ways I couldn't explain.

Drops of blood poured down my chin, and I spat on the ground. My brethren surged forward from their hiding place, engaging the remaining mages. The girl remained limp on the forest floor, her body still pinned down by the blade. After ensuring our enemies were being taken care of, I approached her cautiously.

Her face was covered in burns and bruises. She stared unblinkingly toward the trees as if not seeing anything at all. If I hadn't sensed her blood and her heartbeat, I might've thought her dead.

She looked . . . broken. And for some reason, this sliced

through me, filling me with regret. I thought of the spirited ball of fire she'd been when we'd last met.

That girl was gone, leaving nothing but a hollow shell behind.

Carefully, I stooped to lift her into my arms. She shifted slightly, but not aggressively. It was as if she wanted to fight me off but lacked the strength. I cradled her to my chest and caught another whiff of Ronaldo.

Yes, I was certain of it. She'd been in the same room as him.

My blood raced with excitement, but I squashed it down. If she had answers about my brother, I would have to extract them carefully. But first, she needed to recover from her injuries.

"Fret not, Little Nightmare," I said in a soothing voice. "You're safe now."

I glanced up at the fray. Miguel had just rendered the last mage unconscious. The other mages lay motionless on the ground, some sporting bloody wounds.

Miguel wiped blood from his mouth and approached me, his eyes wild from the fight. "What should we do with them?"

I stared at the unconscious mages for a long moment. *Kill them,* a sinister voice within me whispered.

But they were merely obeying orders. My coven followed a code. If I broke it, what would that make us?

It would make us no better than the Count.

And yet . . . one of the mages smelled of my brother. I inched closer and inhaled deeply.

Yes, the scent was there. This mage had been *covered* in my brother's blood. Though the man's hands were clean now, I smelled Ronaldo as clearly as if the mage had bathed in his blood.

My entire body went still. Fire roared within me, demanding justice. For a moment, conflict warred in my mind as I was torn between the principles of my coven and the cry for revenge in my blood.

Ronaldo would preach of forgiveness and mercy.

But Ronaldo wasn't here. And right in front of me were the men responsible for that.

The monster within me roared, and I glanced down at Brielle again. Her vacant eyes stared emptily at the forest, but pain was etched into her face. A long, bloody cut ran down her arm, and her clothes were soaked in blood, sweat, and grime. She'd lost so much weight since I'd last seen her that she looked gaunt.

Those mages had done this.

Forgive me, Ronaldo.

I fixed a hard gaze on Miguel. "Finish them."

I turned away and carried the girl toward the caves. Behind me I heard the cracking of bones and the slurping of blood.

But I felt no sorrow or sympathy. Instead I thought of my brother—who was most certainly dead—and how I had taken the first step in avenging him.

30

BRIELLE

A MONSTROUS ROAR CONSUMED ME. FIRE BURNED everywhere. Children screamed. Women sobbed. Men yelled in anguish. Metal clashed. Blood soaked the ground, filling the air with a metallic smell.

But it smelled wonderful. *Delicious,* even.

And I reveled in it.

My eyes flew open, my whole body jolting as consciousness slammed back into me. I sat up quickly. Too quickly. Spots danced in front of my eyes, obscuring everything from view. I blinked impatiently and raised a hand to my head, trying to rub away the faint throbbing that pulsed incessantly.

As my vision cleared, my jaw dropped. I was inside a cave. But it was unlike any cave I'd ever seen. The ceiling climbed higher than a cathedral, putting even the ornate ceilings of the castle to shame. I gazed upward, craning my neck, and found a few small openings in the cave ceiling.

Sunlight filtered through in small chinks, providing the smallest slivers of light to fill the room.

Yes, *room*. That was the only way to describe it. A fur rug lined the smooth floors. I was sitting on a king-sized bed with fur blankets and soft pillows. A large, wooden wardrobe rested in the far corner, and its open doors revealed a stunning collection of satin gowns and frilly lace shawls. Lanterns had been built into the rocky walls, though they weren't lit since the sun provided enough light.

Slowly, I swung my legs over the bed and rose to my feet. The ground felt cool against my bare feet, and it was as smooth as marble. Though the walls were rocky and bumpy, there were no stalactites or stalagmites. It was as if someone had smoothed the top and bottom of this cave, transforming it into comfortable living quarters. A safe place. A *home*.

I glanced down at my toes. They were clean, though I'd certainly remembered them covered in grime in the forest. And I was dressed in a thin white shift that barely covered my naked body. My skin had been scrubbed free of dirt and blood. I tried rolling my shoulder and winced, hissing in pain. With a glance behind me, I realized someone had bandaged and cleaned the wounds on my shoulder and arm, though they still throbbed.

I rubbed my arms that prickled from the chilly cave air. Though the air smelled faintly of demon, it had a musty, mineral smell that mingled and almost made the scent . . . pleasant. It smelled earthy. Ethereal.

Magical.

I pushed the thought away, reminding myself I was

among enemies. These caves belonged to Leo and his coven, who had attacked the castle—attacked *me*—on multiple occasions. They probably saw me as an enemy too.

Though I couldn't help but notice I was in some kind of guest room—or guest *cave*. Not a prison cell.

Which already put my host in a higher standing than the Count.

"The dresses in the wardrobe are available for you to wear," a soft voice said from the mouth of the cave.

I yelped and darted to the side, hoping to shield myself from view.

My visitor chuckled softly. "Fear not, Little Nightmare. I can barely see you. I won't come too close anyway, what with the sunlight."

I crossed my arms and peered toward the mouth of the cave, though all I saw was darkness. "Leo?"

Leo sucked in a breath and laughed. "Such informality. And yet I do not know your name, Little Nightmare."

I rolled my eyes at his nickname for me. "Brielle Gerrick."

A pause. Then, "An exquisite name. Though surely you're not French?"

I groaned. "*No.* I'm not French. My mom just thought the name was pretty. You can call me Brie if it bothers you."

"It doesn't bother me. It's quite beautiful."

I shifted my weight from one foot to the other, unsure of how to respond. "Erm . . . what happened to the mages?"

Leo was silent for a moment. "They left when my men emerged. They knew it was a battle they could not win."

Goosebumps rose on my skin at the thought of this demon coven fighting . . . for *me*.

"Thank you," I mumbled, dropping my gaze. The words didn't feel like they were enough.

"It wasn't for you." Leo's voice was tight. "They were trespassing. We were protecting our home."

"I know," I said quickly. "That doesn't mean I'm not grateful."

Leo said nothing.

I rubbed my arms. "So, uh, who dressed me? And bathed me?"

Please don't say it was you. Please don't say it was you. The idea of Leo with his hands on me like that made my skin crawl.

"Guadalupe."

My body sagged with relief. "Oh. Who's Guadalupe?"

"My cousin."

I cocked my head, waiting for more information. "And she . . . ?"

Leo laughed again. "What would you like me to say? She's a demon. A part of this coven. A shapeshifting vampire like me."

My hand instinctively flew to my neck, but I found no puncture wounds.

"She would not bite an unwilling victim." Leo's voice sounded terse.

Anger flared within me. "Why not? *You* did."

Leo barked out a laugh. "Need I remind you that you attacked me first? It was a matter of self-defense."

I scoffed. "Hardly. You could've easily just left me there *without* drinking my blood."

"Ah, yes, but you would've followed me. Wouldn't you." It wasn't a question.

My mouth clamped shut, and I couldn't keep the corners of my mouth from twitching. *Yes. I would've.* I shook my head to clear my expression. "Can you come forward just a little? It's creepy talking to nothing but a shadow."

Leo sighed and edged closer. Though he was still mostly concealed by shadow, the nearness of the light helped me make out his figure. His long hair was tied behind him, and he wore a loose, casual tunic. No waistcoats. No ascots or cravats.

I once again remembered I was in nothing but a transparent nightgown, and I drew my arms tighter around my chest.

Leo smirked. "As I said before, you are welcome to the dresses here." He waved a hand toward the wardrobe.

I gazed around the room, curiosity overwhelming me. "Whose room is this?"

Leo's lips pressed together, and his eyes danced with amusement. I got the distinct impression he was trying not to laugh at me.

I leveled a hard stare at him. "What's so funny?"

"It's amusing how many times I must remind you that most of us are vampires in this coven. We don't sleep. And many of us are uncomfortable in the sunlight." He gestured toward the bed and the light filtering through the ceiling. "This is our guest room."

I dropped my arms. "Oh." Embarrassment washed over me, warming my face and bringing with it a twinge of annoyance. "And does your shapeshifting vampire clan get many *guests*?" I raised my eyebrows.

Leo's face sobered. "We used to."

All feeling fled from me, leaving me cold and empty. *Oh. Before the time loop, he means. Before he lost his brother and his sister.*

Ronaldo. I straightened, suddenly remembering. "Leo, I . . . I met your brother."

Leo went very still, his dark eyes boring into mine. "Ronaldo?" he said softly.

I nodded.

In just a few strides, Leo emerged from the shadows until he stood only a few feet in front of me. Sunlight blazed on his face, and his jaw went rigid. His fingers clenched into fists, but he still stood in front of me, watching me. His eyes burned with intensity. "What happened to him?" His voice broke, but I couldn't tell if it was from emotion or the pain of being in the sun.

My mouth opened and closed. I glanced up at the sunlight and pointed to him. "You don't have to—"

"*Tell me.*" He stepped even closer to me, his chest rising and falling with ragged breaths.

I swallowed. "He's dead. Or at least, I'm almost certain he is."

Leo stared hard at me for several seconds as if waiting

for me to say I was joking. "How?" he demanded, his tone icy.

I took a deep breath and told him everything—that Ronaldo had tried to rescue their sister. That Lilith had taken over, and Lucia's body had given out. That Ronaldo was imprisoned and tortured. When I told Leo about how the Count and his mages had cut off Ronaldo's legs, Leo swore and whirled away from me, running a hand over his face.

I stopped talking, waiting for him to process everything. Then, still facing away from me, Leo waved a hand and said weakly, "Go on."

I told him of how Ronaldo had sacrificed himself to help me escape—how *all* the demons had come to my aid. How without them, I never would've made it.

And Izzy. I owed her my life.

When I finished, I closed my eyes, feeling the weight of those traumatic memories sink into my stomach, dragging me down.

"Why?" Leo said in a haggard whisper. "Why did he sacrifice himself? For *you*?" He practically spat the word.

I flinched. I couldn't help it. Though I'd always seen Leo as my enemy, he'd been nothing but pleasant toward me. Flirtatious. Arrogant.

To see—and *feel*—such hostility from him was surprisingly jarring.

"The Count revealed to us that he was the one who cursed the city," I said. "He's responsible for the time loop."

Leo's brows knitted together. "Impossible."

"He told us himself. He's a Jumper."

Leo cocked his head at me. "A what?"

I shook my head. "A Teleporter. He can get out of the city. But he chooses not to. He cast this spell to trap everyone here so he could find Lilith's cursed witch. So he could find . . . me."

There it was. The truth. I couldn't hide from it now.

A small, insane part of me was hoping Leo would end my life right then and there. It was because of me that the Count imprisoned and killed his brother and sister. The Count had been looking for me the entire time. How many people had suffered because of it?

Leo straightened and lifted his chin. "If my brother saw you worthy enough to die for, then . . . I must offer you my assistance. For his sake. And for Lucia's."

I stilled. "You don't owe me anything, Leo. I've done nothing to deserve anyone's help."

Half of Leo's mouth curved upward, but the anguish lingered in his eyes. "On the contrary, Brielle. Lucia died because she wasn't strong enough for Lilith's soul. If I can help you in the ways I failed her, it will feel like I have . . . redeemed myself somehow."

Something within me jolted, and it took me a moment to realize why: it was the first time he'd used my name. I tried to ignore how pleasant it sounded, rolling off his tongue with his accent.

"And if working with you will help break this curse," Leo went on, "then I will feel the same satisfaction in regard to my brother."

I stepped toward him so we were almost touching. "You aren't responsible for their deaths."

"Perhaps not directly. But if I'd done more—if I'd found a solution sooner—they might still be with us."

His words struck a chord with me. *If only I'd had the foresight, the wisdom to refuse Councilman Solano—to flee when he told me he was taking me away, I wouldn't have ever come here. This city would never have been endangered. And I'd still be with my family.*

But I swallowed down those thoughts, determined not to drown myself in regret and possibilities of what might have been.

"Leo," I said in a broken voice, unable to look him in the eye. "You need to send me away. Lock me up. Strap me down or *something*. I'm the one responsible for killing innocent people, for destroying this city. You shouldn't give me a damn guest room to sleep in." I waved a hand toward the bed behind me. "You should chain me up! I'm a danger to *everyone* here."

Leo stared at me. Something unreadable stirred in his eyes. "I would never chain you up."

I shook my head. "Leo—"

"The Count may have believed you were doomed from the start. But I don't. I didn't believe it of my sister, either. I *will* find a way to free you."

"And if you can't?"

Leo said nothing. For a long moment, we watched each other as if waiting for the other to give in. To concede the staring contest.

But I knew why he couldn't answer—because he had no solution. If I *was* doomed to surrender myself to Lilith, there was nothing he could do.

Except kill me.

Leo changed the subject. "There's something I don't understand." His gaze grew distant, and the silver rings in his eyes glinted with the sunlight. "If the Count can Teleport, why didn't he just apprehend you himself?"

I thought for a moment. "Because I wasn't supposed to know about his powers. If he used them out in the open and tried to find me, people would know. Your coven might've found out. He couldn't have that. He needs people to believe he's as innocent as the rest of us with this time loop."

Leo frowned. "Yes, you've said that before. 'Time loop.' What does that mean?"

I quickly explained the year that repeated itself and how Leo's coven had finally broken free.

Leo's face went pale, though his skin was already paper-white. "So, every year—for years, we . . . we never . . ." He broke off and swallowed. "Merciful Lilith." He exhaled long and slow. "We knew he'd formed a magical barrier around Segovia, but we didn't realize the entire city was repeating the same year over and over."

"How did you do it?" I asked. "How did you break out of the time loop?"

Leo shook his head. "We were trying to find a way out of the city. Past the barrier. Using my research, we cast a spell, but we assumed it didn't work. Then, we felt *something*. A similar feeling to when we enter the Castillo de Coca. We discovered he'd cast *multiple* enchantments—not just surrounding the city, but the castle as well. And we'd broken through the castle's spell. So, we sent word through our spies, luring the Count and his men to us so we could attack the Castillo and investigate for ourselves."

My brows knitted together. "But I found you in the armory trying to steal weapons."

Leo chuckled and rubbed his jaw. "Yes, well . . . we had other needs too." His eyes flashed with amusement. Suddenly, he stiffened. His face went taut, and the veins and tendons of his neck popped. "Forgive me." He drew away, retreating to the shadows.

Chagrin washed over me. He'd been in physical pain that whole time, and I'd just stood there chatting with him. Forgetting about his needs. *Idiot,* I chided myself.

"You must be Second Tier," I said, referring to the pecking order of demons. When a demon performed a specific blood ritual, they Ascended to another Tier, tapping into more and more power with each Ascension.

"I am." He paused. "Does that frighten you?"

"Not in the slightest."

Leo laughed.

I cocked my head at him. "How old are you?"

Humor danced in his eyes. "How many years have I lived, or how old is my body?"

"Both."

"I have lived for sixty-five years. But this body is nine-teen years old."

A jolt of surprise rippled through me. I tried to smooth the shock from my face, but he must have noticed. His eyebrows lifted. "You're surprised?"

I shifted my weight. "A little. I thought you were older. I mean, coven leader, Second Tier demon . . ." I waved a hand toward him. "Your facial hair." It had all been terribly misleading.

Leo flashed a wide grin at me. "I need the illusion of maturity to lead. To frighten my enemies. If they knew how young I was, they wouldn't see me as much of a threat."

I frowned and nodded, understanding the logic behind this. It was still jarring to know he wasn't much older than I was. Well, his *body* wasn't. But even his vampire years were a shock to me. I'd been expecting him to be hundreds of years old for some reason.

Leo exhaled. "Well, I will leave you to dress, Little Nightmare. Someone will fetch you for dinner shortly."

The shadows around him rippled before swallowing him up, concealing him like a dark curtain. Then, a flapping sound echoed in the cave, and he disappeared, leaving me completely alone.

I stood there for a long moment, feeling like I'd forgotten to say something. Discomfort swirled within me until I finally realized what it was: I'd never apologized for attacking him. For abducting him. For interrogating him. And it seemed he didn't harbor any negative feelings toward me for that.

Nausea roiled in my stomach at the thought. I felt vile.

Like I was no better than the Count for the methods I used to get what I needed.

With that sour thought, I collapsed on the bed, dropping my head into my hands as regret and anguish smothered me.

31
BRIELLE

To my dismay, all the clothes in the wardrobe were floor-length satin gowns. I chose the least conspicuous one—a black gown with gleaming silver buttons on the bodice. I fidgeted with the many layers of fabric until someone cleared their throat from the cave entrance.

I jumped with a yelp, whirling to see who the intruder was.

A woman stood leaning against the rocky wall, dressed in a blood-red dress with a plunging neckline. Her alabaster skin shone, even in the shadows. Her long dark hair fell over one shoulder in elegant tresses.

I swallowed, realizing my heart rate had picked up and my face was on fire. For one wild moment, I'd thought Leo had come back, and the idea of him witnessing my struggle with this damn dress would've been mortifying. Though I wasn't sure why.

"You look as if you could use some assistance," the

woman said, her voice a low, soothing timbre. Her dark eyes gleamed with the same silver rings that Leo's had.

I watched the woman carefully. I didn't like the way she eyed me—like a predator. "I'm fine, thanks."

The woman chuckled, pushing off the wall and striding toward me, her skirt sweeping gracefully along the floor. "Nonsense. I won't bite." She smirked at me, and I felt a chill race down my spine. With a swift movement, she took the gown and sifted through the layers. "Besides," she added. "I've dressed you before."

I stiffened. "You're Guadalupe then?"

"I am."

"Nice to finally meet you. I'm Brielle Gerrick."

"So I've heard. Leo calls you *Lady Pesadilla*." Guadalupe helped me into the gown and then spun me to fasten the buttons.

My eyebrows lowered as irritation prickled through me. *Pesadilla* meant "nightmare."

Guadalupe laughed, no doubt sensing my annoyance. "He only behaves like that because your reaction fuels him."

"I know." That didn't make it any less irritating.

Guadalupe tightened the strings at the back of my dress. Then, she patted my shoulders. "A vision."

I gazed up and down my body and wrinkled my nose. "I look like an old lady at a funeral."

Guadalupe cocked her head at me and frowned.

I shook my head. "Never mind. Thank you."

"You know this is a dress ordinarily worn by commoners, right?"

I shrugged. "I don't care."

Guadalupe crossed her arms and looked me over. "Why are you here, Miss Gerrick?"

I fidgeted under her scrutiny. "Because the Count has to be stopped."

Guadalupe studied me, her eyes gleaming. "No, I don't think that's the whole reason. You see, if you wanted to stop the Count, you would have just returned to the Castillo yourself. Why are you *here*?"

I sucked in a breath. "Because I can't do it alone." The words actually caused me physical pain. I clenched my fingers into fists. "Because I'm dangerous. And I think Leo is the only one who can help me."

Guadalupe's eyebrows shot toward her hairline. "Leo?" she repeated. Then, she laughed again. "You refer to him so informally."

I rubbed my forehead. "Yes, well, where I come from, that's the norm."

"And where is it you come from?"

"Somewhere far away. Somewhere no one around here has even heard of."

Guadalupe's eyes glinted with interest, but she made no reply.

My stomach growled, and I grimaced. "Sorry, uh . . . do you know when dinner will be served?"

Guadalupe smirked at me, and in that moment, she looked just like Leo. "Most of us don't eat like the mortals do. Are you sure you wish to be a part of it?"

Discomfort roiled in my stomach, but I lifted my chin. "I

don't expect your coven to pander to my needs. I can make do."

Guadalupe frowned, looking impressed. "Very well. Follow me, Miss Gerrick."

"You can call me Brielle."

Guadalupe's lips pinched as she suppressed a smile. "As you wish."

Guadalupe led me back into the shadowy cave entrance, and I struggled to keep up with her loping strides. The darkness engulfed her almost completely. I squinted and barely made out the glow of her white skin that served as my only light. We weaved through a narrow tunnel, and my shoulders bumped against rocky edges. My feet ran into a wall several times, and I uttered many unladylike sounds in the process.

Guadalupe only laughed. "I forget how hard it is for you mortals to see in the dark."

"I am not a *mortal*," I grunted as I sidestepped another rocky surface. "I'm a witch." Though I wasn't entirely sure this was true. Most witches and warlocks could live much longer lifespans than mortals due to the magic within them. But how did that work when my magic was so broken?

Guadalupe slowed for a moment and sniffed the air. "You don't smell like a witch."

"I know," I grumbled. Had Leo not told her I was cursed? I imagined that was a big piece of information everyone in his coven ought to know.

"I should warn you," Guadalupe said, leading me onward. "Many of the demons here might not take too kindly to your presence. They know you've lived in the Castillo for a long time. They think you are a spy."

I nodded, expecting this. "I understand."

Guadalupe was silent for a moment. Then, she said, "This does not bother you?"

"I expected Leo to throw me in prison as soon as I arrived here. I expected to be treated with hostility and suspicion. Of course it doesn't surprise me. Up till now, this coven and I have been enemies."

"And still you sought us for help?"

"I had no other choice," I muttered.

The winding cave tunnels finally widened into a large cavern about twice the size of my room. Dim lanterns hung from the cavern walls. Large round cushions formed a wide circle in the middle of the room where several figures were seated. My stomach did a backflip. At first glance, it looked like the figures were wrapped in a sensual embrace, but when I looked closer, I realized they were vampires feasting on—

My stomach lurched forward painfully. The vampires were feasting on *humans*. I could smell the mortals—their sweat and excitement; the stale smell that meant an absence of magic. It was what most demons smelled when they encountered me.

The vampires were on their knees behind the cushions, drinking freely from the humans' throats. Some humans were men, but most of them were women. Their heads were thrown back to expose their necks, and a look of pure ecstasy filled their faces as they lounged comfortably on the cushions.

They looked like they were hookers. Or on drugs. Or both.

Guadalupe, who stood a few feet in front of me, turned to see why I'd stopped in my tracks. The corners of her mouth quirked up in a knowing smile, as if she reveled in my disgust. She gestured to the few remaining cushions that were unoccupied. "Have a seat."

"I—what—what's to stop them from—" I stopped short, my words choking off.

Guadalupe's smile faded. "We never feed from unwilling Donors." Her voice was hard. "No one will harm you. Not unless they want to incur Leo's wrath."

My limbs were stiff as I shuffled forward, trying to swallow down my discomfort. *Your dad's a demon,* I tried to remind myself.

But this was different. My dad was a warlock. He just practiced dark magic.

These creatures, however, were dark creatures. Feasting on humans was in their nature.

I shook my head, knowing that wasn't the case for all demons. My dad was an advocate for law-abiding demons. There were plenty of them who didn't kill or attack innocents. Perhaps this coven was like that too.

I found an unoccupied cushion and slowly sank down to it. The vampire closest to me broke away from his Donor to eye me up and down. Blood dripped down his chin, and his fangs were bared. The look in his eyes made my skin crawl.

The woman he drank from groped for him blindly, whimpering. The vampire obliged, sinking his fangs into her neck again.

I shivered. The Donors really *were* like junkies.

"Don't look so disgusted," said a low voice.

I turned and found another vampire watching me with narrowed eyes. Unlike Leo and Guadalupe, this vampire's eyes were as black as night. Blood stained the corners of his mouth, and his arm was outstretched. Drinking from his wrist was a human Donor—a man who gripped the vampire's wrist so tightly he looked like he might rip right off.

"Have you ever tasted vampire blood?" the vampire whispered.

"No," I said. I couldn't keep my eyes off the human, whose loud gulping echoed in the cave.

"Then, you couldn't possibly understand the power it provides." The vampire lifted his chin defiantly. "It grants inhuman strength and protection. Clarity and focus. It's a gift."

A few other vampires drew away from their Donors as well. I watched as the vampires sank their fangs into their own wrists and stretched their arms out to the Donors just like the vampire who spoke to me.

"One word from you," the vampire went on, "and I'll gladly gift my blood to *you* as well." He grinned widely, showing his bloody fangs.

I leveled a stare at him, squashing down my discomfort. "No, thanks."

The vampire chuckled as if I'd told a joke. He jerked his head toward the back of the room. "In that case, there are refreshments available for Donors. You are welcome to partake."

I followed his gaze to find a buffet of fruits, cheeses, and slices of bread. My stomach growled again, and I stood, ignoring the hungry look in the dark-eyed vampire's gaze as he watched me walk past him.

There was something familiar about him. Then again, I'd probably seen him before.

On the day I'd abducted Leo.

I strode over to the food and popped a few grapes in my mouth. Then, I grabbed a heel of bread and turned to face the display of feasting vampires.

The dark-eyed vampire was murmuring something to his Donor, but the human didn't respond. Then, the vampire waved his hand, and dark tendrils of smoke pooled from his fingertips. The magic engulfed the Donor's face until he broke away from the vampire's wrist and fell backward on the cushion, unconscious.

I stiffened, suddenly remembering the vampire's name. It was Jorge, the one who'd threatened me with his black magic after rescuing Leo. Leo had had to talk him down from jumping at me.

No wonder he saw me as prey. He probably would love nothing more than to sink his fangs into me.

Gradually, Jorge's Donor rolled off the cushion and staggered to his feet. Jorge muttered something and pointed to the table of food. The Donor stumbled drunkenly toward the food—toward me.

I edged out of the way, providing him full access to the buffet.

The human's eyes were dark and wild, and a few drops of blood spotted his neck. The red liquid coating his lips made me shudder. He drew a handkerchief from his pocket and wiped his mouth. Then, his gaze settled on me.

"Are you a Donor too?" he asked.

"No," I said quickly. Too quickly.

The man's head reared back. Then he shook his head. "It isn't what you think. Yes, there's a sort of . . . thrill to it. Something euphoric. But when that feeling fades, it's replaced by unencumbered strength and clarity."

I just stared at him doubtfully.

The man laughed. "You'll see. Come find me when it's not feeding day and I'm a bit more lucid." He nodded to me. "My name is Marco Romano."

"Brielle Gerrick."

Marco frowned slightly.

Before he could ask if I was French, I said hastily, "How long have you lived here, Marco?"

"Oh, I don't live here. I only visit once a month. But I've been participating as a Donor for . . . just over a year now."

My eyes widened. "You don't . . . stay here?"

Marco shook his head. "I live in the village. Many of the Donors *do* live here in the caves and are well taken care of. But I have a family, you see, and . . ." He paused and glanced at me. Then, he straightened. "Well, it would be better if they didn't know what went on here. It would be safer for them."

Something cold slithered down my spine. *He has a family.* "So why do you do it? Why do you still come here?"

Marco arched an eyebrow. "As I said before, their blood gives me strength. And the coven here provides protection. I'm able to work harder and earn more money to support my family."

A figure entered the cavern, and my gaze shifted. My heartbeat thrummed against my chest. It was Leo. Like before, he wore a loose tunic and no waistcoat. His hair fell to his shoulders in soft curls.

He strode into the cavern hand-in-hand with a woman with light brown hair tied up into an elegant bun. Her cheeks were pink with excitement.

She was human. His Donor.

Something hot bolted through me, though I couldn't tell if it was anger or . . . something else.

Leo guided the woman to the cushion and coaxed her backward until she reclined before him. The way he hovered over her, with her gaze sensual and beckoning—it made me feel like I was intruding on an intimate moment.

I tore my gaze away, swallowing hard. I found Marco watching me.

Clearing my throat, I asked, "Do all the vampires feed from you? Or just the one?"

"Only Jorge. We share a bond. He knows when I'm in danger, and I know when he thirsts."

I nodded, though my brows knitted together.

"It's a small connection," Marco went on. "Just a small tingle within me. Nothing to interrupt my life. But enough to keep us linked. To protect us both. Other Donors—the ones who feed more often—their connection is more potent. More of a presence in their lives."

More potent. My brain conjured the image of Leo bending over his Donor with her head thrown back in rapture. I sensed Leo's movement across the room, but I kept my gaze fixed determinedly on the table of food. I snatched another piece of bread and tore through it with my teeth.

"So, if you aren't a Donor, then what are you doing here?" Marco asked. His eyes were curious and unguarded, and his forward questions were so unlike the formality I was used to in the castle.

"I—well, I just—I'm here for protection," I sputtered, rubbing my nose and dropping my gaze.

"From what?"

My mind worked furiously for a response. "My own coven. They forced me out and hunted me. I'm seeking refuge until I can find a safe place to go." It wasn't a complete lie.

Marco nodded, his eyes swimming with sympathy. "I'm sorry you were forced from your home. The Serrano coven will take care of you, though."

I eyed him. "They don't . . . frighten you?"

"They did at first. I'm sure everyone is frightened by a demon at first glance. But they allowed me to visit several times before committing to becoming a Donor. They never pushed it on me or threatened me. It was simply an invitation. An offer. Almost like employment."

I looked back at the vampires, most of whom had broken free of their Donors. Some used magic to break the connection gently, like Jorge had, and others simply pulled away and gestured to the food table. Several Donors stumbled toward us as incoherently as Marco had.

The vampires plopped down on the cushions, reclining casually and chatting with one another as if they'd done something as simple as arrive home from work. A few dabbed at their mouths and wrists with handkerchiefs like Marco had.

My eyes settled on Leo, who was drinking freely from his Donor. He gripped her arms and leaned into her. Heat seared through me as I watched them, so I turned away again.

A few Donors approached the table, and I scooted away to give them free access to the food. For a long while, I stood in the corner munching on my food, watching the vampires converse and avoiding looking at Leo with his Donor. A few Donors at the table glanced at me with interest, but none of them approached me like Marco had. They looked around sleepily for a moment before lumbering away, no doubt to sleep off their blood transfusion.

Though the sight of the coven no longer made my stomach roil, I still felt empty and alone here, surrounded by people who didn't know or understand me.

All I wanted to do was get out of here and be on my own. At least by myself I would be in good company.

My eyes found Guadalupe, who relaxed on a cushion, her eyes clearer than they'd been when she'd first escorted me here. She looked at me with raised eyebrows as if asking me a question. Slowly, I nodded.

She hopped up from her cushion and approached me. "Shall I escort you to your room?"

"Yes, please."

I followed her out, keeping my gaze averted from Leo before stepping into the shadows again.

32
BRIELLE

I DREAMED OF FIRE AGAIN. FLAMES AND destruction. Screams and sobs. With every death, with every drop of blood I shed, I felt the power rising within me. Swelg. Growing stronger.

And I loved it.

When I woke, I still felt the euphoria before it faded from me. The racing of my heart from exhilaration.

My eyes opened and found a faint chink of moonlight filtering in through the cracks of the cave. It took me a moment to remember where I was.

And then I realized I was smiling. Not a soft, kind smile, but an insane, bloodthirsty one. A wicked grin of revenge and power.

My blood chilled, and the smile vanished, though I still felt a presence within me laughing.

Whether it laughed at me or out of pure joy, I couldn't tell.

But I had no plans to fall back asleep. Just imagining the horror and devastation in my dream made me shudder.

And the idea that it brought me *joy* made me want to puke.

Goosebumps erupted on my skin, and I shivered. Climbing out of bed, I hurried over to the wardrobe to wrap a shawl around myself. The cold, smooth floor felt like ice against my bare feet.

I turned, ready to leave my room, and then faltered. The narrow passageway was even more impossible to see through at night. And even if I *could* find my way, where would I go?

Something within me deflated. As I glanced back toward my bed, bile rose up my throat. I shook my head.

No, I thought firmly. *No more sleep. I'll just find my own way around the caves.*

I strode forward purposefully until I slammed straight into a cave wall.

"Ow," I muttered, rubbing the top of my forehead. Clenching my fingers into fists, I tried again. Slower this time.

I extended my arms, reaching out blindly for jagged edges and shifting away from them to avoid injury. The blackness consumed me, suffocating me—but it was a welcome change from the flames in my nightmares. With this darkness, the presence within me was quieted.

Even if it made me uncomfortable, it was a small victory knowing that presence had been silenced.

For now.

After what felt like hours, the winding tunnel opened up to a dimly lit cavern that was a bit smaller than my bedroom. Lanterns hung on the walls, similar to the dining room. The rocky walls had been smoothed, creating a clean, dome-like room. It was easy to forget I was in a cave. A few squashy armchairs surrounded a desk, and rows of bookshelves lined the walls. It wasn't nearly as impressive as the Count's library, but it seemed less overwhelming. Cozier.

The books were untidy. Some were turned to the side. Others were flipped open to a random page. When I saw the clutter, I perked up.

Perfect.

I surged forward, my fingers itching to busy themselves. But when I reached the first set of shelves, a soft voice made me jump.

"I may be wrong, but I was under the impression witches *sleep* at night."

I stiffened and whirled around, my heart racing. A figure leaned against the wall in the corner with one book open in his hand. He snapped it shut and stepped forward into the light.

It was Leo. He wore a loose black robe open at the chest, revealing a contour of muscles that made my skin feel hot. He wore no pants or shoes.

I had the sudden insane fear that his robe would spill open and flutter to the floor, leaving him stark naked.

The idea was both terrifying and thrilling. It was a baffling array of emotions, so I quickly shoved the thought from my mind.

"Can't sleep." I turned back to the bookshelves and prayed the dimness of the room masked my blush.

"So, you thought you'd help yourself to my collection of books?"

I huffed a sigh. Without looking at him, I snapped, "I won't read any of them. I just need to . . ." I shrugged. I didn't know why, but I didn't want to tell him about my compulsive tendencies. It sounded weak to me, and I hated the idea of exposing that part of myself to someone I still vaguely thought of as an enemy.

"Hmm." The light padding of his feet told me he'd moved away from the corner. Closer to me.

I finally turned to face him, only because I didn't like the idea of him sneaking up on me while my back was turned. His silvery eyes glinted in the faint light.

"You are welcome to visit my library anytime you wish," Leo said softly. "But I would caution you against roaming these caves so freely at night. Many of my brethren don't like to be disturbed. Vampires don't sleep, you see. And we have our habits and rituals that we like to maintain."

"Rituals?" *Like blood rituals?* It made sense—they *were* demons. But the idea of these vampires sacrificing innocent lives to gain power didn't sit well with me. It contrasted starkly with the idea that they didn't feed off of unwilling Donors.

Leo laughed. "Mild rituals. Animal sacrifices, prayers, and that sort of thing."

"Prayers?" I raised an eyebrow. "You don't strike me as the pious type."

"Because I'm a demon?" He stepped closer to me.

I instinctively drew away, pressing my back against the bookshelves. "No. Because you're *you*. You make a mockery of everything. I can't imagine you being serious for long enough to worship anything. Or anyone."

Leo's grin widened. "You know me well, then. Ronaldo was the most devout of all of us." His smile flickered and then vanished. "And look where that got him."

"He died for a greater purpose," I said quietly. "He told me he was satisfied with his sacrifice. That he would be rewarded for it."

"He can believe that all he likes," Leo said darkly. "But if it isn't true, then it means he died for nothing."

I lifted my chin. "I don't believe that." Or rather, I wouldn't let myself believe it. I had to trust that Ronaldo had gone to a better place. That his existence hadn't just *ended* with his sacrifice.

"Oh?" Something sparked in Leo's eyes. "So, you believe in an afterlife then? A higher power?"

I shrugged. "Maybe. How else do you explain magic?"

Leo frowned in contemplation. "A fair point. But that doesn't necessarily mean there is an afterlife."

I scoffed. "How can you *not* believe in an afterlife? Seers and Thinkers have been communing with spirits for thousands of years. What, you think those spirits are just hanging out in an empty void, waiting to be summoned?"

Leo's brows knitted together, and I knew I must've confused him with my modern jargon. "You make a good argument, I suppose." He cocked his head at me. "Where are you from, Brielle?"

Shock rippled through me at the usage of my name—again. Why did that affect me? Maybe because he'd called me "Little Nightmare" for so long that I wasn't used to him actually using my name like a civilized person. "What do you mean?"

"I mean, you speak Spanish, but your name is French. You don't speak like us, and you don't look like us. So where are you from?"

"Cuba," I blurted without thinking. It was the first thing that came to mind. Besides, blonds in Cuba weren't entirely unheard of. My dad was blond, after all.

Leo's head reared back. "Cuba? Where is that?"

"It's an island in the Caribbean. Near the Americas. Some Spaniards settled there . . ." I trailed off, racking my brain. "About two hundred years ago." *I think.*

Leo stroked his short goatee. "I see. And how did you come to be here? In Segovia?"

I stared at him, finally realizing how little he actually knew. He'd only just found out about the time loop, so of course he wouldn't know about the portal or where the guests of the castle came from.

I hesitated before responding. Though I no longer had any allegiance to the Count, I still felt loyal to some of my friends back in the castle. Izzy, in particular. Maybe even Riker, if I could let go of the pain festering inside me from his betrayal. His refusal to help me.

Even though I understood why he'd done it.

Instead of answering Leo's question, I asked, "What do you know of the residents in the castle?"

Leo watched me for a long moment. "They come from many places. Some of them speak differently. Like you." His eyes glinted as he gave me a calculated look. "But, also like you, their arrival here is a mystery."

I didn't like the gleam in his eyes. It reminded me of a predator stalking its prey. I tried backing up, but I was out of room. A hard shape pressed into my back—a book, no doubt. I had nowhere left to run.

"Do you care to enlighten me?" Leo asked, stepping closer to me.

I swallowed. "Maybe. If you give me something in return."

Leo barked out a laugh. "Haven't I given you enough? I've provided you with refuge from the castle. I saved you from the mages who were trying to abduct you. The way I see it, *you* should be offering *me* a favor."

"I came here to fulfill your brother's dying wish," I said. "It was as much for your benefit as it was for mine."

Leo's expression turned cold. "I doubt that."

I leveled a stare at him, unflinching. I refused to back down.

Leo sighed, dropping his hands. "Name your terms."

"Let me look through your library."

He raised an eyebrow. "Is that all?"

"You told me things about Lilith's curse," I said quietly. "Of how to fight off her influence. I need . . ." I trailed off, realizing I was about to expose myself. My fears. I swallowed. "I need to find a way to survive. To push her out. Your brother said there was a way."

Leo scrutinized me. "Did he?"

I nodded.

Leo rubbed his chin, his eyes distant. "There is . . . more to the tales than I originally told you. I'd be happy to show you everything I have regarding Lilith's curse."

I exhaled in relief, but the feeling was short-lived. Leo stepped even closer. Close enough for me to smell him. A sharp scent mingled with something spicy that made my head spin.

"I must ask something else of you," he purred. His face was so close that if I turned my head, our noses would touch.

My trembling hands gripped the shelf behind me. "What is it?" I rasped.

"Consider it a bargain in exchange for my hospitality. In exchange for *not* imprisoning you as an enemy to this coven."

I gritted my teeth, waiting. But he just smirked at me. Like he knew how uncomfortable I was. "Well?" I snapped.

He chuckled, his soft breath tickling my face. "I could use your expertise in crafting spells. Ronaldo's sacrifice was valuable in that I know about this 'time loop' and who cast it to begin with. But I have been researching ways to break the Count's enchantments for months now. We finally broke through his wards only to discover we had unlocked a different spell." He paused, pressing his lips together in a way that made my stomach coil. "I must admit I'm at a loss where to look next."

"And how am I supposed to help?" I asked, struggling to keep my voice even.

"You have cast unusual spells before. Spells I've never heard of. How?"

"I wrote them."

"You . . . *wrote* them? What does that mean?"

I sighed. *Must I spell everything out for him?* "I invented them myself. I created them. I formed them in my mind." I spread my arms. "Need more explanations than that?"

Leo waved a hand in irritation. "No, that's quite enough. I just wasn't aware . . ." He trailed off, frowning. "I have tried for years to write my own spells and haven't been very successful. How do you do it?"

I shrugged. "I just use common phrases found in the Grimoire. Put them together and make sure it rhymes. It doesn't always work. You have to have the right intent."

"Intent?"

"I mean, your goal has to align with the magic as well as your level of abilities. Like if I tried to set this whole room on fire, it wouldn't work because that's too much power. Or if I tried to heal a stab wound by concentrating on an illness, that wouldn't work either." I thought of Riker and his vision and how I'd healed him from it. My stomach wound itself in knots. That was the day we'd kissed.

Leo stroked his chin thoughtfully. "I see."

"It's easier to do the spells in English," I added. "There's a wider vocabulary."

Leo smirked at me. "*Sí, pero es mucho más delicioso usar mi lengua materna.*" *Yes, but it is so much more delicious to use my native tongue.* The words poured from his lips like a caress, and I resisted the urge to fidget again. "We have a deal," he murmured, his voice smooth. "You have access to my resources here in exchange for your help with spells— and your answers to my questions."

I nodded stiffly, my throat dry. "Fine."

Leo grinned widely, and I was close enough to make out the tiny points of his fangs. He stretched an arm out, gesturing to the armchairs. "Shall we?"

"Now?" I sputtered.

"Unless you suddenly feel tired enough to return to your chambers?" He arched an eyebrow at me, his eyes dancing with amusement.

My nostrils flared. *No way am I sleeping anytime soon.* My heart was racing far too quickly, and at any rate, I had no desire to succumb to my nightmares again.

I huffed a breath and strode away from him toward the chairs. Being free of his scent and his piercing gaze made me feel like I could breathe again. I collapsed in a chair, sinking backward into the soft fabric. Leo took the seat opposite me, lounging with one arm stretched out but still looking as regal as a prince.

"Where should I start?" I asked.

Leo's eyes gleamed with anticipation. "Start at the beginning. Start with where *you* came from."

33
LEO

I SAT IN MY CHAIR FOR A LONG WHILE AFTER BRIELLE finished answering my questions. My back was rigid, and my body hadn't moved in over an hour, save for my lips uttering questions.

It couldn't possibly be true. It *couldn't*—

But it was. Down to my bones, I knew the Count would stop at nothing to achieve his goal. I just hadn't realized he had done *so much* in the name of finding Lilith's cursed witch.

Finding Brielle.

That bastard had drawn a dozen innocent young casters to his prison of a castle, all with the intent of torturing each of them if it meant finding Lilith.

I stared vacantly at the smooth, cold floor under my bare feet. I rubbed my chin. Despite the horror of it all, I could acknowledge one thing: I had what the Count wanted more than anything. I had Brielle.

Of course, it meant little now that I knew Lucia and Ronaldo were dead. But perhaps if I delivered Brielle to him, he would agree to lift the curse. Then, my coven could escape this "time loop" and be free. We were innocent, after all. Now that we knew *who* Lilith's cursed witch was, it only made sense to free everyone else.

My eyes shifted to Brielle. Her brown eyes appraised me, her brows knitting together as if she were trying to read my expression.

I smoothed my face and raised my eyebrows. "Is that everything?"

Her head reared back. "You were expecting *more*?"

I lifted one shoulder. "I'm no longer surprised by your shocking revelations." I smirked. "I've learned to expect the unexpected with you, Brielle."

She shifted in her seat, her blood warming from my words. But she fixed me with a fierce scowl that almost made me laugh. "So, what's your plan then?"

I blinked. "I beg your pardon?"

"What's your plan for finding a cure for me?"

I stared at her for a long moment, knowing I couldn't disclose everything to her. I needed her to trust me—even though I certainly didn't trust her.

I took a breath. "My sister spoke of the monster within her. We assumed she was speaking of Lilith, but over time we realized there was another . . . presence inside her. Another being."

"*Three* beings?" Brielle asked incredulously.

"So it would seem. She was terrified that Lilith would

take the creature. Lucia wanted to keep the creature safe from Lilith's influence. But in the end, she wasn't strong enough." Regret filled my throat, but I shook it off before it consumed me. "But if *you* prove a strong enough vessel, then you should be able to push Lilith out."

Brielle shook her head. "I don't know *how*."

"Is she possessing you now?"

She snorted. "Of course not."

"Why not?"

"Because . . . I'm awake." Her voice was uncertain.

"When was the last time she possessed you?"

Brielle thought for a moment. "In the dungeon. At the castle. A few days after we spoke in the courtyard. No more than a week after that."

I smirked. *Spoke in the courtyard.* What a gentle way to say *abducted and interrogated.* "And she hasn't possessed you since then?"

"No. Well, I still have nightmares." She clamped her mouth shut like she hadn't meant to disclose this information.

Gallant man that I was, I chose to ignore her confession. "Why do you think she hasn't possessed you again? She took over your mind completely, yes?"

Brielle nodded, her face ashen. "I . . . scorched the wall. Or the creature did. I don't remember any of it."

I went still. "Did you kill anyone?"

She shook her head.

I stroked my chin, frowning in contemplation. "What

was different this time? Was this the first time she possessed you?"

"Yeah."

"So, what changed?" I asked myself more than her, but she still responded.

"Well, the Count was torturing me," she bit out. "I was starving. Weak. I had no motivation."

I snapped my fingers, and she jumped. "You gave in to her?"

Brielle's mouth opened and closed.

"You succumbed?" I clarified. "You let the creature take over?"

"I . . . guess?"

I stood and strode over to a stack of papers scattered along the desk. Flipping through them, I finally found what I was looking for: a journal entry of Lucia's I'd been studying. "Lucia often spoke of 'giving in' to the creature. Of freely offering up herself."

"To Lilith?" Brielle asked in horror.

"No. To the creature—whatever it is."

"I don't understand. If she gives herself up, then won't she be surrendering to Lilith instead?"

"She spoke of the creature as if it had its own soul. As if it were a separate entity. Separate from her *and* Lilith."

Brielle was silent for several moments. Then, she said quietly, "Your sister died, Leo. I don't think giving myself up freely would be the right choice."

I sighed and sank back into the chair, staring hard at my sister's familiar, curly handwriting. "Ronaldo suspected

Lucia was struggling because of the creature and not Lilith."

Brielle's gaze snapped to me. "What?"

"He believed Lucia's body wasn't strong enough to handle a full transformation. That she tried to release the creature, and it didn't work."

"And . . . what do *you* think?"

I didn't answer for a while. "I don't know," I whispered. "But if Ronaldo is correct, then that means the creature tried to free itself and it died along with Lucia in the process. It is easier for me to blame Lilith and link her together with the creature—since it is because of them my sister is dead." Darkness swirled within me, and something solid hardened in my chest.

My eyes flicked to Brielle, and fear stirred in her expression before she quickly composed herself.

"If the creature died with your sister, how am *I* accessing it?" Brielle asked.

"The way my sister described it, the creature was tethered to her magic. Without her magic . . ." I trailed off with a shrug. "It wouldn't be able to survive. Ronaldo speculated that Nightcasters each have their own creature tied to their magic, and that is why Lilith targets them."

Brielle frowned in contemplation, her brows knitting together. Silence fell between us, and I was suddenly returned to those dark days just before Lucia's death.

I blinked to rid myself of the haunting memories. "Even so, I feel it is noteworthy that you have resisted Lilith's influence for months now."

All the color drained from Brielle's face. "What?"

I stilled, reading the horror and confusion on her face. I frowned. "You said the last time Lilith controlled you was in the dungeon, yes? A week after you abducted me? That was several months ago."

Brielle shook her head slowly. "No. That can't be right. It wasn't even summer when . . ." She trailed off, her eyes growing distant.

I leaned forward in my chair. "What do you remember?"

Brielle swallowed. "I remember being in the Count's dungeon. But I don't know how long I was down there. The Count withheld food from me, so it *couldn't* have been months."

"Well, I assure you, it's harvest season. Don't you recall the cooler weather when you traveled here?"

Brielle's mouth opened and closed, her eyes blank. "Merciful Lilith. You're right. The trees were bare when I came here. The leaves were dying. It—it *is* autumn. I can't believe I didn't . . ." She shook her head again. "Normally I'm always cold, but with the powers inside me, I didn't feel the chill at all. I just assumed . . ." She broke off again, blinking rapidly before looking at me. "How is this possible? Does time pass differently outside the castle?"

I looked at her for a long moment, trying to discern if she was playing a trick on me. But the blood pounding in her body betrayed her fear, as did the lack of color in her cheeks. Her eyes were wide with horror.

The truth then. "My sister was often consumed by the fire of the creature within her. The worst of her fits was when she was unresponsive for three months. We all felt her heart beating and her blood pumping, so we knew she hadn't passed. But she didn't move. She was—"

"Catatonic," Brielle supplied.

My brows furrowed.

"It's a word used in my time," she said quietly.

"Well, we thought that was it. That Lilith had claimed her, and her body was no more. But then, months later, she returned to us as if it had only been hours or days. Like nothing had changed."

"But . . . how did she survive that long without food? Or, I guess, blood? And what did Lilith do with her during that time?"

"I don't know," I answered honestly. "But as for blood, I could smell the blood within her from her last feeding. It was like her body had been . . . preserved through time. Unaltered. Unchanged. Like she—"

"Traveled through time," Brielle said in a soft whisper.

I sighed. "You must stop doing that."

Brielle's lips twitched with a smile. "Sorry."

The sight of a smile on her face—even a faint one—made me grin. "I feel I am at a loss conversing with you. Your vocabulary is much more advanced than mine due to our—what was it? Three hundred years' difference?" Just the thought sent my mind spiraling, but I kept the easy amusement on my face.

Brielle's mouth suddenly twisted in a grimace, and her skin took on a greenish tint. "I—are you telling me I *time traveled*?"

My brows knitted together. "I am suggesting you endured the same thing my sister did. That Lilith preserved you and sent you forward."

"But *why?*" She rubbed her arms, still looking ill. And I couldn't blame her. Knowing Lilith had taken over her body for *months* for unknown reasons would've unsettled me as well.

I remained silent as I watched her, trying not to pity her. But something in my heart ached at the sight of her forlorn expression.

Brielle gasped, lifting a hand to her mouth. "If it's been *months,* then that means those at the castle . . ." She paused and placed a hand to her forehead. "Merciful Lilith. *Izzy.*"

I frowned as she jumped from her chair and strode toward the cave tunnels. Then, she stopped short and turned to me. The belligerence and strength in her face had returned. Her jaw was rigid with determination.

"I need to rescue my friend from the castle," she said in a commanding voice.

I laughed. "No."

Her eyes narrowed. "You of all people know what the Count is capable of. The other casters in the castle are *innocent.* I only got out because of your brother—and because of Izzy. I've got to help her. With me gone, the Count will suspect her first. He knows we're friends. And if it's been *months,* then she might already be in trouble."

Slowly, I rose from my chair and crossed my arms, looking down at her. "I am *not* risking my men's lives to rescue your friend. We risked enough taking you in. The best thing we can do for the people in the castle is to reverse the Count's curse so they can leave the city. And with the Count's mages gone—"

"Gone?" she repeated sharply. "What do you mean, gone?"

I lifted my chin. I wasn't sorry for the order. It had to be done. "We killed them."

Something like horror struck her features, but then it was quickly smoothed away by a reluctant acceptance. Slowly, she nodded. The conflicting emotions on her face made her blood pulse with unease. My head throbbed from taking it all in.

"What about the other mages?" she asked in a hushed voice. "The ones who don't live at the castle?"

I shrugged. "The Count will undoubtedly send for them. But it will take time." I paused. "As I was saying, with the mages gone, the Count is at a disadvantage. He's weak. Now is the time for us to strike."

"Exactly. Now is the time for us to strike the *castle* and rescue my friends."

I held up a hand. "Friends? I thought it was just one person."

Brielle threw her hands in the air, groaning in frustration. "What does it matter? You're obviously not going to help me."

"And why should I? You haven't exactly been trustworthy toward me since we met."

Brielle glared at me, her nostrils flaring. "Can you blame me? You attacked the castle. That was my home."

I took a step toward her. "Can *you* blame *me*? That bastard tortured and killed my siblings. I would've done anything to rescue them. To relieve their suffering."

Fire burned in the space between us. I could feel the heat rolling off her body in waves. It made my head spin.

We glared at each other for a long moment. Then, to my surprise, Brielle exhaled, conceding. "You're right. I don't blame you."

I blinked. *What the hell?* I truthfully believed she would fight me right then. I'd almost wanted her to.

I cleared my throat and nodded. "Good. Well . . . let's—"

"But I'm still going back for Izzy."

I exhaled in exasperation. Of course she wouldn't have given in that easily. I shot her a sharp look. "*No.*"

"Leo—"

"If you go back there, the Count will do *everything* in his power to trap you again. And who's to say he hasn't convinced the others in the castle that you're the enemy? That you aren't to be trusted? What if he's convinced your friend as well and she betrays you?"

"She would never."

"You don't know that."

She crossed her arms and glared at me. "What happened to the old Leo, the one who was kind and gentle when I first got here? The one who promised he'd do everything in his power to help me?" Her cheeks were red, but her eyes blazed with an intensity that made my blood boil.

I drew closer to her, enjoying the way her pulse quickened at my nearness. "He's still here. And still willing to help you. *Here* in the caves."

"But—"

"We don't have much time," I said, my voice growing louder and my blood pulsing in anger. "You told me your priority is to find a way to escape Lilith's curse. *My* priority is breaking free of the Count's time loop. And now you suddenly have a *new* goal you want to pursue? This is madness!"

"Leo, I *have* to!"

I gritted my teeth. "You are *not* free to roam about, Brielle!"

"Why not?" she snapped.

"Because I don't trust you!" I cried.

Her eyes widened briefly.

Dammit, Leo, I said to myself. I hadn't intended to reveal this to her just yet, but I couldn't ignore the rage building inside me. It was either yell at her, or drink her blood— which, obviously, would've crossed a line. "You have fought me every moment since we met until it served *your* purposes and *you* needed help. Then, you expected me to meet your demands and provide you with refuge. I have been nothing but hospitable and accommodating to you, which is more than I can say of *you* when my life was in *your* hands. And now, despite the mysterious circumstances of you showing up here unannounced, you expect me to travel *back* to the home of my enemy—the place where my family was killed—and sacrifice my men to rescue someone I don't know." I stared down at her, cocking my head. "Do you not understand why I would be suspicious? Why I might suspect you to be leading me to a trap?"

Indignation and fury swelled in her eyes. She gritted her teeth. "I am *not* a spy, Leo."

I lifted my shoulders and frowned. "Your actions have given me no reason to trust you, Brielle."

"If you don't trust me, then what the hell have I been doing here?" Brielle shouted. "What about our conversations, the things we've said to each other? Why would you talk to me like that if you still saw me as an enemy?"

I leaned close to her until I could taste her sweet breath and feel the anger rippling through her body. Something within me growled like a hungry beast. "Because it seems you and I treat our threats differently, Brielle." I paused, and my gaze darted briefly to her lips. She wet them, and the beast within me rumbled in response. "And just because I don't trust you doesn't mean I see you as an enemy."

I gathered my shadows around me and shifted to my bat form. Ignoring her anger and confusion and the fact that I'd unintentionally revealed my mistrust, I flew from the room before I did something else I regretted.

34
BRIELLE

STILL REELING AFTER THE STRANGE ARGUMENT WITH Leo, I stumbled my way through the caverns until I made it back to my own room. My heart thrummed anxiously in my chest, my head spinning from what I'd learned.

I time traveled. It's been months *since the Count imprisoned me.*

Izzy could already be in danger.

If Leo thought I would just sit here in this luxurious guest cavern without doing anything, then he was an idiot.

A part of me knew he was right—that my time was limited. That Izzy's life would mean nothing if I exploded into a fiery beast and killed her. I *had* to find a way to push Lilith out.

But I couldn't ignore my friend. Not after she risked everything to get me out.

I'll bring her here, I told myself. *Then, we'll all work together to find a way to get rid of Lilith.*

A small voice nagged within me, still unsatisfied. But I pushed it away, determined to focus on rescuing Izzy. She could already be imprisoned. Tortured. Or even killed. I *had* to save her.

But I needed to keep up appearances with the coven. The vampires had sharper senses than I did. If I tried sneaking out right away, someone would figure it out.

I had to wait until the right moment. Until they were all feeding.

Over the next few days, I bided my time, trying to observe the vampires' schedule and get my bearings in the confusing tunnels. I wandered the caves, sometimes stumbling awkwardly into another vampire's room and blustering my way through an apology before rushing out.

At night I slept fitfully, my dreams plagued by flames and screams. I often woke covered in sweat with that same disturbing euphoria taking over me.

I didn't go back to sleep after the nightmares. Instead, I wound through the tunnels, trying to familiarize myself with the complicated network of paths.

One afternoon, I found myself in the dining room. The cushions were spread in a circle and unoccupied, though there was one vampire feeding on his Donor. My heart sank when I noticed them. If he was feeding, then it meant the coven staggered their feedings. So not all of them would be preoccupied at once.

Which I should've figured out. It would've been stupid to leave the coven defenseless during feeding time.

I strode toward the snack bar like I belonged there,

ignoring the vampire and his Donor. They seemed completely enthralled by each other; the Donor had her body wrapped around the vampire in a tight embrace.

I munched on a few slices of cheese and gathered some bread and apples in my skirts for my journey. Then, I noticed a knife used for cutting fruit. I buried it between the apples and casually strolled out of the cave.

The darkness of the tunnels pressed in on me, blinding me. I ran my free hand along the edges of the cavern, feeling for the sharp crevice I remembered during my last trip through the caves.

But I didn't find it. Frowning, I stumbled farther into the tunnel. Low murmurs reached my ears. Then, a high-pitched giggle.

I stopped short. This definitely wasn't the way to my room.

A deep voice said something quietly, and the girl laughed again.

I swallowed, my throat dry. I *definitely* shouldn't be here.

But . . . maybe whoever it was could point me in the right direction.

Gathering my courage, I plastered a look on my face that I hoped seemed innocent. Then, I strode forward, hefting my skirts up to conceal my stolen food. The tunnel opened to a wide cavern. A vanity rested on one end of the wall, covered with jewelry and combs. Next to it was a wardrobe thrown open wide, revealing several silky gowns.

On the opposite wall was a king-sized bed, and two figures were tangled in the sheets.

My heart lurched in my throat, and my face burned. *Idiot, idiot, idiot.*

I whirled, hoping to flee, when a voice stopped me.

"Brielle?"

I was so startled I almost dropped the food from my skirts. My insides froze, and I slowly turned. The sheet fell forward to reveal Leo in bed with a woman with light brown hair. I recognized her as his Donor.

Heat rushed through me, fierce and embarrassing. I shook my head numbly. "I—sorry. I got lost. I . . ."

Leo laughed, waving a hand. The sheet slipped farther down, revealing a sculpted torso of scars and hard muscle. The sight made my tongue feel like sandpaper. "You can join us, if you like."

The girl uttered a shrill squeal and slapped Leo's arm playfully. "Oh, stop. He's just teasing." She turned to me with a superior look on her face. Her eyebrows lifted just a bit, like she felt she needed to explain Leo's behavior to me. Like I was a child.

I resisted the urge to glare at her. "Right. Um. Sorry to intrude."

My face was on fire as I turned and ran from the room. Leo and the girl's laughter echoed behind me, and anger swirled within me. I couldn't tell if I was angrier at myself for getting into this position, or at Leo and the girl for laughing at my expense.

As I weaved blindly through the tunnels again, I focused on another unpleasant feeling worming its way through me

—a mixture of discomfort and embarrassment. Leo *slept* with his Donors? Was that even allowed?

Well, obviously. The girl sounded like she was enjoying herself.

Which sent another confusing array of emotions through me. My skin burned again, and I pushed the thoughts from my mind. Gritting my teeth, I surged forward until, finally, I reached my bedroom. I placed the food and knife in a sack and shoved it under my pillow. Then, I sank onto the mattress with a deep sigh. Exhaustion prickled at the corners of my eyes, and my body sagged. The sleep deprivation from the past few days was wearing on me.

Every part of me longed to leave this place. I had to get Izzy out of the castle.

But . . . then what? Go into hiding with her? Doom her to be slaughtered by the monster within me whenever Lilith saw fit?

I covered my face with my hands. More than anything, I wanted to be with my family again. They would know what to do. Between the Count torturing me and Leo suspecting me of being a spy, I yearned to be with people who trusted me. Who loved me. People I could trust not to turn on me or try to kill me.

If Mom, Dad, and Angel were here, I knew they'd work with me to find a solution—one that didn't kill me.

"Are you all right?" a soft voice asked.

I yelped and nearly jumped out of my skin. Guadalupe leaned against the opening of the cavern, watching me with an unreadable expression.

I couldn't believe I hadn't smelled her. Being in these caves—surrounded by vampires—had dulled my senses. The whole place reeked of vampire, so I could never tell when one was approaching.

Which made my own scent even more obvious. I tried not to let that deter my plans to sneak out and find Izzy.

Now that I noticed it, a faint, flowery smell reached my nose, mingling with the dulled scent of vampire that I'd grown accustomed to.

I rubbed my forehead and forced a smile. "Yes, I'm fine."

Guadalupe cocked her head and took a hesitant step forward, careful to avoid the sunlight filtering from the ceiling. "You don't need to lie. I know you're enduring a lot right now."

I watched her for a moment, remembering her confusion earlier when it seemed like she didn't know I was cursed. "What do you know about me?" I asked slowly.

Guadalupe shrugged. "Only what Leo has told me. You were imprisoned and injured by the Count. You escaped and came here."

I blinked, waiting for more. But that was it.

That's all he told her?

It seemed stupid. Why wouldn't he warn his coven about me?

"He didn't tell you anything else?" I asked.

Guadalupe said nothing for a while. Then, she murmured, "My cousin keeps many things from us. He's our leader, and he's earned his privacy. I know there is more to you than what appears, Brielle. But if Leo isn't prepared to divulge that information, then I must respect that."

He keeps many things from them. That didn't surprise me. But then I thought of his sister. How many people knew about her and her fate? How many knew that Lilith had tried to possess her?

If Lucia had been kept a secret, then it would make sense that Leo would conceal the truth about me as well.

But that made me insanely curious. *Why?* If his coven was so important to him, why would he remain closed off like that? His sister was gone. What harm would it do to open up about her? Besides, Ronaldo had told me that demons revered Nightcasters because they were seen as holy vessels for Lilith. Surely, revealing his sister's curse would've been a *good* thing, right?

"You seem to understand about keeping secrets," Guadalupe said suddenly, her eyes appraising me shrewdly.

My gaze snapped to her. "What do you mean?"

"You haven't told us anything about yourself—who you are, where you came from, or why you're here. You're as elusive as Leo himself."

I shifted my weight on the bed, suddenly uncomfortable. *I am* not *like Leo.*

But her words speared through me. I'd been thinking about how ridiculous it was that he hadn't opened up to anyone here. But how long had it taken me to open up to Izzy about my secret? And I'd *never* opened up to my family about how alone I'd felt.

I'd always been so determined to be strong and capable. I'd seen opening up as weak.

In many ways, I still saw it that way.

I rubbed my nose. "It's hard to know who to trust. I thought I could trust those in the castle, but . . ." I trailed off with a shrug.

Guadalupe chuckled without humor. "I understand." She strode closer—as close as she could get without touching the sunlight. "I want you to know, Brielle, that you are under our protection. You are an honorary member of this coven now. As long as you are with us and don't betray us, you will be safe."

I almost laughed. "I'm a light witch. I can't be part of this coven of vampires."

"You certainly can," Guadalupe said in a firm voice. "We consider the human Donors a part of our coven as well. Your species—your magic—makes no difference. You are still ours to protect."

A lump formed in my throat, and I looked at her. "You can't mean that. Why would you trust me?"

"I never said we trust you. I don't even trust Leo half the time. But the Count has made an enemy of you just like he has with us. In a sense, that makes us allies."

Enemy of my enemy . . . I pressed my lips together and nodded slightly.

The corners of Guadalupe's mouth curved upward in a smile. "We feed in an hour. You are welcome to join us." She inclined her head and left the cave.

My heart jolted in my chest, waking me from the emotions swirling within me. *One hour.*

As soon as Guadalupe's flowery scent vanished, I jumped up, wriggling out of my ridiculous gown and into the trousers I'd arrived in. Thankfully, someone had washed them, but they still reeked of blood and dirt.

I didn't bother putting on a shirt. Instead, I found a jacket in the wardrobe and wrapped it tightly around myself, then used a belt to tighten it further. My chest left much to be desired, so it wasn't like anyone would see anything exciting anyway. Besides, I had no other shirts to wear, and I couldn't exactly move stealthily in those stifling gowns.

I slid the knife into my pocket, grabbed my sack of food, and looked at myself in the mirror. The jacket covered me well enough. In fact, I looked perfectly appropriate if I'd been in my time.

My time. I didn't even want to dwell on that. But once I thought it, I couldn't push it from my mind. Would I be stuck here forever? Would I ever see my family again?

Shut up, Brie, I snapped at myself. *One thing at a time.*

When I deemed myself ready, I approached the tunnels and listened hard.

Nothing. I sniffed deeply, closing my eyes and trying to filter through the smells. Guadalupe's scent lingered, but it was stale. Nothing else but the musty scent of moisture and rocks.

I took a deep breath and raised my free hand.

"*Magic above and powers that be,*

Light the way in front of me."

A faint blue glow emanated from my outstretched hand, illuminating the path before me. I surged forward, knowing my time was limited. The glow was like a beacon, alerting the others to my presence. If anyone noticed it, they would investigate.

So I ran through the tunnels, using the light to guide my way. I noticed the crevice I'd found earlier and turned right, away from the dining room. I paused for a moment, sniffing again. Foliage. Dead leaves. A chill in the air.

Yes, I was close.

I kept going and uttered a spell to remove the light when I noticed sunlight just ahead. My chest swelled with excitement.

Freedom. *I'm coming, Izzy.*

I stopped short when a familiar voice drawled, "Going somewhere?"

35
LEO

BRIELLE'S PULSE RACED, HER EYES WIDE WHEN THEY locked onto mine. I smirked and crossed my arms. Did she honestly think she could escape so easily?

My arrogant expression made her blood boil, and I laughed. "Come now, Brielle. We've already discussed this."

"You don't want to risk your coven? Fine. I'll go myself."

"And reveal my secrets to the Count? I don't think so."

Brielle stepped forward, her nostrils flaring. "I am *not* abandoning my friend."

I stepped closer to her too, and she shrank away from me involuntarily. I felt her heart race, giving me a sense of power. "You were the one who begged me to chain you up when you first got here. Because you were dangerous. Say you rescue your friend and escape the castle. Then what? Doom her to die by Lilith's hand?"

She flinched, and for a moment I regretted my words. But no, she needed to hear this. I vividly remembered the explosion in the Castillo de Coca when my sister had met her demise at Lilith's hand.

Brielle needed to know about this.

"Are you strong enough for Lilith?" I asked in a soft voice. "Because if you aren't, I've seen what happens when she tries to take over. It's catastrophic. Do you really want to subject your friend to this fate?"

Brielle gritted her teeth. "You don't know that."

"Very true. But your friend is probably living comfortably in the castle right now."

"Or she isn't because she's living with that monster."

Something inside me swelled with satisfaction hearing her speak of the Count with such hatred, but I shoved the feeling down. "I know you aren't accustomed to following orders," I said slowly. "But my order is final. Do not cross me, Brielle."

She lifted her chin. "Or what?"

A challenge. Fire roared within me in response. I cocked my head at her. "I've bested you before."

Brielle dropped her sack to the ground. She drew a knife from her trousers and brandished it toward me. "You won't succeed again."

I threw back my head and laughed. Then she tackled me, pinning me to the ground. My shadows swirled around me in response, but before I could shift, she muttered a hasty spell.

"*Magic above, hear my call,*
Stop this demon from changing form."

Something shifted in the air, and I stared at her, momentarily frozen.

Then, I realized what was different—the spell was in Spanish.

Blue magic poured from her fingertips and wrapped around me, suffocating me with the nauseating scent of jasmine and vanilla. It stung my nostrils, and I coughed. The shadows around me swirled angrily, but then the blue enchantment engulfed me. My shadows diminished, receding as if retreating from an enemy.

Coward, I told my magic. I tried shifting, but nothing happened.

Seething, I glanced at Brielle, who wore a triumphant smirk on her face.

My blood roared. My fangs emerged, and I hissed at her.

Brief alarm registered on her face, but when I lunged, she tumbled backward instinctively. I grabbed for her again, but she dodged. I summoned my shadows without thinking, and nothing happened. Then, I remembered my predicament, and fury filled me again.

We were both on our feet. Brielle sidestepped my movements easily, and the arrogance in her expression was so familiar to me.

It mirrored my own.

She had goaded me. I had fallen right into her trap. The smugness in her face was like a slap. It jolted me. Awakened me to how juvenile I was behaving.

I hadn't realized I was hunched over until a solid realization hit me. I gradually relaxed my posture and withdrew my fangs. Clearing my throat, I smoothed my ruffled hair.

But Brielle was unconvinced. She crossed her arms and raised her eyebrows. "Not fun being 'bested,' is it?"

A low growl rumbled in my throat, and I drew closer to her. "You forget yourself, Little Nightmare. You don't want to make an enemy of me."

Brielle scoffed. "We were enemies the instant you attacked me in the armory."

Well, that was true.

Familiar scents wafted behind me. I didn't need to turn to know Guadalupe and Miguel were close by, ready to assist their leader. I lifted a hand to hold them off. I didn't need help.

What kind of leader would I be if I couldn't handle this petite girl with no magic?

I grinned at her. "You're a worthy foe, Little Nightmare."

Her blood pounded in response to the irritating nickname, and I laughed at the indignation in her expression.

She attacked again, swiping her blade so it nicked the skin of my neck. I hissed, jumping backward in alarm.

Trust your instincts, I told myself. I couldn't shift, but I was still a fighter.

Brielle swung her fists. I ducked, then jumped. I tackled her from below her waist, and we collapsed to the ground. Her arms flailed, but I pinned them down, pressing my hips against hers to hold her in place.

"Get off me!" she grunted, still thrashing against my grip.

"Not until you yield."

"Never. You'll have to suck me dry."

I chuckled. "Don't tempt me, Little Nightmare."

"Go ahead!" she spat, glancing behind me. "Go ahead and drain an unwilling victim in front of your coven."

I stilled. Something in my chest rang from her words.

She leaned her face closer to mine. "Do it," she hissed.

I stared at her. Her labored breaths tickled my face, and her scent overwhelmed me. She smelled like the sea after a storm. Her panting made my stomach clench. She caught her lower lip between her teeth, and the beast within me rumbled. I was suddenly aware of the contours of her soft body pressed against mine. I felt the rapid beating of her heart, the heat rising in her cheeks at our proximity.

I leaned closer. And she did too.

Then, a burst of magic tickled the air. I stiffened, raising my head. A sudden fierce wind stirred the leaves in the trees, hissing against the forest. The wind intensified, spinning like a cyclone and tousling my hair. Shouts of alarm echoed behind me.

I jumped to my feet and helped Brielle up, our quarrel forgotten. The wind surged, stinging my eyes and pushing against me. I staggered, clinging to Brielle's hand as we struggled to return to the shelter of the caves.

Then, lightning crackled in the sky. A burst of white light consumed the forest. I cried out, shielding my face from the burn of the light.

Three figures materialized in front of us. The storm subsided, and the lightning died. Gradually, my vision returned, and I squinted at the visitors. A blond man stood next to a woman with dark, curly hair streaked with gray. A girl stood beside them, about Brielle's age, with black hair and bronze skin.

Alarm raced through me, but I heard Brielle suck in a sharp gasp, staggering backward in shock. Her wide eyes drifted over the three visitors, her face slack with disbelief.

"Who are you?" I demanded loudly. I had the sudden urge to draw Brielle close to me, but I ignored it.

Brielle answered my question. Her voice was a hushed whisper. "They . . . they're my family."

36

BRIELLE

I felt like I was dreaming—because that was the only time I saw my family. When I wasn't cursed with nightmares of fire and devastation, my parents' and sister's faces often swam in my head, taunting me. Reminding me I would never see them again.

Yet here they were.

They wore traveling cloaks and leather trousers like they belonged in this time period. Their faces were worn and haggard, and Dad had a strange burn on one side of his face that had scabbed over.

They glanced at each of the vampires who had gathered at the cave entrance to investigate the disturbance. Mom's face was pale as her eyes quickly flitted from each face until they finally settled on mine. Our gazes locked, and my heart lurched in my chest as if finally realizing this was *real.* This wasn't a dream.

"Mom," I said, my voice breaking.

"Brie!" She surged forward, and several vampires lunged, including Leo. Mom threw her arms out, and two vampires soared backward from her Telekinetic magic.

"Take her!" Leo roared.

"No, wait!" I shouted, raising my hands.

Dad summoned a ball of fire in his palm, his expression fierce. Angel drew two blades from her belt, her jaw rigid and her teeth clenched. I almost staggered back a step in shock. I'd never seen her fight in my entire life. But here she was, standing battle-ready with a fierceness in her face that made her unrecognizable.

Shadows swirled around me. The vampires growled and hissed as they moved toward my family.

I had to do something.

I yanked my arm free of Leo's grip and lifted my hands before uttering a spell.

"Magic above and powers that be,
Freeze the vampires next to me!"

Blue magic poured from my fingertips and engulfed the coven surrounding me. Several pairs of dark eyes fixed on me with shock and anger. But I ignored them and weaved through the array of frozen bodies before rushing toward my family.

Mom opened her arms, her face streaming with tears. I fell into her embrace, and something within me shattered. Like the tiny bit of resolve I'd had left was finally gone. Seeing them here had broken me, destroying the thick, defensive wall I'd built in my heart. My face crumpled as Mom's familiar sweet scent filled my nose. Tears stung my eyes, and I pressed my face into her shoulder. Her arms circled around me in a warm embrace.

"Oh, Brie," she sobbed, stroking my hair. She drew back to look me over, her eyes rimmed with red. "You . . . you've lost so much weight." Concern filled her eyes as she cupped my face in her hands. Her brows knitted together. She scrutinized me, no doubt seeing darkness in my face that hadn't been there before. "What happened to you?"

"What happened to *you*?" I shouted, glancing at Dad and Angel behind her. Angel's eyes were filled with tears. Dad looked at me briefly before returning his gaze to the coven behind us.

"Careful!" Dad said sharply.

An agonized shout echoed from behind me. I recognized it immediately. Leo.

I whirled as Leo broke free of my enchantment and shifted into bat form, flitting straight for us. I faced him head-on, blocking his path to my family.

"Leo, stop!" I shouted, lifting a hand. "Don't make me cast another spell. You know I will."

The bat hovered in front of me for a moment, and I could almost feel the anger radiating from him. Then, he shifted again, his silver eyes gleaming. He crossed his arms, his gaze roving over Mom, Dad, and Angel. "Who are they?" he demanded.

"My *family*," I said again slowly.

Leo glared at me. "Yes, but I don't know who your family is. I don't even know *you*, Brielle. What are they doing here?" He glanced behind them. "Were they followed? Did the Count send them?"

"No one sent us," Dad growled, stepping toward Leo. A ball of fire still swirled in Dad's hand. "We came looking for our daughter. She was thrown into a magical portal months ago, and we haven't heard from her since. Now we know why." His eyes blazed as he stared at Leo, nostrils flaring.

"Dad, no," I said quickly. "It wasn't Leo's fault. It—Lilith, it's a long story." I glanced at Leo. "Is there somewhere I can speak with them privately—to explain everything?"

Leo's jaw tightened, his face a mask of fury. I knew what his answer would be.

"Please," I begged, my voice cracking. "We'll go deep into the forest, away from your coven if that's what you're worried about." I stepped closer to him. "They're my *family,* Leo." I widened my eyes at him, knowing how close he'd been with his brother and sister. What if they'd shown up here out of the blue?

He seemed to read the implication in my eyes, and something stirred in his gaze. His face softened but then quickly wiped clean, as if he hadn't meant to reveal that tenderness. Waving a hand, he muttered, "Very well. Half a mile east. When you're finished, Brielle, you return *alone.* I'll send my men to ensure they aren't a threat."

Relief filled me, followed instantly by indignation. "You didn't seem all that threatened when *I* showed up here."

Leo's gaze fixed on me, and that infuriating smirk

spread across his lips. "You were no threat, Little Nightmare."

I clenched my fingers into fists. A soft chuckle sounded behind me. I glanced over my shoulder and found Angel fighting a smile. Rolling my eyes, I relaxed my hands, my anger vanishing instantly.

I exhaled. "Thank you, Leo."

His eyes glinted as if he'd *known* how irritating he was being. He waved a hand at the vampires behind him, and they followed him back inside the cave. All except Jorge, who remained a moment longer to stare at me, his expression full of suspicion. His dark eyes speared through me, conveying a solid threat.

I stared him down, unflinching. He could glare at me all he liked. I wasn't backing down.

Slowly, he turned and disappeared into the cave. I released a breath, my body sagging slightly and my eyes stinging with exhaustion. I turned and caught a glimpse of my dad's brown shirt and gold hair before he enveloped me in a tight embrace. Angel wrapped her arms around my other side, half laughing and half sobbing. I felt Mom's fingers on my shoulders as she joined in too. For a long moment, the four of us clutched each other desperately, clinging to the sweetness of our reunion.

We walked through the forest hand-in-hand, our steps slow and precise. We weren't in any rush. I felt safe with them next to me, and it was nice to enjoy the quiet solitude of the forest together. It was like we were taking a family hike.

After half an hour of walking, I said, "Here is fine." I collapsed, propping my back against an oak tree and resting my head against the trunk. My eyes closed for a moment. I smelled Angel's raspberry scent as she sat next to me. Something different mingled with her smell—like roasted peanuts. And charcoal.

I opened one eye and found my parents sitting cross-legged in front of us. My eyes rested on Dad's new scar.

"What happened to you all?" I asked, leaning forward slightly. "How did you get here?"

"Your mother feared the worst when we never heard from you," Dad said gravely. "We tried your cell, but it was dead. We reached out to every contact we had at the Council. No one could provide us with any information."

I waited for more, but Dad fell silent. Something dark stirred in his eyes, and he exchanged a meaningful glance with Mom.

I straightened. "What is it? Just tell me."

Dad's face went rigid, and Mom jumped in instead. "You have to understand how desperate we were, Brie. It had been six months. We hadn't heard from you. For all we knew, Solano had sent someone to have you killed. We would've done anything—and I mean *anything*—to get you back."

The way Mom's voice emphasized "anything" made my heart twist with apprehension. *What did they do?* Though fear raced through my heart, I wasn't afraid of what they'd done; I was afraid of what they'd left behind. Had they ruined their lives in Miami just to find me here?

I shook my head. "Whatever it is, you can tell me. I've—I've been through a lot here, too. I've done terrible things." I thought of the nightmares that plagued my dreams, the screams that sounded so real. Each time I woke with that strange euphoria it felt like I had actually killed people—and that I'd enjoyed it.

"We crossed a lot of lines, Brie," Mom said quietly. "Your dad had to use some . . . creative methods to get his coworkers to talk."

Creative methods. I thought of my own methods of getting Leo to talk in the castle courtyard. Swallowing, I nodded. "I understand."

Mom and Dad shared another look. "I don't think you do, Brie," Dad said slowly. "I broke laws. I tortured high-ranking members of the Council. Including Solano."

Solano. The man who had taken me away. Who had delivered me to a Jumper and sent me through a portal with no way back.

I actually didn't feel all that bad about Solano being tortured.

I exhaled and leaned forward. "Whatever you guys did to get here—even if you killed people—I don't care. I just need to know you have a way to get back. Please tell me you can go back."

Mom's eyes went wide, her brows knitting together in confusion. "Brie, what . . .? Do you want us to *leave*?"

"She wants to go back home, obviously," Dad said, but his eyes were uncertain.

"Well, *yes,*" I said. "But that isn't all. You—you all can't stay here. What about Angel and her medication?"

"I haven't had a single seizure in the months we've been here," Angel said in a soft voice.

I stilled. "What? How?"

"I've run a few tests on her aura," Mom said. "I suspect her condition has improved because there is less magic clouding the air. Less magic to interfere with her visions."

"Do you think that was what caused her problem?" I asked.

Mom shrugged. "It's just a guess. It could also have to do with the lack of technology, cell towers . . . or a smaller population . . . less pollution. But whatever it is, this time period seems to have cured her."

Relief spread through me, but it was tainted by the dread in my heart from knowing my family was here. That they would witness the devastation at my hand. That they might die because of me.

"That isn't all," Angel said, reading the conflict on my face. She touched my shoulder. "Brie, what is it? Tell us."

My throat felt tight, but I took a deep breath and told them everything. The portal that took me through time. The other casters in the castle who had problems like me. The Count and his secrets. The demons he had imprisoned. When I told them how the Count threw me in the dungeon, Dad's face contorted with rage, his eyes filling with a darkness that chilled me to my bones. I quickly dropped my gaze, afraid if I watched their reactions then I wouldn't have the strength to finish my story.

I finally ended by detailing my escape to Leo's coven and our agreement to work together to cure me.

Silence filled the space between us, broken only by the birds and insects lurking in the forest. I still couldn't look at my family, but I felt the shock and horror emanating from them like radio waves.

"So you're . . . you're Lilith's cursed witch," Angel breathed in a tight voice. "It really *is* true?"

I nodded grimly.

"But this Leo guy says he can cure you," Mom said quickly. "You can find a way to fight this. If anyone can fight this, it's you, Brie."

I shook my head. "I can't. She already took over. The— the fire. So much fire." I closed my eyes to ward off the incoming tears. "She's too strong." But remembering my conversation with Leo, I had no idea if it was Lilith who was too strong . . . or the creature within me.

I couldn't reconcile the idea that the creature lurking inside me was *innocent* and deserved to take over me. No matter what Lucia believed, I couldn't possibly accept that.

I looked at Dad and found his face sickly, his green eyes wide with realization. He shared a horrified look with my mom.

"What?" I asked, straightening. "What is it?"

"You said . . . fire?" Dad asked slowly.

"Yeah." I glanced from Mom to Dad and then to Angel.

"It can't be," Mom whispered to Dad.

"Tell me!" I shouted, my heart racing frantically.

Mom blinked and looked at me. "I cast a time travel spell to get here, Brie."

I frowned at her and shook my head. *What?*

"I've cast it before. You and I, we possess a sort of . . . genetic mark. Something that allows us to travel through time. Something that makes us Timecasters."

"Timecasters," I repeated numbly.

Mom nodded. "Your dad and Angel possess a similar mark, but it's different. They can travel, too, but they're more like Timewalkers than Timecasters."

I shook my head, irritation prickling through me. "What the hell are you talking about, Mom?"

"Watch it," Dad growled.

Mom leaned forward, her eyes intent. "Listen to me, Brie. I cast my first time travel spell long before you were born. I got into a whole lot of trouble for it, and I was almost imprisoned for unsanctioned time travel. I vowed never to cast it again or risk disrupting the timeline. We tore the page from the Grimoire so you two wouldn't get any ideas.

"Over the years, I've spent countless hours researching how the time travel spell works and why some people can cast it and others can't. I was able to examine my genetic makeup as well as your father's, and that's where I found the markings. And they are *different*. Your father has cast the spell before, too, but it didn't work the right way. It wasn't the same as when I cast it.

"I found the marker on *you*, too, Brie." Mom paused,

biting her lip. "When your dad found the portal you went through—when he tracked down the Jumper who brought you there—I inspected it with my tech. I found it was tethered to another person's soul. That person has the same mark that you and I have, Brie. That mark was embedded into the portal, preventing anyone unmarked from entering."

My mouth fell open. "Are you saying that only Time— Time-whatevers can go through the portal?"

"Timecasters, yes."

"But *why*?"

"Because of Lilith," Dad said in a low voice. "History tells us she is reincarnated through witches across time. She requires that genetic code in order to possess another person's soul."

Horror chilled my bones, rippling down my spine. Nausea swirled in my stomach until I thought I might puke. It was the Count—it had to be. He engineered this time portal so only those who were marked could pass through.

All so he could find the one marked caster he was looking for—the one who was cursed by Lilith. The Nightcaster.

"Brie, that isn't all," Mom said softly.

My gaze jerked to her, my heart fluttering in anticipation. "What is it?"

"When we first arrived, it was spring. We showed up in the middle of a village. And . . . we saw a creature. A fiery creature attacking the city."

My heart dropped like a stone. "No," I whispered numbly.

"The creature . . . slaughtered the city," Dad said in a tight voice. "Brie, it killed hundreds of people. The area was blockaded by wreckage and debris. We were trapped. Separated. We couldn't get to each other for days. When we finally did, your mom barely had enough ingredients to cast the spell again. We assumed we'd arrived in the wrong location when we cast it the first time. So, we tried again. We arrived here, in front of those caves."

"No," I said again, closing my eyes.

"Brie," Angel said quietly.

I shook my head fiercely. *Don't.* I didn't deserve her sympathy or her pity.

Because I finally registered what my parents were saying.

Those months when Lilith had possessed me—she had taken control of the creature. She had used me to slaughter a village full of innocent people.

37
BRIELLE

THUNDER ROARED IN MY EARS. I COULDN'T SPEAK. Couldn't move. Horror numbed my entire body, freezing me in place. I stared unfocused at the forest floor. A chill swept over me.

Mom was speaking, but I didn't hear her.

I heard nothing but the screams of my nightmares. The roar of the monster within me.

It had all been real. I had really killed all those people.

Someone shook my shoulder, and I blinked. Awareness slammed into me, followed by a wave of nausea. I swallowed down bile. Angel met my gaze, her hand still on my shoulder.

I wanted to shake her off. To run away from them before I hurt them.

They'd been in the village during the attack. My eyes found the scar on Dad's face. I could've killed them.

I didn't deserve their pity. I deserved their hatred and scorn.

The Count had been right about me.

"Brie, talk to us," Angel whispered. "We're here for you."

Anger roared within me, and I jumped to my feet. "You shouldn't have come."

My family exchanged glances before they all stood too. Mom drew closer to me, but I paced away from her, deeper into the forest. Toward the Castillo de Coca.

"Don't say that, Brie," Mom said. Her quiet steps behind me told me she was following.

I whirled around to face her. "I'm dangerous! I'm going to destroy this entire city! Now that you're here, I'm just going to kill you too!" I groaned, rubbing my forehead. "There—there isn't any way for you to go back?"

Mom shook her head. "We used all the ingredients to travel the second time. I might be able to cast the spell if I can get the ingredients again, but . . ." She trailed off and pressed her lips together.

"But what?" I snapped.

"But we don't have a home to go back to," Dad said, approaching behind Mom. Angel stood by the oak tree, her arms crossed as she watched us from afar. "We gave up our lives to come here, Brie," Dad went on. "We're wanted fugitives in Miami. If we go back, we'll be imprisoned."

A lump formed in my throat. "It's better than dying at the hands of your daughter," I said in a tight voice.

Mom stepped closer, grabbing my hands. "Brie, it *won't* come to that. We're here to help! You said this Leo guy was supposed to find a way to cure you, right? Let us help too! We're from the future—we know modern spells and potions. We can help!"

Dad nodded encouragingly, and his eyes were so full of hope like Mom's that I found myself nodding along with them.

But I didn't believe it.

It was one thing when I wasn't hurting anyone. When it was just nightmares haunting me every night. But now I knew it was real, and I was a danger to *everyone.*

They weren't just dreams anymore. And we were out of time.

"Let's just take this one step at a time," Dad said slowly, rubbing his chin. "What do we know? What do we know about Lilith and the creature?"

I shrugged helplessly. "The creature is made of fire. It . . . craves death and suffering. Although I can't tell if that's Lilith or the creature." I shook my head, revolted with myself. "Nighttime is when I'm most vulnerable. When I sleep. Leo says Lilith's cursed witches are called Nightcasters."

Mom looked at me, her blue eyes solemn. She glanced at Dad. "It's still 1735, right?"

I nodded.

Mom's lips twitched in a smile, and she exhaled. "I can't believe we cast that spell and only traveled forward a few months." She shook her head, meeting my eyes. "It was worth it to find you, Brie."

Angel strode toward us, her eyes contemplative. "The creature—do we know what it is?"

"I always pictured it as a dragon," I whispered. "What else could cause so much death by fire?"

Dad shook his head. "It's not a dragon. It's much smaller. I shot it with my water and doused its flames for a moment. I was able to catch a glimpse. It's about the size of a falcon."

I stiffened. Something within me stirred to life, awakening from his words. I remembered reading about the different creatures Lilith's beast could be, and the answer came to me as clear as day. "A phoenix." My voice was hushed, and it resonated within me. I wasn't sure how I knew—but I did.

"Phoenix," Mom repeated in a quiet voice. Then, she nodded. "That makes sense. The brief moments I saw it, it was completely on fire. It could breathe fire too, and it disappeared into the sky on a whim. It was . . . incredible. And terrifying."

"It needs to be killed," I said sharply. "Before anyone else gets hurt."

"I don't think it's that simple," Dad said slowly. "When I used my water against it, it . . . *whimpered.* Like it was in pain. Like it didn't want to be there. It shied away from me in terror until something overcame it and it took to the skies again."

I stared at him. The monster had a chance to kill my dad —but it hadn't.

Like it didn't want to be there.

My throat felt tight, and I closed my eyes.

Dad changed the subject. "What else do we know?"

"I only have a few months left," I said. "At the year's end, the time loop will reset. It ends with me destroying the city."

Mom took my shoulders with a fierce look in her eyes. "Brielle, listen to me. That creature is *not you*. You can't fly. You can't light yourself on fire. You never left that dungeon! It is *not you*."

My eyes stung as I shook my head. "Then, how? How is this happening? I see it in my dreams. I hear the roaring and the screams. It *is* real, Mom. It's happening because of me."

"No, because of Lilith," Dad said in a hard voice. "She wants to control you. She wants to control the creature. It's *her* who's wreaking havoc and destruction. We just have to find a way to push her out."

I can't do this. My head was spinning. Panic and despair swirled in my chest until I felt I couldn't breathe.

I knew only one thing. I would die before letting Lilith kill my family.

But I had to make them believe I was on board with finding a solution. That I wasn't about to do something reckless.

So, I arranged my face into a calm expression and said, "I should head back. It'll be dark soon, and you all need a place to sleep." I forced myself to meet their gazes, struggling to remain composed. "Let me talk with Leo. I'll come

back for you. He's just . . . he doesn't trust strangers."
Including me.

"Of course," Mom said, rubbing her arms. She shared a look with Dad that told me they were still worried. But for now, it seemed I'd appeased them. "We'll wait for you, Brie."

I nodded and offered a weak smile before turning away from them. My feet moved forward automatically, but my mind swirled with thoughts of fire and devastation. The real screams that pierced through my dreams—they'd belonged to actual people. People *I'd* killed.

I didn't care what my parents said. If the beast lived inside me, then I was responsible for the deaths it caused.

I reached the mouth of the cave as the chill of dusk wrapped around me, seeping into my bones. But I welcomed it. If I was cold, it meant the monster wasn't trying to take control. Lilith was quiet—for now.

A dark figure waited for me at the cave's entrance. I knew before I recognized him that it was Leo. His silvery eyes locked onto mine as he leaned against the rocky wall. Though he was the picture of ease, I knew it was just a ruse. He was frightened of my family. Of what their arrival meant.

"Did you have a nice conversation?" he asked idly.

I shook my head, not in the mood for his games. "It was fine. Can they stay here?"

He popped off the wall and strode toward me. "I'll need to speak with them first."

I stared hard at him. "Speak with them. But not fight them."

Leo watched me for a long moment. Then, a predatory smile spread across his face. "Of course."

I didn't like that look. I sighed. "I'll come with you."

His brows knitted together. "That won't be necessary." His eyes roved over my face. "You're exhausted, Brielle. You must sleep."

Not happening. "I'll be fine. Let's go together." I strode toward the forest again, but Leo caught me by the wrist. I stilled, my skin warming from the softness of his fingers.

"Brielle," he murmured, and I nearly trembled at the tenderness in his voice. "What's bothering you?"

I gritted my teeth, avoiding his piercing gaze. My brain ached from shoving my emotions away, and my body sagged with fatigue. The ruse with my parents had taken all my energy. I didn't have anything left to convince Leo.

And even if I had, he'd see right through me. He had a knack for that.

I swallowed. "Why didn't you tell me?" I finally met his gaze. My vision blurred with tears.

He frowned. "Tell you what?"

"There was an attack in the city," I whispered. "The monster killed hundreds. My parents were stuck there, trying to get out." I pressed my lips together. My face felt like it would split in two as I tried to hold it together. But despite my best efforts, tears streamed down my face.

"Brielle," Leo said again, drawing closer until his spicy scent filled my nose. "I—I didn't know." His chest was so close to me. All I had to do was inch forward and press my face against him. I was almost certain his arms would wrap around me. Despite the anger and mistrust between us, the tenderness in his face was undeniable. All I wanted to do was sink into his embrace.

But I stepped back and sniffed. "My parents want to work with you to find a cure for me. If that's okay."

Leo watched me for a long moment, his expression unreadable. Then, he nodded. "Of course. Assuming I don't uncover anything malicious when I speak with them."

I snorted and rubbed my nose. *Malicious? Hardly.* "I'm sure they'll pass your little test with flying colors."

Leo's brow furrowed, and I almost laughed at the bewilderment on his face. I turned to leave, but his hand still clasped my wrist. He wouldn't let me go.

I raised my eyebrows at him expectantly. Something dark flashed in his eyes.

"Whatever you do, Brielle, promise me you won't return to the Castillo de Coca," he said in a low voice.

I stilled. *How could he possibly know I'd planned to do that?* "I'm not an idiot," I said. My voice trembled, betraying me.

"If what you say is true—if this monster attacked a village—then it happened under the Count's watch. If you go back there, it will happen again, and you will only hurt more people. Do you think he cares about the lives of commoners? He just wants to draw Lilith out. He doesn't care what it takes."

"But what if he's just trying to protect the city?" I asked before I could stop myself. "What if the lives of a few are worth sacrificing if it means the entire city can be saved?"

Leo brought his face closer to mine, his jaw rigid and his eyes fierce. "If you believe that, then ask yourself where he draws the line. He summoned a dozen innocent casters to his castle. He has imprisoned and tortured countless demons from my coven. My *family*. How many lives will he sacrifice in the name of protecting his city?" He paused. "And if you're wrong—if he is only looking to protect himself—then he might be willing to sacrifice every life within this time loop in order to succeed."

My blood chilled at his words, and I looked at him, unmoving. His eyes held me there, freezing me in place. I couldn't look away from him. The intensity of his gaze was like a magnet drawing me in.

At long last, I nodded slowly. "I understand."

Leo relaxed his grip on my wrist. "Good. Now, let's go talk to your parents." He glanced over his shoulder at something near the cave. A few dark figures peeled off the cave wall like shadows.

I suppressed a shudder. How long had they been there? Had they heard me break down and cry?

I recognized the first figure as Jorge. He fixed a fearsome scowl on me. The other man was one I'd seen before, but I didn't know his name. He watched me, his features softer than Jorge's but still guarded.

Leo grinned at me. "Shall we?"

38
LEO

I COULD FEEL BRIELLE'S ENTIRE BEING QUIVER AS WE walked through the forest. The soft footsteps of Jorge and Miguel behind me provided a comfort to me—but Brielle's gaze kept darting back to them, and I knew they made her nervous.

What did she have to fear?

That's a foolish question, I chided myself. She was as mistrustful of my coven as I was with her.

And now her family was here. I remembered the panic that filled me when Ronaldo had stolen into the castle on his own. The numbing fear that wouldn't release me. That gripped me like a vise.

I edged closer to Brielle. She straightened slightly but then relaxed again, her heartbeat soothing into a more comfortable rhythm. My arm brushed against hers, but she didn't jerk away from me.

Brielle's family stood when we approached. The father's eyes were wary as they fixed on me. I could tell this one was a demon from the way he smelled. But the two women were witches—light casters.

Interesting.

When only a few feet separated us, I stopped and plastered an easy smile on my face. "My name is Leo Serrano. I'm the leader of this coven. Before we open our home to you, I have a few questions. What are your names?"

The man exchanged a glance with the woman next to him before answering. "My name is Oliver. This is Desi and our daughter Angel."

I eyed the girl. *Brielle's sister.* They looked very different. Angel was much darker—darker hair, darker eyes, and darker skin. Her gaze lacked the ferocity and strength that often speared through me when I met Brielle's gaze.

"A pleasure to make your acquaintance," I said with a low bow. "Please explain to me how you found my cave."

Oliver spoke, detailing a mysterious spell that took them through time. Desi chimed in, explaining that she had used essences of Brielle's aura to tether the spell to her. It just so happened that the spell deposited them to the mouth of the cave—precisely where Brielle was.

The idea that a spell was capable of transporting a family three hundred years into the past made my head spin.

And it seemed far too convenient that they happened to show up at the entrance of my home.

But I kept the smile on my face as I asked them more questions, such as why they were looking for Brielle in the first place, who they had come across in the city so far, and how they intended to leave.

Desi and Oliver exchanged a glance before Desi answered my final question. "We don't know if we'll be leaving."

I went very still at her words. "Why not?"

Brielle shifted slightly, her heart racing.

"We don't have the ingredients to cast the spell again," Desi explained. "And we won't leave until we figure out a solution to Brie's problem."

Problem. That was too mild of a word to describe what was happening to Brielle.

"I must confess I do not have the resources or the lodging to accommodate you permanently," I said slowly.

Oliver shook his head. "We won't be staying here."

Brielle stiffened. "We won't?"

"No," Oliver said in a hard voice. "We won't overstay our welcome with a coven of vampires we know nothing about."

I felt Miguel and Jorge bristle behind me, and my own blood boiled with Oliver's implication. I smiled coldly. "I assure you we have been nothing but hospitable toward your daughter. And we abide by the laws of magic. We do not feed on unwilling Donors."

Oliver's lips pressed together. "So you say."

"Dad," Brielle hissed.

"With all due respect, Mr. Serrano," Oliver went on. "I'm a demon myself. I work among men like you. Men who claim to follow the law but operate under their own set of rules when it benefits them. And I won't be taking that risk. Not with my family." His eyes roved over the men behind me. "Though I'm sure your coven is delightful."

Jorge hissed behind me, surging forward. I flung out an arm to stop him and stared hard at Oliver. "And where do you intend to go?" I asked. "I presume Brielle has told you of the curse on the city that has us all trapped."

"She has," Oliver said. "We've made some friends in the village we came from. I'm sure they would be more than happy to welcome us, since we saved their lives during the attack."

Brielle flinched next to me. It was so subtle that her family didn't notice, but I felt her blood pumping furiously. She started trembling again. I instinctively drew closer to her, and Oliver tensed, balling his hands into fists.

I shifted away from Brielle and pretended I hadn't noticed her father's reaction. My eyes fell to a large sack resting on the ground behind the family. I pointed to it. "My men will have to search this before you enter my home."

Oliver's eyes tightened. "Of course."

With a sigh, I waved my hand forward. "You may join us in the caves. For now." I looked at Jorge. "Search them before they enter." Then, my gaze found Brielle's wide eyes. "I must speak with you in private."

Brielle nodded. I sensed Oliver's movement and felt his

blood boiling with anger, but I ignored him. I grasped Brielle's elbow and led her in the direction of the cave, allowing Jorge and Miguel to handle her hotheaded father.

"What is it?" Brielle hissed, glancing nervously over her shoulder at her family.

"I simply wanted to anger your father," I said with a smirk.

Her eyes blazed, and she violently shook her arm from my grip. "You're a dick, you know that?"

I raised an eyebrow at her. The fire in her eyes only ignited the flames within me as well. How could I resist goading her?

She gritted her teeth and turned away from me, but I caught her arm again.

"Brielle," I said softly, my smile fading. "To be perfectly frank, I *did* have something I wanted to discuss with you."

Her furrowed brow smoothed, and she scrutinized me, her eyes still wary. "What is it?"

"Once your family is situated in the caves, I'd like you to meet me in my library."

"Why?"

I leaned closer and said in a low voice. "I assume you won't be sleeping tonight?"

Unease stirred in her eyes. She swallowed and shook her head. Despite the dark circles under her eyes, the blatant fear in her face told me she had no desire to sleep. Especially not after learning what the monster had done to that village.

I nodded once. "Very well. Then, we might as well get to work finding a cure for you."

Her lips parted in surprise. "I—" She stopped, clearly at a loss for words. For once.

I watched her. The darkness I'd seen in her face earlier was still there—the darkness that told me she'd try to go back to the Count and sacrifice herself.

I knew if I didn't help her find a solution quickly, she'd take matters into her own hands and do something reckless. Something that might get herself or others killed.

I couldn't have that.

"What if there is no cure?" she asked in a whisper. Her eyes met mine, her face taut with unabashed fear. I'd rarely seen her emotions exposed so plainly before me. She was usually so guarded, and to see her raw, naked fear here in front of me was sobering enough to push all thoughts of teasing her from my mind.

I ran my thumb along the line of her jaw. To my surprise, she didn't jerk away from me. Instead, she closed her eyes, and her breath hitched. I felt her pulse racing, though I couldn't tell if she feared my touch . . . or craved it.

"There must be a cure," I said in a soft voice. "You are a warrior, Brielle. If you can't fight off Lilith, then no one can."

The corners of her mouth twitched, lighting up her face just a fraction. I longed to see a real smile from her, though I knew it was unlikely.

She remained silent as we strode back to the cave together. Twilight darkened the sky, giving way to the early moon and the hint of winter's chill. The space between us felt lighter and more comfortable as we walked in silence. But deep down, I felt a nagging sensation—a sense of foreboding.

The end of the year was fast approaching. And I knew something dark waited for us just around the corner.

39
BRIELLE

LEO'S MEN SPENT AN UNNECESSARY AMOUNT OF TIME searching my parents—their bags, their clothes, even their shoes. I could tell by the way Leo smirked in the corner of the cave that he was enjoying the show. Particularly my dad's anger. Dad's face was beet red by the time Leo and his vampires were finished. I watched my father's blazing eyes send daggers toward Leo as he snatched his clothes back from Jorge and hastily put them back on. It hadn't been a picnic for Mom and Angel, either, and I swore Dad was about to punch Jorge in the face when he took his time going through Angel's pockets.

Leo was taunting Dad. I couldn't tell if it was because he enjoyed making people angry—*that* was a given—or because he thought he was a threat.

I hadn't forgotten the strange, tender moments Leo and I had shared today. Part of me cringed inwardly at the thought of how I'd sobbed like a baby in front of him. Or how I'd opened up and revealed my fears to him. I hated appearing weak, especially in front of someone who was supposed to be my enemy.

But the longer I stayed in the caves, the less Leo felt like an enemy to me.

A few vampires dragged some cots into my bedroom. I offered the huge bed to Mom and Dad, but they politely refused and settled into their cots, dragging them to the other side of the room for some privacy. I watched them huddle together, their eyes soft and far away as they whispered to each other. Mom's face was pink, and she pressed a kiss to Dad's cheek. They had that look of nostalgia in their eyes—the look that told me they were thinking of some memory they'd shared long ago.

When I saw that look, sometimes it made me curious. What were they reminiscing of? Other times, I didn't care. As a kid, I'd thought my parents' displays of affection were disgusting.

But now I wondered what other secrets they'd kept from me. Were they reminiscing of how they'd time traveled together? Or was there some other huge secret I didn't know about?

"I know it's crazy," Angel whispered as she slid into bed with me. "It took me weeks before I could look at them the same."

I blinked at her, realizing *she* had time traveled too. She'd spent months in the year 1735 with Mom and Dad—even after finding out about the time travel spell.

The fact made me feel strangely alone.

"What's even *crazier* is how friendly you are with the coven leader," Angel went on, propping her head up on her elbow and raising her eyebrows at me.

I scoffed and scooted into bed next to her—but only for show. As soon as she fell asleep, I'd slip out to find Leo.

The thought made my face burn, only making me look more guilty.

Angel snickered quietly. "Brie, I can't believe you! A shapeshifting vampire . . . and a coven *leader* at that. That's pretty bold of you."

I shoved her arm. "Stop it. There's nothing going on. Besides, he's *super* friendly with his Donors." I wiggled my eyebrows suggestively. "It would make me uncomfortable to pursue someone who's that . . ."

"Hands on?" Angel asked with a snort.

I laughed too. "Yeah." To say nothing of the fact that just being around him made me boil over with anger. And we didn't trust each other. And I'd tortured him, and he'd sucked my blood.

Yeah. Definitely nothing going on there.

Angel's face sobered as she looked at me, her eyes worried. I knew that look. I wanted to sigh and turn away, but I was so grateful she was *here* that I couldn't bring myself to.

"Brie," she said quietly. "I know you. You're trying to suffer through this alone. But you don't have to. You have nothing to prove to me. Or Mom and Dad. You're the strongest person we know. Hands down. And with all this happening to you—well, no one would blame you if you broke down or asked for help or, Lilith forbid, actually *showed* some emotion." She smiled, trying to ease the tension. But it didn't work.

I swallowed and nodded. "I know. I'm just . . . trying to process everything. That's all." And that was all I *could* tell her. Because if my family knew I wanted to sacrifice myself to save them, they would try to stop me.

But I would die before letting that monster kill them. I swore on my own life I would never let that happen.

As soon as Angel's soft snores filled the cave, I gingerly rolled out of bed. My bare feet padded softly against the smooth, cold floors. I approached Mom and Dad's cots, which were angled near the exit. Pausing momentarily to make sure they were sleeping too, I took a breath. Then, I slid between their cots, weaving through the cave tunnels that had become more familiar to me over the past few days.

I wasn't sure what I was expecting. As I crept down the narrow tunnel, a chill swept over me, and I was reminded of those days in the Castillo de Coca when Ignacio had murmured words in Latin—the strange spell he'd used to awaken the monster inside me, and the blood pooling from my hand.

I suppressed a shudder, squashing the thoughts down. Though I told myself it would be different this time, I wasn't sure if I believed it. Like the Count, Leo was willing to do anything to save this city and get his people out. Even at my expense.

The thought filled me with fear—putting my trust in a

man who didn't trust me—but I couldn't blame him. If it meant saving everyone, including my family, then I would gladly ask him to end my life.

When I arrived in the library, I found Leo poring over books in the armchair, his long hair disheveled as it framed his face.

"Welcome," he said without looking up. "Please, have a seat."

I frowned at his formal tone and sat opposite him with raised eyebrows, waiting.

Leo sighed and ran a hand through his hair, then met my gaze. "I am reading everything I have about Night-casters and Lilith's curse." He paused. "So far, the only thing remotely helpful I've found is something that refers to 'uniting with the beast.'"

My brows furrowed. "Can I see?"

Leo handed me a thick textbook with worn pages, and I squinted as I read the Spanish words. *When Lilith is reborn, the Nightcaster may resist her influence by uniting with the beast. This task solidifies the bond between Nightcaster and beast, unifying their souls so there is no space remaining for Lilith to reside.*

I looked up, my gaze distant. "Reborn," I whispered. "Of course."

Leo cocked his head at me.

I raised my eyes to meet his. "The beast is a phoenix."

He blinked, and his eyes widened. "A firebird reborn in the ashes."

Suddenly, the pieces started sliding together. I raised a

finger, my heart racing as my mind spun through the information. "The phoenix and Lilith . . . they both need a host who can travel through time. Someone who can travel with them when they are reborn." *Someone with a mark like me.*

"And that person is you?" Leo asked uncertainly.

I nodded.

Leo leaned forward, propping his arms on his knees. "Brielle, I know you won't like this suggestion, but I stand by what I said to you before. I think the way to solidify this bond with the beast is to turn yourself over to it. Like my sister."

I went still. My mouth opened with an automatic objection, but then I remembered something Dad had said about the phoenix. *It whimpered like it was in pain. Like it didn't want to be there.*

Like someone else was controlling it. Someone like Lilith.

"You may be right," I whispered.

Leo stared at me, his mouth opening in surprise. "I—I beg your pardon? I must have misheard you."

I shook my head. "I said you may be right."

Leo chuckled and leaned forward, tilting his ear toward me. "I must be going mad, because it *sounded* like you were admitting I was right."

"Shut up," I snapped, crossing my arms. But my mouth twitched, and when I caught a glimpse of Leo's crooked grin, I had to return it.

Leo cleared his throat, his face sobering. "I propose we invite the creature. That you succumb to it but try to remain in control. Don't fight it, but don't surrender completely either."

My head was spinning. That sounded frustratingly difficult. "How the hell do I do that?" I paused, and in a quieter voice, I said, "And how can we guarantee I won't hurt anyone?"

Leo considered this. "I'll stay with you."

I stiffened and looked him over, trying to detect a trick.

He raised his hands in surrender. "I won't harm you. But I remember when my sister got her fevers, that was when the beast took over. If I notice the same signs I saw in her, I'll rouse you."

"What are the signs?" I asked before I could stop myself. I wasn't sure I wanted to know—but I had to hear it.

Leo's eyes darkened. "Violent tremors. Burning heat. And . . . steam. Sometimes steam would rise from her. Her body would twitch and thrash like she was struggling." He swallowed and dropped his gaze, his jaw rigid.

Idiot, I told myself. I hadn't been thinking of how it would feel for him to relive his darkest memories. The memories of his dying sister.

"I'm sorry," I whispered.

Leo met my gaze, his eyes softening. "It isn't your fault, Brielle. My sister would be happy to know that in her death she provided a way for you to survive when she couldn't."

Silence fell between us as our gazes locked. Something solemn spread in the space between us, linking us together like chains. For the first time in months, I felt understood.

The feeling was so foreign that I wanted to instinctively

shove it away. Especially when I faced Leo, whom I didn't trust as far as I could throw.

"I need you to promise me something," I said quietly.

Leo watched me, his silver eyes glinting. "Anything."

I was so startled by this that I gaped at him, momentarily forgetting what I was about to say. Then, his eyebrows lifted, and I cleared my throat. "I, uh—if I start to show these signs and if you can't wake me—if it seems like the worst has happened and Lilith *has* taken over"—I swallowed and took a breath—"I want you to kill me."

Leo straightened, his eyes widening. "I will not," he growled.

My nostrils flared. "You *have* to."

"Brielle—"

"No, *listen* to me," I said over him, balling my hands into fists. "I can't do this anymore. I can't keep up this sick dance with Lilith as we grapple over whatever phoenix is living inside me. And if she takes over again, more innocent people will die. It could be my parents next." I paused, and then decided to use a different tactic. "Or your coven."

Darkness clouded his eyes, and his jaw ticked back and forth as he considered this. I knew I'd won him over. He would do anything to protect his coven.

At long last, he said in a low voice, "I will station sentries outside the cave. If one of them notices the beast, he will inform me."

I held my breath, waiting for him to say the words. *I need him to say it.*

He finally met my gaze, and something unreadable

stirred in his eyes. Something that almost looked like regret. "If the firebird poses a threat to our coven, then I will intervene."

Intervene wasn't nearly a strong enough word for me. My body tensed, waiting for the words I needed to hear: *I will kill you.*

But he didn't say them.

I couldn't tell if I was relieved or disappointed.

He seemed to read the conflict in my face. "There are other ways to weaken you besides killing you, Brielle."

I stilled, thinking of the blissful numbness that had taken over my body when he'd drunk my blood. Fury coursed through me as I remembered how weak and useless I'd been after that, but I squashed the feeling down. He was right. Sucking my blood would weaken me—hopefully enough to weaken the phoenix as well.

"If that doesn't work . . ." I said softly.

"For Lilith's sake, Brielle, if you want me to end your life, you'll have to do better than that," he snapped, his eyes blazing.

My head reared back in surprise. Rage filled his face as his piercing gaze speared right through me.

He was . . . *angry* that I was asking this of him. But that made no sense to me.

"I don't take pleasure in killing," he said, his voice deep and menacing. "Though it's in my nature, it is a crime against humanity. It makes me become more animal than man, and that's something I will not relinquish."

I stared at him, my chest swelling with his words. Something fierce resonated inside me, rising from within. *More animal than man.*

Or more beast than woman.

I nodded slowly.

"You have nothing to fear, Brielle," he said softly, the rage in his face now gone. "I will keep you and your family safe."

I nodded again, unable to find my voice. I wrung my hands together, my gaze fixed on the floor, until I realized Leo was watching me. Waiting.

My eyes locked onto his, and understanding flowed between us. His eyebrows raised with a question.

"Okay," I said in a firm voice. "Let's do it."

40

BRIELLE

I WAS SO EXHAUSTED THAT I COULD'VE FALLEN asleep instantly—if I'd been alone.

But with Leo in the same room, sleep was far from my mind. I convinced him I needed to be alone to clear my head, so he left me in the library, though I knew he remained close by.

I sagged backward into the armchair and stared at the flames dancing in the lanterns on the wall. I focused on breathing and letting my thoughts roam freely. My instinct was to be on guard, to search inwardly for the phoenix or Lilith's presence, but I fought the instinct and instead released the hold I had on my mind and body. Eventually, my vision clouded, and unconsciousness claimed me.

Let go. Let the phoenix take you. Those were the last coherent thoughts I remembered.

Fire scorched my skin. A piercing roar rumbled around me. I was consumed by the flames.

No. I *was* the flames.

My eyes opened. My arms were outstretched and covered in fire. Wind and mist streaked across my skin, sizzling against the flames around me.

I was flying. The midnight air surrounded me like a cloak, and my fire only burned brighter by contrast.

Hunger pulsed through me, but not for food. A scream built up inside me, desperate to be unleashed. I wanted to hold back, but my own words echoed in my mind: *let go.*

So, I sucked in a breath and released the scream. It tore through the air like a shrill screech. Flames poured from my mouth, burning against my throat. Satisfaction swelled within me, and I roared again. With each scream, the energy from inside me released, bringing with it a sweet relief that numbed my body.

I coasted through the air, the misty clouds tickling my wings. I wanted to fly lower, but something within me warned me not to.

Was the voice Lilith? Or myself?

I couldn't tell. And I was too afraid to decide what to do.

A flash of memory, and then I knew the phoenix's mind had taken over. Women and children screamed and sobbed. Fire consumed buildings. Concrete crumbled to the ground. A mighty roar filled the air.

The phoenix's heart filled with sorrow. Anguish. And in that moment, I knew the euphoria, the strange bloodthirsty hunger for death and blood—it hadn't been me *or* the phoenix.

It had been Lilith.

Clarity burst through my mind, and I could see as plainly as if I'd been wearing a mask my entire life. The phoenix was born of fire and magic. It needed a magical host to survive. Like Lilith, it was reborn—and it needed someone marked by time. Someone who could pass through portals. Like me.

But the phoenix couldn't survive unless it was tethered to my soul. To the soul of a magical being.

Over the past several months, I'd fought its presence and tried to push it out, thinking it was Lilith.

But this only gave Lilith more opportunities to take over my body. She, too, was looking for a host. And if she could take over my soul, then she could bind herself to the phoenix and push me out entirely.

As I soared through the sky, I searched within myself, looking for the soul of the phoenix.

There it was. Like a second heart beating inside me.

I wasn't the phoenix. We were separate beings. Separate souls. But we were fueled by the same source of magic. My magic had never manifested itself because it had been keeping the phoenix alive.

Leo had said I was called a Nightcaster because Lilith only took over when I slept. But now I realized that my unconsciousness allowed the phoenix to awaken as well. It was like by dreaming, I'd allowed another part of myself to wake up. To live. To survive. And then, when I'd woken up, that part of myself had gone to rest again.

I wanted to smile. To laugh. To close my eyes and bask in the relief of this knowledge, the answers I'd yearned for my entire life. But my body was not my own anymore. The phoenix was in control. And I gladly let her take over.

Her. Yes, the phoenix was a female. I knew it down to my bones. I could see her soul—her essence.

I'll call you Nix, I decided. Another joyous sound poured from the phoenix's mouth. She liked the name.

Where am I? I wondered vaguely.

You are still asleep in the caves, a soft voice said in my head. It sounded like a whisper or a murmur. I couldn't tell if the voice was low or high. I *felt* it more than I heard it. Like a gentle rumbling in my mind.

And where are you? I asked Nix.

Somewhere high in the sky. I am not sure where.

How did you leave the caves? I wondered, thinking of Leo and how wild it would be if a phoenix exploded to life in front of him.

I was never there. I rest in the Astral Realm while you are awake. When you sleep, I appear in different places, usually somewhere close to you since we are connected.

Where is the Astral Realm? I thought, my head spinning with this information.

I do not know. It is neither here nor there. It is inaccessible to mortals.

But I'm not mortal—I'm a witch.

I felt Nix's smile as she responded. *Even a witch like you cannot reach this place.*

Where have you been? I asked her. *Why haven't I felt you before I came here to Segovia?*

Because Lilith was waiting for you here. Before you arrived, you and I were balanced, shifting power back and forth. I was careful and subtle enough to not draw attention when I took over. But when you fell through the portal, Lilith's influence came between us.

Darkness crept into my mind at the mention of Lilith, but I pushed the thought away, not wanting to invite her into our conversation.

Nix flew on and on, stretching her wings and breathing fire when she was high enough to avoid detection. Each breath of flames was like stretching sore muscles. She'd been dormant for so long that she needed to release the magic built up within her. *My* magic.

I relinquished complete control, drifting off as my mind wandered in a dream state. Familiar faces swam before me: Mom, Dad, Angel, Leo, Izzy. The Count's menacing glare drilled through me. I tried to escape, but he was there, waiting for me. Watching me.

Then, his face morphed into someone I'd never seen before. A woman with inky black hair that surrounded her like a curly mane. Her eyes were all black, and her skin was ashen and pale. She looked like a corpse.

Her mouth spread wide when she saw me, revealing rotten teeth stained with blood.

I tried to run from her, but her long fingers wrapped around my wrist. Jagged fingernails scraped against my skin, and I screamed.

"You are *mine*," she hissed. Her voice sounded like hundreds of whispers blended into one. It made my skin crawl.

"Let go!" I shouted, but my voice was gone. All I saw was this woman. Her deranged face. Her lidless eyes. Her wide, sickening smile. And I knew exactly who this was.

Lilith.

41
LEO

Brielle scowled even in her sleep. It shouldn't have surprised me.

As soon as I felt her heart rate decline and her breathing slow, I crept back into the room and sat across from her. She was huddled against the crook of the armchair, her head nestled against her shoulder. She looked extremely uncomfortable, and yet she slept soundly. Her eyelids shifted, and her head twitched slightly. A low murmur escaped her lips.

I stiffened, waiting for something to happen. When Lucia had her fits, she would speak in her sleep as if she were arguing with someone. But after a moment, Brielle went still again. I relaxed but kept my eyes on her. The features in her face were soft, and for a moment she looked like nothing more than a child. A fierce protectiveness came over me, and desperation pulsed through me. I wanted to save her. I *needed* to save her. The burning desire pounded through me until I thought it would burst from my chest. I didn't know where this came from. I hardly knew the girl. But when I looked at her, I saw my sister. My brother.

If Ronaldo were here, he'd tell me God had given me a second chance. A chance to save a soul from Lilith when I'd failed with Lucia.

I rose from my chair and approached the cave wall with clenched teeth. Anger built up within me, and I pounded my fist against the wall. "Damn you, Ronaldo," I growled. Even after all these years, his ridiculous pious nature still resonated in my brain.

I wanted to be rid of it—but I also clung to it because if it left, my brother would truly be gone.

I cannot be you, Brother, I thought, as if he could hear me. He had been devout and rigid with following rules, but he had also been reckless. Careless. He'd acted from the heart instead of from the head.

For years, I'd wondered how he could make such rash decisions based on what his heart told him. But here and now—watching Brielle sleep and vowing to do what I could to protect her—I finally understood.

Brielle twitched again, her head turning. "No," she muttered.

In an instant, I was by her side, sweeping her blond hair away from her face. Her skin burned, and her forehead was sticky with sweat. Alarm raced through me. *This is it.* Lucia's fits always began with a fever.

Brielle's breaths came heavy and fast. Her head turned this way and that, her brows furrowing in her distress. "No!" she shouted.

I shook her shoulders. "Wake up, Brielle!"

She wouldn't wake. Her body continued to thrash. I shook her again so violently her hair flopped over her face. But still she wouldn't wake.

I stared at her, wracking my brain. My blood pulsed hungrily within me, as if it realized before I did what I had to do.

Resistance tugged at me, freezing me in place. I couldn't —not when she was defenseless. Not when she hadn't consented.

Brielle began to buck with such intensity she almost fell off the chair. I had to do this. Even if she despised me for it afterward.

I almost laughed. *She already despises me.*

I leaned in, peeling her sweaty hair off of her neck before plunging my fangs into her throat.

The sweet, tangy blood filled my mouth. I'd forgotten how delicious she tasted. Then came the sharp bitterness laced within, marking her as someone different. Someone I'd never tasted before that first day in the armory.

A Nightcaster.

My blood called out to her, drawing her into me. I felt her stiffen against my grasp and then relax, succumbing to my venom. Her body sagged, and I caught her in my arms to keep her upright. I drank, gulping down the savory blood that beckoned me further.

Stop.

I knew I had to stop before I killed her. I broke contact so suddenly my mouth burned and my stomach heaved.

Brielle made a gagging sound, but her eyes were still closed. She was most likely too weak to wake.

But she was no longer fighting. And her skin had cooled slightly.

I swallowed down the last few drops of her blood and then raised my wrist. Using my fangs, I pierced two holes into my skin and lifted my wrist to her lips.

"Drink," I urged her. A few drops of blood wept from my wound and onto her mouth. She wet her lips with her tongue, and something rumbled in my stomach at the sight. She swallowed and smacked her lips, tilting her head up for more.

I pressed my wrist against her lips, trying to ignore the softness of her mouth or the delicious way she gulped down my blood. A low moan escaped her lips, and I closed my eyes. She leaned into me, and a fearsome roar swept through me as our blood bonded together. Though the energy within me faded from the loss of blood, I thrived on the power of that bond. The need. The hunger. The seductive desire.

I leaned against her, pressing my hips to hers. We were cramped together on the armchair, but I needed to be closer. I needed to be one with her.

Brielle's eyes flew open and met mine. Her face paled, and she shoved my arm away from her.

"Get the hell off me!" she shouted, struggling to extricate herself from my grip.

I drew away, my head feeling fuzzy, and rose from the armchair. Brielle staggered to her feet and then swayed, blinking rapidly. I tried approaching, but she raised a hand, her eyes blazing.

"I—" She stopped and straightened. Clarity burned in her eyes, and I knew what she was feeling. That strange energy. That euphoric thrill.

Her gaze hardened as she stepped toward me. "What the hell did you do to me?"

I backed away from her, despite the way her blood pulsed through me, calling to me. I desperately wanted to taste her again. To *feel* her again.

But I buried that desire deep down, knowing I'd crossed a line. Knowing we couldn't have the same connection I had with Estrella.

"I had no choice," I said quietly, raising my hands in surrender. "You were burning up. I recognized the signs. Lilith was trying to claim you."

Brielle's face slackened in shock, and then the blood drained from her face. "Lilith." She shivered, rubbing her arms. "I . . . I saw her. She was there, in my mind. I—" She looked around as if she'd dropped something. "Where's Nix?"

I frowned at her. "Nix?"

"My phoenix. Where did she go?"

"She's tethered to you." I cocked my head, still confused.

"But Lilith," Brielle said breathlessly, her eyes wide. "Did Lilith take her?"

I drew closer to her. "She can't take her when you're awake. Not without your permission. Lucia only had her fits after a feeding—when she was most vulnerable. As a vampire, she never slept, but Lilith still tried to strike when her blood was fresh and she was open to a connection with another. Like a bond shared between vampire and Donor."

Brielle leveled a steely gaze at me. "Like what you forced on me."

I shook my head. "Brielle, I wouldn't have done that if I hadn't thought your life was in danger."

"But you *gave* me your blood," she said angrily. "You took blood from an unwilling Donor, and then you solidified a bond between us! I didn't give you permission to do that!"

"If I'd left you there after drinking your blood, you could have died after your fight with Lilith," I said, my own anger rising. "You told me to do whatever it took to keep you from killing, to keep your family safe. Would you prefer I'd killed you?"

"Yes!" she cried, spreading her arms. "I would rather die than be bound to a vampire against my will!"

I stilled, my insides chilling at her words. *She would rather die than be bound to me.*

My chest hardened, closing off my emotions before I could examine them. I forced the easy smile to my face and raised my eyebrows. "It's in my nature, Brielle. There was a problem, and I trusted my instincts." I shrugged, trying to brush off her hatred and resentment. "I won't apologize for my decision. I stand by what I did. If it's so offensive to you, you are welcome to ask someone else to end your life. I'm sure Jorge would be more than willing." My mouth stretched wide into a grin.

Brielle balled her hands into fists, her jaw rigid. She stepped toward me. "You bastard."

I laughed, remembering our first encounter when she'd called me that. "Perhaps I am. But you're alive, and Lilith is gone . . . for now. I consider that a victory."

Brielle glared at me, her nostrils flaring. She opened her mouth to argue with me when I raised a hand, recognizing Miguel's presence. He shifted forms, appearing in front of us as a vampire. His eyes were wide and wild, and my body tensed at once.

"What is it?" I asked.

He gestured behind him, panting. "We're under attack."

42

BRIELLE

Leo immediately snapped into action, forgetting our argument entirely. Though anger still burned through me, my heart stilled at the words: *We're under attack.*

I wanted to ask who, but I already knew. It was the Count.

"How many?" Leo asked, striding out of the library with Miguel. I quickly followed, my ears straining to hear Miguel's response.

"At least a hundred. All armed."

"What kinds of weapons?" Leo asked. I hurried to match his urgent strides.

"Mostly swords and daggers. Some of them have rifles."

Leo swore. "Are the wards intact?"

"For now. But the Count and his casters are hitting it with their magic as we speak."

I stopped short. "Casters?" I repeated numbly.

Leo and Miguel stopped to look at me in surprise as if just realizing I was there.

Merciful Lilith, I thought in horror. The Count had brought the casters with him. Izzy, Riker, Armin, and all the others were out there now, ready to fight us.

Ready to fight *me.*

"With half his mages dead, he needs all the magical help he can get," Leo said softly, though his eyes were blazing.

I swallowed and looked at him, gritting my teeth and finding my resolve again. "What can I do?"

Leo stared at me for a long moment, contemplating. "Return to the library. Start crafting a countercurse."

I blinked. "What?"

"I need to get my people out of the city," Leo said sharply. "My Donors, the people under my protection—they can't all fight. I have to find a way out, and breaking the Count's curse is the only way to do that."

"Leo, I'm a fighter! Let me help!"

"You can." He stepped toward me. "But write the spell first. We need you, Brielle. This is the most important thing." He shook his head, his brows knitted in frustration. "I put it off for too long. I should've worked on the spell with you from the beginning."

But that had been my fault. First, I'd insisted on searching for a cure for myself. Then, I'd thrown a fit over trying to rescue Izzy. Then, my parents had shown up.

There'd been no time. It was now or never.

Reluctantly, I nodded. "All right. When I finish, where can I find your weapons?"

"We're headed to the armory now," Leo said. "Follow us to grab what you need in case anyone breaks through our defenses."

Without waiting for my response, he turned and continued down the tunnel with Miguel. I took a breath and hurried after them.

We took several turns I'd never been down before, finally ending up in a small cavern the size of a linen closet. There was only room for one of us inside, so I awkwardly stayed in the tunnel with Miguel while Leo rummaged through armor and weapons.

"As I said to you before," Leo grunted, his voice carrying through the tunnel, "we are quite low on weaponry. Had you not confronted me in the armory of the Castillo de Coca that day, we might have had more." He flashed me a grin, and my stomach twisted with guilt.

Leo tossed a breastplate to Miguel, who slid it on. After a few minutes, Leo emerged with his own breastplate and two long swords strapped to his back. His hair was pulled back, and his muscular arms were bare beneath the armor. For a moment, I wondered why he only wore a breastplate—then, I remembered he was a vampire. His only vulnerability was his heart.

"What would you like, Brielle?" Leo asked pleasantly as if we were having dinner together. "Sword or dagger?"

"Dagger, please."

Leo nodded and passed me a small blade with a decorative hilt. I glanced up and down my nightgown uncertainly until Leo handed me a belt with a hilt attached. He smirked knowingly at me, and I rolled my eyes.

"Thanks," I muttered, wrapping the belt around my waist and sliding the dagger in the hilt.

A deafening boom shook the ground, and I teetered, pressing my hands against the rocky wall for support. I shared a worried glance with Leo, whose jaw went rigid.

"The wards won't hold much longer," Miguel said gravely.

I stiffened, suddenly remembering Angel and my parents. "My family!" I turned to Leo. "Where are they?"

"I have sentries posted outside. They'll keep them within the wards if they try to leave the caves." Leo paused. "If they're smart, they'll stay in your room."

I knew they wouldn't. My parents were fighters. They'd been in battles before.

But Angel hadn't.

Without another word, I surged forward, weaving through tunnels and only pausing to regain my bearings. I finally wound down a familiar path until it opened up to my room. The first thing I saw was my parents' empty cots, and my heart lurched in my throat.

Then, a voice hissed, "Brie!"

I jumped, my eyes roving around the room until they rested on a few dark figures huddled in the corner. The faint moonlight twinkled from the holes in the ceiling.

I rushed forward and found Angel and my mom

crouched together, obviously hiding in case an enemy searched the caves.

"Where's Dad?" I asked.

Mom straightened at my approach, her eyes fierce. "He volunteered to fight."

A lump formed in my throat. I looked from Mom's determined expression to Angel, whose face was filled with fear.

"You go," I said to Mom. "I'll stay with Angel."

"I'm not a baby," Angel snapped, though her trembling voice betrayed her.

"You're not a fighter, either," I said.

"I've been training these past few months," she said, lifting her chin in defiance. "I can fight."

"Come with me," I said, dragging her arm. I glanced over my shoulder at Mom. "Be safe!"

"You too," Mom said before we parted ways.

"Brie—" Angel protested, but I continued dragging her through tunnels. Another boom shook the ground, and we both yelped as we bumped into each other.

We made it back to the library, which was empty now. I dropped Angel's hand and hurried toward the bookshelves. "I need your help," I told her.

She was silent for a moment. When I looked at her, I saw the defiance still showing in her face. The desperation to prove herself. To be something fierce.

I knew that feeling all too well. In that moment, I saw myself reflected in her eyes.

"What do you need?" she asked at last, stepping forward to help.

I grabbed a handful of books and then froze, my mind racing with possibilities. My first thought had been to look through the Spanish spells, but then I remembered Ignacio and the other mages. When they'd cast spells to try to unleash Lilith, they'd spoken in *Latin.*

"The spell is in Latin," I whispered. I blinked and looked at Angel's confused expression. "Find whatever books you can about Latin spells. Use my translation spell if you need help."

Angel nodded and fingered through several books before propping one open.

Urgency pulsed through me, but I knew this wasn't something I could rush. The cave rumbled frequently as we searched, and my blood boiled with the desire to fight. To take action.

I jotted down notes and phrases from other similar spells, pausing occasionally to think of the Count and what I knew about him. I had to match his intent. He cast the spell to locate Lilith's cursed witch so she could be destroyed.

"Locator spells, banishing spells, spells about altering time," I muttered. "Anything you find that relates to that will help."

"Spells that alter time haven't been written yet," Angel said. "But I can give you what I remember from when Mom cast the spell."

The time travel spell. For a minute, my heart leapt in my

throat, reminding me of that monumental secret Mom and Dad had kept from us.

But I shoved it down. *Now is not the time.* "That would be helpful. Thanks."

I wrote down phrases like *pythonissam*, *maledictum*, *tempus*, and *excindo*. I also wrote down synonyms of *banish* and *curse*, since there were multiple forms.

Lilith, this will take forever.

"Here," Angel said, sliding a piece of paper toward me. "These are all the rhyming words I found in the spells."

I wanted to hug her. I exhaled with relief, pulling the list toward me. "Thank you."

We worked silently for a few more minutes, occasionally gasping or crying out when the ground shook again. Angel passed me her notes and kept researching while I worked on crafting the spell. I cursed this time period and its lack of erasers as I scribbled through phrases over and over again.

Then, another explosion shook the caves, this one more massive than the others. The walls shook. The ceiling quivered. Rocks and pebbles rained down on us. Angel and I ducked, covering our heads with our hands.

A tickle of magic wafted in the air. It smelled sharp, like the vampire coven. But then the scent was overtaken by another more subtle scent. The smell of ash, onions, and seaweed. A smell that filled me with memories of staying in the castle.

The Count.

A ripple of magic washed over us like a splash of cold water. I sucked in a gasp, my wide eyes meeting Angel's.

The wards were down. We were out of time.

Something powerful hammered into the caves, and Angel shrieked, covering her head again. More rocks tumbled from the ceiling.

I snatched the papers closest to me, tugged on Angel's hand, and pulled her forward. "Come on!"

We raced out of the library as the ceiling cracked and crumbled. Boulders slammed into the ground around us. Angel screamed. I stopped short as large rocks poured from the ceiling, blocking our path.

Angel's hand trembled in my grip. Panting, I glanced behind me, knowing there was no way out but forward.

But we were trapped. And the cave was collapsing around us.

"Help!" I shrieked. It was probably no use, but I had to try. "Is someone there? *Help us!*"

I'm here, a voice whispered.

I jumped and whirled around wildly. "Who's there?"

"Brie," Angel whispered uncertainly, her eyes cast toward the ceiling. "No one's there."

"No, I heard something—"

I'm here, Brielle. I can help.

I went very still. Fire burned within me, just waiting to be unleashed. "Nix?" I asked.

Yes, the voice replied. *I am here.*

My heart froze, and for a full beat, time seemed to stop as I homed in on the voice inside me. *Nix.*

My blood raced, and an unfamiliar energy buzzed through me. *Leo's* energy.

His blood was inside me. And I recalled what had happened when the Count forced me to drink Ronaldo's blood. Lilith had taken control of Nix. But now that Nix and I had connected, Leo's blood had simply awakened her inside me.

Even though I was also awake.

"Brie," Angel said urgently, her wide eyes darting to me with that "she's crazy" look.

"Nix, what can you do?" I asked. "I can't exactly fall asleep right now."

The cave rumbled again. Angel screamed and tugged on my arm, dragging me back toward the library as more rocks rained down on us. Something heavy collided with my shoulder, and I fell over.

We are bonded, Nix said to me. *We have united. The transformation will be easier now. Clear your mind and give yourself over to me.*

I swallowed. Her words jolted me, and a ripple of unease swept through me. *Give yourself over to me.* It sounded dangerous. Like something Lilith might say.

"What—what about my sister?" I asked. "Can you get her out?"

Yes. Tell her she must hold onto you. Your body will be lifeless when I take over. I will extinguish my flames so you both can hold onto my talons. But only for a moment. Once we are freed, I will need to fly and ignite my flames again to recharge.

I sucked in several sharp breaths. Angel was still watching me warily, but I squeezed her hand. "We'll be all right," I told her.

"Oh, are you talking to me now?" she asked hysterically. Dust coated her hair, and her face was smeared with dirt.

Cast a protection spell on you both, Nix said.

I closed my eyes and flexed my fingers toward Angel.

"*Magic above and powers that be,*

Protect us from harm and injury."

My hands glowed blue, and Angel yelped as her body began to glow.

"Hold still," I warned her.

Angel obeyed, her body stiff as my magic swept over her. Then, the blue magic rippled over my own body as well.

When the blue glow faded, Angel blinked at me. "What was that for?"

"I'm—I'm going to release the phoenix."

The blood drained from her face. "*What*? Brie—"

"There's no time!" I shouted over the noise of another explosion. "This cave will collapse on us any minute. She says she'll put out her flames so you can grab hold of her talons."

Angel was shaking her head. "The last time the phoenix came out—"

"I know," I said, closing my eyes briefly. "But that was Lilith. Not the phoenix. Nix and I are bonded now. We can communicate. She'll keep you safe, Angel. But when she's free, you'll need to hold onto me. I won't be conscious."

Angel's wide eyes remained fixed on me, and her body trembled with terror. In that moment, *I* felt like the older sister. The one tasked with protecting her. I'd always felt that way about Angel.

But I couldn't protect her if she didn't trust me.

Our eyes locked, and she nodded slowly. "Okay."

You both should back up, Nix advised.

I guided Angel to the opposite side of the cave tunnel. Then, I closed my eyes and sat back on my rear, trying to ignore the chaos of sounds around me. The fire in my chest roared to life, ready to respond. I felt Nix's soul nestled next to mine. She was ready too.

I inhaled deeply. Images flashed through my mind: Mom, Dad, Leo, the Count, my friends at the castle—but I struggled to shove them down, to release my thoughts. I exhaled through my mouth, long and slow. With each steady breath, Nix's presence grew stronger.

When I opened my eyes, I saw nothing but fire. The flames burned in my chest, desperate for release. I opened my mouth to oblige, but Nix stopped me.

Not yet, she whispered.

I let her take over.

In an explosion of rocks and debris, she crashed through the cave ceiling and landed on the ground, stretching her wings wide. Angel shouted in alarm, but Nix ignored her. With monumental effort, Nix withdrew the flames. They boiled within me, threatening to burst, to explode. It felt like knives clawing at my insides.

Nix flapped her wings, soaring toward the gaping hole in the ceiling. A heavy weight tugged on her talons, and I knew Angel had grabbed on. In the recesses of my mind, I vaguely registered another limp figure alongside Angel.

It was me. *I* was the limp figure. It was surreal, to think and feel as if I were Nix, but know my body was right there in the bird's grasp. I felt the girl's body attached to Nix's talons as if she were a doll—as if she weren't me at all. The thought made my head spin.

With a roar, Nix released her fire, spewing the flames onto the ceiling like molten lava. Angel screamed, and Nix shot forward, bursting against the ceiling and crashing through. Rocks and boulders rained down, but Nix broke free of the wreckage and spiraled high into the sky. She spun, arcing around the caves and toward the forest where flashes of light marked the battle between the demons and the Count's men.

Nix pivoted toward the fray, aiming for the long line of armored soldiers advancing toward the caves. Some men shouted and dived out of the way. Those that remained aimed their swords and guns toward Nix, but she breathed fire, igniting them with her flames. The weight on her talons released, and I knew Angel had let go. I hoped she had taken me with her—that my body was safe.

If I died while Nix was free, would I feel it at all?

A sharp pain split through Nix's skin, and she roared. Agony roiled through her, emanating in my own chest and searing my skin. I tried to scream, but I was trapped in Nix's mind. The phoenix shrieked and crashed into the ground before slumping over, motionless.

43
LEO

I FOLLOWED MIGUEL OUT OF THE CAVES TOWARD THE edge of the forest. Most of my coven was already outside and fully armed. A full moon bathed the woods in an eerie glow that mingled with the blue sparks flying in the air. Half a dozen mages were positioned at the front, closest to the caves. Next to them, a line of young light warlocks stood with their hands outstretched as they murmured enchantments, no doubt trying to pierce through my wards.

My eyes fell on the lone witch standing at the end of the line. Her stark white hair was familiar to me.

Yes, I remembered. This was Brielle's friend—Izzy. I stared hard at Izzy, thinking of how desperate Brielle had been to rescue her. Yet here she was, fighting on the Count's side.

But as I watched her, my eyes narrowed. A dizzying array of smells assaulted my nose: perspiration, light magic, metal, gunpowder. But I smelled something faint emanating from the girl.

Fear.

Izzy's hands trembled as she flexed her fingers. Sweat poured down her brow. Her eyes shifted nervously to something behind her. I followed her gaze and found the Count dressed in armor from head to toe. I almost wouldn't have recognized him, but his helmet visor was up, and his icy stare was fixed on me.

When I met his gaze, I smirked at him, burying my unease and keeping my smugness at the surface. Agitating my enemies was my strong suit.

My eyes roved over the row of light warlocks, suddenly seeing what I hadn't noticed before. Half of them looked as conflicted as Izzy, their arms stiff and trembling, their faces betraying their reluctance.

When my focus returned to the Count, he was smiling. Like he knew what I'd just figured out. I had no doubt he'd coerced these casters into fighting for him—perhaps he'd threatened their families or their lives. He was desperate, after all. I had what he wanted most: Brielle.

If I could find out how the other casters were bound to him, perhaps I could free them and convince them to switch sides.

Jorge shifted and appeared next to me, his face pale. "Two hundred armed soldiers," he said breathlessly. "Not to mention the mages and casters."

"What about the Donors and their families?" I asked.

"Guadalupe snuck them out the east end of the forest. She'll hide them in the village."

"If this battle goes poorly, that will be the first place the Count will look," I said grimly. *We need to get them out of the city.*

"I know," Jorge said, his eyebrows knitting together. "But it's all we can do for now."

My gaze flicked back toward the caves. Brielle was now the only one left inside. *Make haste, Little Nightmare,* I thought. We needed that countercurse.

The ground rumbled, and I swayed, barely catching myself before falling over. Looking up, I found a line of white cracks floating in the air, marking the transparent wards that surrounded the caves. The casters were breaking through. It wouldn't be long now.

I turned to face my coven—my family. With a swift movement, I drew both swords from the sheaths at my back. My very bones trembled with anticipation, and my body yearned for blood. For victory.

For revenge.

I lifted my sword and shouted, "Prepare yourselves! We take no prisoners today!" I paused, thinking of the casters fighting against their will. "Spare the casters if you can." I turned to face the army waiting for us and leveled my gaze at the Count. "And Antonio de Silva is mine."

More cracks formed against my barriers. The ground rumbled again, but I remained upright. I stretched my arms, brandishing my swords. The energy racing through me was exhilarating. Intoxicating. I'd forgotten the thrill of battle.

A crash echoed behind me. I glanced over my shoulder and found boulders crumbling from the cave ceiling. It took me a moment to realize why my blood was pulsing with urgency.

Brielle was still in there.

I straightened, fear chilling me to my bones. *No.* I glanced at Jorge, who watched me with understanding in his eyes. He shook his head slightly, indicating he hadn't seen her.

I swallowed, reluctantly turning back to face my enemy. I couldn't abandon my coven just before battle, though my body screamed at me to run inside and search for Brielle.

I closed my eyes, inhaling deeply and focusing on the taste of her blood. The scent of her skin. My own blood roared in my ears, hungry for more of her delicious nectar, but I shoved it down, searching inward for our bond.

There it was. Brielle's blood still pulsed, though it raced with fear. She was still alive—for now.

Something else tainted her blood. Something dark and fiery that boiled forth. It was foreign to me—I hadn't tasted it when I'd drunk from her.

It had to be either the firebird . . . or Lilith.

My eyes opened, and I exhaled long and slow. Brielle was a fighter. I had to trust that she could fend for herself.

Movement caught my eye at the edge of the caves, and a vaguely familiar scent stung my nose, filling me with dread and alarm.

Brielle's parents, Oliver and Desi, strode toward me,

their faces set with determination. Rage and fire danced in Oliver's eyes, so familiar to me. In his eyes, I saw a reflection of myself. My own hatred. My own energy.

I blinked and glanced behind them for their daughter. When I frowned, Oliver answered my unspoken question.

"She's with Brielle."

Merciful Lilith. I looked back toward the caves as another boulder crumbled.

Desi stiffened, her face going pale. Her hand reached for Oliver, her eyes wide with warning.

"Did they make it out?" Oliver demanded, gazing around the forest for his daughters.

"I haven't seen them," I said gravely.

Desi's face paled, and Oliver went very still.

Another explosion burst in the air, followed by a deafening crack. The feeble remains of my protective barrier shattered, scorching the air and singeing my nostrils. Magic rippled in the air and poured downward like a falling curtain. The smell filled me with nostalgia—I'd been with Lucia and Ronaldo when I'd constructed the wards. Their magic had helped to build the barrier.

I gripped my swords tightly in my hands as the soldiers and casters shifted their weight, readying for battle.

"On me!" I shouted, raising my sword. Then, I surged forward, a battle cry pouring from my mouth. I felt the pounding of footsteps behind me, the accompanying shouts of my men. The Count's soldiers and casters rushed forward as well, and when I was almost upon them, I shifted to my bat form. Darkness clouded my vision, and I flitted my wings, pivoting in the air before landing in the middle of the soldiers. My swords slashed three of them before they had even registered what had happened. The clang of metal rang in my ears. Blood poured from their wounds, igniting the fire within me.

Not now, I scolded it. I could feed later. Instead, I drowned myself in the heat of battle. My blood thrummed, and I swung my swords, aiming for shoulders and armpits where their armor was weakest. I felt my fangs emerge as my body sensed the bloodbath around me.

But I refused to break my rule. I would *not* feast on unwilling victims. Even in battle.

Here, I was a man fighting to protect his home. If I submitted to the monster, I would become something else entirely.

I thought of my brother, so devout in his faith yet so reckless with matters of the heart. I could almost hear him cheering me on from the other side, rooting for my survival.

I will protect our people, Brother.

I sliced my swords through two more soldiers. I sensed a man lunging for me from behind, and I vanished in a puff of black smoke. My bat form lifted me higher and higher, and when I landed, I speared my sword into the soldier's eye. He fell over, motionless.

Another explosion rattled the ground, and I stared, frozen, toward the caves. My people's caves—our home— crumbled before my eyes, collapsing inward on itself.

My eyes widened, and a deafening roar filled my chest. I

took a step toward the caves as panic pulsed through my veins.

Brielle.

Agony flooded through me in nauseating waves. My instincts barely returned in time to dodge the swinging sword of a nearby soldier. The blade nicked my arm, and I blasted the man backward with a burst of my magic.

A bloodcurdling scream shook me to my core, and I knew without looking that it was Brielle's mother. Loud crashes echoed behind me, and I whirled to find Desi using her Telekinetic powers to sweep away the rubble of the caves. Her face was red and covered with tears. Oliver reached for her, trying to stop her, but she pushed more boulders out of the way as if she could find her daughters' bodies among the debris. My blood chilled from the sounds of Desi's sobs, and for one wild moment, I wanted to join her. To mourn with her.

But Brielle was a fighter. She would want me to fight.

I turned away and slashed my swords again, taking down two soldiers at once.

Then, a burst of fire drew my attention to the caves. The firebird soared from the rubble in an explosion of flames, its mighty roar rumbling in the air and rattling my ears. A collective gasp echoed around me as soldiers on both sides gaped at the magnificent phoenix soaring into the sky.

Then, the Count shouted something to his men, and they aimed their crossbows.

"No!" I roared, shifting and flying toward them. But I was too late. The whizzing tickled my ears as the men fired.

I shifted back to my vampire form, following the trail of fire as the phoenix went down. A figure crumpled nearby from the impact, and I rushed toward it.

"Brielle?" I cried, turning the girl over.

It was Angel. Her dark hair was covered in ash and dust.

A war of emotions took over me. Relief that Angel was safe. Terror that it wasn't Brielle. My gaze found the firebird, whose flames were doused. It lay weakly on the forest floor, moaning and turning its head.

A dozen soldiers surged toward the creature, and I brandished my swords. *I'll take on all of them if I have to.* They moved toward me, and I sprang into action. Cut. Slice. Strike. Blood drenched my arms. Men fell. Sharp stabs of pain pierced my skin as I withstood their blows.

They could bleed me dry, but without a stake, I would just keep healing. Keep fighting.

"Enough!" roared a familiar voice.

The soldiers stopped cutting at me and straightened obediently as the Count emerged, parting his men like the sea. His eyes drilled into me, but he glanced hungrily at the fallen phoenix.

"I have worked too hard to be thwarted by a vampire *boy* who doesn't know his place," the Count spat, his jaw quivering. He aimed a rifle at me.

I laughed loudly. "Go ahead. I'll just get back up again."

He fired the gun, and pain slammed into my shoulder, knocking me backward. Agony pulsed through me in waves, and my vision darkened. I cried out, clawing helplessly at something in my shoulder.

The Count approached me slowly, his smile smug as he stood over me. "My men created a unique bullet made of wood. The same holy wood used to destroy your kind." He aimed the rifle at my face. "Tell me, Mr. Serrano. Have you ever been staked in the eye?"

Before he fired the gun, I shifted and flew toward his face, clawing at his skin and his eyes. The Count roared, swatting his hands. I shifted again, slamming my full weight into him as we toppled to the ground. My swords lay forgotten on the forest floor behind me, but I clawed my fingernails into his forehead and eyes. Blood welled from the cuts, and the Count screamed. My body yearned to feast, and for a brief moment, I considered it. This man was the vilest of monsters. Shouldn't I release my own monster to match him?

My hesitation cost me. The Count slammed the butt of his rifle into my face, and I toppled over dizzily.

The familiar smell of the sea filled my nose, and something whooshed past me. The Count roared in pain as a blade sank into his exposed shoulder.

Relief blossomed in my chest as I turned and found Brielle standing there, her body poised for battle. Fire burned in her eyes, and her body and clothes were lined with scorch marks. Her hair was pulled back in a messy, tangled braid, and she still looked ridiculous in her shift tied together with the belt I'd given her.

But she was still the most beautiful thing I'd ever seen.

"Finish him, Leo," she growled without looking at me.

In an instant, I was by the Count's side, holding his head

upward to expose his throat. I felt his blood pulsing with fear. My skin prickled with movement from behind me, but Brielle engaged the soldiers, buying me time. I sensed Jorge and Miguel joining her.

They knew what this moment meant for me.

I bared my fangs and hissed. The Count closed his eyes, his lips trembling. I leaned in and froze, suddenly hearing my brother's voice.

Don't give in, Leo.

I paused, only a breath away from the Count's throat.

Suddenly, light magic tickled the air, and I fell backward in an explosion of blue smoke. When I righted myself, the Count was standing, his eyes blazing. With a jerk, he yanked the dagger from his shoulder, which bled freely. The blade glinted with his blood as he brandished it.

My arms itched to grab the swords on my back, but I knew they weren't there. Fury boiled in my blood, and I leveled a fierce gaze at the Count.

I didn't need weapons. I *was* a weapon.

I lunged, and the Count vanished with a *pop.* He reappeared behind me and sliced the dagger into my arm. I hissed, whirling, but he disappeared again in a puff of blue smoke.

I heard Brielle shout something, but I couldn't make out her words.

The Count reappeared and hurled his dagger, but I shifted to avoid it. In my bat form, I flitted higher and higher, out of the Count's reach. He murmured a spell, and a jet of blue fire soared toward me. I barely dodged the flames as they scorched my wings.

I vaguely registered Brielle as she, too, uttered a spell. The scent of her light magic filled the air and swarmed around the Count. I shifted back to my vampire form and stood before him, cocking my head.

The Count smirked at me and then stiffened. He glanced around, wide-eyed, until he found Brielle grinning smugly at him.

"What did you do to me, you filthy whore?" the Count roared, stepping toward her.

In one quick motion, I spun him around and wrapped my hand around his throat. Rage pulsed through me so powerfully it made my limbs quiver. I shoved him until he was pinned against the trunk of a tree. He reeked of light magic and fear. The smell of his terror only made me smile.

My fangs longed to bury themselves inside him, but I remembered my brother's words. *Don't give in.*

Clinging to my brother's voice, I slammed my forehead against the Count's, rendering him unconscious. Then, I took his bloody dagger, raised it high above me, and buried it into his throat.

"That's for my brother," I hissed. I tugged it free, and blood soaked the earth. I raised it again and slid it across his throat. The Count slumped over, collapsing to the ground. He gurgled and choked and then went still, his blood pouring from him like a river.

"And that's for my sister." My voice sounded hollow in my ears, my blood singing with satisfaction.

For the first time in my life, my hunger for blood was absent. My body and soul rejoiced as one, reveling in my act of vengeance. My vampiric needs were silenced.

Ronaldo was right. The man within me had taken over the monster. And I'd won.

44
BRIELLE

I'D FELT NIX'S PAIN. HER AGONY. WHEN I'D COME TO, she was gone. I couldn't even feel her fire within me. Her presence.

I only felt cold and empty.

But I'd woken in the heat of battle, so I couldn't stop to search for her. A soldier slashed his dagger, and I ducked to avoid it. I kicked him in the chest, and he stumbled backward. I dropped to the ground, sliding my legs under his until he crashed to the ground. With a grunt, I kicked him in the head and snatched his dagger.

Then, I saw Leo and the Count. Though I knew Leo was more than capable, I couldn't help myself.

I owed the Count all the pain and suffering he'd caused me.

So, I hit him with my dagger, buying Leo some time. Then, I'd uttered a spell to freeze his powers, just like I had with the Jumper from the Council before he'd thrown me through the portal.

And when Leo ended the Count's life, I felt a stir of emotion within me. Horror. Disbelief. And a small sliver of satisfaction, knowing he wouldn't be around to cause any more harm.

"Brie!" a voice shouted.

I glanced up and found Angel fighting a soldier armed with a long sword. I surged forward, but before I got there, Angel twisted the soldier's arm around and buried the sword in his neck. The man fell in a pool of blood.

Breathing heavily, Angel looked up and met my gaze. Fire blazed in her eyes, making her unrecognizable. All I could do was stare at her speechlessly.

"Brie, are you hurt?" Angel asked, hurrying toward me.

I blinked and shook my head. My gaze roved over her form. Aside from a few scorch marks, she looked unharmed. "You?"

"I'm fine. The phoenix covered us with her wings when we escaped the cave." Her mouth opened and closed. "I—I can't believe you did that, Brie. That you summoned her. That she *saved* us."

A soldier lunged for us, and we both ducked.

"We'll talk about it later," I said, slicing the soldier's leg with my dagger. He howled and fell over while Angel embedded her sword in his throat. I stared as my sister took another man's life with ease—and it made me wonder what else she was capable of.

Something heavy collided with my head, and I stumbled

backward, blinking stars from my eyes. A soldier wielded two swords and slashed them toward me. I dodged, but one of them cut into my side. I gasped, staggering backward. Dropping to the ground, I spun and buried my knife in his kneecap. When he fell, I slit his throat.

I looked up and found Angel sparring with Riker.

My heart jolted in my chest. Riker burst forward, wielding an athame. His face was pale and sweaty, but his eyes were determined. I knew he would kill my sister.

I hurried forward, ignoring the stabbing pain in my side, when Angel suddenly went rigid, dropping her sword. Her limbs quivered and her mouth fell open. Her eyes rolled back until they were all white. Even Riker stilled in surprise.

An ethereal voice poured from Angel's lips. "On this day, a choice will be made. A threat will emerge, powerful and afraid. Darkness will rise and cover us all. And then her magic will make us fall."

My blood chilled, and I stared at my sister in disbelief. It was almost exactly the same prophecy Riker had uttered when he'd had that vision. The same day we'd kissed.

Riker's face drained of color, and I knew he recognized the words. His gaze slid to me, and for a moment, the three of us just stood there awkwardly while the battle raged around us.

Then, I lunged for him. Angel remained upright, her body quivering. I had to protect her until she woke from her vision. I slammed my shoulder against Riker's until he stumbled backward.

"Brielle—" he said, but I didn't let him finish. I kicked him in the shin, and he bent over. I jerked my knee up between his legs, and he howled in agony before collapsing.

"Stay away from my sister," I growled.

"I . . . can't," Riker rasped.

I stiffened. "What're you talking about?"

Riker sucked in a breath and looked up at me with pained eyes. "The Count. He bound our magic together. We *have* to fight."

"The Count is dead," I said, glaring at him.

Riker shook his head. "But his spell . . . will keep going. He used demon blood. As long as the demons live, the spell carries on."

My brows furrowed. *He's lying.* But even as I thought this, I knew his words had truth in them. Why else would the Count keep those demons alive in his dungeon? He couldn't possibly have suspected all of them of being Nightcasters.

"Brielle," Riker said urgently, staggering to his feet. His eyes burned with urgency. "If the Count is dead, then we're all in danger. He included a failsafe in the time loop. If he dies—"

A deep rumbling shook the ground. Riker and I collided and tumbled to the ground. Light exploded in the midnight sky like fireworks. I looked up, my eyes wide. A bloodred smoke curled in the sky, spreading like an infection. The crimson shadows bled farther and farther until the entire sky was consumed by redness.

Horror chilled me to the bone. "What the hell is that?" I whispered.

"The failsafe," Riker said in a grim voice.

I stared at him numbly. "What does it do?"

"The time loop will collapse on itself. Obliterating the city."

My heart dropped to my stomach. As if the Count were right next to me, I could almost hear his reasoning for this: *If I don't survive, no one will.*

Curse that bastard.

I had to find Leo.

I darted away from Riker, weaving through soldiers and demons who had stopped fighting to stare in horror at the bloody sky. *Where is he? Where is he?*

"Brielle!"

I turned and found Leo running toward me. A long, jagged cut ran along his jaw, and his wild, curly hair had come loose. He held a sword in each hand, and for a moment, I stared at him, overwhelmed by the fierceness of him—clad in armor, wielding swords, sporting injuries. His face was taut and determined. He looked like a soldier. A man defending his people. Not at all like the sneaky vampire I'd first met.

Leo pointed skyward. "The spell?"

I nodded. "It's the Count."

Leo swore and raised a hand to his forehead. "I feared this would happen."

I stepped toward him. "What do you mean?"

"I hoped that with the Count's death, the curse would be

broken. But I knew it was a possibility he'd built in a reaction to his death."

"You knew this might happen?"

Leo leveled a hard gaze at me. "Save your judgment, Brielle. Did you write the spell? The countercurse?"

Something within me jolted as I remembered jotting down Latin phrases with Angel. That had felt so long ago. I reached behind me and pulled out the folded sheets of paper I'd stuck in my belt.

"Here goes nothing," I muttered.

"Wait," Leo said, drawing closer to me. He raised a hand to the cut on his face and rubbed his jaw until his fingers were smeared with blood. Then, he pressed his bloody hand against my side—my injury.

I hissed and backed away from him. "What the hell?"

Leo took my free hand in his and rubbed our blood together. "Nightcaster blood and demon blood," he said in a low voice. "I have no doubt the Count used powerful ingredients when he cast the spell." He pointed to the red sky. "This indicates demon blood used with light magic. Hopefully, the power in your blood will counteract the other ingredients he used." He nodded toward me. "Go on."

I took a deep breath and uttered the spell I'd written on the paper.

"*Hoc vocat justo. Audi me voca.*

Intende in adjutorium meum, et sana.

Circumdate civitatem hanc. Defendat.

Frange hoc augurium. Adiuva nos effugeret.

Quaerite de illo anathemate venefica eis.

Nos furore suo. Nos eramus servientes.
Fero quod ex urbe inlectus dimitte nobis.
Super spiritibus, voca me audies."

My hands shook and glowed blue. Magic coursed within me, racing through me. Fire bubbled in my chest. I closed my eyes, waiting. Hoping.

Then, the magic within me died. I opened my eyes, and the blue glow on my hands was gone.

It didn't work.

I looked at Leo in alarm.

He nodded again, but I could see the unease in his face. "Try again."

I nodded and uttered another spell I'd written down. But like the first, it did nothing. I gritted my teeth and swore loudly.

"Here." Leo drew close enough for his spicy scent to fill my nose. It mingled with sweat, blood, and dirt, filling my nostrils. I exhaled, trying to clear my head.

Leo pointed to the phrase *venefica eis.* "Try *pythonissam* instead. It means 'witch.' And this phrase here, try saying *nos incantationem.* So the words align."

I nodded slowly. *To make the spell rhyme.* "Okay." I opened my mouth and tried again.

This time, the blood on my hand burned when I spoke the words. I clenched my fist, trying to ward off the pain, but it spread through me like wildfire. I dropped the paper from my hands and closed my eyes. Magic swelled within me so rapidly it made me feel sick. I hunched over as blue magic poured from my fingertips and jetted toward the sky. Cracks formed in the red clouds above us.

Fire scorched my insides, and I fell to the ground.

"Brielle!" Leo was at my side, touching my arms and shoulders. "Brielle, can you hear me?"

My vision blurred. The redness in the sky faded, but everything swam before my eyes.

A soft voice hissed in my ear, "You are nothing." But it wasn't Leo's voice.

A woman stood before me. I'd seen her before. Her all-black eyes stared at nothing, but her wide smile made me shudder.

It was Lilith.

I shook my head, trying to back away from her. But I was frozen in place. I glanced around. We were alone in the forest. Leo, the soldiers, and the demons had all vanished.

"You're gone," I said numbly. "I pushed you out when I bonded with Nix."

Lilith's grin widened, and she laughed. "It was a valiant effort, little one. But it was de Silva's magic that kept me at bay—not yours."

De Silva. The Count.

Lilith spread her arms wide and threw her head back in rapture.

No, I thought in horror. No, this couldn't be happening. "Nix!" I shouted desperately.

Lilith sighed with contentment and lowered her head to look at me. "Your firebird is long gone. It sacrificed itself to save you."

I shook my head, my throat filling with emotion. "No. You're lying."

Something in my chest resonated from my accusation. *She's lying. Lilith can't survive without the phoenix's energy.*

I tried to calm my panicked breaths and cling to that knowledge within me. The knowledge that the only reason Lilith targeted me was because of the phoenix.

Nix had to be alive.

But where was she?

The ashes, said a voice in my head.

I blinked, glancing down. At my feet was a pile of ashes as small as an anthill.

A lump formed in my throat. *Nix.*

I looked up at Lilith, but her hands were pointed toward the sky. Words in Latin poured from her lips, and blood-red magic emanated from her fingers.

The red smoke in the sky. It had been *her.* Trying to break through.

And then I'd broken the Count's curse and let her in.

I dropped to the ground and cupped my hands around Nix's ashes. Closing my eyes, I thought desperately, *What do I do? Nix, what do I do?*

Focus on my fire, she whispered. *Remember my soul. My aura. You can bring me back, Brielle. Because we have bonded.*

I nodded even though she couldn't see me. My brows knitted together as I focused on the flames within me that I'd tried to ignore for so long. The heat in my body. The presence of another inside me. Nix's soul. Her desire for peace. Her longing for safety.

Her love for me.

A loud screech pierced the air, and Lilith stopped her enchantment. I felt her gaze drilling into me, but I kept my hands pressed against the ashes.

An explosion of red magic slammed into my chest, and I tumbled backward.

"You are *nothing* without that firebird," Lilith spat. She drew closer, standing over me with triumph etched in her face. "And you're too late, little one. I've already taken over."

With a grunt, I climbed to my feet to face her. My hands clenched into fists. "If I'm strong enough to let you in," I growled, "then I'm strong enough to push you out." I raised my hands, and fire burst from my palms, scorching Lilith's face.

Lilith shrieked and stumbled backward. I dropped my hands in shock, and the fire vanished. Smoke rose from my hands.

Nix? I asked.

I'm here. But my body is not strong enough to take over. You must defeat her without me.

Terror gripped my body. *How?*

Use my fire. Use our magic.

Our magic.

Lilith roared in fury and shot more red magic toward me. I ducked, narrowly avoiding her spell. My hands shot forward, sending fire toward her, but she countered it with her own magic. Red and orange lights burst against my eyes as our magic collided.

I need more than just a few flames to defeat her, I thought angrily.

Focus, Brielle, Nix said. *Use your entire body. Let the flames consume you.*

I closed my eyes, remembering how it felt when Nix succumbed to the fire. When the flames built up inside her and poured from her mouth.

Heat churned in my stomach, escalating until they climbed up my throat. When I opened my mouth, fire exploded in front of me. I saw nothing but the whiteness of the fire. I felt nothing but the burning heat of the flames.

I screamed at Lilith, inching closer as the fire intensified. My entire body was burning. Every inch of me was covered in red-hot coals.

I could smell Lilith's fear. I felt her rage. She shot her magic at me, but it glanced off my flames as if I wore a shield. She shrieked and shouted, but I couldn't make out her words.

End her, Nix said.

With my firebird's magic, I sprinted forward. Though I couldn't see, my senses told me Lilith was right in front of me. I leapt for her, pinning her to the ground and pressing my flames against her. Suffocating her. She writhed and struggled under my weight, but I held her still, forcing my fire on her.

"We are fire," I hissed, leaning closer to her. "And we will defeat you."

Lilith screamed, and my ears throbbed from the shrill-ness of her voice. Her red magic burst against me, and my skin burned from the impact. Agony spread through my body, and I screamed along with her.

I will end her, I told Nix. *Even if it kills me.*

Then we are in agreement, Nix said. *Do whatever it takes to finish her, Brielle.*

Fire consumed me. I pressed the flames against Lilith, bringing myself further into the red magic pulsing from her in waves. Waves of pain erupted on my body. My chest burned. Her magic tore through me like knives. I felt my body disintegrating, but still I pushed on.

Further and further until I became one with the fire.

45
LEO

"LEO."

I looked up from my book of Latin spells. Exhaustion pulled at my body, and I marveled at the feeling. It felt so *human*. I ran a hand along my face and squinted at the interruption.

It was Jorge. His brows knitted together as he approached me. His eyes roved over the bedroom—the roaring fire in the fireplace, the stacks of papers and books on the table, and lastly, the body lying on the bed.

Brielle's body.

She hadn't woken since the battle two months ago. But I knew she was still alive. Just as surely as I'd known Lucia would return when she had her fits.

But perhaps if I could find a spell to awaken her—similar to the spell she'd cast—then I could bring her back sooner.

"You must feed," Jorge said, crossing his arms.

"I am well, Jorge," I said, dropping my gaze to the text again.

"Don't lie to me. And this isn't just about you. Estrella—"

"Don't talk to me about Estrella." I waved a hand. Every time I thought of her and the bond we shared, my blood was reminded of a new bond that had been forged. The bond between my blood and Brielle's.

I needed Brielle. In more ways than one.

"She can find another vampire," I went on. "She has my blessing to become a Donor for another. Guadalupe perhaps."

"Leo," Jorge said again, drawing closer to me until I was forced to look up at him. "You can't keep doing this. Our coven needs a leader."

"And so you have one. But Brielle is part of this coven. She sacrificed herself to save us. To break the Count's enchantment. I owe it to her to bring her back."

Jorge sighed and sank in the chair across from me. "What does her father say about it?"

"Her parents have tried to revive her. Her mother even brought in some strange instrument to inspect her soul." I frowned, still confused by the strangeness of it. "Desi says both souls are still there—but she can't tell if it's Brielle and her firebird, or Brielle and . . ." I trailed off, unable to say the words.

"Lilith," Jorge said grimly.

"Yes."

Jorge leaned forward. "You can't abandon your people for this girl, Leo."

I gritted my teeth. "My people wouldn't be here without her."

"You're right. But spending your days drowning in books and notes won't bring her back. If you keep this up, you'll lose your coven. You'll starve."

I threw my hands in the air. "Then I'll starve!" I roared.

Jorge fell silent. He dropped his gaze and shifted his weight. Then, he said softly, "Lucia's death isn't your fault."

I went very still. I hadn't told *anyone* about Lucia. Ronaldo and I had been the only ones to know about her condition. And her fate.

I raised my gaze to Jorge's. His face crumpled in grief. "Ronaldo told me," Jorge said. "Before he left for the Castillo de Coca." He paused. "But Leo, why didn't *you* tell me?"

I didn't have an answer for that. I stared at the floor, my blood thundering with anxiety and shock. Finally, I said quietly, "I feared losing my coven."

"They wouldn't have cared. Leo, you're *family*."

I shook my head, slamming the book shut. "I know that. But I'd just lost Ronaldo. Lucia was gone. I had to appear strong. And this was a weakness. When I speak of her, I am weak, Jorge. I—I couldn't relive that again. Not in front of my men."

Jorge sat back and raised his eyebrows at me. "So, it seems I know *all* of your weaknesses now."

I frowned at him until I found his gaze had moved to Brielle lying on the bed.

Anger surged within me, and I rose to my feet. "Don't," I growled.

Jorge said nothing as I approached Brielle. Her eyes were closed, and her expression was filled with peace. I touched her wrist again—as I had every time I'd seen her—and it still felt hot to the touch.

"Brielle," I whispered.

Her eyes flew open. She sucked in a rattling gasp, her chest rising.

I dropped her hand and stumbled backward in shock. Jorge was on his feet, his eyes wide.

Brielle took several deep, shaky breaths and blinked, looking around in confusion. "Where—where am I?"

I couldn't speak. I could barely move. All I could do was stare at her, wondering if I was dreaming.

"Villeguillo," Jorge answered for me. "Just north of the Castillo de Coca."

Brielle sat up and raised a hand to her head, her expression crumpling in agony.

I overcame my shock and rushed to her side, crouching down to her level. "Are you hurt?"

Brielle looked at me in confusion. "Leo. You're here."

"Yes."

"No, I'm not hurt."

"What happened?"

Brielle scooted forward, but I pushed her back down. She glared at me. "I'm fine." She stood and scrutinized her body, no doubt taking in her fresh clothes and healed injuries. "Oh, hell." She grimaced and met my gaze. "I traveled, didn't I?"

I nodded and took her hand. "Brielle, *tell me* what happened."

She took a breath. "It was Lilith. I fought her with the phoenix's power. Then . . . she vanished."

"Vanished?"

Brielle nodded. "Nix and I were prepared to die in order to defeat her. I think Lilith knew this, so she gave up. But Nix says she still senses her. Lilith's presence is faint, but she's still there. She'll return again, looking for another host." Brielle met my gaze, and determination blazed in her eyes. "I'll be ready for her when she does."

I exchanged a look with Jorge. "Brielle, I need to take you to your parents," I said.

Brielle's eyes widened as if she'd forgotten her family was here. "Are they okay?"

"Yes. Your sister is fine too. But . . . they were talking of bringing you back. To your time."

Brielle's face slackened in surprise. "What?"

"Your mother believed that medicine and spells from your time might help you."

Brielle shook her head. "No, they can't. They're criminals. And Angel, her seizures—"

"They have told me all of this," I said. "But they thought *you* might want to return. Since you did not choose to be here."

Brielle remained silent. Her eyes grew distant as she

considered this. Then, she looked at me with clarity burning in her gaze. "I want to stay."

Something within me swelled with relief and joy, and I couldn't stop the smile from spreading on my face. "Really?"

Brielle rolled her eyes and shoved my arm. "Don't flatter yourself, Leo. You're the only one who has answers about my . . . condition." Her gaze flitted to Jorge.

Jorge crossed his arms, his nostrils flaring.

"He knows," I said quickly.

Brielle looked at me again. "Besides, my family is safer here. As long as it's what they want, then I'm staying." She paused. "That is, if you'll allow me to remain with your coven."

I wanted to laugh, but my instinct was to remain composed. I smirked at her, and I felt her blood boil with irritation. In response, my own blood sang with satisfaction. *She's staying.*

"I suppose," I said slowly, stroking my chin. "But you will have to contribute to our coven if you are to live among us."

Brielle nodded. "That's fine." Suddenly, her face paled. "I—what happened? In the battle? My friends, they—"

I raised my hands to stop her. "They are fine. Only four perished in the battle, but your friend Izzy tells me you didn't know them well."

"Which four?" Brielle asked.

"I don't know their names. Three of them Izzy referred to as 'douchebags.'"

514

Brielle's head reared back. Her lips twitched, but then her face sagged. Conflict warred in her eyes. I could tell she was deliberating between relief that these *douchebags* were dead and sorrow that lives had been lost. She blinked and said, "What about Izzy? How is she?"

"She's fine. She asks after you constantly. My coven and I were able to reverse the Count's spell on them using our blood. We've agreed to let them stay here as long as they abide by our rules."

Brielle gaped at me. "Really?"

I raised my eyebrows. "Don't sound so shocked. I *can* be civil. Occasionally."

Brielle grinned, and it was the most beautiful thing I'd ever seen. "And your coven? How many were lost?"

"Fifty." The reality of it settled in my chest like a weight, reminding me of why I'd so eagerly dived into my research. Part of me wanted to forget the loss I'd suffered. To immerse myself in something else.

Brielle touched my shoulder, and I looked at her in surprise. "I'm sorry, Leo," she said quietly.

Jorge cleared his throat from across the room. "I'll go fetch your family, Brielle." He inclined his head stiffly before he left.

Brielle stared at the door after Jorge exited. She rubbed her arms and stepped away from me. "The mages?"

"We killed them all. No one is left who worked for the Count."

Brielle nodded, her eyes briefly clouding over with darkness. Then, she blinked and glanced around the room. "What about the caves?"

"Gone," I said. "For a moment, we'd thought you—" I stopped, knowing if I kept speaking, my voice would betray my feelings.

Brielle's eyes softened. "Nix got us out just in time."

"Nix is your . . . firebird?"

"Yes."

I looked around as if the phoenix would show itself. "Where is she?"

"She's dormant right now, but I can still feel her. We share magic. We both can't be awakened at once. If I give over to her, then my body is useless while hers comes to life. Then, she sleeps when I return."

I nodded, my head spinning from this information. "Fascinating. You won't . . . unleash her on me, will you?"

Brielle's eyes danced with amusement. "Only if you provoke me."

I laughed and stepped closer to her. My fingertips brushed against her palm, and her breath hitched. I laced my fingers through hers and raised her hand to my lips, pressing a kiss against her skin. I felt her blood thrumming in response, and her cheeks reddened.

"It's wonderful to have you back, Little Nightmare," I murmured against her skin. It still felt hot to the touch, and her saltwater scent overwhelmed me. The hunger within me rumbled, but I squashed it down, focusing instead on the relief of having her here—feeling her breathe, smelling her scent, and hearing her speak.

I expected her to draw away from me. To shove me or glare at me as she usually did. But instead she watched me, and something unreadable stirred in her eyes. Her breathing was shallow, and the blood rising in her cheeks made me roar inside.

Our gazes held for a moment longer before she answered. Her voice was a shaky whisper, but her eyes were warm as they regarded me. "It's good to be back, Leo."

What will Leo and Brielle do when a werewolf pack shows up in their city? Find out in Book 2, The Fallen Demon!

ACKNOWLEDGMENTS

I am grateful and humbled to have so many wonderful people in my life to support and encourage me. Without their help, none of this story would've come to life.

First of all, thank you Kaitlin for your incredible editing skills and your support and encouragement. You've been a wonderful friend to me during my writing journey.

A huge thank you to my critique partners: Jenni, Tori, Melanie, Kari, Melissa, Katherine, and Heather. Thank you so much for your feedback. Your comments and suggestions helped shape this into such a fantastic story.

I am so lucky to have such an amazing and *huge* ARC team! Thank you Janete, Darcy, Darian, Scarolet, Bianca, Jodee, Asreen, Devika, Tyler, Cheryl, Pamela, Andrea, Rachael, Jamie, Lillian, Sara, Olivia, Jennah, Kirstey, Amelia, Jess, Virág, Sam, Nicole, Joanna, Roxanne, Elizabeth, Erica, Oliver, Liz, Nicole! I'm so grateful for your willingness to read my story and give me helpful feedback.

And lastly, thank you to my amazing husband and children. For your patience and encouragement. For your endless support and love.

ABOUT THE AUTHOR

R.L. Perez is an author, wife, mother, reader, writer, and teacher. She lives in Florida with her husband and two children. On a regular basis, she can usually be found napping, reading, feverishly writing, revising, or watching an abundance of Netflix. More than anything, she loves spending time with her family. Her greatest joys are her two kids, nature, literature, and chocolate.

Subscribe to her newsletter for new releases, promotions, giveaways, and book recommendations! Get a FREE eBook when you sign up at subscribe.rlperez.com.

Printed in Great Britain
by Amazon

36062659R00300